Praise for

MW00984296

"Liasson writes with humor and heart."

—Jill Shalvis, *New York Times* bestselling author

SEASHELL HARBOR SERIES

Coming Home to Seashell Harbor

"Picking up a Miranda Liasson novel makes me feel like I'm catching up with old friends!"   —FreshFiction.com

"If you're looking for an engaging, feel-good, contemporary romance for your summer reading, take a trip to the beach with Miranda Liasson's *Coming Home to Seashell Harbor.*"   —TheRomanceDish.com

Sea Glass Summer

"Soul-stirring... A sweet, sensitive charmer."

—*Publishers Weekly*

"Liasson aims straight for the heart in this book and does not miss."   —TheRomanceDish.com

ANGEL FALLS SERIES

"Step into the delightful world Miranda Liasson has crafted in her Angel Falls series, a fictional small town bursting with warmth, romance, and nosy neighbors."

—*Entertainment Weekly*

All I Want for Christmas Is You

"A scrumptious holiday treat." —*Publishers Weekly*

"*All I Want for Christmas Is You* has yummy cookies, Christmas miracles, and a sensational seasonal love story."
—FreshFiction.com

The Way You Love Me

"A sweet, homespun romance that tugs at the heartstrings in all the right ways." —*Entertainment Weekly*

"Liasson's work here is among the best of its kind."
—*Akron Beacon Journal*

Then There Was You

"Emotional, heartwarming romance you can't put down."
—Lori Wilde, *New York Times* bestselling author

"Liasson will make you laugh and melt your heart in this can't miss read."
—Marina Adair, international bestselling author

"Ably tugs at the heartstrings with this poignant contemporary." —*Publishers Weekly*

The Summer of Second Chances

Also by Miranda Liasson

SEASHELL HARBOR SERIES

Coming Home to Seashell Harbor

Sea Glass Summer

ANGEL FALLS SERIES

Then There Was You

The Way You Love Me

All I Want for Christmas Is You

The Summer of Second Chances

MIRANDA LIASSON

FOREVER

New York   Boston

Copyright © 2023 by Miranda Liasson

Cover design by Yoly M. Cortez
Cover copyright © 2023 by Hachette Book Group, Inc.

Forever
Hachette Book Group
1290 Avenue of the Americas, New York, NY 10104
read-forever.com
twitter.com/readforeverpub

First Edition: July 2023

Forever is an imprint of Grand Central Publishing. The Forever name and logo are trademarks of Hachette Book Group, Inc.

The publisher is not responsible for websites (or their content) that are not owned by the publisher.

Forever books may be purchased in bulk for business, educational, or promotional use. For information, please contact your local bookseller or the Hachette Book Group Special Markets Department at special.markets@hbgusa.com.

Library of Congress Cataloging-in-Publication Data

Names: Liasson, Miranda, author.
Title: The summer of second chances / Miranda Liasson.
Description: First edition. | New York : Forever, 2023. | Series: Seashell
    Harbor
Identifiers: LCCN 2023003949 | ISBN 9781538736319 (trade paperback) |
    ISBN 9781538736302 (ebook)
Subjects: LCGFT: Romance fiction. | Novels.
Classification: LCC PS3612.I227 S86 2023 | DDC 813/.6—dc23/eng
    /20211105
LC record available at https://lccn.loc.gov/2023003949

ISBN: 9781538736319 (trade paperback), 9781538736302 (ebook)

Printed in the United States of America

LSC-C

Printing 1, 2023

May you have the kind of friends who will call you out when you need it and who always have your back.
And may you live every single day with a sense of love and gratitude.

Chapter 1

THE REASON DARLA Manning had bought the most sprawling, contemporary beachfront house in Seashell Harbor, New Jersey, had nothing to do with proving her success. Nope, she'd bought it because she knew beyond a doubt that Nick Cammareri, six feet two with eyes of blue, would never set foot inside any structure that wasn't— well, vintage. No quirky curves, outlandish gingerbread trim, or a turret...no Nick.

Ha.

Nick was the construction manager of the Cammareri Vintage Remodeling Company. And her ex-husband—her youthful mistake and the man she'd divorced almost a decade ago. Keeping him out of her home and her life sounded so good in theory. But in practice, it was another story.

Darla ascended the twenty-two steps up to the aqua-painted double doors of her home with her bulging suitcase and the backpack containing her precious laptop in tow.

She couldn't even see the ocean yet, but its salty tang awakened all kinds of feelings. Love of her town. Of her friends and her family. A sense of finally being home, and also a bone-deep sadness that she wasn't going to stay.

What ifs were as plentiful as dandelion seeds. It was best to blow them away to the wind and be done with them for good.

She'd bought her house a few years ago, but she'd spent the past year in California taking advantage of a wonderful position to teach at a college creative-writing program. It had been hard being a continent away, trying to purge her mind of Nick, but it had been good for her, and she'd done it. All she had to do these next few weeks was make certain the feeling of being over him stuck around long enough for her to put her house on the market so that she could return to accept the permanent position she'd been offered.

She'd already gotten the wheels in motion, calling the premier real estate agent in town to list the house.

At the top of the steps, she glanced over the railing just as the mid-June sun was taking its final plunge over the water. In the waning light, the row of beachfront houses was a pastel ribbon of salmon, aqua, and pale yellow.

It took her breath away. The familiar coastline, the cheery colors, the ocean as her backyard, with its endless white-capped waves playfully rolling in as if nothing sad in the world could ever happen. She had so many wonderful memories growing up along this sunny shore.

The other memories—of her failed marriage, of her hard road to overcoming cancer—she tried hard to forget.

She was very, very grateful to be a Hodgkin's disease survivor. But sometimes, even three years after she was declared cancer free, she felt that she was still in survival mode, not living mode.

She punched a code—which was, ironically, HERE2STAY—into her door lock and pushed. The doors opened with a surprisingly loud squeak, probably from not being used much in the past year. She took that as a reassuring sign that Nick had definitely stayed away—because the fixer in him would *never* tolerate a squeak like that.

A gust of sea breeze blew through the great room, fresh and clean. Definitely not the dust-laden stillness of a house that had been shut up for a year. There was something else in the air—the scent of rich, bold coffee. It instantly brought Nick to mind because he loved craft coffee. Did home invaders make coffee?

More surprises awaited. Her new kitchen backsplash was a stunner—a blue iridescent tile with a pattern that reminded her of waves sparkling in the sun. She touched the tiny tiles, admiring the intricate and artistic design, and a glance at the enormous wall of windows showed one of the glass sliders fronting the beach to be open.

It occurred to her that maybe she should drop everything and run before she ended up like the poor hapless victims in the bestselling thrillers she penned. But just as she stood there contemplating her next move, a head popped up from the couch.

A big, massively furry head, with a long pink tongue and a *very* bad haircut.

"Woof!" the interloper said, placing his massive paws on the back of her very expensive couch, done in a color her designer called "aqua heaven," a blue that perfectly matched the color of the ocean outside.

"You're not a scary home invader," she said. The dog made a move as if to scramble over the sofa but appeared to suddenly remember his manners.

Unlike her best friend Hadley, who owned an animal shelter, Darla was not enamored of pets. And she had no idea what kind of dog she was looking at. A sheepdog, maybe? White face, gray ears and back. Hair seriously in need of a stylist (probably even more than hers was after nearly twenty-four hours of air travel). With one lethal shake of his head, dog hair flew. All. Over. Her. Couch.

Yikes.

She did *not* almost laugh out loud at the expression of insta-love on the dog's dopey, drooly face as he cocked his head to the side, assessing her. Despite herself, she took a cautious step closer.

"Well, hello to you too," she said. She was wary of animals and wasn't sure if she should reach out a hand.

There was a bit of a standoff as the dog assessed her. Apparently deciding that she would do just fine as a petter, he struggled for purchase on the plush cushions and then galumphed over the couch to get to her quicker.

"Ouch," came a groggy voice from the couch. "Watch it, Boss Man."

Darla froze, her hand midpet, as the tones of that voice vibrated through her in a startling, unwelcome way. It was low and deep and gravelly from sleep, and so heart-stoppingly familiar that she was hit with a truckload of unwanted emotions.

Shock. Surprise. And yes, anger that speak-of-the-devil Nick was, indeed, in her home. *Calm down, emotions,* she warned herself. *You've worked hard to be in control. Don't screw up now.*

She was ambitious. Driven. Fiercely independent. She'd conquered her rogue feelings about Nick. This was only a test, one that she would pass with flying colors.

The dog jumped up and licked her, this time on the face, probably because, in her distracted state, she'd slacked off on the petting.

"Down, Boss!" her male visitor reprimanded, but not very harshly. Nick was easygoing, slow to anger, and typically didn't demand much of people. Or pets, apparently.

Or himself, as their five years together had taught her. The ginormous Boss lived up to his name by ignoring Nick's command and bounding over. Darla shook his massive paws, trying not to get thrown off balance by a dog who was nearly as tall as her own five feet two, gently placed them on the floor, and patted him on his shaggy head.

Naming a dog Boss was asking for trouble from the beginning. That dog should be named Fireball or Tornado or Chaos. That was how she succeeded in her job as a top-ten thriller writer. She had careful control of words, sentences, and of course, her characters.

That was how she kept cancer out of her mind.

And that was how she planned to keep Nick out of it too.

"Sorry about that," Nick said, flying off the couch and attempting to finger comb his dark, wavy hair, which was completely the opposite of her fine, curly, blond hair. And which made him hot in the way that attractive guys are who don't give a fig about their appearance.

Which threw her off balance in a completely different way.

"The backsplash is beautiful. Thanks. The floor looks great too." Darla kept her gaze everywhere but on Nick, trying not to focus on the fact that her ex-husband happened to be shirtless. With fine, broad shoulders and a tapered-down waist. And, she noticed with chagrin, he was barefoot in a faded, worn pair of jeans. Feelings tumbled around her head willy-nilly—he had beautiful long-fingered working hands, beautiful feet. Okay, fine, he was gorgeous everywhere. And his laid-backness clearly didn't extend to his workout routine. Because the ripples of muscle on his chest were prettier than sunshine on the bay.

"Hey, Darla." After all this time, she still felt the burn of Nick's gaze as it flicked quietly over her in assessment. And the rumbly cadence of his voice vibrating through her, reminding her of a casual, careless cowboy who'd just slugged a shot of tequila.

"What is it?" she asked. He was staring at her.

He pointed to her head, rotating his finger in a circle in the air. "Your hair. It's…"

Her hand flew upward. "A mess. I took the red-eye, but we had a rain delay in Denver. Long night."

He reached over like he was going to gently finger a curl. Then he seemed to realize that wasn't appropriate and dropped his hand. "It's…long."

It had finally reached her shoulders, a real feat with curly hair that just kept…curling up. At last, it was the length it had been BC, *Before Chemo*. Before she'd found a little, seemingly insignificant lump in her neck that had changed her life forever.

On the outside, she now looked just as she had before

all of that. But she doubted she'd ever feel like her old happy, carefree self again. The battle for her life had banished that woman forever. But she'd always attacked all her problems with a vengeance. She prided herself on that. To the world, Darla Manning appeared to have her shit together. She'd made certain.

She shrugged. "It's been three years." And if she made it through her upcoming barrage of blood and other screening tests without a sign of the cancer returning, the prize was relative relief from worry... until next year. The fear and overwhelming sense of dread that was now at its height would temporarily abate. She'd have a ticket to ride the bus of life through another year to continue her plans and dreams.

"Three years," he mused. "It's a milestone."

"One I'd like to forget," she quipped. Then immediately bit her lip. Nick tended to make things come out of her mouth—honest things—that she later regretted.

"No," he said, his gaze bearing down on her with a solemn, intense expression. "It should be marked. Celebrated."

She waved her hand in a dismissive gesture. "I'm not sentimental like you."

"Yes, you are," he said. "You just don't show it."

"You don't get to analyze me anymore," she said quietly.

"You're right," he said, his tone dry. "Because we don't have a relationship, do we?"

"What does that mean?" She threw her hands up in the air. "Of course, we have a relationship. We're exes."

He gave a lazy shrug, but the intensity was back in his gaze. "We were best friends for years."

She snorted. "A lot's happened since then."

"Just to clarify," he said, "I'm not looking to be best friends. Just *friends* would be nice."

She held up her hands in surrender. "I have nothing against being friends." If only she could squish Nick Cammareri firmly in the friend box and shut the lid. Trouble was, he kept spilling out.

Oddly, he grinned. "Good." He petted Boss, who was now sitting patiently at his feet. "So why did you come back a day early?"

Shouldn't she be asking him why on earth *he* was here? While she tried to figure out a calmer way to ask that, she said, "I'm on a deadline, and I have a million things to do." She thought about telling him that she was headed right back to the West Coast as soon as she could, but she didn't quite know how to bring that up. Or, more truthfully, she was avoiding the subject.

She noted the subtle disapproving lift of his brow. "Writing *and* teaching. Still working yourself to the bone, I see."

She waved her hand in a *whatever* gesture. "The price of success." *Add your marriage into that calculation too,* a little voice inside of her whispered. That had been a victim of her success too.

"Yeah, well, as far as your health is concerned, maybe that's too high."

"My health was fine until I walked in and you made my blood pressure skyrocket," she snapped.

"I've always been good at that," he said with a pointed expression that told her he wasn't talking about anger. Why did he look at her like that, with a gaze that reminded her of things he was capable of doing that she had no business remembering?

That caught her off guard and made her blush—again. Before she could think of a clever retort, he said, "All I'm saying is that your friends are worried about you, but they don't want to say anything. Maybe I'm just concerned too."

"Thanks for that. But I think we'd better just stick to the facts. Like, what are you doing here?" Darla switched to her no-nonsense voice. The one that made her twin five-year-old nieces stop fooling around and listen up immediately.

"Oh. That's...a long story. Can I get you a drink?"

He was asking her if she wanted a drink? In her own home?

The familiar irritation welled up, fortunately tamping the sex appeal down. "No drink, Nick. Just answer the question." Her house was just twenty years old, not one hundred–plus like nearly all the homes in their charming beach town. She'd caved and given him a key to redo her kitchen backsplash, at his insistence. And okay, he'd also offered to sand and refinish the wood flooring while she was away. But those projects had been done months ago.

Also, she knew him well enough to know that he was stalling.

He sighed heavily. "My roommate just found out he's leaving for air force training on Monday. His fiancée had to switch her shifts at the hospital to get the weekend off and—"

Why did a thirty-seven-year-old man have a roommate? She bit back the question. Their old friends had all settled down with jobs, relationships, and houses. His lack of doing so was even more evidence of his continued lack of maturity. Too bad she still found herself trying to avoid looking into his soulful eyes that, come to think if it, sort of matched the dog's.

As if Boss read her mind, he rolled over on his back and gave her that *you-know-you-love-me-already* look.

"And you came *here?*" She practiced calming breathing, like her therapist said.

The goal was to get him to leave, not engage him. Yet, after five minutes, here she was, irritated as all get-out.

He gave a lazy shrug. "Far be it from me to stand in the way of young love."

She rolled her eyes.

"The truth is, they're really noisy. The bed squeaks, the headboard knocks against the wall, and..."

She held up a hand. "Okay, spare me the details." He was messing with her, being Nick. She could tell by the mischievous twinkle in his eyes as he embellished the facts. Or at least, she hoped he was embellishing. Unfortunately, her brain had taken that info and twisted it into things she didn't want to recollect. She shook off the old memories, peeled his gray T-shirt off the back of her couch, and handed it to him, trying not to notice that it was soft and warm and smelled like his soap. The same familiar scent from so long ago, her nose remembered perfectly.

He didn't take it.

Please take it, she wanted to say, *and cover up those pecs already!*

"Maybe you can go to your dad's." There. She had no problem being assertive with anyone else in her life.

"Except Dad has Mayellen over, and I feel awkward going there." Mayellen was his dad's longtime love, and Darla was so happy for him. He deserved happiness after raising all three of his kids alone. With a pang, she remembered how much she missed Angelo. Divorce did bad things to a lot of your other relationships too.

That was just like Nick. Assuming he could stay here. Using his charm to get what he wanted.

He hadn't changed one bit.

With big, broad shoulders, the callused hands and rugged tan of a working man, and thick, wavy hair that was never completely in place but looked perfect anyway, Nick still had every single trait that pushed all of her attraction buttons. And all the traits that irritated her to death too.

Nick placed his hands on his hips. "I texted you, but when I didn't hear back, I assumed it was okay. Hadley told me you were flying in tomorrow."

"Wait, you—" she scrolled through her phone and found the text. Hey, Dar, something's come up. Okay if I stay over at your place this weekend? Call me back and I'll explain.

He did sometimes text her. About tile colors. The flooring. All the little details of her remodel. If they stuck to basic conversation like that, they were fine. Because bad things happened when they started to veer off the road into emotional territory. More evidence that it was time to end it. For both their sakes.

"How about going to Tony's?" His brother was dating her best friend Hadley, and the quaint, old cottage they'd bought was in the middle of a huge renovation.

Nick let out a heavy sigh and leveled a practical gaze at her. "Dar, please let me stay for tonight. Tomorrow I'll figure something else out, all right?"

Dar. No one else called her that. She used to love how he said her name. But now he said it like she was the one being unreasonable, not him.

Was she unreasonable? She threw up a mental flag, too exhausted to argue. Besides, her house was huge. If he stayed in one of the extra bedrooms, she probably wouldn't even see him. "Fine."

"Great." He flashed a smile that threatened to make her knees go weak. "You won't even know we're here."

Right. "Okey dokey," she said.

Nick wheeled her suitcase past the kitchen toward her bedroom. "Hey, I made some pasta. With broccoli. You hungry?"

Broccoli? she almost said. She couldn't recall Nick ever eating anything green.

Her stomach gave a loud rumble, but she ignored its complaint. "Thanks, but I ate at the airport." She stifled a yawn. "And I need to get to work early, so I'd better go to bed." She gathered her purse and her computer. There was a time when she would've sat down with him and shared food and asked about his family. His dad was surely getting close to retirement age. And his sister, Lucy, who was just finishing her first year at the Culinary Institute of America in upstate New York; how was she taking the move with her almost four-year-old daughter? But chit-chat wasn't going to do anything but muck up her feelings even more.

"Of course you do." He said it like nothing had changed.

She would always be Darla the workaholic, and he'd always be laid-back Nick.

"Well, good night." As soon as she started down the hall, he stopped her.

"You sure you want to go to bed?" He turned red. "I mean, are you sure you want to go to *sleep*?"

It was her turn to blush. "What?" Did she hear that right? "You aren't propositioning me, are you?" Because that would be...embarrassing. And of course, nothing she would *ever* want.

"No! Of course not." He sounded adamant.

Oh, okay. *Good.* She should have felt relief, but she was too confused. "I really have to go to the bathroom."

He hesitated. "I—um—maybe that's not such a good idea."

She raised a questioning brow. "It is if I don't want to pee on the floor."

He hiked a thumb behind his shoulder, pointing to the wing of the house opposite her bedroom. "Maybe you could use that bathroom."

"Good night, Nick," she said in a firm voice. Enough was enough. She finally broke away, wheeling her bag down the hall.

Now she just had to break away mentally too.

Chapter 2

NICK SAT DOWN on the couch, the dog glued to his side, glancing at the second hand on his watch. Five, four, three, two…he braced himself for impact just as Darla came running back into the living room.

She appeared in front of him, her hands balled into fists, lips pursed as she clearly struggled for calm.

Even now, Darla could enter a room and leave him not knowing what hit him. Mowing down his common sense. Filling his senses with her beautiful face, her curly blond hair, and her warm brown eyes. Looks that were deceiving because she often presented a tough don't-mess-with-me demeanor. But underneath lay a warm heart and a wicked sense of humor that made her unlike anyone he'd ever met. Tangling up his emotions and filling him with wanting. *Still.*

He cursed silently. "I started on your bathroom a little late, and the tile was delayed. Sorry it's a mess in there."

He'd meant to tell her, but she'd thrown him by showing up a day early. And just being in the same room with her again had made all his thoughts scatter.

"Did we actually *talk* about redoing my master bathroom?" Now she was waving her arms. Not good.

"No, but you told me you hated it. And you did pick out that tile." She probably thought he'd procrastinated, but he hadn't. Nor could he blame it on the fact that he'd had papers and projects for his MBA program, on top of working full time with his dad. She didn't know this, but the tile she'd fallen in love with had been out of stock for months. Finally, he'd managed to order it—from Italy. But it had gotten stuck on a cargo ship somewhere out at sea. He'd meant to surprise her with the whole project being done, but now she was coming home to a mess.

"I hate a lot of things. Crowds. War. Brussels sprouts..." She counted on her fingers.

Somehow, he was relieved he didn't make the list. On the other hand, if she kept going, he was certain she'd call out his name.

The Nick she used to know would've been quick to make excuses. But he didn't have to make them now.

He was great at irritating her, sometimes on purpose. That hid the attraction that still flared between them. Yes, it was much better to have her think he was a deadbeat because he felt too much in her presence. Wanted too much.

And he'd hurt her enough.

Oh, he hadn't cheated on her. But he'd been jealous of the time she'd spent building her career at a time when his was languishing.

She'd filed for divorce. And in his anger and hurt, he'd said *fine.*

He hadn't fought for her. Like his own mother when he was young, who'd left him, Tony, and Lucy silently in the middle of the night, never to return.

No stick-to-it-iveness. His dad had made it a point not to criticize their absent mother, but that was what was implied.

"The tile just arrived to the shop," he continued, shaking off the memories. "It'll take me a week tops to put your bathroom back together. And now that you're home, you can give me your approval on the fixtures that I thought would look nice."

Something in her eyes softened. "Well, it was nice of you to tackle my bathroom. So...thank you."

He nodded the *you're welcome.* Seemed like he was always trying to show her that he'd changed. He'd fixed her rotting porch roof with the slow, undiagnosed leak. Redid her plain, boring backsplash. Her kitchen floor. And now her master bath.

He'd fixed everything he could get his hands on but their broken relationship. Done everything but tell her how sorry he was that he'd screwed things up between them.

Maybe it was time for him to move on and let the past lie, like she clearly wanted to do. But that was the thing about living in this town. You saw your whole past every single day—every person, every mistake. It was actually one of the things he loved about it—there was no running.

He did his best every day to show that he'd turned into a capable, hardworking person, even if he couldn't quite shake the image of the immature young adult he'd been.

"Nick, I—I just wanted to tell you something," she said. Her eyes were the kind of gentle brown that reminded him of a doe, a comparison she used to hate. He remembered being eighteen and thinking he'd never seen anyone with eyes like that, with gold flecks that could look cool or fiery, depending on her mood. And he still hadn't.

"Sure. What is it?" A thought occurred to him. What if she was about to tell him that the cancer was back? That sent a shudder through him. "Are you—are you okay?"

"Of course, I'm okay." Her irritation was barely disguised. "It's not always about my health."

"Sorry. I shouldn't have jumped to conclusions." It was just so hard when he was the last to know anything. But he couldn't tell her that.

Her face crumpled. "No, I'm sorry. I shouldn't have snapped." She rubbed her temples. "It's been a really long day."

Always with the apologies. Both of them were quick to smooth things over without ever going deeper. "I've got a crew coming here first thing in the morning so we can get that bathroom done." She looked super unhappy at that, so he added, "I'll tell them to come at ten. That way you can sleep in a little."

"Okay, thanks," she said. "I appreciate it."

"What was it you wanted to tell me?" He vowed not to jump to conclusions, whatever she said.

She gave him a wave as she headed toward the hallway. "Not important. I'm going to crash. See ya."

"Oh, I almost forgot." He got up and fished around in his pocket. "My guys were back there drilling out the floor, and I found this on your bureau."

As he held out the antique ring, she recoiled. Which threw him, because he knew it was important to her. "I trust my crew," he said, "but sometimes we have delivery people coming in and out, and I didn't want it to lie around and take a chance that some dishonest person—"

"Thanks. It belonged to my great-great-grandmother." Together they examined the large, sparkly gem with an old-fashioned filigree band. There was no mistaking it for a unique piece. It wasn't a precious gemstone, but Nick knew it was precious to her in other ways. "I would hate to lose it."

He looked up at her, so close that he could reach over and kiss her cheek. "The ancestor who started the home for unwed mothers, right?"

Darla nodded. "Yep. She was amazing."

He knew a whole lot more about that ancestor than Darla thought he did. She stood there, palm open, waiting for him to drop the ring in. "Well, it must run in the family then," he said, which made her blush.

He was digging himself a hole. He decided at the last minute to place it carefully into her palm, curling her fingers around it.

Her lashes fluttered, and she looked at him.

His heart gave a jolt. She was still just the same. A complex mix of vulnerability and emotion, shielded by a huge suit of invisible armor. He knew who she was underneath the armor, and he yearned to connect with that person.

Nick saw everything in that look. Confusion, pain, annoyance. But something else too.

A tiny flicker of attraction. Heat. Still there, after all this time.

And despite himself, he felt a strange sense of hope.

Chapter 3

DARLA DID NOT want that ring. Yes, her great-great-grandmother Amelia Manning was a kick-butt trailblazer and way ahead of her time.

The ring was pretty too, at first glance looking exactly like a diamond, but it was really one of thousands of bits of quartz that had bumped their way down watersheds from the Catskills, getting polished and hewn along the way, and often ending up on local beaches—and then in a lot of the local gift shops.

It wasn't a diamond, but it was priceless to Darla. Amelia had left a bad marriage, bought the ring, and pretended to be a widow so she could buy property. Hence the "amazing" part.

The property she bought was an old Victorian with a wraparound porch a few blocks from Main Street, taking in unwed mothers who had no place to go, teaching them life skills like personal finance and childcare. She helped them get jobs and sometimes, when she could beat down the summerhouse mansion doors of the very rich and plead her case, even educational opportunities or apprenticeships.

Darla often bolstered herself by thinking that just a hint of her ancestor's gutsiness might run in her blood. Could courage be inherited? She hoped so.

The weird thing was that Hadley and Kit, her two best friends, had both found love while wearing the ring. It had been Darla's idea to give it to each of them over the past two summers to serve as a little shot of courage when they'd needed it most.

But Darla was interested not in *finding* but in *forgetting*, and she didn't even take the ring to California.

Also, the irony was not lost on her that the ring had just been handed back to her by the guy she'd spent the past year trying to forget.

As much as she yearned to learn more about her bold ancestor, there was *no way* that she was going to put that ring on now with Nick standing right there. So she set it on her bedside table, vowing to put it somewhere for safekeeping in the morning.

She sought out a bathroom in the same part of the house Nick was sleeping in, but as far away from him as possible. She skipped the shower and just brushed her teeth, hurrying back to her bedroom as quickly as possible.

Then she threw on her favorite T-shirt that read I'M AN ENGLISH MAJOR, YOU DO THE MATH and sleep shorts and climbed into bed with her laptop, settling in to write just a few words until she got sleepy.

Any words counted at this point. *Stalker X*, the book she

was contracted for, was coming out more along the lines of an enemies-to-lovers romance. No terror, no suspense. She'd been struggling for the past three weeks to turn it into the book she was supposed to be writing.

But Darla was tired. She couldn't even remember the last time she'd taken a full weekend off. It seemed that the more successful her books became, the faster her publisher, Crime Scene Publishing, wanted her to write them. Which had initially seemed like a good problem to have. She'd handled the stress and strain of deadlines without missing one in all this time. But for the first time in her career, the winds had blown her way off course.

She picked up the ring and tried it on, examining its sparkle. "Hi, ring. Instead of a man, please bring me an idea so that I can save this book." She let out a chuckle because—well, she was appealing to a ring. "Although being married to my work is probably not a good idea. But what I really need is a mysterious man named Stalker X that I can invent to save my neck."

As Darla looked at the tiny, glinting facets, she wondered again about her ancestor. Internet searches that she'd done hadn't turned up much about Amelia's life. While Darla was home, she vowed to stop by the library or historical society and get help with some local research.

Darla felt certain that Amelia had faced a lot bigger problems than fixing a book. She'd led her life boldly and bravely and against the grain. She hadn't let anything stop her.

Like fear. Which reminded Darla that her cancer checkup was forty-eight hours away and counting. *Tick tick tick.*

Maybe she *should* wear the ring. To remind herself to be brave too.

A few minutes later, she'd dozed off for the tenth time, only to jerk her head up to find that she'd left an entire paragraph of *zzzzz* on her screen. She was exhausted. She was stressed. And distracted by the bizarre presence of her hot-but-troublesome ex right down the hall.

Rubbing her temples, she did the math for the thousandth time. Two thousand words a day times a month till her deadline was still doable but felt impossible unless the ideas started flowing. Finally, she shut her laptop, slid it under the bed, and immediately sank into a deep sleep.

She was awakened sometime later by her doorbell ringing, followed by banging at the front door. Giant "woofs" sounded out, and doggy toenails clicked on her polished wood floor. She threw on her robe and charged down the hall, suddenly having to contend with a one hundred–pound dog excitedly running circles around her while the knocking continued.

"Boss! Hey, get over here," Nick said, grabbing the dog by the collar as he approached the door from the opposite side of the house.

One glance showed him to be wearing a sleepy expression from just being awakened and little else. He was shirtless—again—with soft gray sweats, his thick, wavy hair tousled and sticking up a little on one side, once again stirring up memories of tender moments she didn't want to remember.

As the light from the hall fell on his smooth planes of muscle and his toned arms, she froze. A rush of heat flared up inside, and for a second she forgot about the pounding, which was now accompanied by giggling and laughing, meaning in all likelihood that her friends were on the other side. Nick glanced up and caught her staring at him full-on. Which made him break out into a slow, sure smile.

Darla put her hand on the doorknob. "I am *not* staring at you," she said. Just in case he was thinking that.

He held up his hands in surrender. "Hey, I never said you were." But his smirk proved he thought otherwise.

"What time is it?" she asked.

"Almost midnight." He looked through the sidelight. "I don't believe this," he said.

Darla walked up behind him. The sharp, spicy, masculine scent of soap and shaving cream wafted toward her. Yep, fresh from a recent shower would be her guess.

Darla tried to shake the scent out of her nostrils. It was just that she hadn't dated anyone in a year. Which made her way too susceptible to cloves and menthol, that was for sure.

Sure enough, outside the door stood Darla's two best friends. Hadley, whose light brown hair was up in a ponytail, stood there staring back and holding a pizza box. Kit, who had long dark hair, waved excitedly at her side.

Nick's brother and Hadley's fiancé, Tony, was there too, and so was Kit's fiancé, Alex de la Cruz.

Her best friends, ironically with *his* two best friends.

"I think they've been drinking," Darla whispered to Nick. "They look way too happy."

"At this point, I wish I were too." His glance slid over to her. Suddenly she knew what he was thinking—imagining the fallout when their friends saw them together looking like—

"Maybe they won't notice," she said, her cheeks on fire.

He lifted a brow. "Too late now," he said with a shrug. "They've seen us."

"Why don't you have a shirt on?" Her words slipped out in an irritated tone.

"Um, because I don't sleep with a shirt." He flashed her a pointed look.

She felt another blush overtake her face. Because she knew that that wasn't all he didn't sleep with.

"Also, I rushed out here to save you from potential home intruders. I didn't have time to put one on."

Darla sent him an *oh well* glance and threw open the door.

"You're back!" Hadley cried, passing the pizza box to Tony, who caught sight of Nick, his brows immediately shooting up in surprise.

Darla went into a hug huddle with her two oldest and dearest friends. Except that the giant dog tried to join in. Hadley, who ran an animal shelter, crooned to Boss, making him even more excited.

Despite the antics of the hairy party crasher, it was a thrill to see her friends again after so long. That made her happy but also hurt her heart because California was a long way away.

"Oh!" Kit said, a hand suddenly flying to her mouth. Her expression grew puzzled as she looked from Darla to Nick and back again.

Oh fricking no.

Darla looked down at her pink robe. And her T-shirt. And dragged her gaze over to Nick, who was standing there in all his shirtless glory. Except Nick hadn't flinched. Whereas she was wrapping her robe tightly around herself and wanted to disappear into the floor.

Tony, a big guy with a tight end's body, gave a fake cough. "Hope we're not...interrupting." Tony, a young-Tom-Brady-kind-of-famous football player until an injury sidelined his career, had returned to Seashell Harbor, reassessed his life, and opened up a crazily popular restaurant called Cam's Place. Most people called him Cam, but Darla never had, probably because she'd known him since high school. Nick loved his brother and had never resented his fame, but calling Tony *Cam* seemed, to her, to omit the fact that Nick was a Cammareri too.

"Oh, Darla." Hadley, who was always exuberant, immediately wrapped her arms around her. "You guys got back together. I knew it would happen!"

Over her embrace, Darla telegraphed Nick a *do-something* look. And in response, she got...a shrug.

Yeah. Like either of them could actually fix this mess.

"It's not what it looks like—" he offered.

"What exactly is 'it'?" Hadley bit down on the insides of her cheeks to keep from laughing.

Darla tried to sound as controlled and no-nonsense as usual. "Nick was here when I got in, working on some projects. He needed a place to stay for tonight."

"Right," Kit, her kind, empathic friend who tended to believe everyone, said like she didn't believe it at all.

"Projects." Tony looked his brother over with a huge grin. Alex cleared his throat and suppressed a laugh.

"Oh," Hadley said in an overly cheery tone, "that makes complete sense. We actually believe it."

"I was crashed in the guest wing." Nick pointed down the hall. "And Darla was...over there." He waved his hand in the opposite direction.

"*Way* over there," Darla said. "Complete opposite sides of the house." They sounded…ridiculous. Even worse, they sounded *guilty*.

"Well, hope both of you are hungry," Hadley said.

"Were you all out having fun?" Darla asked them. "Why didn't you call me?"

"Tony and I were being spontaneous," Hadley exchanged a mischievous glance with him. "We brought all this pizza from Giovanni's, and we decided to get everyone together. Come on, let's eat before it gets cold."

"We should go out on the deck," Alex suggested. "It's a great evening." He winked at Kit, who smiled back and blushed a little. Ever since those two had started dating last summer, Darla had never seen Kit happier. Alex too, for that matter. Kit's six-year-old son, Ollie, was blossoming too. They'd all had hard times since Kit's first husband, an air force pilot, died while serving, but this past year had changed Kit's life in every way.

Of course, it was just a coincidence that Kit had been wearing the ring.

"Great idea," Darla walked toward the kitchen. "I'm not sure if I've got anything to drink—" As she opened the fridge, she gave a little gasp, finding it fully stocked. Coke. Beer. Even milk and OJ and actual food like a hunk of cheese, eggs, and a carton of blueberries.

Her mom had probably done it on her way to work her twelve-hour ICU shift at the hospital, which, come to think of it, she should just be getting off from now.

Before she could say anything, Nick shrugged and reached past her to pull out the beer. "Nothing worse than coming home to an empty fridge," he said with a grin as he grabbed a pizza box and headed outside.

Okay, shocker, not her mother after all.

Nick stocked the fridge…for her? With other things besides beer? Who was this man, and what had he done with Old Nick?

A few minutes later, they were all gathered outside on Darla's expansive deck, sitting around a softly glowing firepit under a starry summer sky, beautiful enough to take your breath away.

"I really missed you," Hadley said over the gentle lap of waves beyond the deck as she pulled out a giant slice of pizza, trailed by a long, stretchy string of cheese. "Don't ever leave again."

"That was a really long year," Kit said between bites. "But I'm glad you had a great experience in the writing program. We're just so glad you're back."

Darla opened her mouth to tell her friends about accepting the job when Hadley grabbed her hand and held it up. "You're wearing it."

Oh no. She must have dozed off before she could take the ring off.

"It's your turn," Kit said matter-of-factly before Darla could say anything. "Whether you believe it or not. And just to remind you, you're the one who started this. So wear it and good luck."

Darla shook her head. "Um, I suggested wearing the ring because Hadley was so down, remember? I'm more interested in finding out a few things about my ancestor." But how would she ever make time for that?

Hadley smiled. "The ring came through for us just

when we needed it the most. So whether you like it or not, it's on your finger, babe. Kit's right. It's your summer."

"And you've been working so hard," Kit said. "It's time to slow down and enjoy life. Maybe the ring will help remind you of that."

Kit and Alex sat side by side on a couch, glancing at each other like... well, a couple in love. Tony and Hadley sat next to each other too, sipping from the same beer. Darla and Nick sat across from them—each alone on chairs, as far apart as it was possible to be.

Boss was collapsed at Nick's feet, softly snoring. So even Nick had somebody, even if he was hairy and a hundred pounds of deadweight.

Equally strong as feeling quite alone was the feeling that Darla couldn't help wanting just a smidge of that happiness for herself. A quiet but insistent voice in her head whispered, *Is it too late for me?*

"Should we tell them?" Hadley glanced at Tony as she polished off her last slice and set down her plate.

Uh-oh. Darla caught Kit's gaze. Kit smiled and gave her a thumbs-up.

She would guess that excited reaction probably meant a baby or a wedding or both.

Tony grabbed Hadley's hand in a sweet gesture that made Darla's eyes mist over.

On what seemed to be instinct, Darla darted her gaze over to Nick to find him staring quietly at her. Instead of shifting his gaze, he sent her a little shrug that signaled he was just as surprised as she was.

"We have an announcement." Hadley beamed at Tony. "We're getting married."

Kit gasped. Darla held her breath. But Alex voiced what they were all thinking. "Congrats you two, but, um, we've heard this before, like, a long time ago." Hadley and Tony had planned their wedding all last year, and it had gotten bigger and more elaborate with each passing day, the consequence of Tony's star status. Finally, they'd put their plans on hold until they could think hard about the more intimate wedding they really wanted.

"This time it's for real," Hadley said, her eyes dancing with happiness.

"There was a sudden cancellation at the Seaside Inn," Tony said, referring to the crown jewel of their town, a century-and-a-half–old Victorian right on the water, a coveted venue for weddings. "We can have the ceremony and the reception there, so it's a nice, simple solution. No muss, no fuss."

"But I thought you two wanted it in your backyard," Kit said. According to updates from Hadley, she and Tony were smack in the middle of renovating a quaint old cottage that sloped right down to the bay.

Darla was thrilled for her friends. But she found herself waiting to hear when the wedding was going to take place. After her deadline, she silently hoped. Which maybe was selfish of her, but she wanted to have the freedom to celebrate with her best friends.

"We did," Hadley said, "but our remodel's not going to be done for a few more months. And I'm expanding the cat side of Pooch Palace and Tony's so busy with the restaurant…"

"Basically, life is not going to stop for this wedding," Tony said.

"So when the venue had an opening," Hadley continued, "Paula Shearer thought of me. It worked out like a charm." Hadley turned to Darla. "It's like…fate. I know this is sudden, but you're home now and it's summer and…and it just feels right."

"We know we're springing this on everyone," Tony said. "But does the last Saturday of the month work for everyone? Just say the word if it doesn't."

Darla suppressed an anguished groan. That happened to be the exact date of her book deadline. Two weeks away.

Not to mention she had to put her house on the market. And her bathroom looked like a tractor had just plowed through it. She felt a little dizzy. But everyone was piping in with their congratulations and offering to help.

How could she tell them she was leaving now? Ugh, how could she leave these friends of her heart at all?

"The venue takes care of everything—food, music, drinks," Hadley said. "So all you guys have to do is show up and celebrate with us."

Tony nodded, putting his arm around Hadley's shoulders. "What we want is a simple, quiet ceremony surrounded by our family and best friends. Nothing complicated. We hope that making it simple works for everyone."

Darla pushed aside the sense of looming dread that tugged at her insides. She wanted to be all-in for them, but common sense told her that weddings were never uncomplicated.

Hadley was hugging her. "We waited for you to get here, and you're done teaching. So you have time, right?"

"Of course," Darla mustered a bright smile. "I'm so excited for you. And I'll do anything you need to help."

She meant it. She would do *anything* for her friends.

And she really needed to tell them all that she was leaving. That made her stomach churn with even more dread, so she pushed it aside. Right now, it was Hadley's moment.

"You sound like you two have got it covered," Kit said. "So we should plan a few activities over the next two weeks for all of us to spend time together."

"We'd love that more than anything," Hadley said. She gave them both a quick side hug before joining Tony as he chatted with the guys.

Weeks of fun? It all sounded amazing, wonderful...if they were any weeks but *these* weeks.

"Are you all right?" Kit looked her over with concern. Darla had to work extra hard not to alert Kit's mom radar, which was always up and running.

"I'm just a little exhausted from the trip," Darla said without hesitation. "It's going to be great to spend time together."

"You and I both know that Hadley underestimates any work normal humans have to do to plan an event. She's going to need stuff." Kit counted on her fingers. "The cake, flowers, a dress, maybe a bachelorette party..."

"She has the dress, right?" Darla said. Didn't Kit remember the painstaking, time-consuming process they'd gone through months ago with Hadley's mom and grandmother? Kit was staring at her, not saying anything, and that made Darla's heart sink even more. Of the three of them, Hadley was the one who took hours deciding on clothes. Literally. Hours. And shopping gave Darla hives.

"She said something about looking for another one," Kit said.

Oh my. The hectic events flashed before Darla's eyes. Events that would doubtless include Mr. Shirtless and Barefoot.

She wouldn't have the choice to boot Nick out of the wedding fun. But she could definitely boot him out of her house. Which she planned to do ASAP.

Guilt welled up that she felt so conflicted about something so joyful involving her favorite people in the world. As if Nick had read her mind, she caught him staring at her again, a look of concern on his face. But he turned away quickly to talk to his brother.

Maybe Hadley noticed because she dropped her voice and said, "Are you okay with hanging out with Nick? I'll do my best not to pair you off together, but..."

"First of all," Darla said quickly, "no matter what it looks like, nothing's going on between us. He's just being...Nick. He brought that giant dog, and he's camping out here tonight so his roomie can spend time with his fiancée. And he's been tearing my master bathroom to pieces."

"Oh, Darla, that's so sweet," Kit, who always thought the best of everyone, said. "He's redoing your bathroom as a surprise?"

"I didn't ask him to do that," Darla said firmly. "And I didn't expect to come home to chaos."

Hadley suddenly looked worried. "If this is too much right now..."

"Oh, Hadley, no. Never. I'm thrilled that you waited for me to come back. It's going to be an amazing wedding."

She would deal with the chaos and her deadline and her annoying-but-still-hot ex...somehow. And she'd do everything in her power to help her friends have the best wedding ever.

Chapter 4

THE NEXT AFTERNOON, Darla stood on the front
stoop of a clean-lined mid-century home in a very non-
Victorian part of town. Before she could knock, her sister
Rachel threw open the door and engulfed her in a giant
hug. "You're back!"

"Hey, watch the cake!" Darla laughed as she shielded
the boxed confection she'd brought straight from Mimi's,
the best bakery in town. It felt wonderful to be enveloped
in her big sister's embrace. It almost made her forget
about tomorrow's big doctor's appointment, which kept
creeping into her mind like a sliver of left-behind splinter
you just can't quite forget. "I missed you too," she said,
suddenly teary eyed.

Rachel took the box. "Sorry to make you pick up the
cake for your own welcome-back barbecue. But thanks for
bringing it."

"No problem. Where are the little angels?" Darla

glanced around the too-quiet foyer. She set her purse down on the dining room table and placed a shopping bag on the floor. "And Wallis. Where's Wallis?"

"You mean my fourth child?" Rachel said with a chuckle, referring to their sweet but giant goldendoodle. "He's pretty much glued to the kids' sides." With a mysterious air, she said, "So everyone's really excited to see you, but there's something momentous going on right now, and you've arrived just in time." Rachel gestured for Darla to follow her as she rushed through the family room.

Before Rachel could explain, the pattering of two pairs of little feet echoed down the hall. Well, make that four pairs because Wallis came bounding along too.

"Aunt Darla, Aunt Darla!" came the sweet voices of her twin five-year-old nieces, who nearly tackled her by wrapping themselves tightly around her legs and jumping up and down. She was shocked at how much they'd grown since Christmas when she'd last seen them. As she promptly gathered them up and smothered them with kisses, a bittersweet pang hit her. She was going to miss the simple happiness of being showered with love—and okay, yes, even doggie kisses.

"Teddy just pooped in the potty," Phoebe, who was blond with pigtails, announced. "We helped him." She crinkled up her cute freckled nose. "But we didn't wipe his butt."

"I wanted to," Maisie, the take-charge one, who had dark brown hair like her dad, said, "but Mommy said she'd do it."

"I'm so glad you two are cheerleaders for Teddy," Darla said, tugging affectionately on one of Phoebe's pigtails. "I missed you both so much."

"Did you bring us something?" Maisie's big blue eyes grew wide as she spotted the shopping bag Darla had deposited near the door. "From Fornea?"

Fornea? Suddenly, it dawned on Darla that Maisie was not talking about an island in the far reaches of the Pacific. "From California! Yes, well, maybe I did." She turned to her sister and whispered, "Sounds exotic, like Borneo."

"Or forbidden, like fornicate," Rachel whispered back.

Just as Darla was rolling her eyes, a small boy with no pants on came flying down the hall with a giant grin on his face. "We been waiting all day for you, Auntie." Teddy, her almost-three-year-old nephew, grabbed her hand. "C'mon, see my poop. It's a *big* one."

"That's amazing!" she said, noting the obvious pride in his face.

"Did you bring us books?" Phoebe asked, tugging on her shirt.

"Phoebe wants to write books like you, but I only want to read them." Maisie tried to see in the bag. "I want to be a sturgeon like Daddy."

Darla and her sister exchanged glances. How did her sister keep from bursting out laughing with this 24-7 comedy show going on? She wondered if Greg, who was in his last year of a general surgery residency, knew his occupation had suddenly become very...fishy. "I know you're going to be a great surgeon," Darla said, completely serious. "And you're right. Surgeons need to read books and get smart before they can operate on people."

Phoebe was tapping her on the arm. "What's your new book about? I wanna read it."

Darla's heart melted. She didn't play favorites, but

Phoebe reminded her so much of herself as a kid. Free-spirited and creative. "When you're older, you can read all my books, pumpkin."

"Uncle Nick did," Maisie said, nodding. "*All* of them."

Well, that was interesting. Darla jerked her head up at Rachel, who had lifted Teddy up and was hauling him down the hall, butt up in the air, for cleanup.

Darla followed them. "*Uncle* Nick?" Darla was not going to have mercy for her frazzled sister.

Rachel finished helping Teddy put his pants back on. Once freed, he bolted out of the bathroom to find his sisters while Rachel disposed of the prize and sterilized the field.

"Okay, so there's been a development," Rachel said as the scent of lemon-scented Clorox wipes filled the small space.

Darla crossed her arms. "A development?" She knew that Greg, her brother-in-law, was close friends and golfing buddies with Nick. "We discussed this *uncle* thing before, and I thought you were with me on the kids not calling him that."

"Well, I was, until…"

"Mommy," Maisie called in a singsong voice, "Phoebe spilled juice."

"Just put a paper towel on it, honey." Rachel tucked the wipes in an upper cabinet and washed her hands. "Nick has a house-flip business now, you know that, right?"

"No, I hadn't heard."

"Okay. Well, a few months ago, he bought the house next door."

Darla felt dizzy. Must be Clorox overload. "You're joking."

"Nope. The Dooleys moved to North Carolina to be near their grandkids."

"So he's renovating the house *next door*?"

"And living in it. And sometimes his air force buddy stays there too. Anyway, he draws the kids like a magnet, and he and Greg are buds, and—"

"And you let the kids call him *uncle*?" It felt...traitorous.

"I'm sorry." She shrugged, lifting her arms. "It just...happened."

"I thought you were on my side."

"It seemed disrespectful to have them just call him Nick," she said. "And calling him Mr. Cammareri is a mouthful."

"This town is way too small." Darla shook her head. And...*all* her books? She knew Nick had read a book of hers for the very first time before she left last year. But *all* of them?

"I'd love to stay here and inhale bleach fumes and chat more, but you probably have juice footprints through the entire kitchen. I'll go work on that."

"Great! Now I have time to actually pee by myself. Love you," her sister said as she closed the door.

Darla cleaned up the juice mess on the kitchen floor, which the dog "helped" with by lapping it up but then walking through it. Then she said, "Come here, little kittens. I have something for you." The kids gathered around while she pulled rectangular packages out of her bag.

She'd brought the kids picture books autographed by the author, a friend of hers (job perk), and shared some insider info about the characters, which the kids loved—like the fact that Morris, the one-eyed gray tabby in one of the books, was actually named after the author's own cat.

As the kids cleaned up the gift paper and ran to play outside, Rachel said, "Thanks for the presents. You know, they're so amazed that you're an author. We're all so proud of you."

"Well, I'm so proud of you." She smiled at her sister. "They're amazing, Rach."

"I agree with that on most days," she said, but she couldn't suppress a telltale look of maternal pride. "They're so excited to have their aunt Darla back."

As Darla let the stab of guilt pass, Rachel stopped at the sliding door that led to the back deck. "There's one teeny tiny little thing I forgot to mention."

Darla stood on tiptoe, scanning over her sister's shoulders. Peering into the backyard, she gasped. "Rach, no." The "thing" was six feet two and broad shouldered, definitely not teeny tiny. "He's *here?*"

Standing near the grill with Greg was Nick, holding a reusable water bottle and laughing. All three kids, let loose from the confines of the house, darted straight toward him. He set down the bottle and intercepted each kid in turn while her friends watched nearby.

Ugh. It was clear from the sounds of happy screams and childish laughter ringing through the air that they adored him.

In all honesty, who didn't? Nick was a charmer. Handsome and easygoing and funny. One of those people with a relaxed way about him who could always make you crack a smile when you were down. Being on the serious side herself, she'd loved the way he could lighten anyone's spirits in an instant with his laid-back joking around.

After all, he'd captured her heart during a ten-minute

walk home from the library nearly twenty years ago, and she was still fighting the impact.

Her sister had to be held accountable for this torture. "Rachel?" she said as ominously as possible.

"It's your welcome-home barbecue," she said in her I-just-couldn't-help-it voice.

"But why—"

Suddenly, Nick caught sight of her. "Hey, Darla," he said from across the yard. Immediately, his hand went to his chest and lingered there. Then he seemed to catch himself, pretending to rub his chest then dropping it awkwardly to his side.

Darla froze, her heart suddenly pounding in her ears. He'd started to do something she hadn't seen him do in years. Way back when, they'd had a little sign, something like a wink, just between the two of them. It was corny and weird, but Nick had always done it, part of his romantic nature, she guessed. But this time, he'd realized what he was doing and stopped.

Nick broke eye contact, grabbing Teddy as he flew by. He flipped the giggling toddler in the air before setting him down on his feet. Teddy landed a little dizzily, a crooked grin on his face.

As the kids gathered around Nick, lifting their arms and begging to be flipped, she got lost in a memory from long ago.

She and Nick were in the high school library studying—or, trying to, anyway. Nick kept tapping his tennis shoe under the table, trying to get her attention, and Mr. Howard, the librarian, kept shushing them.

Suddenly, Darla became aware that Nick was sending

her some weird signal, opening his hand over his chest, tapping it twice, and then pointing at her.

"Something go down the wrong hole?" she whispered.

He shook his head.

"Heartburn?" she tried again.

His expression intense and serious, he again tapped his hand over his heart, nodded, and then pointed to her.

She sucked in a breath. Was he saying something ridiculous like his heart belonged to her? She barely knew this boy, and he had a reputation for being sort of a flirt. He'd kissed her one time, when he'd dropped her off at her door, and her mom had turned the porch light on and flung it open, so that was that. But that slight peck of a kiss had caused a shock wave to reverberate clear through to her bones.

She leaned across the table and kept her voice low so Mr. Howard wouldn't hear. "I don't get it."

Nick got up, grabbed his book bag, and walked around the library table until he was standing behind her, pretending to peruse her calculus homework. His nearness made all the numbers blur, and not only that, the entire library spun around her. He bent down and whispered in her ear, "I'm falling in love with you."

And then, before she could catch her breath or her balance, he walked away. Leaving her reeling.

"Come on," Rachel's voice startled her, bringing her back to the backyard full of her family and friends, "everyone wants to say hi."

As Darla let Rachel pull her into the fun, she couldn't help thinking that ever since she'd touched down, Nick had been everywhere, filling her senses and her life. She was riding an emotional rollercoaster. How could she get off?

* * *

"Darla, honey, there you are! My baby girl's home!"

A slight shiver went through Nick as Darla's mother called out across the lawn and Darla ran to greet her. Tricia Manning was a force. A fiercely dedicated neonatal ICU nurse, she had standing up for the underdog baked into her nature, professionally and personally.

That's not what scared him. Nor did her often stoic expression or her short, no-nonsense haircut and personality to match. It was the fact that she'd never, after all these years, forgiven him for all the grief of the divorce. Which she blamed him for exclusively. And try as he might over the past decade, he could do nothing to get into her good graces. Oh, she wasn't terribly rude. And she still talked to him, which was a plus. It was just that she conveyed with practically every sentence how much he wasn't her favorite person.

He tried not to hold a ten-year grudge against her, because Nick didn't hold grudges against anyone. Except she'd done one thing he had trouble forgetting, even if he'd forgiven it. She'd made sure he didn't get within a mile of Darla during her chemo treatments.

It still left a bitter taste in his mouth, because he'd always felt that Darla hadn't had a say. Even though he hadn't been on Darla's Favorite Person list back then, he'd desperately wanted her to know that he still cared. Darla never knew how hard he'd tried to help her during that rough year.

Tricia was hugging Darla and patting her back, and they were both crying.

"You look thin," her mom said, holding her at arm's length. "And your hair is so long. It's so good to see you, honey!"

It *was* great to see her. Just seeing her walk out of the house just now made him emotional, brought him back to older times. He needed to get a grip.

"You too, Mom." Darla half laughed and half choked. "But I can't breathe."

"Oh, sorry, I just can't help myself." As Tricia released her daughter, she looked over and saw Nick standing there. The smile immediately faded from her face. "Hi there, Nick," she said, with about .001 percent of the enthusiasm she'd just expended on her daughter.

"Hey, Mrs. Manning." He forced a little smile. And yes, he wasn't proud of it, but he still called his former mother-in-law *Mrs. Manning*, just like he had when he was eighteen.

She turned immediately back to Darla. "Carol Drake from the realty office let it slip that your house is about to go up on the market. Are you really leaving us?"

What? Nick darted his gaze to Darla, who suddenly turned the color of the geraniums growing alongside the patio.

"I was going to tell you when I got in yesterday," Darla said hurriedly, "but you were at work."

"Tell us what?" Hadley piped in as she and Kit walked up.

"You're selling your house?" Kit asked.

Everyone had gathered around. Darla let out a heavy sigh and addressed her best friends. "My writer-in-residence year at Stanford went really well," she said, "and they invited me to stay on as faculty and teach some classes. It's an opportunity to help create a new track in their writing program. I'm really excited."

Nick knew exactly what *excited* sounded like for Darla, and what he was hearing didn't jive. She seemed to be trying hard to sell her new adventure to everyone. Or maybe he was just completely thrown.

"I planned to say something," she continued, "but then the wedding was such a surprise, and I—I just didn't think the timing was right." She turned back to her mom. "It was a great honor to be asked. Like you've always said, financial security is important, and being a writer—"

"You're moving *across the country?*" Rachel looked stunned.

Tricia wrung her hands nervously.

Nick felt a little shocked himself, but part of him almost smiled. Tricia had always been worried about Darla becoming a writer for financial reasons. But Darla had done it anyway and made a great success of it. So he knew that money wasn't an issue, but it was an angle her mom would understand.

But why was she leaving? Was there a guy in California? What else could possibly take her away from her family and her posse of friends who were closer than sisters?

"I'm so proud they want you to keep teaching," Tricia said. "It's just...so far away."

"Really far away," Hadley said with a sigh.

"Wait—you're leaving?" Kit said, as if her brain had to catch up with her emotions. "You're actually *leaving?*"

"That wasn't the plan," Hadley said. "All of us were supposed to be together, remember?" She paused. "I'm sorry," she backpedaled, rubbing her temples. "It must be the wedding stress. That sounded really selfish. I'm just a little shocked."

"We'll miss you, Darla," Alex said. "But, wow, Stanford. And to think, I remember when you used to doodle plot points on napkins in the high school cafeteria. Just like J. K. Rowling."

"Those weren't plot points," Hadley corrected. "They were notes she was passing to Nick."

Darla didn't look happy about that comment.

Tony seemed to be quietly taking everything in. He was also staring at Nick over his beer. When Nick caught his eye, he lifted his brow in question. Nick didn't get a chance to respond because Tricia spoke again.

"What about your medical records?" she asked. "Dr. Ag knows you so well and—"

"Mom," Darla said quickly, "Stanford has one of the best cancer hospitals in the world."

Tricia looked like she was fighting tears. "It's just . . . well, to be frank, after all you've been through, I thought we'd have you close to home."

Yeah, Nick got that. In fact, he thought about it a lot, the fact that they'd almost lost her. Actually, he personally almost lost her twice—once to divorce, and nearly again from the cancer. Ironically, the loss from the divorce was the more permanent one.

Darla seemed at a loss for words. Teddy tapped on Darla's leg while he wiggled his butt. "I got to go to the bafroom again. C'mon, Auntie, help me."

Darla looked down at Teddy's earnest little face and smiled. "Oh, that's so exciting. Let's go!" Teddy immediately took her hand and started pulling her away, and Darla seemed way too happy to go.

"I'm going to go get the burgers from Greg," Rachel said, also seeming eager to leave. Their friends went into a semi-huddle, processing the big news.

And as for Nick, he didn't feel angry. Or sad. He felt shook up. He realized in that moment how much he'd been counting on Darla to stay. Actually, he'd assumed it.

As the women stood and talked, Tony walked over to Nick with two beers and offered him one.

"Thanks," he said to his brother. "But I already know what you're going to say."

"Have you told her?" Tony asked.

At least he didn't come out and ask him how he felt about Darla leaving. "In all fairness, she just got back. I haven't had time." Grateful for the beer, he twisted it open and took a swig.

"It's a small town," Tony said, eyeing him carefully. "She could hear it from any number of people, even though you've done your best to keep it quiet."

Nick winced, even though he was used to his brother digging into his psyche, as brothers do. Maybe it was extra with Tony because he'd been like a parent as well as a brother to him after their mom left.

Which was mostly good. But all of Nick's feelings about Darla were complicated, and he wasn't in the mood to get called out on them.

Tony was referring to a house Nick was flipping— an old frame Victorian with a giant wraparound porch just off Seashell Harbor's main street that had sat vacant for years.

Darla's great-great-grandmother's house.

"I haven't quite figured out what to say." In truth, he had no idea how he was going to tell Darla about the house. He'd bought it because...well, because it rightly belonged to her, and he was the one who could fix it up the way it deserved to be fixed up.

And it had become a mission. Something he'd done because he'd followed his gut, which was unusual for him. Nick was a careful planner about everything, from his MBA to his house-flipping business, to scheduling his daily workouts.

He'd bought this house against the better judgment of his practical side and to the chagrin of his brother and his dad and the few other people who knew what he'd done.

He'd just had the feeling Darla would fall in love with it.

And it wasn't lost on him that he'd dreamed of it being a way to keep her in town, of course. That is, before she'd just blindsided everybody with her announcement.

"Well, you might want to say something as soon as possible," Tony said.

He shot his brother a don't-you-think-I-know-that-already look, but before he could tack on a sarcastic comment as well, Tricia took him by the elbow and pulled him away. "Hi, Tony," she said. "Hope you don't mind if I borrow Nick for a minute." She pulled him through the yard to a grassy spot near the swing set, out of everyone's hearing.

Yikes.

"I heard you're staying with her," she said in a low voice.

How in the world...He opened his mouth to respond, but she said, "Hadley was talking about the wedding and let it slip." She looked angry, and that caught Nick even more off guard.

Tricia had never really liked him, but ever since he and Darla had eloped right after college graduation, her dislike had been cemented.

"Darla's chosen to live her life without you, yet you keep hanging around. Always volunteering to do things in that house as a way to get close to her. This time, you barely let her get off the plane. You're a likeable guy"— she waved her hand toward the gathered family—"but I'm asking you to please stay away from my daughter. Let her live her best life. And that's one without you in it."

Ouch. Between the shock of Darla's bombshell announcement and now Tricia's clear stay-away message, Nick had to summon all his inner strength. "Respectfully," he said in a careful, steady voice, "you're wrong about me, Tricia. I'm not trying to get back together with Darla. I just want to be friends." There. He'd said her given name. And the sky hadn't fallen. But did he really have to rush to explain himself? He wasn't sure if he was still trying to win her over after all these years or if she still just frightened him so damn much that the words just tumbled out of their own accord.

She gave a huff that indicated she didn't believe him at all. "Why is it so important to pursue friendship? To appease your conscience?" She paused long enough to make him even more uncomfortable. "I take solace in the fact that she's leaving, if only because she won't have to watch you march your parade of girlfriends through town. Then maybe she can finally move forward."

He opened his mouth to defend himself, but how could he?

He'd never had a "parade of girlfriends," whatever that was, but he had tried to move forward with his life. But Tricia had also said something very interesting. Was Darla bothered by the women he dated? And how exactly did he prevent her from moving on?

Tricia only saw the old Nick, the one who had caused Darla pain. She was right about that—he *had* caused pain. For that reason alone, maybe he shouldn't be so eager to pursue Darla's friendship. But shouldn't Darla be the one to decide that?

Chapter 5

AFTER DINNER, CAKE, and sunset, and after Darla's mom had gone home to rest up before tomorrow's long shift, Rachel brought Darla a glass of wine, and they sat together on the patio, watching the guys run around the yard with the kids.

Darla *really* needed that wine. She was still shaking inside from the fact that her mom had blurted out her news. Her friends looked upset and disappointed. *She* was upset and disappointed. She didn't want to leave the place she loved that was full of all the people she loved. But she just couldn't control certain feelings about Nick that surfaced whenever he was around.

He was wrong for her. She understood that. She had to move forward and beyond him. Yes, yes, yes. It all sounded so logical and simple.

And she'd seen her mom pulling Nick aside, and she was worried about that too.

If she hadn't been the guest of honor tonight, and if her sister and Greg hadn't gone to such lengths to celebrate her return and feed half their neighborhood in the process, she'd be curled up in bed in her pj's drinking this wine on her own. Because to top it all off, watching Nick run around with those kids, laughing and fooling around in the best way, was making her heartsick.

She loved the kids and the fact that her sister had a great marriage and was happy. But this was the exact life she used to envision for herself—full of laughter and chaos and children. That dream had been doubly crushed—by the divorce and then by the long and grueling course of her cancer therapy. The dark yard and starry sky reminded her that she and Nick sometimes used to lie on an old sleeping bag in the tiny postage-stamp backyard of their rented duplex and look up at the stars, holding hands and discussing naming the kids they wanted to have.

"Edgar, Allan, Poe, and Wollstonecraft," Nick had said in his easy, joking way. "In honor of the fact that their mother's going to be a famous author."

"You're going to name a boy after Mary Wollstone-craft?" she asked, laughing.

"Why not? We'll call him Woolie for short."

"Sounds like a dog. Or a rock star."

He smiled that lethal weapon of a smile that always made her melt. "It's unique."

"Right. But aren't you planning for any girls? We need girl names." She couldn't wait to hear what he'd say to *that*.

"Virginia, Louisa May, Jane, and Woolf," he'd said without missing a beat.

She'd shaken her head at his antics. "This tells me something I never knew—that you paid more attention in lit class than I thought. And also, you're ridiculous. I am not calling a baby Woolie *or* Woolfie."

He'd slowly turned toward her, his eyes soft and warm in the dim light. "There's only one thing you need to know about me. I'm crazy for you."

Rachel's voice snapped Darla back to reality. "Sooner or later, you're going to have to come to grips with your feelings for him," she said, not unkindly. "Maybe you can do that right here instead of running away to California."

Darla sighed. "I'm not running," she said defensively. But her sister called her out by flashing her an *oh-yes-you-are* look.

Okay, she was running. But it was self-preservation.

"When I first moved home, I thought that I could do it," she said honestly. "But being in the same town with him really messes with my head. I think I just need a few more years…"

Rachel gripped her hand. "Try harder. We almost lost you a few years ago, and now that you're okay, I don't want you clear across the country. I want you right here." Rachel nodded her head toward the yard, where the kids were happily giggling. "Have you discussed these rogue feelings with him?"

Absolutely not. "I don't want to get back together with him. I think I'm just… a little lonely, you know? Hadley and Kit are so happy. I think I'm just vulnerable right now."

Rachel stopped her right there. "My advice is to talk."

Darla couldn't help smiling. "You've given me plenty of great advice in my lifetime, but I'm not going there.

Everything about our divorce was so painful. There's no way I'd want to relive any of that." She'd survived cancer, but she could not survive another heartbreak like that again.

Rachel shook her head. "You were so young, Darla. You've both grown and matured. It could be really good between you now."

Darla shot her sister an incredulous look. "I can't believe you're our mother's daughter. If she caught you saying that..."

Rachel shrugged. "I see Nick a lot. And I don't just mean because he lives next door. I mean, I see him in a way Mom never does."

In the yard, Nick was running around showing the kids how to get fireflies to land on their hands but not squish them. They were all gathered around, enraptured, as he held open his hand, where a bug was crawling, and explained about all its parts and its light.

"Mom suffered a lot of hurt from Dad," Rachel said, "but she never let it go, you know? All men aren't like Dad. You do know that, right?"

Darla rolled her eyes. "This is not about Dad. Logical people do not remarry the man they divorced because there were good reasons why that happened. And maybe with all this time we're going to spend together for Hadley's wedding, I'll get a chance to remember every single one of them."

Her sister sighed. "Okay. You're the boss of you. Here's to annoying, stinky exes. How's that?"

She tapped her wineglass to her sister's. "To annoying, stinky exes."

With the kids gathered around him, Nick bent down so they could see. With the lull in the conversation with Rachel, Darla couldn't help overhearing what he was saying. "From the outside, it just looks like a plain bug. But on the inside, it's magical."

"It lit up!" Teddy said, his eyes wide.

"Yep," Nick said. "They talk with light. Every lightning bug sends a special signal to the lightning bug it loves in a special language that only that bug understands. So they get the right bug's attention. The one that's right for that bug alone."

"Is the light hot?" Maisie asked, more interested in science than lightning bug romance.

"There's no heat in the light," Nick said. "The bug doesn't waste any energy trying to light up. It's really efficient."

"What's efficient?" Phoebe crinkled up her nose.

Nick smiled. Darla could tell he was loving being with the kids. "It means they're really good at glowing."

"I want to hold it," Teddy said.

Nick straightened out a little. "When I was little, we used to put them in jars. But we know better now that this little creature deserves to bring its light to the world and be free. So we're going to send it on its way to be awesome."

"So sappy," Darla said, pretending she had something in her eye. What he'd said had touched her. Because the kids were completely engrossed. Because his message was sweet. And lastly, because he weirdly had an amazing bank of knowledge about lightning bugs.

The bug flew away, and Rachel and Greg rounded up

the kids for bed. Nick walked over to where Darla was now sitting alone, which made her steel herself for anything. "I think the firefly is your spirit animal," he said.

He always did that—threw her off-balance in unexpected ways. But she played along. "Is it because I emit a natural glow? Because I'm efficient? Because I don't want to be put in a jar?" She had no idea what he was getting at. But he looked so good standing there in front of her on a summer evening, dressed in shorts and flip-flops and wearing a bemused expression directed right at her.

He shook his head and sat down in the chair Rachel had just vacated. "You have quite an imagination, you know that, right?"

She shrugged. "My job, remember? I sit and make things up all day."

"I was thinking unique, lit from within, not afraid to glow."

"Not afraid to glow?" Was he teasing her? Because that was about as far from the truth as could be. She was afraid of…well, everything.

"Yeah. You take life by the balls. You set a goal and accomplish it. With your writing. With your teaching. With overcoming cancer."

She waved her hand dismissively, uncomfortable with talking about herself. "You're making too much about all of that. Besides, the flashing is all about sex, you essentially just said that to the kids."

"I beg to differ. He sends out the signal, and if she likes him, she responds."

She narrowed her eyes. "What if she doesn't like him?"

"Maybe he's ruined for life because she won't give him

a chance. Or…maybe he goes out and has a beer with his buddies and tries to forget her." He quirked a smile she'd still call adorable. "I don't know." He looked directly at her. "I wonder what happens when it works—when the signals match? When they manage to connect with each other?"

Her pulse sped up. Because…were they really talking about bugs here?

Nick kept going. "Did you know there's one species of firefly where the female lures the male in with flashes and then eats him? But mostly, they connect, and the rest is history. And here's one last fun fact: when the female lays her eggs, they glow too. And so do the baby larvae."

"You know what I think?" She cracked a smile.

"What's that?" Even in the dark, with the glow of fireflies all around them, she could see the intensity of his gaze.

She shot him a pointed look. "That you know way too much about fireflies."

He shrugged. "I think it's all very romantic."

"Personally, I really liked the part about the female luring in the male and having him for dinner."

He burst out in a good, hearty laugh that she hadn't heard in quite a while. And it sent a warm feeling washing over her.

"Why does it not surprise me you write scary books? Think about it." He swept his arm in an arc over the backyard. "Two little fireflies in the universe sending signals out there to each other over and over until they connect. What could be more amazing? So the old adage is correct."

She hated to fall for the bait. But she did anyway. "Okay, fine. What old adage?"

He looked at her long and hard and unmistakable. "When you know, you know."

She rolled her eyes. "That's ridiculous." But in truth, she felt just as mesmerized by him as the kids.

"Maybe." He assessed her a little too carefully. "But you like it."

"Why do you think that?" She shook her head but felt unnerved.

"Because you're blushing."

"At least you didn't say that I was glowing."

"I was going to, but I thought you might smack me."

Was he...no. He couldn't be flirting. He was just... being Nick.

The life that had gotten interrupted—doubly, first by divorce and then by cancer—seemed to be standing right in front of her, bowling her over with what ifs as plentiful as those fireflies.

Nick was annoying. And stubborn. Which was often true.

If only he didn't have to be so damn appealing too.

* * *

"Hey, Nick, we're taking off now." His friends Stephanie and Zander were approaching, thank goodness. Because Nick was feeling the same old feelings all over again, falling into the same fun, teasing interactions that made him want Darla all over again.

He wasn't going there. He was going to show her that he was responsible. That he wanted to be her friend.

Friends, friends, friends.

Plus, she was leaving for good. He was still shocked by that. And hurt. Flirting came easily but difficult conversations did not. And he wasn't sure how to bring that up.

He rose to shake Zander's hand. "Hey, buddy, thanks for stopping by."

"It was great to meet your friends," Stephanie, Zander's fiancée said. "Everyone was so welcoming."

Nick turned to Darla, who rose from her lawn chair. "Meet my friends Zander and Stephanie. They're engaged." Then he turned to his friends. "This is Darla, my...my ex-wife." He stumbled over the words. Seemed he'd never get used to thinking of Darla as his ex-wife.

Darla shook hands with them. They were standing together, Zander's arm around Steph's waist. Young and in love. Totally. Not so long ago, he and Darla had been just like that.

"I'm sure you heard that Nick is letting us stay in his house this weekend." Zander gestured to the freshly painted white-frame house next door.

"We couldn't be more grateful," Stephanie said, giving her honey a squeeze.

"Oh, is that right?" Darla had confusion written all over her face.

"I sublet my place because I was supposed to be deployed last week," Zander explained, "but they delayed me a few days." He lifted his beer. "So, thanks, buddy."

"Hey, happy to help," Nick said.

"Nick's done a really nice job with the house," Stephanie said. "It's really charming."

They chatted for a few more minutes, until Zander and

Stephanie moved on. Nick walked over to a nearby cooler and threw open the cover. "Diet Coke, water, beer..."

"Diet," Darla said, but he was already reaching for it. He wiped the can off on his shirt before handing it to her.

Laughter rang out from the patio. Darla looked over nervously, as if she didn't want to be caught alone with him. They should go back and rejoin their friends. Call it a night. He opened his mouth to say so, but something else came out instead. "Want to see the house real quick?"

"Sure," she said without hesitation, which made his heart jump a little.

"Oh, I almost forgot." He handed over her phone.

"How did you—" She suddenly patted her pockets in confusion.

"Phoebe's got a mind like some of the mastermind villains in your books. Our goal should be to get her to use her powers for good. Oh, and the photo of the floating treasure really made my day. You must be a very proud auntie."

"The floating..." It took her a few seconds as she flipped through her photos. "Oh! The poop." She chuckled. "I am a proud auntie. But Phoebe took the photo. When she stole my phone, obviously."

As she took her phone back, their hands grazed. Her touch felt like fire. He wanted to tell her so many things. Like he was sorry for his immaturity. That he wanted to be friends again if she would allow it.

Instead, he walked her over to the house he'd been working on for the past year. It was colonial style and built in the 1940s, with shuttered windows and a brick patio in the back built around a large maple tree and surrounded by a garden.

Inside, he'd redone the kitchen and the floors, and knocked down a wall to make the family room more accessible. It was clean and bright and functional—and he hoped she'd see that he was proud of his work.

"It's very sweet," she said, surveying the kitchen. "You've always been an artist."

He burst out laughing. "I definitely wouldn't call myself an artist." Inside he was secretly pleased that she understood the hard work involved. "I figured I'd put my knowledge to use and build a side business."

She ran a hand along the smooth surface of the white quartz countertop. "It was nice of you to let your friends use your house."

"I know," he said with a grin.

She rolled her eyes.

"Seriously, I know what that's like. To be in love like that and far away from each other. How could I not help out?"

She went to the door and looked out over the patio. He wondered if she was thinking of the same things that he was thinking about. "Remember your editorial internship in Philadelphia?"

She laughed. "I fell in love with writing that summer... but not editing."

He was remembering something else—how in love with each other they had been. But he didn't say that. "Every Friday, I'd finish work and borrow my brother's car. He let me take it as long as I had the money for gas. And I'd drive the hour and a half to see you."

She gave a soft laugh. "Sometimes you'd pay a lot for a parking spot for the weekend."

"That was better than squeezing his car into that parking garage where the cars were packed tighter than sardines. I was terrified that if I'd dented my brother's car, he wouldn't let me use it to see you ever again."

She smiled. "We ate cheesesteaks. Saw a Phillies game. Ran the art museum steps." She fell silent. They did other things too, that he saw in full, brilliant detail in his mind. Was she remembering too?

"Good times." He gave a little laugh. "Every single Sunday you'd cry when I left."

"Well, I'm a crier." She looked up at him, quietly assessing him. He had no idea what she was thinking. "And...I didn't want you to leave." She cleared her throat. "We were in love."

Yes. Madly, wildly in love. "I never wanted to leave," he said quietly.

They hadn't been the best at communicating when they were married. He'd been the one to shut down, mostly, not exactly being a star at conversation. He knew now that they would never be able to chip at the surface of their iceberg of problems unless he made an effort.

And for some reason, it felt really important to try.

"You're leaving," he said, their gazes still locked.

"Yeess." She said it like, *What didn't he understand about that?*

"But this is the first I've heard of it." He knew he was hurt, but he realized then that he was angry too. Couldn't help it.

"Yes again," she said. She didn't sound mad. She sounded evasive.

"Why didn't you tell me?" Okay, not even five minutes and the frustration was seeping out. Not good.

She looked away, over his head. "I didn't think it was important."

"You didn't think it was important?" Okay, he had to do better than repeating what she'd said in an octave higher than usual. And also, what he really meant was, *You didn't think I was important?*

"There was hardly time, and let's be honest, we don't…we don't communicate about things like that." Now she was looking at the floor.

Let's be honest. Something they hadn't been for a long time.

"Yeah, but…" He was trying not to react but… California. He raked his fingers through his hair.

"Nick, we text about the house. But we don't *talk*."

Her words poked at him like tiny daggers. Did she think so little of him that she wouldn't tell him she was moving across the fricking country?

"It's—it's not like that at all," she said.

Oh no, he'd said that out loud, hadn't he?

"It's a once-in-a-lifetime opportunity at a prestigious university, and I—couldn't pass it up." She was looking just past him. At his shoulder. Or at the wall, maybe.

She'd always done that when she wasn't quite telling the truth.

"But you moved home for family. You bought your house with the intention of staying." He paused before plunging into deep waters. "Is there—is there a guy? Maybe what's his name? The superfan."

She folded her arms, giving him a *don't-go-there* look. "I'm not going to answer that."

"He knew every last detail about your books."

"His name is Sam," she said in defense. "He loved and appreciated them."

Nick gave an ironic chuckle. "I've never seen such an enthusiastic fan. He struck me as being a little odd."

Nick knew he'd gone too far even before Darla's brows knit down in a frown. "You know what strikes *me* as being a little odd? The fact that you've dated more women than..." Her voice trailed off and she took a deep breath. "You know what? I'm not going to discuss this. Anyway, there is no guy." She waved her hand dismissively in the air. "It's just time for me to move on and take an opportunity I can't get here."

Besides being angry, she sounded melancholy. But it wasn't his business to pry. It wasn't his *right*. So he backed down. "I'm sorry to mention the guy." He couldn't bring himself to say his name. "I'm happy for you, Dar. Look at all you've accomplished. I always knew you'd go places."

"Apology accepted."

Nick tapped his fingers together. Okay, maybe that was it. He should let this go.

Or maybe not. "You're...you're important to me. You always will be. Your news blindsided me. I—I don't want to be shut out of your life." There, he'd finally said what he felt.

Her eyes widened. Maybe in shock. It had been a long time since he'd spoken his mind like that.

"This is what you want, right?" He pressed her one last time. Because he wanted to hear it from her. Direct.

"Yes," she said so quietly that he almost didn't hear. "It's what I want." He could sense turmoil. Sometimes when she looked at him, her eyes got soft with what looked like tenderness. Like maybe she wished things between them were different.

But these were only flickers when she was caught off guard, like now. Then she shut down so fast that it left him wondering if he'd seen it at all.

"I'm sorry I didn't tell you," she said. "To be honest, I didn't know *how* to tell you. Like it or not, we've been here in this town together since the beginning."

"Yes, we have." A sudden vivid image entered his mind of getting on the school bus in third grade, where he saw a pretty girl in pigtails crying because she'd forgotten her lunch. He'd sat down next to her and given her his entire lunch, including his Power Rangers lunchbox, because he just couldn't stand to see her cry.

"Do me a favor," he said softly.

"What's that?" she asked, her voice hoarse and raspy and clogged with emotion.

His gaze never wavered. "Give me the benefit of the doubt sometimes, okay?"

She nodded.

"Don't always think the worst of me."

Her brows shot up. She looked startled. "I don't think the worst of you," she hedged.

Now that she was leaving, he had nothing to lose. He got up close and circled his finger in front of her face. "I can see it in your eyes. Maybe I disappointed you years ago, but not all flaws are permanent and lethal, Darla. We were young. I didn't make the best choices. But I'm different now." He paused long enough to debate his word choice. But then he let loose with it anyway. "I'm a grown-assed man."

She blushed, and he got a strange satisfaction in thinking that it might just be because she was remembering that he was, indeed, a man.

"I respect that you're a grown, successful *person*," she said. "But people don't really change. The things that made us not work...they're still there."

Her words were harsh, but a flicker of doubt seemed to pass in her eyes. And another look entirely. *Wanting.* It caught him off guard. But he knew her too well not to know what it was.

It made him push even further. "What about the things that *did* make us work? Are they still there too?"

Her gaze locked with his and held. Something crackled and buzzed between them, and it wasn't anger.

She shook her head, as if she were trying to shake him out of it. "Anyway, these few weeks aren't about us. They're about our friends. I'll do everything I can to make this the best wedding ever. Even..."

"Get along with me?" he asked, still feeling a little hurt.

"Yes. We can set our differences aside. For our best friends."

"Agreed. We both love them enough to do whatever it takes to make their wedding perfect." He extended his hand. "Shake?"

"Shake," she said, all business.

His hand wrapped firmly around hers and shook.

But that simple let's-make-a-deal threw him for a loop. Because her hand, deceptively dainty and small like the rest of her, felt just as it had the millions of times he'd held it before. When he'd had permission to hold it. When his touch was welcome and wholly reciprocated.

And that filled him with longing.

Her gaze flicked up to his, and for a moment, he saw a struggle. Like she might still be attracted to him, but she sure didn't want to be.

The slider suddenly opened, and Hadley and Tony walked in, followed by Kit and Alex.

"We were looking all over for you guys," Kit said, sounding a bit panicky.

"You're not going to believe this," Hadley said, looking up from her phone.

"Our venue flooded," Tony said, looking distressed. "A pipe burst."

Hadley blinked back tears. "We'll never find another one this late in the game."

"No, honey," Darla said, "there's got to be a solution." Her gaze wandered over to Nick's, and he gave a nod of affirmation.

"We'll call around." Nick ticked off possibilities on his fingers. "Places that do beach weddings. Parks, outdoor spaces. The courthouse. There's got to be another option."

Darla nodded. "Absolutely. We're on it."

She telegraphed him a look of agreement. All right then. They would work together to help their friends. Not only that, but he was also determined to prove to her that he'd become a responsible human being.

He was going to show Darla that he was worthy of being friends. And be satisfied with that, regardless of what his heart wanted.

Chapter 6

AT 7:30 A.M. Monday morning, Nick was flipping a lemon-ricotta pancake in Darla's kitchen. He'd already made a list of all the potential wedding venues in town that might be available at this late date. He also had his notes open on his laptop for his upcoming finance exam. Boss, who hadn't stirred from his location a few feet from the griddle—praying, no doubt, for a pancake to fall—ran to greet his new favorite person as she entered the room.

"I can smell those clear down the hall." Darla slid onto a stool around the big island. Boss immediately leaned his head against her leg, the big flirt. "Your famous pancakes, yes?"

"You're just in time." Nick flipped one onto a plate and slid it in front of her.

She looked him over and chuckled.

"What? Why are you laughing at me?" Then he realized he'd put on a floral apron he'd found in a drawer.

Smoothing it down, he said, "It matches my shirt, don't you think?"

"Flowers look good on everybody," she said graciously. "But if you bought pancake mix, does that mean you're staying even longer?"

He leaned over the sparkling quartz counter that was the color of sand and stared directly into her eyes. "First of all, I made them from scratch. No mix." He pushed a mug of coffee toward her.

"That's even more stuff you must've gone to the grocery store for," she said. Joking was a good sign, but she was tapping her fingers nervously on the island. And she wasn't exactly digging into the pancake.

"Thanks for letting me stay an extra night," he said. "Steph and Zander will be out of my place today."

She nodded but was strangely quiet. He could guess the undercurrent of worry she was trying to hide. He'd found a sticky note by accident near her purse with "Dr. Ag 9 a.m." written on it, along with her medical insurance card.

That's what made him run out to the grocery store and set him to making her favorite breakfast. And some gourmet coffee.

But she'd barely taken a sip.

She had on a flowered sundress and sandals. He couldn't repress a slight smile because she still loved flowers and bright colors. In his mind, she was still the cute bookworm oblivious to her own beauty.

"Why are you smiling?" She ran a hand over her head. "Did I forget to brush my hair or something?"

"What? All these luxurious curls?" He reached over

and playfully ruffled her hair. She gave him a look of mock horror and batted away his hand. "I was just remembering the first time I really talked to you. You were sitting in the library with a giant stack of books."

She turned those brown eyes on him, the same pure, warm hue that never failed to send a thrill through him. The flash of vulnerability in her gaze made his heart irrationally speed up.

"You carried them all," she said.

"It was an opportunity for conversation I couldn't pass up."

He'd known he'd have one and only one chance with her because she'd flat-out rejected a few of his jock friends. The fact that he was popular with the girls did not impress her. Or that he played football.

He'd gone up to her table, picked up the top book, and said, "You actually read this stuff?"

The world's worst pick-up line. The book was *Pride and Prejudice*. Which was on their English lit reading list for later in the semester. Smartie pants that she was, she was undoubtedly getting a head start.

His awful attempt at striking up a conversation didn't work at all because she'd stabbed him with a stare and then gone back to her book, which happened to be *1984*, their current lit assignment.

Flipping through the pages, he tried again. "Why is this so great, anyway?"

She set down her book facedown on the table and gave him a cool stare. "*Pride and Prejudice* is the most romantic story in the world." She tapped the book in his hand. "And it is *riveting*."

"Well, how about you tell me all about it on the way home?" So he'd walked her there, listening to her talk about why she loved it. When he got to her house, he slipped her copy into his bag.

The next day he handed it back and said, "I think I get some of the reasons why it's such a great book."

"You took my book?" Her eyes grew wide. He noticed for the first time they held pretty gold flecks.

"Borrowed," he corrected. "And read it too."

She frowned. "Did you stay up all night reading that to impress me?"

Ignoring that, he leaned close. "These two clearly misjudged each other. So I think maybe you should give me a chance too. Although my name isn't Fitzwilliam. That might be a disadvantage because how can you not fall instantly in love with anyone with a name like that?"

She laughed at his nonsense. "How do I know you're not just flirting with me?"

"Because I *did* stay up all night reading, but I still have to help my dad rip out somebody's kitchen after work today."

And then she laughed and looked at him like...well, like someone who would give him another chance. And the rest was history.

As he watched her not eating the pancake, he vowed that one day, he'd get that look again. In a purely platonic way, of course.

She crossed her arms and laughed. "You never even figured out that I put that giant pile of books in front of me on purpose because I knew you'd offer to carry them for me."

He jerked his head up. "Say what?"

She shrugged. "I had tactics of my own."

"Oh. So you thought I was hot all along, didn't you?"

"I thought you might be arrogant because you could get any girl you wanted. But I also knew that you couldn't pass up helping anybody who needed it. And yes, I thought you were hot."

Emotions pummeled him and made him say stuff he normally wouldn't have said. "I never wanted any girl but you, Dar."

Their gazes locked and held, and silence fell like a curtain between them. The smell of smoke snapped him back to reality. *The pancakes.*

Nick rushed to the rescue, but they were black discs sending thick curls of smoke into the air that made him cough as he flipped them straight into the trash. Even Boss slunk far away.

When he got things under control and turned back, she was wearing a cool and distant expression.

Except something within him was different than the Old Nick. He could handle things better now. He could refuse to accept that she was impenetrable. And he really wanted to help her through this morning.

He flipped a decent pancake onto her plate and made a sweeping motion with his hand. "Mangia. Eat."

"You sound like Hadley's grandma, trying to get me to eat," she said. "That's really weird, even for you."

He shrugged. "Secretly, I have the soul of an Italian grandma. Didn't anyone ever tell you breakfast is everything?"

She took another bite—a mouse-sized bite, like she was just doing it to get him off her case.

Boss made a snorting, gobbling sound under the counter like...wait, did she toss him part of a pancake?

"Well, I appreciate the coffee and breakfast." She narrowed her eyes. "But...aren't you usually working by now?"

He looked at his watch. "My dad's coming over with a crew. We're going to tackle your bathroom. So...I'm early for work today." He chuckled. "I have a list of wedding venues to call. Want to see it?"

She nodded and took the list from him. "You're always early for everything," she said, which was true. He was always up at the crack of dawn while she always got a second wind at midnight. He recalled times after they'd made love where he dozed off to the sound of the computer keys ticking away as she got up and wrote. Setting down the paper, she looked at her watch. "I can't think of any others, but I'm happy to help make some calls. I wish I could stay to say hi to your dad, but I've got to run."

She picked up her plate and headed for the sink. He was running out of time. He had to say something quick before she left.

"Are you...is it a doctor's appointment by any chance?"

She stopped in her tracks. Her expression almost made him wish he hadn't said anything.

He nodded toward her purse. "I saw your medical card. I could drive you, you know. Or even wait in the waiting room until you're done."

"Thanks, but I don't need company." Looked like tough Darla was back to stay.

"Why should you go alone?" he asked. "I wouldn't want to."

"It's just my annual checkup. No big deal." But she'd barely touched her favorite breakfast. And it was clear that she was stressed.

He leaned over the countertop. "Dar," he said softly, "you don't have to do this all by yourself."

"I appreciate that you want to help me," she said in a dismissive tone. "And thanks again for breakfast." She loaded her dishes in the dishwasher, every move efficient. Then she grabbed her purse and ran for the door faster than if the house were on fire.

She'd brushed him off.

He poured himself more coffee and tried to go back to studying but found himself reading the same sentence ten times over when he heard a knock. "Hey," his brother Tony said, walking in and looking around. His eyes lit on the kitchen with its giant island. "Nice job on the backsplash."

"Thanks. Dad here yet?" Tony had come to help haul tile in before he went to work at his restaurant.

Glancing at his watch, Tony said, "No, but he'd better be on time. I'm meeting our seafood rep in a half hour." He did a double take. "You okay?"

"Yeah. Just have an exam coming up." Nick shut his laptop. "Want a pancake?" He pushed a plate toward his brother.

Tony examined the stack. "Dad's lemon-ricotta recipe? I think I will."

As Nick passed his brother a fork, he said, "Darla's got her cancer checkup this morning. She didn't want to talk about it."

Tony swallowed a bite. "Wanting her to trust you

doesn't magically make that happen. These are delicious, by the way."

Why had Nick started this conversation? It was stress, that's what it was. He was worried about her. Nervous for her appointment too. "If I could do anything to reverse that, I would."

Tony studied him in his big-brotherly way. "Why are you doing this now?"

"Doing what?"

"I don't know. Regretting. Wanting to confess, that kind of thing. Some people do that more for themselves than for the other person. Like, if they're lonely. By the way, every time I run into Lauren, she asks about you."

Nick shook his head. "I broke it off with her a year ago and she still wants to get back together, but she's not the one. And I had two dates last week. Frankly, I'm sick of dating. I can't seem to connect with anyone the way I connected with Darla. I miss our friendship."

"Just friendship?" He lifted a skeptical brow.

"I want her to understand that I'm different. That I'd be there for her no matter what." That was what friends did, right?

Tony swallowed another big bite of pancake. "In my opinion, you've tried to be there for her. Maybe it's time to forgive yourself and accept that some things just don't work out."

Nick just couldn't seem to do that. Because...because why?

Maybe Tony was right. It was time to move on. But deep down in his gut, something told him that he and Darla just weren't finished.

Chapter 7

I AM CALM, Darla told herself as she closed her eyes and listened to the quiet gurgling of the fountain in the very zen waiting room at the oncology center. Her writer's brain catalogued more calming touches—tranquil music, warm lighting, and even a real rubber plant in the window. When a nurse showed her to an exam room, she thanked her politely, changed into a paper gown, and sat down on the exam table, mindlessly scrolling through her phone but not registering a thing.

She was not calm. She was freaking the hell out.

And when the door opened, she nearly jumped out of her skin.

"Hi, honey," Dr. Agrawal said. "California looks great on you."

Darla brought a hand up to her cheek, remembering she still had a tan from running on the beach. "Hi," she said to the kindly gray-haired oncologist, who walked in wearing a lab coat with her shortened name that everyone called her, DR. AG, embroidered in royal blue thread over the breast pocket. "It was a fun year."

The doctor took a seat in front of a desk holding a computer screen and keyboard resting on a metal arm. "Your mother's thrilled to have you home. Every time I run into her in the hospital, she tells me that she's been counting down the days."

Darla's stomach flipped with nerves. Dr. Ag had been through a lot with her and her family, and she was used to being truthful with her. "Stanford offered me a permanent position in their writing program, and I took it."

"Oh." Darla picked up on the surprise in Dr. Ag's voice. "Well, congratulations on the honor. You must be very excited."

"Mixed feelings," she said honestly. "I love being home and near my family."

Dr. Ag assessed her carefully. "Being a cancer survivor, you're more aware than most people how finite life is. Family is important, but on the other hand, adventure is good. I'm sure you've put a lot of thought into your decision."

"It's really complicated," she admitted.

Moving away from memories and feelings she didn't want to deal with—was that bold or cowardly? She honestly wasn't sure. Even worse, was she trading being with her family for peace of mind from thinking of Nick?

And worst, maybe there was no peace of mind from Nick.

But she wasn't here to think of him, so why was she thinking of him anyway? Apparently, the man could aggravate her remotely too.

"Darla?" Dr. Ag said. "Are you all right?"

"I'm sorry," she said, forcing herself to focus. "Lots going on. Plus, today's the day."

"Ah, yes. Happy cancerversary. Three years cancer free."

Darla managed a nod, but honestly, her nerves were making her shake. Even her lower jaw was trembling, which was weird. "Thank you. Maybe I'll feel more celebratory after I know everything's okay?"

Dr. Ag smiled and patted her arm. "I know you want to get this appointment out of the way as quickly as possible. It's just going to involve a physical exam and sending you for some routine tests. So tell me how you're feeling."

"Physically, I feel fine. No complaints."

"And mentally?"

Her oncologist, like only a handful of people in her life, had seen her at her rock-bottom worst. "Busy writing, ready to put my house on the market, and Hadley and Tony have finally picked a wedding date...and it happens to be in two weeks."

"Oh dear, that is a lot."

"So I'll be seeing my ex a lot," slipped out of Darla's mouth.

Dr. Ag nodded sympathetically. "Hard to move on with an ex in a small town."

"Exactly." She stabbed the air with her finger. "How did you do it?"

She quirked a smile. "It's not as hard if you're not in love with him."

"Oh no, I'm not still in love with Nick." *Definitely not.*

"In my business," Dr. Ag said in a philosophical tone that she used often, "cancer is often a wake-up call. And you'd be surprised what people decide their priorities are when they really have to choose them. Some people really do get back together with their exes."

Darla shook her head adamantly. "I'm too smart to go back down that road." Like her mom always told her, *A man is a mistake you never want to make twice.*

"Well, I can tell you from experience, whether you move away or not, you'll still have to navigate your relationship with him."

"Trust me, I want to navigate as far away from him as possible." As soon as she survived these next few weeks. And this appointment.

After Dr. Ag finished examining her, Darla sat up and asked, "My lymph nodes are behaving?"

"I don't feel anything abnormal." Dr. Ag typed something on the keyboard. "And the rest of your exam is fine. We'll screen your thyroid today. And do some blood tests. You aren't due for any scans today, but we'll do a mammogram."

Darla knew the drill. Make sure the cancer is really gone, and make sure the treatment didn't cause some other kind of cancer. It would be a way of life, being vigilant. Being *reminded.*

Dr. Ag must have picked up on Darla's nerves because she added in a positive tone, "You don't smoke, you exercise and eat well, and you don't drink. Overall, you're looking great."

Dr. Ag was encouraging, and Darla knew how lucky she was to be healthy and cancer free. But something was still on her mind. "Does this get easier?"

"Dealing with the risks?" Darla gave a careful nod. Dr.

Ag let out a quiet sigh, as if to prepare for a complicated answer. "People have different ways of handling the stress of the unknown."

"What do you mean?" Maybe she would learn the magic recipe for controlling this stress. Yoga, running, meditation, and clean eating hadn't worked so far. Maybe she needed more ice cream in her life.

"Well, the way I would *not* recommend handling it is alone. There's no prize for being tough and independent. Cancer is a frightening foe when you don't let the people you love support you. So let the people in who want to help."

"I want everyone I love to forget that I ever had cancer." Truthfully, she wanted to be able to wave a magic wand and forget too.

"I wish it were that simple," Dr. Ag said sympathetically. "But while these visits are stressful, remember, you've beaten it. Your odds are terrific that you're going to continue to do well. And if anything should go wrong, we have an excellent chance of catching it early." She looked at Darla intently. "Did you hear that, Darla? *An excellent chance.* Which brings me to the next topic. Life goes by quickly. And you seem very, very busy."

Darla tried to absorb the positive vibes Dr. Ag was sending her way. "Is that you telling me to slow down?"

She reached over and patted Darla's knee. "You're cancer free and very much alive. I just don't want you to forget to embrace every single moment."

Dr. Ag smiled. Darla smiled too, as best as she could. Dr. Ag was right, of course. She *was* very grateful for her life. She totally understood the importance of squeezing out every single drop of it. But she felt so tangled up in a web of worry.

"Anything else?" Dr. Ag asked.

Darla had barely gotten out a no when Dr. Ag rolled her chair toward her. "Now, I have a favor to ask. And I'll be right up-front with you, it's going to cut into your time. But...it's important."

Darla braced herself, knowing full well that Dr. Ag would stop at nothing to help her patients. And Darla had a sneaking suspicion that, whatever her ask was, it was going to involve at least one of them.

"Do you know the Pearsons?"

"Michelle and Jason?" They owned Seaside Books and Antiques, a fun combination of things all in one place that was popular with tourists and townsfolk alike. "My mom works with Michelle on the Socks for Santa project every year."

Dr. Ag nodded. "Mackenzie, their oldest, gave me permission to tell you that she has Hodgkin's. A lymph node in her neck just like you. She took a leave from college this past semester while she gets through her chemo."

"Oh." Darla's first thought was that that sucked. "She's so young to go through all of that." She had a vague recollection of Mackenzie, or Mac as everyone called her, as a young teen with braces who helped out in the bookstore and who always had her nose in a book.

Dr. Ag cut to the chase. "I wondered if you might pay her a visit."

Darla tamped down a sudden wave of panic. "I'm all for giving back," she said carefully. "Remember when you had me sign and donate books? I'd always do anything

for a charity. But I'm not sure if I'm ready to revisit—
all of that." She waved her hand in the air. As if a hand
wave could swish away chemo, radiation, and the feeling
that you were constantly holding your breath for the next
health battle, whatever that might be. "Maybe next year
when my life—"

"This is a bit of a different situation." Dr. Ag didn't
hesitate to press her case, even if it caused discomfort.
Darla realized with a sinking feeling that Dr. Ag knew
that Darla would do anything she asked because Darla
literally owed her everything.

Dr. Ag punched a few buttons on her phone. "Not only
is she from our town, she's also an enormous fan of yours."
Dr. Ag looked over her fancy jeweled reading glasses. "You
would be a valuable connection for her right now."

For a few heartbeats, Darla met Dr. Ag's gaze, which
never wavered. Finally, Darla threw up her hands. "Okay,
fine. You know I can't say no to you."

"Job perk," Dr. Ag said with a smile, pushing a button
on her phone that made a whooshing sound. Then she
slipped the phone back into her lab jacket.

"I'll be in touch about your blood work in a few days.
And I'll call you when your mammogram result lands on
my desk."

Darla's own phone pinged with the incoming text,
surely containing Mackenzie's contact information. "Is
this how you got through med school, by being pushy?"

Dr. Ag grinned. "You bet." She tapped a stack of papers
on her desk. "You'll like Mac. I think you can both learn a
little something from each other."

Chapter 8

"HEY, DAD," NICK said a little later as his father sat down across from him at Darla's kitchen counter. Nick poured him a coffee amid the sounds of hammering and drilling, compliments of the crew working on the bathroom. He accidentally spilled a little, probably because he couldn't stop thinking about Darla's appointment.

His dad, a silver-haired lion of a man, looked up from his mug. "This isn't that fancy-schmancy coffee again, is it?"

"Sure is," Nick said. "We work hard. It's nice to start the day with a great cup of coffee." Nick's monthly coffee subscription was a little expensive, but a great cuppa to kick each day off right was worth it.

"The bargain canister from the warehouse club suits me just fine," his dad mumbled, taking a sip. But Nick could tell from the way his thick brows lifted that it hadn't hurt going down.

"Smooth, huh?" Nick said. His grin was probably a little self-satisfied.

The only thing his dad couldn't swallow was his pride—and admit how good it was.

But oh well. Nick was used to it.

Aaron Steinfeld, one of their best carpenters, walked into the kitchen. "Hey, Mr. C. Hey, Nick. We're almost finished ripping stuff out back there. Can you come back for a consult in a few minutes?"

"Sure," Nick said. "Just give a holler."

As Aaron walked back to the bathroom, Nick's dad said, "I think you're spreading yourself too thin." His dad always seemed to use the moments they were alone together to express his worry about all of Nick's life decisions. "Don't you have a test coming up? And that house on Bay Street. That thing cost you a bundle. How do you find time to work on that with everything else you do?"

"My house is almost done," Nick said. "I'll be putting it up for sale, and then I'll need another project. Besides, the payoff when I sell is always worth it. You know that. No one does the work like we do."

His dad didn't seem to take the compliment. Instead, he said, "You tell Darla about that house?"

The mention of her name made him think about how on edge she'd seemed at breakfast. And started him worrying all over again.

"She just got back to town, Dad," he said cautiously. "Of course, I'm going to tell her."

Nick knew his dad thought he'd bought Darla's ancestor's house as an impulse decision. Which, admittedly, it was, but Nick had it under control. He'd been managing numbers since he was a kid, and he'd learned how to make smart investments. But his dad didn't seem to see that.

His dad took a bite of his white-bread sandwich, ham and cheese with yellow mustard, the same sandwich he'd been eating for thirty-five years, and said, "Okay," in that dubious way that made Nick feel like he was eighteen again.

"Don't worry, I'll tell her about the house. If she doesn't want it, someone else will." But in his mind, the house was Darla's. Only hers.

His dad made a noise that wasn't optimistic. "I worry about you getting your hopes up."

Nick frowned, not sure where this conversation was going. If it involved Darla, he definitely didn't want to go there. "About what?"

"About Darla." Okay, he guessed they were going there. "I mean, it's been ten years, right?"

Since the divorce, he meant. "Yes," Nick said carefully, wondering how a conversation that began with coffee had ended up here.

His dad set down his sandwich, another ominous sign. "Just be realistic, is all I'm saying. If you're thinking she's going to see what you've done and want to get back together—"

"It's not like that," he said firmly. "I just grabbed the opportunity. No worries. My finances are solid." And while they were at it, he was going to use that to segue into something else. "You know, you could go fishing more often if you left me in charge." He'd already redone their entire bookkeeping system. Made the way they'd purchased materials more efficient. Streamlined their inventory. Basically, he'd learned the business from the ground up, used what his dad built, and was pointing the company into a future of financial security.

Except Nick knew that his dad didn't want to leave the company he'd built from nothing in the hands of the son who'd never wanted it in the first place.

Oh, his dad would never say that. Tony was and always would be the star of the family, and Nick would be the angry kid who'd seen the writing on the wall. During the time he was married, it had felt like family obligation would keep him in Seashell Harbor his entire life working construction while Tony traveled the word collecting Super Bowl rings.

Not that he ever begrudged his brother. He loved his brother. A lot.

But that had been hard.

But eventually, it had also been... transformative. Nick didn't feel that way anymore. He loved the business. He only wished his dad would start treating him more like a partner.

His dad gave him the side-eye. "Are you pushing me to retire?"

"No, of course not. But you've been at this for thirty-five years. It's okay to take a break once in a while." *And show me that you trust me.*

Because he sure trusted Tony, as evidenced by letting his brother handle all his personal finances, set up retirement accounts, and help him make stock market investments.

But Nick had been the one taking care of the business books for years. Now that he was just shy of his MBA, he was ready to take over. Yet his dad seemed to see him as the second kid, the one who didn't shine.

"Hey, Nick," Aaron appeared in the kitchen. "Sorry to bug you again, but we've got everything but the bathtub torn out. Mind taking a look now?"

"Sure. No problem," Nick said as he slid off the counter stool.

"Nicholas," his dad called after him.

"Yeah, Dad?"

His dad looked up and gave a half smile. "Good coffee."

Nick couldn't help grinning back. It was a small concession. "Thanks, Dad."

"I just don't want to see you hurt again. You got that?"

"Got it. Love you too, Dad."

Nick knew his dad loved him. He just didn't fully trust him.

Just before he turned to go, his dad pulled a card out of his wallet and held it up.

Nick squinted. "What is that?"

"It's my ordination certificate," he said proudly. "I just got it in the mail."

"That's great." *Yikes.* "Isn't Reverend Jackson doing the wedding?"

"Yes, but maybe Tony and Hadley would want me to do it instead."

Hmm. Okay. "Why don't you ask them?"

"I was thinking you'd ask for me. You know, so they don't feel obligated."

"Dad, you ask. I gotta go." Yeah, he was definitely sticking to looking for a venue and letting Tony and his dad duke this one out.

Nick gave some direction to the guys on the crew and returned to the kitchen a little later to find Darla walking in at the same time.

"Angelo!" she said. His dad stood and embraced her in a giant hug.

Nick hung back, watching carefully. Unlike Darla's mom, Nick's dad held no grudges. He'd loved Darla ever since the first time Nick had brought her home.

"Darla, sweetheart," his dad said, drawing back to assess her, "you look just like you did when you were eighteen. Except more worried. And too skinny. How's life as a famous author?"

She swiped at her tears and sat down next to him. "I miss you," she said fondly. "No one calls me young *or* skinny anymore." He chuckled and offered her a cookie. Not the store-bought kind, but one that looked like a homemade Italian wedding cookie. She bit into it immediately. "Oh, life's okay. And this is delicious. You made it, of course."

"Of course," his dad said with pride. "I'm excited for my son to finish his fancy-schmancy MBA so I can spend my days fishing. And cooking."

Nick stopped eavesdropping and walked into the kitchen. So his dad just admitted that he wanted to fish after all?

"You're getting an MBA?" Darla asked, wearing a shocked expression.

He quirked a brow to remind her that she'd under-estimated him again. "Four classes and a thesis before I take over the company." He shot his dad a look.

"He's already taken over the books," his dad grumbled. "In fact, they aren't even books anymore, they're all in the computer. And CAD drawing. And he started that flipper company."

"You don't have to bore her with the details," Nick said quickly.

"You guys sound as busy as ever," Darla said.

"Yep." Nick patted his dad on the back. "The company is thriving. Maybe it *is* time for some fishing."

"See that?" his dad gestured with his hands. "My son's trying to get rid of me."

"I think it's really exciting," Darla said. "Looks like Cammareri Vintage Remodeling will be around for years to come."

Nick took hold of Darla's elbow, steering her toward the hall. "I'm taking Darla back to see the bathroom, Dad. I'll be back in a minute to unload that next truckload."

"Take your time," his dad said with a wave.

Darla didn't fight him for once. She was light on his arm, and she smelled like lemons.

"Sounds like you've made a lot of changes for the better," she said. "I'm impressed."

"Wish my dad was. He talks the talk about retiring, but I'll believe it when I see it. Hey, guys," Nick called, glancing at his crew as they carried a large soaker tub with gold jets down the hall. "Watch the wall when you turn that corner down there, will ya?"

"Okay, boss," one of them called.

"Boss, huh?" Darla asked.

He shrugged. "Someday."

"It sounds good on you. Like…it fits."

He made a face. "It's a tough job, but somebody's got to do it."

She frowned and crossed her arms, assessing him. "You should give yourself more credit."

He'd wanted her approval, but now that she was complimenting him, it felt weird. But good weird. "You know more than anyone that I fell into this job."

"But you're doing amazing things with the company. And getting an MBA while you're doing everything else."

"Well, you're the one who taught me to reach for the sky."

She looked at him a little funny. "What do you mean?" As they approached the master bath, he let go of her elbow. Good thing, because his fingers were tingling. Also, he'd just dropped sort of a bombshell there. "Look at you. You had a goal, and you achieved it. It's pretty remarkable."

"No," she said quickly. "Not remarkable. Just the result of being stubborn."

"Well, we're both pretty stubborn," he said.

"For better or for worse." She scanned his face, looking like she might want to say more.

Silence fell. He wondered if she was thinking how, in their marriage, both of them had been really great at digging in their heels.

He changed the subject. "Everything go okay at the doctor's?" He paused. "I hope you don't think I'm prying. I just... wanted to know."

"I got my usual exam and routine blood work." She must have seen the worry because she added, "Hey, I'm three years cancer free. If my tests come back okay, I get to wait a whole half a year for my next appointment."

"I'll buy you a drink to celebrate." He leaned his arm on the wall and scanned her face. "I'm sorry you have to go through this waiting game." So far so good, provided her tests came out okay. Which made him utter a silent prayer.

"My reality. But as my oncologist reminded me, I'm very much alive and well."

He grinned. "Good to hear."

"I'm sorry I was abrupt earlier. It was nerves. I want you to know that I appreciate your concern."

So he'd been right about her nerves. Also, he would've forgiven her for anything short of a capital offense just for looking at him like that, her gaze full of sincerity, her naturally long lashes fluttering against her cheeks.

"Apology accepted." He couldn't help smiling. "Keep me posted, okay?"

They entered the haze of dust and the piled-up debris.

"Hey, Nick," Sam, Aaron's partner for the day, said. "Okay if we grab some lunch now?"

"Sure," he said, "but skip the martinis, okay?"

"Yeah, I don't think a martini goes very well with PB and J," Aaron said with a chuckle.

"Hey, Ms. Manning," Sam, said, "I bought your last book. Think you'd autograph it for my grandma?"

Darla waved her hand dismissively. "Oh sure, I'd love to."

"Great," he said as they passed. "I'll bring it in after lunch."

As the guys cleared out, Nick unfolded a magazine page from his pocket. "Sorry again about the mess."

"Yes," she said with mock seriousness. "But I'm going to really miss cleaning all those jets."

"Anyway, your tile's right in there"—he pointed to a pile of boxes—"but we need to talk about the rest of the bathroom."

She glanced around the torn-up room. "I'm a little sad that you're making it beautiful when I'm about to move out."

"Then don't" flew right of his mouth.

Startled, she jerked up her head. Suddenly the air seemed too still, the space too small. He wanted to grab her by the shoulders and tell her he didn't want her to go. But that would be...ridiculous. Finally, he pushed back from the wall and pointed to the still-standing marble slabs that had surrounded the bathtub.

"Doing this remodel will increase the resale value because everything was dated. And hopefully it will make the house sell more quickly. Besides, it's too late for regrets. We just have to move forward." He felt like he was only half talking about the bathroom.

"I'm all for moving forward," she said. "Tell me what I have to do about picking out the fixtures."

He handed her the magazine page.

She took a glance at it and then frowned. "This is the photograph I showed you months ago when I asked you about the tile. I told you—I told you I loved this bathroom."

Whew. Glad she still felt that way or he'd be in trouble. "Yeah. Well, if you're okay with me going forward, we're going to get you that bathroom right there."

Looking incredulous, she shook her head. "I never meant to hint—"

"You didn't hint. But I could tell you really liked it. I do too." This was something he could do for her, something he was good at. He'd really wanted to do it, and he didn't want her to feel bad. "So...do you trust me?"

"Yes?"

He held his chest like she'd just wounded him. "I'm going to show you what I can do. And it's going to knock your socks off."

"I can't wait to be impressed." She paused. "Thank you."

His gaze held hers. And again, he felt like they weren't really talking about remodeling bathrooms at all. But then maybe it was just a weird day.

Being this close to her was making him remember things. Like a time when, after all this back and forth, she'd be in his arms, laughing and giggling and definitely *not* getting down to business. Or rather, getting down to a completely different kind of business.

"What's this?" He pointed to her midarm. He lifted her sleeve a little to reveal a Disney princess Band-Aid.

She glanced down. "Got my blood drawn."

"You hate needles." He traced over the Band-Aid with his fingertips before he realized that wasn't a good idea and dropped his hand.

"Yeah, well, I still do. Only difference is now I can joke about it a little. Hence the Disney Band-Aids." She tapped her arm. "The lab techs know me too well."

He tried to think of something funny to say about the cartoon characters, but he was at a loss. "It killed me to watch you go through that cancer," he blurted instead.

Whoa. Where had *that* come from? He didn't really know. The words had just…poured out.

She sucked in a breath, looking completely thrown.

"I've never felt so helpless in my life," he added. Okay, his mouth diarrhea was not stopping, and he had no control.

She stared at him. Swallowed hard. "We were divorced quite a while by then. I didn't want you hanging around because of pity."

"You confused pity with caring." He said it quickly, forcefully, the words fast as the snap of a rubber band.

And...he'd just told her he cared.

It was the most honest moment that had passed between them in years. Which was probably pretty sad. But she noticed too, because her eyes suddenly got watery, but she blinked fast.

"We were best friends for a long time before we were lovers," he said, not letting this go. "Not being able to be there for you...it was devastating."

"Why are you...why are you telling me this now?" Her voice was hoarse, choked with emotion.

"Because you're leaving for good, and if we're not truthful with each other now, we never will be."

He realized they were standing amid the rubble, reminiscent of their rubble of a marriage. Too bad relationships couldn't be remodeled as easily as bathrooms.

"Do you—um—do you think we could be friends again?" she whispered.

"Darla, I never stopped being your friend." He couldn't prevent the crack in his voice. Or the quickening of his pulse at the words she'd just said. He could barely stop himself from taking her in his arms.

Who comforted her? he couldn't help but wonder. Oh, her friends were wonderful, but who held her? Who helped her through this battle she'd probably never really stop fighting, in one way or another?

He wanted to. He wished he could.

He took a step closer. Her eyes were round and wide, and in them, with her defenses lowered, he finally saw the same woman he knew from so long ago. And that made him giddy with relief. Did she remember the good times before the divorce, before the mistakes and the miscommunication, like he did? The tenderness in her eyes told him she might. Before he could stop himself, he leaned forward, driven by some force he could not control, to place a kiss on her pretty, full mouth.

Her lips were soft and warm, and she gave a little gasp on contact, but she didn't pull away, and that gave him hope that she was feeling the same wild, short-circuiting connection that he was.

He'd just brought his hands up to hold her, to kiss her more thoroughly, to take her in his arms for real, when someone called Darla's name. She stepped back quickly and cleared her throat. And he stood there, dazed, trying to figure out what the hell had just happened.

"There you are!" Hadley said, coughing a little from the dust and trying to wave it away. "Hey, I need to talk to you."

"Sure." The only evidence that Darla might have been a little thrown was that she briefly touched her lips.

"Is this an okay-Nick-you-can-leave-now problem?" Nick was already making his way out of the mess.

"No, it's more like a wedding disaster problem." That made him halt his steps.

"Another one?" Darla asked, then quickly clapped her hand over her mouth. "Sorry, I didn't mean that."

He felt a little shaky, his pulse hammering in his ears. Had he just imagined that kiss?

Hadley's words poured out. "Reverend Jackson's mom is having hip surgery...the day before our wedding! Of course, he's flying to Ohio to be with her. Maybe it's an omen."

Oh no. The news snapped Nick back to reality.

He frowned. "An omen?"

"I'm starting to feel our wedding is jinxed." The way she was biting her lower lip made him realize she wasn't joking.

Darla turned to Nick, her face full of concern. "Did you have any luck calling those venues?"

Actually, he'd just finished calling a bunch of them before Darla showed up. "It's high season, and the whole town is booked to the gills." Nick shook his head. "Sorry, Had."

"Thanks for trying, but the wedding is off." Hadley sounded sad and resigned. "We thought about having it in our yard, but the city won't approve that kind of gathering with all the construction going on. Luckily, we only have close relatives coming, but both our grandparents have already booked their flights. It's just disappointing."

"Don't give up yet," Nick said. "I don't believe in jinxes."

Hadley smiled politely and gave him a *thanks-anyway* look.

"There *is* another alternative." Nick rubbed his chin thoughtfully.

"In town?" Darla asked. "That would be a miracle."

"I'm thinking beachfront," Nick swept his arm toward the beach, which they could see through Darla's bedroom windows. "Big enough to accommodate everybody." Nick grinned widely, tapping his boot on the dusty floor. "Right here at Casa de Darla."

Chapter 9

DARLA WAS SENDING Nick daggers with her pretty, gold-flecked eyes.

He wondered which she was more upset about—the fact that he'd just offered up her house as a wedding venue for their friends, or that he'd kissed her.

Probably both. What had he been thinking? He'd felt a closeness that he hadn't felt in years, and that had led to...

Near disaster.

Yeah, he'd better make this right ASAP.

Hear me out, he signaled by shrugging his shoulders and lifting his brows.

She frowned and sent him a little shrug back, which he interpreted as *Okay, you've got thirty seconds to make your case.*

He almost cracked a grin because the private, wordless language they used to use so often actually still worked.

Hadley seemed oblivious, too stressed out to really take note of Darla's reaction. "I couldn't do that to you," Hadley said to Darla. "You just got home, and you're getting ready to move."

"It actually might be a good idea." Darla surveyed the bathroom destruction and turned to Nick. "Can you get all this done by then?"

"Let's think about it," Nick said, his mind churning as he stepped out onto the deck and envisioned the setup. "We can have the ceremony down at the beach. And the reception right on the deck. It's perfect." He walked to the doorway of the bedroom and looked out the wall of windows overlooking the massive deck. "It's big enough to put a band in the corner. And turn it into a dance floor when everyone's done eating." He turned to Hadley. "How big's your guest list?"

"Less than fifty. Just family and intimate friends."

"Perfect. It's all doable." He took to examining the condition of the deck until Darla called his name.

"Nick, the deck is fine. Please stop looking at it that way."

"What way?" he asked innocently.

"Like you can't wait to put down a coat of sealer."

Busted.

Darla turned to Hadley. "So we would need food, booze, and music."

Hadley rubbed her forehead. "Let me talk to Tony." She grabbed Darla's arms. "This is a lot to spring on you. Are you sure this is even on the table? We all know Nick can convince a princess to kiss a frog, so please be honest. How do you really feel about it?"

From Nick's point of view, it was a no-brainer. But

then, Darla had a lot on her plate. And, observing her now, something seemed a little off. She was smiling a little too brightly, trying a little too hard to be casual. He knew because her right hand was fisted into a ball. And her posture was ramrod straight.

Darla looked Hadley straight in the eye. "Honey, we've got the ball rolling on this, so why not keep it rolling? I'd be honored for you to get married here. It would be a great way to say goodbye to the house."

Hadley suddenly burst into tears, and Darla comforted her. Knowing when to make a quiet exit, Nick left them alone.

Weddings. They were disastrous events that brought out all the emotions, that was for sure.

But he was a romantic at heart. His mind was already churning about making a wooden bower for his brother and Hadley to get married under and placing it on the beach right in front of the house. Darla could pick the flowers for it, and it would look stunning while the sun was setting. He could practically see it now.

Hadley came out of the bedroom, wiping her eyes with a tissue. Nick walked her to the door and when he came back, he found that Darla had kicked off her flip-flops and was pacing back and forth in front of her bed while she talked on the phone.

The breeze was blowing the sheer curtains. Backlit by the sun, her wild curls were shimmering in the light, and she looked so lovely—and so familiar—that it sent a stab of longing through him.

Plus, they were in her bedroom, which brought back a whole different flood of memories.

He had to admit that this wedding plan was appealing for a completely different reason. And that reason was standing right in front of him.

"Wait," she said, completely engrossed in the call. "They need the blurb for the next book this week? I've had a lot going on since I've gotten home and—"

Nick pulled out his tape measure and pretended to measure something.

"I understand they want it for the new cover but I—okay, I get it. Yes, see if next week would be okay. Thanks, Julia. Talk soon."

Ah yes, Julia. Darla's longtime agent. Whatever it was she was asking, it sounded stressful.

Darla slipped her feet back into her flip-flops. "I've got to get right to work," she said. "I'll just set up my computer in one of the bedrooms down the other hall."

"Not so fast," Nick said.

"Excuse me?" Color raced into her cheeks.

"Did you eat lunch?"

Her anger deflated. "No. But I—"

"Bet you're hungry," he said before she could apologize. Which he could see coming.

"I'm not—"

"You look a little pale." He nodded toward her hand, which was still fisted. "And stressed."

Her hands flew up to her face. "I'm not—"

He cracked a smile. "Okay, I was exaggerating the pale part. But I'm getting a giant stress vibe. Want to talk about it over some good food?"

She cast him a wary glance. "What would your dad say if you took a fancy-schmancy lunch?"

He glanced down at his watch. "Well, since I've been working since 6:30 a.m., I don't think he'd mind holding down the fort for a little while." He pulled out his cell. "I'll ask him to supervise the demo until I get back." He typed in a message and sent it.

In seconds, his phone dinged. "I'm good. Let's go."

He pointed to the sliding door that opened onto the deck.

"Wait a minute," she mumbled to herself. "What am I doing?" She turned to him and threw up her arms. "You kissed me back there!"

He rubbed his neck. "I guess I got a little emotional. Swept away in the moment. It was just…" He didn't know what it was. "It won't happen again. I want to hear about what's bothering you. As…friends."

That's what he wanted, right? To be friends.

Too bad other parts of him didn't seem to be on that same page. But he'd get them in line ASAP.

She looked relieved, so whatever he'd tried to awkwardly say, it must have worked well enough. "Want to know the truth?" she said. "I can't tell my friends about my stress."

"Well then, maybe you can count me as your friend too."

"I could *really* use someone to talk to. And food sounds good too."

"Wow."

"What is it?"

"You just admitted that you can trust me with your secrets…a little."

"Don't be too flattered. I'm a little desperate here. And I don't keep secrets from my best friends. This is just something I don't want to kill the wedding joy with."

"Well then, I'll just take what I can get," he said as he opened the sliding door.

* * *

It was Darla's fault that she let Nick pick the Dancing Crab, a casual restaurant on the water with a killer view. And an old sentimental favorite of theirs from when they were together.

That's what she got for letting her guard down, she thought as she looked over the menu. Memories catapulted her from all sides. From all the old favorites that hadn't changed in a dozen years to that kiss. Like, he'd kissed her and now they were having lunch as if nothing had happened?

Also, pure, unleashed honesty had brought on that kiss. So did that mean it was better not to be honest?

Darla couldn't stop thinking about it. It was just a simple kiss—there hadn't been time to make it anything more. But that simple touch of his lips on hers had ratcheted up her pulse and worse, filled her with longing. If Hadley hadn't interrupted, she would have leaned in and given it all right back to him, and God knows what might have happened.

She told herself it was leftover feelings and physical attraction, the things that always got her into trouble with Nick. Soon she'd be far, far away from him, and then she'd be able to really start over. Away from the pheromones he seemed to exude from every pore.

Except for now, here she was, sitting across from his handsome face. He wore an old gray T-shirt and faded blue jeans the color of his eyes that were just this side of worn, and work boots, making him the picture of Totally Hot Working Guy.

But she wasn't here to salivate over him. She was here to talk, and he'd offered to listen. She must've been desperate to take him, of all people, up on that offer.

"I don't see salad on the menu," she said.

Nick tossed her a look that was half puzzlement, half amusement. "Has salad *ever* been on the menu?" They sat in the dappled sunshine, half shielded by a big red umbrella with a crab happily dancing a jig on it. Seagulls swooped and squawked over the deep blue water, and the breeze carried an unmistakable salty tang. Basically, it was a fine summer day. Nick took about ten seconds with the menu before closing it.

He quirked a smile. "If it doesn't fit in a basket with paper underneath to soak up the grease, it's not a popular item."

She rolled her eyes. "Haha."

He didn't look like the Nick she'd known intimately for so many years. Oh, he had the same strong nose and the same determined jaw. The same full, expressive mouth. But tiny crinkles lined his eyes, and if she wasn't mistaken, a gray hair or two appeared among his dark waves. The overall effect was that of a mature man who was even more sexy than before.

Stick to the salad, she told herself. But she was so distracted and overwrought that she could barely read the lines of the menu.

And also, how had her home become the wedding venue?

"Come on," he said in a teasing tone, "you know you want the battered hot dog bites with wow-wow sauce."

That threw her. Not the wow-wow sauce, because she

knew that he loved that hot-and-spicy concoction. But because it had been a long time since he looked at her like that—with fun, mischief, and…something more that made a rush of warmth run straight through her.

Too bad he wasn't wrinkly and old.

Except she had the terrifying feeling she'd still like him even then.

"Please, please tell me you're not going to order a salad," Nick reached out and lowered her menu, breaking her wayward thoughts.

"I don't eat fried stuff anymore." To prove it, when the waitress approached, she ordered a garden salad with chicken and a Diet Coke.

Nick looked appalled. "I'll take a double order of puppy-dog bites, a large basket of fries, and some wow-wow sauce on the side. And I'll take a Diet too."

As their waitress took their menus and left, Darla leaned over. "I thought you didn't poison your body with things like that anymore either."

He shrugged. "I'm in a nostalgic mood."

She shook her head. "Also, naming battered hot dogs—or anything you eat—after puppies…not a good idea."

He shrugged. "It's the most popular item on the menu."

"If you think I'm eating one of those, you're wrong."

"Okay." He smiled a *we'll see* smile.

On the bay, sailboats floated with pure white sails. The warm breeze was sun-kissed. And for a fleeting moment, Darla's stress loosened. "I forgot how breathtaking the view is."

He shot her a pointed look. "Maybe it takes going away and looking at it again to see what you've missed."

Before she could process that with anything other than a blush, he asked, "So what's going on?"

"You know that book deadline I mentioned? It's the same day as the wedding." She was actually grateful to talk about something concrete.

"You always have a book deadline, and you always turn in your books on time," he said. "Even during chemo."

She frowned. "How did you know that?"

"Darla, you didn't talk to me, but I still asked about you." She didn't want to be touched but somehow his words hit her straight in the heart. "Besides, I know you take your work seriously. It's who you are."

Darla chewed on her lower lip. It was so odd sitting here, just like they had sat and chatted together so long ago. Except everything was so different and confusing now.

Her emotions were so jumbled, swinging back and forth like a pendulum. From the joy of sitting outside in the sunshine and bantering back and forth as they always had, to the sadness of all that they had lost.

Also, he'd just talked about her work in a complimentary way, not like it had been a major source of tension in their marriage.

"What are you thinking about?" He was studying her carefully, unnerving her even more.

"Just that we're sitting here, like we have a hundred times before. Yet everything turned out so differently than we'd imagined."

He took his time answering, and when he finally spoke, it was with measured words. "I look at it a little differently. I'm a big believer that things can be better than before. We're adults now. We wouldn't want to go back to those innocent days, when we didn't know ourselves—or the world—very well."

The waitress brought their drinks. Darla opened her straw and wound the paper around her finger. "If we'd been wiser, maybe we wouldn't have made the mistakes that we did."

"I don't consider us a mistake." His gaze was leveled straight at her, and there was no escaping it. She had no idea what to say—or feel—but her heart was fluttering despite her telling it not to.

He leaned forward, folding his arms on the table. "Now, tell me what's going on so we can help everyone's favorite thriller author."

She couldn't help smiling. He was joking a little, trying to make her feel better. "I started writing another kind of book entirely. I—I'm not really sure why. Something that was in my heart." Confessing this much felt like a relief, but she was never going to tell him that it was inspired by feelings she'd traveled three thousand miles to forget.

"Isn't that what an author does, write the book of their heart? What kind of book is it?"

Maybe it was because Darla was a little overwhelmed, but she told him the honest truth. "It's a book about a couple who screwed up."

He lifted a brow. "Does she end up killing him?"

She laughed. "No killing. No mystery."

"No suspense?"

"Well, only the suspense of how the book is going to end, because I honestly don't have a clue." She supposed she'd started by pouring out their love story to get it out of her head, but it had grown into a unique story of its own. A new story that she simply couldn't put down. But it wasn't what her readers—or her publisher—expected.

Which was defiant—maybe even irresponsible—and not at all like her.

Their food arrived. The waitress set down warm baskets of fries and a giant bottle of ketchup, which made her mouth water. And her salad, which unfortunately didn't, although it was a very nice salad. The hot dog bites smelled salty, beefy, and garlicky, and they were calling her name.

So was Nick, apparently. He was holding out the basket, shaking it gently in front of her face, just enough so she could smell the warm deliciousness and get an up-close view of the crispy, golden coating. "Try one."

She lifted a brow. "If I try one, I may eat ten."

"What's wrong with that? Live a little."

Dr. Ag's words about living life echoed in her head. But if she gave in to the hot dog bites, *he* could be next. "Thanks, but...no thanks. I love lettuce." To prove it, she shoved a giant forkful into her mouth.

Proving that he wasn't the kind of guy to throw in the flag, Nick tried another tack. Setting the basket down, he picked up a hot dog bite, dipped it in ketchup, and brought it to her mouth. "Open up. This doggie wants to go into the doghouse."

It was so ridiculous that she burst out laughing. And, on impulse, opened her mouth. He made like he was going to toss it in, but ended up very carefully placing it on her tongue. The gesture was a little...hot.

She accepted the food and bit into it, very aware of him watching every move. The hot dog bite overwhelmed her tongue with the tang of ketchup, the crispy coating, and the juicy, salty meat. She closed her eyes. "So good!"

"See what you've been missing?"

That made her eyes fly open. All this double talk.

She rolled her eyes. "It's fun to reminisce, but there's a reason I don't have a steady diet of this." Or of Nick.

"Why is that?"

"Because it would kill me." It almost did, divorcing him. And she couldn't ever forget that. Also, since the Hodgkin's, she'd become somewhat of a health fanatic. No sugar. No grease. Lots of veggies. Daily runs along the beach.

"Okay, I can respect that," he said. "Keep going."

"So this book is not even the same genre as what I've promised my publisher, and it has no suspense in it. It would probably be called an upmarket women's fiction novel."

"How much have you got done?"

"I'm almost to the end."

His mouth turned up in a half grin. "Can you invent a killer and make it what your publisher wants?"

"I keep trying to inject some kind of suspense element into it." She absently twirled the ring on her finger. *Bring me a man for my book*, she'd asked it. A mysterious man to make it suspenseful.

He raised a dark, well-defined brow. "But?"

"I didn't say 'but.'" But she was thinking it. That it would be a shame to alter it. But above all, Darla was a professional. "To make my deadline, I'm going to have to. I mean, I can't just do what I want. I have a contract."

They both reached out for a fry at the same time, and their hands grazed.

His was warm, his fingers long and slender, and touching him felt like a jolt, like when you run in your socks across a rug and then touch something.

Snap! Static electricity. Yep, that was it. Part of her wanted to grab that hand and hold on to it for dear life. And the other part wanted to run, run, run.

What had gotten into her? This was her *ex*. Not as in ex-boyfriend. Ex-*husband*. The man who was. Not. For. Her. The man who, once upon a time, had resented her ambition and criticized her for having too much drive.

What was she doing letting him feed her hot dogs and french fries as they sat on the sparkling bright water just like they were teenagers falling in love all over again?

What was *he* doing, being understanding and trying to help her? Getting MBAs and preparing to take over his father's business. Helping out deploying soldiers who needed places to stay. Helping *her*.

Fast as wildfire, she drew back her hand. "Then that's what I have to do. Get the book written, whatever it takes, and turn it in." She'd done it before, sacrificed everything in her life to get a book finished. She could do it again and dig herself out of this mess.

"Tell me something," he said, seemingly unaffected by their one-second hand bump. "Is the book you're writing good?"

"Honestly, I don't know. It just…came out of me." That was the most she could say without telling him the full truth. Which was that the words had literally poured out of her, heart and soul, as she tried to make sense of her life. And of her feelings for him.

Now, all those feelings she'd taken a year to tie up in

a perfect bow and shove somewhere deep inside were all threatening to unravel. All because of puppy bites and wow-wow sauce.

"If the book is good," Nick said in a thoughtful tone, "maybe you should just finish it as it was meant to be finished."

She gave an uncomfortable laugh. Probably from imagining the sharp intake of breath and colorful exclamation Julia would make if she told her about this aberrant creation of hers. "If only I knew how it ends."

He shrugged. "Stephen King says that stories come into the world fully formed and the author knows that, deep down in some secret place inside. You just have to unlock the mysteries of it."

Stunned, Darla set down her drink. "Who are you, and what happened to the old Nick?"

He chuckled. "What do you mean?"

She blinked in disbelief. "You read Stephen King's book on writing?"

"I read a lot of stuff." He fixed that blue gaze on her, more brilliant than the deep hue of the water all around them. "I'm just saying that you've spent years building your career. Maybe you don't have to play by all the rules all the time—like, maybe sometimes it's okay if you invent your own, you know? Not in a bad way, but... there must be a reason you wrote this particular book. I'm happy to read it if that would help."

No way that was happening. But... he'd offered to read it. Which was the first time he'd ever done that. "Thanks. I'll think about it."

"So let me get this straight," he said, talking with his

hands. "You have a deadline, but you also have to take part in the wedding *and* put your house on the market. And I just offered to have the wedding at your house. Let's call Hadley and take that off the table."

"Actually, I think a beach wedding in front of my house would be really special." She couldn't help smiling just thinking about it. "I'm thrilled Hadley and Tony waited for me to come home to get married. And I would never ruin their joy with my stress."

She wanted to show him that she knew what her priorities were now. Because at one time he'd accused her of being married to her work.

"I respect your work ethic and your love for your friends," he said, "but I worry that you'd risk your health before you'd ask for an extension. How do you want to handle this?"

When they were married, she'd been trying so hard to become published, working full time at an office job and writing half the night. And it had interfered in their marriage. To be honest, maybe it had even been the start of all their problems.

"I need to be there for our friends," she said. "That's the most important thing. But moving the deadline is impossible."

He didn't question her further. "Well, if that's the way it has to be, then I propose an accountability project."

She laughed. "A what?" She was extremely accountable. Was he suggesting she wasn't?

"Yeah. Listen. I know how responsible you are, but this sounds like dire straits, right?"

"Maybe." *Yes!*

"You get up at the butt-crack of dawn and start writing your heart out," he said matter-of-factly. "I finish your bathroom, take my exam next week, and we both tag team all the wedding responsibilities in between. So we spend evenings with our friends *and* get all our work done. How's that sound?"

He'd made it sound so simple. "You know I'm a night owl," she said.

"Well, maybe for the next two weeks you're not. Just until you pull yourself out of this trouble. Because it's going to be hard to sleep in if my crew is in your bathroom working."

"Okay. I'm in," she surprised herself by saying. What did she have to lose? To be honest, it felt good to have support and understanding when she was feeling over-whelmed. The surprise was that those things had come from Nick.

"Has Carol put the house on the market yet?" he asked.

"She's about to."

He rubbed his hand over his chin in thought. She noticed the faint shadow of his beard, which was way too sexy looking. "Can you tell her to spread the word, but no showings until after the wedding? It's prime property, and she might even be able to sell it off market."

"You make everything seem possible," she said. "But then you were always an optimist."

"It *is* possible," he said with typical Nick determination. "We'll help each other. And our getting along will ulti-mately help our friends as they celebrate their wedding." He held up his Coke. "Deal?"

"It might just be crazy enough to work." She clinked

her Coke with his. "Thanks for listening." She debated whether to continue. "I really needed someone to talk to. You helped a lot."

He glanced up at her over his straw, and their gazes snagged in that same crazy way. How many times had she peered at his oh-so-familiar face across from her, taking for granted that she'd be looking at it forever?

He set down his glass. "Remember when we used to share a Coke all the time because we were constantly pinching pennies?"

Oh, Nick, something deep within her cried. Just when she shored up her feelings, he had to go stab her straight in the heart.

Of course, she remembered.

He reached over and grabbed her hand. "You okay?"

She shook her head. "Sometimes I just…"

He squeezed her hand. "Hey, it wasn't all bad, was it?"

"No." Of course he'd figured out what she was thinking. "It wasn't." Her voice came out low and a little choked.

He rubbed her palm with his thumb. His grip was sure and strong.

"Darla," he said softly. "Maybe we could—"

Before he could get the words out, a woman walked over to their table, calling out Nick's name.

Pretty, bubbly Lauren, the children's librarian whom Nick had dated for almost a year and then had ironically broken up with just before Darla left for California.

During the entire time Lauren and Nick were dating, Lauren barely cast a side glance at Darla. Not that Darla expected warmth and exuberance, but something resembling civility would have been nice.

"Hey, Nick," Lauren said. She tossed a "Hey, Darla," quickly over her shoulder. Then she gave Nick a hug. Like, a big hug. And, Darla noted, a kiss on the cheek.

The lingering kind.

Well, okay, maybe that was an exaggeration. But to Darla, the kiss seemed a lot more than a peck.

"Hey, Lauren." Nick smiled. "You're back. How was hiking out West?"

"I had a great time, but I'm so happy to be home." She gave him another exuberant squeeze. "Being gone really lends perspective."

Lauren had wavy hair the color of wheat fields and bright green eyes. And the way she turned them on Nick...well, Darla was a writer. It was her job to notice things. And if she had to wager, she'd bet the look in Lauren's eyes was *still smitten*.

"I'm having a little get together at my house on Friday," Lauren said, "and I was wondering if you might want to come? Just a few friends. We're going to grill something and hang out on the beach. Text me if you can make it. I'd love to tell you all about my trip. Great to see you." As she walked away, she added, "Bye."

Not, "Bye, Darla." Darla gave a little wave anyway, just as their waitress came back, asking if they wanted dessert. But all thoughts of dessert had gone south. "This was great," she said to Nick, trying to sound upbeat. "So now I'd better go and put my plan into action and get to work." As she rummaged through her purse for a credit card, she started to get angry. At herself.

Nick was allowed to have a life. And she no longer had any claim to it. He was allowed to date people and have sex with them and do whatever he wanted. As was she. But why did she feel like Lauren was sending her a hands-off signal—still, after all this time? And why should she care?

Nick's gaze searched hers. "You sure you don't want dessert? They still make that killer brownie with ice cream and caramel sauce."

"If I ate that, I'd nap all afternoon." What had she been doing, letting him in?

"That might not be a bad idea," he said. "Sometimes it's good to take a little rest."

She went to hand the credit card to the waitress, but Nick had beat her to the punch. As the waitress left, he said, "I invited you, so I got this."

"I'd prefer we split," she said, pulling out a bill.

He suddenly placed a hand over hers, which forced her to look at him. "Please," he said. "I want to."

She swallowed. "Okay," she said, forcing a smile. "Thanks for lunch."

"Yeah, thanks for lunch." His mouth turned up the slightest bit. "It was fun."

Too much fun. She found herself falling under his spell, getting lost in memories, sliding back in time.

All the things she'd vowed not to do.

Chapter 10

LATER THAT AFTERNOON, Nick sat with his laptop on a battered old porch overlooking an equally unkempt backyard, trying to study for his exam. But he wasn't studying—he was thinking of Darla. And how it seemed that just as they were starting to break through to one another, Darla pulled back.

Like she would never trust him again.

On the other hand, if she'd gotten jealous of Lauren—and he knew Darla well enough to possibly detect a glint of that in her eyes—well, that was very interesting.

He got up and went inside the old house on Bay Street, where he'd been working on and off for the past few months and sat down at a folding table he'd set up in the kitchen in front of a bay window. His drawings were still where he'd left them a few days ago—different kitchen sketches because the kitchen was currently a blank rectangular space where just about anything was possible. He shoved a pencil behind his ear and walked around the room, placing big pieces of cardboard on the floor where appliances could potentially go. "Should I put the stovetop on this wall or that wall? I think the sink should be under the window for the view, but maybe that's not the way to go."

"Why don't you just ask Darla the way she likes it?" his brother Tony suddenly said from the doorway.

Nick startled and looked up to see his brother leaning on the doorjamb. "You believe in knocking?"

"No," Tony said with a grin. He walked in and surveyed the room that had been torn down to the studs and now sported new drywall. "This place has got beautiful moldings. How did you make them go around the whole new kitchen?"

"I found someone to make a mold and then create a lot more of them."

"This place is going to be amazing one day," Tony said. "I've got to hand it to you, you've got great natural instincts."

"Tell that to our dad." Uh-oh. That just slipped out. But he didn't want to get into that. So he picked up his cell and held it up. "Why are you here? We have more modern means of communicating than creeping in here and scaring me."

"I was in the neighborhood." Tony sat down at the battered table, unfortunately making himself at home. "It's a nice neighborhood, by the way. Close to downtown, right on the bay." He tapped his fingers on the table. "So how's the 'friendship' going?" He made quote marks in the air.

"I'm not looking to get Darla back, if that's what you're

getting at," Nick said adamantly. He tossed his pencil on the table.

"Maybe you should. Try to get her back, that is."

"No" came out too quickly. What was up with his brother, anyway?

Tony's cell began to buzz. "Hi, Had," he said into the phone. "With Nick. Yes, I'll be sure to ask him. Love you too." As he pocketed his phone, he said, "That was nice of Darla to offer us her house. Except I heard you might've had a hand in that."

"I had the idea, but I'm going to do any work that needs to be done to get things ready."

"Of course, we'll help too." He paused. "Since you two are both spending time together already, the favor I need shouldn't be a big ask."

Nick moved a piece of cardboard that read *fridge* in permanent marker across the room. "Okay, sure."

"ESPN is doing an interview with me and Hadley in my restaurant. But it's at the same time as our cake tasting tomorrow. We wondered if you and Darla would go instead."

Nick laughed. "That is the most undisguised attempt at matchmaking I've ever seen. Reschedule the appointment, dude."

"It'll be the third time we're rescheduling, between both of us being so busy with work. Besides, we have different definitions of the word *cake*."

Nick shot his brother a *what-are-you-talking-about* look.

"Hadley believes anything not containing chocolate is not worth serving. I'm a vanilla person myself. You'd be helping us avoid prewedding conflict." His brother actually managed to keep a straight face when he said *vanilla person*. If this wasn't a setup, Nick didn't know what was.

"You two aren't seriously fighting over cake?"

"No, but the cake is a gateway to other wedding arguments," Tony said, gathering abandoned pencils from the table and lining them up. "Where to cut it, how to serve it. If I can smush it in her face."

"Even I know the answer to that question is always no." Nick moved the cardboard labeled *stove top* across from the fridge piece. "Why not have Mimi decide?"

"My future wife feels like you two know what we like the best and will do an excellent job narrowing the choices down for us. The interview's important and so is knowing when to punt to keep the peace. I'm practically begging."

"Okay, whatever." Nick knew when it was better to just surrender. "I'll ask Darla."

"You're the best." Finished tidying the pencils, Tony sat back and assessed him. "So how's it going, spending time with her?"

"Fine." Would his brother be offended if he walked him to the door now?

"You look like you need to talk about it."

Nick rolled his eyes. "That's exactly what I don't want to do."

"Want and need are two different things." Tony swept his hand over the scattered plans. "You break pencils in half when you're frustrated. I'm counting eight halves here." He gave Nick a pointed look and pulled out a chair. "Come sit."

Nick shook his head at his brother's persistence, which he both loved and hated. He never even made it to the chair before his pent-up words came tumbling out. "I can fix all the backsplashes and floors and bathrooms in her house," he said, "but nothing can make up for someone who didn't have the staying power to stick by her in times of trouble. And that's just the truth. I'm our mother's son." Nothing like a brother to get you to spill all your secrets in ten seconds or less.

Tony crossed his arms. "You're being awfully hard on yourself."

Nick shrugged, not in the mood for Tony's optimism. He walked away, into the adjacent room, a great room with beams and a dark wood-paneled fireplace. The tiles of the surround were cream colored, each painted with a different bright-hued flower. Drop cloths were scattered around, as he was in the middle of scraping out the old grout which had yellowed and crumbled in places and re-grouting the whole thing. A sawhorse was set up nearby, covered with tiles. He picked one up and examined it, but didn't really register what he was looking at.

His brother followed right behind him, not letting the conversation go. "Out of the three of us, you might be the one who looks the most like our mother, but you're making a big mistake when you say you're actually like her."

Nick set down the tile, which held a rose and picked up another one, a blue-and-yellow iris. "I've already shown that I don't have the staying power. Divorcing at twenty-five is not exactly—"

"That's in the past," Tony said quickly. "And don't forget, divorce takes two. Darla served you with the papers."

"I didn't handle things right. I should've fought harder for my marriage."

Tony started poking around the tiles, exactly what Nick didn't want. "You have a lot more staying power than you give yourself credit for. You've worked with Dad for twenty years now, and not only have you two not killed each other, but you've also ensured the success of the company. You did everything you could to be there for Darla during her chemo. You've fixed everything she'll let you fix in her house."

"But not in our relationship."

"That's something for you two to work out."

"She's leaving. It's best to let sleeping dogs lie."

Tony glanced around at the large room. "What you're doing to this place proves that your relationship is not a sleeping dog, bro—it's awake and howling. My advice is to decide how far you're going to take this." Nick must've tossed him a puzzled look because Tony continued, "I'm saying that if you love her and see a life with her, then don't let this chance pass you by."

His brother was bringing up things that hit on all his deepest wounds and made him consider things he never would've given himself permission to consider.

Tony eyed him carefully. "Stop thinking about how people perceive you and decide what you want inside."

"Since when have I cared about what people think?" Nick walked over to the fireplace and started poking at a loose tile to add it to his pile.

"Sometimes I think you think people believe you're an irresponsible kid. And you were never irresponsible. You were angry—at me."

Nick looked up. "I was always proud of your success. I would never—"

"Listen to me." Tony moved closer. "I got the golden ticket, and I left you to man the business with Dad. I know that was never your dream."

Nick sucked in a shocked breath. His heart was thumping in his chest. They'd *never* talked about this. "Just to be clear, I never held you responsible for my future. I'm nothing but proud of you."

"I get it. But you made hard choices because of my choices."

Yes. That was true. And in the beginning, Nick had hated it. "It all worked out."

"Look, you were just a kid when you got married." Tony had a calm, authoritative way of talking that made Nick want to believe him. Desperately. "You know who you are now. And if you love Darla, throw everything you've got into showing her. Decide the course of action based on your goals."

Nick couldn't help cracking a smile. "Spoken like a true football star."

"Hey, football is life." Tony grinned. "Truthfully, it used to be. My life now is so much better."

Nick grinned. "I'm happy for you."

Tony cast him a knowing glance, reminding Nick that he'd had to fight for his own happily ever after. "You've got one more chance before Darla leaves for good. Better to lose than to live a life of regret."

Nick already knew what that was like. He'd been living it for the past ten years.

"Sometimes when Darla and I are together, it feels just

like it used to. But maybe we're just forgetting the painful part." *Poke poke poke.* He worked to dislodge the tile.

"You have opportunities now to remind her of why she fell in love with you."

Remind her of why she fell in love with you. Was that why he'd chosen the Dancing Crab? Without even realizing it?

"And as for the painful part," Tony continued, "you'll have to talk about that too. If you decide you really care for her."

"Whoa." The tile suddenly gave, collapsing inward. On closer inspection, the tile was hinged. Nick worked it back and forth. "Well, I'll be," he said, admiring the hidden craftsmanship. "Come look at this."

Tony looked over his shoulder as Nick opened the tiny tile door to find a rectangular space. "What in the—"

"You know what it is," Nick said, grabbing his phone and turning on the flashlight. "Dad's told us about these." They'd discovered many secret compartments in their remodeling work. Some contained jewelry. Some money. Some mementos. Most were empty, their contents long ago raided like artifacts from pharaohs' tombs.

Nick shone the light into the space. It was small, about the size of a cigar box.

"It's steel, isn't it?" Tony reached in and tapped on it. "Fireproof."

Nick jiggled the box, and it slid out. "It fits in there perfectly."

The brothers walked back into the kitchen, where Nick set it down on the table. It was in decent shape except for flakes of orange rust crusted around its edges.

Tony bent to examine it. "S. T. Manning Construction, 1895," he read from the side.

Nick met his brother's gaze. "Whoa. What?" Darla's last name was Manning. Amelia's last name was Manning. But why did the construction company have that name too? "Have you ever heard of it?"

"I know there were a handful of companies who built tons of homes during the boom, when beach homes were going up left and right for wealthy people to escape the heat of the city."

Nick broke out into a sweat. There was only one logical explanation, and it hit him like a boulder. He had to sit down. "Amelia married her contractor."

Tony's voice was a solemn whisper. "It's a sign, dude."

Nick shook his head in disbelief. If it were true, he'd just accidentally discovered the biggest piece of personal information about Darla's great-great-grandparents ever.

"I'm sweating." Nick pushed the box over to Tony. "You open it."

Tony unhitched two small latches, but the box wouldn't open. Nick got up, rummaged through his toolbox, and came back with a screwdriver. "Let me see it."

It took a few tries, but he pried it open.

In the box sat a photo, old, sepia toned, and curled up at the edges. With a shaking hand, he lifted it out.

A young couple stood with their arms wrapped around each other. The woman was pretty and blond like Darla and, also like Darla, had lots of curly hair piled up on her head, wisps sneaking out to frame her face. The guy's face was turned a little sideways, casting a look at the woman that could only be called adoring. And he appeared to be whispering something in her ear.

The woman was laughing. Not suppressing a smile, or barely smiling with her mouth closed, but a full-on, rambunctious laugh.

Not your typical nonsmiling old photo, for sure.

"There's more," Tony said, pointing to the bottom of the box.

Nick picked up a brittle, yellowed note with ink-blotted script. *My beloved Samuel. You built us a beautiful life. All my love, Amelia. August, 1938.*

"So it's true," Tony exclaimed.

Nick's mind was racing. A dashing contractor. And a woman with Darla's curly hair and big wide eyes.

"Don't be afraid of what you want," Tony said in his wise-older-brother tone.

"Okay, I—I don't even know what to say." Nick placed the paper and the photo carefully back into the box. "Just, thanks for listening. And for being here."

Tony suddenly burst out laughing.

"What?" Nick frowned. "What's so funny?" He was still shaky, his blood still pounding loudly in his ears.

"I actually didn't come here to give you a hard time." Tony looked sincere. "I wanted to ask you another favor. But maybe I should wait." He bit back a smile. "I don't want to give you a heart attack or anything."

Nick gave his brother the eye. He wasn't sure how much more he could take.

Tony put a hand on Nick's shoulder, his expression suddenly deadly serious, making Nick's stomach take another dive. The last time his brother looked like that was when he'd suffered a devastating knee injury that ended his football career at the height of his success.

"I want to know if you'd be my best man." Tony broke out into a wide grin.

Nick, clutching his chest, exhaled a sigh of relief. Before he could speak, Tony continued, "You're my brother and my best friend. You've been through everything with me, through thick and thin, and I can't think of anyone else I'd want more. And Hadley agrees." He looked straight at Nick in a way that saw through him. He did, in a way. No one in the world knew him better. Well, except for Darla. But he couldn't think of that now.

Nick stood up and pulled Tony into a hug.

Tony gave him an affectionate clap on the back. "I love you, man. So stop saying that you quit people, okay?"

That stabbed him. Ever since their mother left, he and his brother had forged an unbreakable bond. They'd been there for each other for everything. "I'd be honored." Nick pulled back. "On one condition."

"What is it?"

"That you never stop interfering in my life." Nick returned the back clap.

Tony shrugged his broad shoulders. "You'd do the same for me."

"Actually," Nick said. "I have an opportunity to do that right now."

Tony looked puzzled.

"You find another officiant yet? Because Dad's campaigning for the job."

"I'm already on it." Tony shook his head, as if he'd accepted his dad's pitch for the job, for better or for worse.

"He showed me his certificate. It's a great idea. Unless he starts telling embarrassing stories."

"Hey, it's Dad. Count on it." Nick got serious. "And by the way, I love you too."

* * *

That night, Darla was dreaming of her agent and her editor, who had just opened a box containing copies of her last book and were tossing them one by one into a giant trash can and laughing gleefully.

As she bolted upright in bed, she discovered two things. One, she was covered in sweat. And two, she was relieved to find that the box of books sitting in the corner of her bedroom was still intact. However, someone *was* knocking on her door. She wrapped her robe around her and bounded down the hall, noticing that it wasn't the middle of the night at all. Outside the windows, the sky was lightening to the color of blue-gray and birds were already chirping up a riot.

And Nick was standing at her front door. She opened it, rubbing her eyes and tugging her robe up on her shoulder.

"Good morning, sunshine," he said in that amiable, somewhat flirty voice.

"Did you come out of the womb that way?" she asked with a frown that was not exaggerated. Too much.

"What way?" His face held a look of mock innocence.

"Chipper. Wide awake." She waved her hands to demonstrate. "It's so annoying."

"Someone didn't have their coffee yet." He was full of merriment and mirth.

"I hate you," she said.

He bit back a smile. "Looks like someone just rolled out of bed."

She stifled a very wide yawn. "I must've slept through my alarm."

"Well, I have just the thing to put some sunshine into your day. Hold on a sec."

She watched him jog back to his truck. He was wearing an olive-green T-shirt and jeans, his hair damp from a shower. And he still had the finest butt she'd ever seen. A pang hit her smack in the chest. She realized now that it was a privilege, being with someone through normal, everyday stuff—like greeting each other as they started the day together. She'd never thought their days together would end. Yet somehow, they'd let each other go.

It was way too early in the day to be accosted by these thoughts. Just as she'd steeled herself against him, he was back, holding out a large paper cup of coffee.

Aw. "Thanks," she said, reminding herself that bringing her coffee was just a nice gesture, not anything more.

Although she had to admit, she felt a little braver having him here. Like his presence was giving her the courage to tackle her manuscript anew. If he didn't distract her to death, that is.

"No need to get dressed on my account." Bad word choice, as evidenced by the blush that spread across his tanned face. "I mean," he quickly clarified, "feel free to get right to work. That's what I'm going to do." He started to head past her down the hall toward the bathroom.

"Nick," Darla called out. "I'm not going to that cake appointment today." Hadley had asked her, and she knew that Tony had asked Nick. And she'd decided that going with him was a very bad idea for a lot of reasons.

He stopped and turned around. "Why not?"

"Because Hadley and Tony should pick out their own cake." That was the most obvious one.

He shrugged. "I sort of got the sense from my brother that it was causing conflict, and this was a way to decrease premarital strife."

"I have enough strife of my own." Plus, she suspected a setup. And spending time alone with Nick was something to avoid at all costs.

He crossed his nicely muscled arms. "You did promise to be there for them."

"Can't I make phone calls instead?" She counted on her fingers. "For the string quartet, the tables, the dinnerware? That's definitely being helpful."

"What's the difference?" Even his casual shrug was sexy. "It all takes time."

"The truth is," she said firmly. "I don't eat sugar." It was forbidden, just like Nick. It also happened to be true.

His brows shot up. "Like, ever?"

"Well, rarely." She wasn't ashamed about being healthy. For her, it was literally a matter of life or death. She didn't expect most people to understand that, but that was how it felt.

"How is life worth living without sugar?" He looked incredulous. And also very cute, she hated to admit. She rolled her eyes. "Life is more than giving in to empty calories."

"It is?" He looked at her like she was completely missing the boat. "I think you're afraid to do this with me."

"Am not," she said too quickly.

"Come on," he said. "What's the worst that could happen?"

"I don't know." Yes, she did. "I develop a sugar addiction." What she really meant was a Nick addiction was far worse. When he frowned, she tossed up her hands. "Okay, fine. I'll go."

"Fantastic," Nick said, still in a jovial tone. Which wasn't quite as irritating because the coffee was starting to kick in. He pointed to her coffee cup. "Want me to set this down in your office? I'm headed that way."

"No, it's all right." She hesitated. "Maybe I—I'll work right here on the couch."

"You sure? My guys are going to be walking back and forth." When she didn't say anything, he asked, "What's wrong?"

"Nothing," she hedged, amazed that he still knew her so well. "Okay, fine," she finally said. "I've never worked in my office." Only sheer, icy panic had made her admit that.

Nick assessed her for a moment. Then he tugged her down the hall until they were standing at her office doorway.

He walked in, noting the light of the new day flooding in and the panoramic ocean view. Joggers and walkers made their way along the beach, often in pairs, the slanted rays of the morning sun accompanying them along the way. "People would kill for this space."

Darla lifted her hands in a shrug. "I know."

He tipped his head sideways, trying to figure her out. "Was someone murdered here?"

"No!"

"In your imagination?"

She tapped her finger against her lips. "Maybe only you."

He snorted. "Then what's the problem?"

She heaved a sigh. "I—I don't exactly know."

"It's like you're punishing yourself for having a nice office. That's just weird."

"Maybe." She grabbed her laptop, headphones, and earplugs, deciding not to wallow in her own quirkiness. "I'm not going to be able to enjoy anything until I make this deadline. So...shoo. I'll figure it out."

"Okay." He let her push him to the door. "But remember, you deserve to be happy."

"Okay, I get it."

"See you at noon," he said over his shoulder. "And I want a report on that word count. Okay?"

"Aye aye, Captain," she said with a salute. Which made her robe slide down a little again, revealing her shoulder and nightgown strap.

His gaze followed the slip of the robe then up again, where he met hers. Heat flooded her, her heart suddenly skipping a beat as a slew of memories suddenly bowled her over. Again.

She thought of things he might have said long ago. Like, "Mmm. Nice." Or done. Like, kissed her shoulder. Taken her in his arms. Let the robe slide off.

"Time to go." He cleared his throat as he took off down the hall, giving her a wave as he walked away.

She tried not to fixate on his fine butt in those worn Levi's. Instead, she conjured up Julia's face when she missed her deadline for the first time.

A minute later, she headed to the great room couch. The

one that faced the wall, not the ocean. As she got busy, she vowed there would be no Internet. No online shopping. No searching for information about Amelia. Just facing up to her scary work.

Maybe she needed blinders too, but even that couldn't stop thoughts of Nick from invading her brain. She wasn't sure how much longer she could keep resisting the urge to laugh with him, flirt with him, or resist the strong pull between them.

She suddenly realized with chagrin that Nick was like cake to someone like her. Once you had a taste, it could be your total downfall.

Chapter 11

"I'M STARVING," NICK said as he walked with Darla down Petunia Street a few hours later. Their town was at its summer show-offy best, baskets hanging from old-fashioned iron lampposts bursting with bright red, pink, and purple petunias, and bright green vines trailing in the breeze. Crowds strolled the street, window shopping. Parents carted little kids in their arms as they dripped ice cream all over their shirts, but everyone was in a happy mood and no one seemed to mind.

Some local residents hated the crowds, but the contagious joy of families on vacation made summer in Seashell Harbor Nick's favorite season, hands down, and never failed to put him in a great mood.

He stopped suddenly in front of a popular shop that sold glass globes, key chains, vials of sand, and of course, Seashell Harbor diamonds.

"What? What is it?" Darla asked with concern.

"When did you stop eating cake?"

Darla shrugged and kept walking. "I just eat really healthy now."

Eat healthy now. As in, after the cancer, he took that to mean. "You used to love cake. Especially cheesecake, remember?"

"That was the old Darla." She directed her gaze at the rainbow-striped Seashell Harbor beach towels displayed in the window, not at him.

He didn't say so, but he missed that Darla. He wished that she'd relax a little and have fun. He was beginning to realize that, although she'd survived the cancer, it still seemed to have a big grip on how she navigated her life.

Not using her office. Not eating anything fun. As if she were hesitating to...well, *live*.

"I just thought of something scary," he said.

"What's that?"

"You and Mimi have a special bond over breakfast bars."

She turned to him and smiled. "I *love* her breakfast bars."

"So do all the seniors," he teased. He touched her arm as they started to walk again, causing her to glance up. "I have a suggestion for this tasting."

She scanned his face. "Okaaay..."

"*Not* to channel breakfast bars." He kept his tone light. But he wanted to push her a little. Because no cake? Ever? That was just plain wrong.

"So what exactly should I channel?"

"Definitely not any strong feelings you might have about oats, bran, or chia seeds." He steered them past a group of window shoppers. "We don't want Tony and Hadley to regret that they asked us to help out."

"Go ahead." Her tone was teasing. "Make fun of healthy eating. We'll see where *your* cholesterol is in twenty years."

First, he shook his head sadly. "Thinking of cholesterol before a cake tasting." Then he reached over and ruffled her hair. "You *definitely* need more fun in your life."

She laughed and playfully pushed him away, which made him laugh too.

In the old days, he would have kissed her and then taken her hand as they walked together down this familiar street. But instead, they just awkwardly stared at each other for a beat as his brother's words came back to him. *If you love her, throw everything you've got into showing her.*

It was one thing to want to make her laugh, he realized, and another thing entirely to want her back. The former was spontaneous and easy, but the latter required determination and commitment. And, even more scary, an ability to accept the possibility of failure. Yep, the laughing part was a whole lot easier.

They entered the bakery, which was one of his favorite places. It was filled with bright sunshine. Maybe the fact that the walls were lemon yellow didn't hurt either. The black chalkboard behind the counter was filled with today's lunch specials interspersed with colorful chalk flowers, and a vase of real flowers stood on the counter.

Mimi, who was in her forties with red hair and a contagious smile, came out from the back, wiping her hands on her chef-grade apron. "Hi, Darla. Hi, Nick," she said. "So I see you two got consigned to coming."

Nick grinned. "It's a big sacrifice, but someone has to do it."

They followed her to a back room where she invited them to sit down at a small table overlooking the tree-lined side street. A yellow cat was lying in a patch of grass in a fenced-in yard outside the window, curling and uncurling his tail, having a lazy day in the sun.

It was the perfect time to sit and eat cake. With Darla. Which was an odd thing to think, but just being here with her was making him... happy.

"I'm oddly nervous," Nick said as he sat down.

"I know! Me too," she confessed, sitting across from him. "I sort of feel like I'm getting ready to take an exam."

Darla flipped through a book with laminated pages full of cake photos from hundreds of weddings. "Do you remember our wedding cake?" she asked.

"Um—yes?"

She lifted a brow, expecting him to elaborate. He was a terrible liar, and she knew it.

"It was kind of round—" He lifted his arms to signify the shape. "And also kind of squared off—"

"Round. Tiered." She used her hands to help describe it, but that still wasn't ringing any bells. "My mom made it. To save money. But it was nice."

"I remember it tasted good," he said. That was safe, wasn't it?

She squinted. "What flavor was it?"

"Um, chocolate?" She'd be great in an interrogation room.

She shook her head in disbelief. "Kit and Hadley made the topper, do you remember? They made the little people look just like us. I was reading a book, and you were holding a hammer. And there was a little banner that said *True Love.*"

"Sorry, but I really don't recall that," Nick said. "I'm sort of glad I don't because...a hammer? Geez."

"It was cute." She propped her chin on her hand. "What *do* you remember?"

He thought about that for a minute. "Feeding you cake." Ah yes, now how could he ever forget that?

She frowned. "As I recall, you didn't smash it into my face."

He lifted an *aha* finger. "Because I'm smart."

"I thought you were sweet. You didn't want to ruin my hair or makeup."

No, that wasn't it at all. "I wasn't thinking about your hair or your makeup or about what flavor the cake was. I was thinking of how lucky I was to be the one standing there feeding you cake. You had this pretty pink lipstick on, and your eyes were sparkling, full of excitement and happiness, and all I wanted to do was kiss you."

Whoa. Where had that come from?

"So we fed each other cake, and then you kissed me." She seemed far away, lost in the memory.

"Yes. Our first kiss outside of the church. I remember that very vividly."

She chuckled. "We got a little carried away."

He touched her arm. "I'm sorry I don't remember the cake flavor. It isn't because it was meaningless to me. I was too busy counting down the seconds until I could be alone with you."

She smiled a little. And stopped making eye contact.

"What flavor was it, anyway?" Nick asked.

"Half vanilla and half chocolate. Remember, we ate the top layer on our first anniversary?"

He laughed. "I was afraid to because it sat in your mom's freezer for a year."

"I had to talk you into it."

He shot her a knowing glance. "And I'm so glad you did."

Darla turned as red as the fire hydrant right beside the sidewalk outside the window. And he knew why—they'd eaten the cake in the bathtub. Amid candles and a bottle of wine. And they'd done a lot more than just eat cake. "Well," she said, clearing her throat, "that was a memorable anniversary."

Time to lighten things up. "Maybe we should have just given up being careful about the cake and acted like one-year-olds. Anything goes."

"Yeah, maybe." She still seemed a little shaken up.

"We can today," he offered.

Which made her laugh, thank goodness, because it broke the tension.

Mimi walked in carrying a large box. "Okay, I've got two cupcakes of each flavor. I suggest sharing one of each pair and taking notes on the notepad. You can take the remaining ones back to Tony and Hadley for their approval. How's that sound?"

"Fun," he said. Darla seemed to be trying her best to look excited rather than act as if she were about to be forced to eat poison.

"Also, I recommend blind tasting," Mimi said.

"What's that?" Nick asked.

"One of you take charge and make the other person close their eyes and taste. When you shut down one of your senses, they say the other ones take over. It might help."

As soon as she left, Nick reached for the box. "It's okay, Dar. Duty calls."

She huffed out a sigh. "I can do anything for our friends."

Nick carefully wrote something down on his notepad. "Close your eyes and get ready."

"Can't we just split them in half and know what we're eating?" He knew that she needed to be in control. He decided then and there to show her how much fun it was not to be.

He picked up a fork and opened the box. "Now be a sport."

Surprisingly, she didn't protest, just scooched her chair to the table, tilted her head up, and closed her eyes.

He sneaked a peek at her lashes grazing her cheeks, her full lips parted expectantly. She looked so kissable it hurt. It threw him so much that he forgot which cupcake to begin with.

"What's taking so long?" She cracked open one eye.

"You look like I'm about to give you an injection or something. It won't hurt, I promise. Now close your eyes."

She did as told. He used the fork to pull off a bite and very carefully placed it in her mouth. "Chocolate," she said, tasting it. "Wow. Like, amazing chocolate." Her eyes flew open, glazed with pleasure. "You taste it."

He took the fork, dug in, and saw her point. "Okay, yeah. Chocolate wins. Except it has a fancy name."

"What is it?"

He read off the sheet. "Dark chocolate mud cake with bittersweet ganache and Swiss-meringue buttercream."

He wrote something else on the tablet.

"You gave it five stars," she said, peering over at his notes.

He shrugged. "When you know, you know. I'm done here."

"You can't be serious." She tipped her head toward the box. "We have five other kinds to try."

Mimi came rushing in. "Oh, you tasted the chocolate. That's my bestseller. That pairs really well with coffee if you're serving that at the reception."

"Are they serving coffee?" Darla asked him.

"Beats me, but this one still wins." Maybe Nick was screwed. Because he understood in that moment that Darla was exactly like that cake, in that he wanted her and no one else. He always would.

Darla set out the next three cupcakes, reading off their names. "Vanilla with raspberry icing, carrot, and vanilla with lemon curd."

"Tart and delicious," Darla said, tasting the lemon curd.

Nick shook his head. "But not chocolate."

"We can eliminate the red velvet right now," Darla said, pulling out another one. "Hadley doesn't like it."

"I'm still going to taste it." He did, offering her a forkful.

She pressed her lips together and shook her head. "I just can't put that red food coloring in my body."

"It's made from beets," Mimi called from the doorway. "Nothing artificial."

Darla held up a hand. "Thanks, but still a hard pass. Red cake just feels weird to me."

"Fine," Nick said, eating the whole cupcake. "Your loss."

"Back in the day," Darla mused, "we didn't know about fancy cake flavors or ganache or meringue." She darted her gaze to him. "We didn't know a lot of things."

Nick nodded in agreement. "I didn't care about us being broke or what kind of cake we ended up with or that our reception was in the YMCA gym." Maybe he should've stopped there. "More maturity would've helped me, but I wasn't short on love for you." As soon as the words spilled out, he knew he should've stuck to tasting cupcakes. So he busied himself cutting another one.

Darla stared at him, swallowing hard. This tasting was going off the rails. "I'm sorry," he said. "I didn't mean to make this into something uncomfortable."

"Wait," she said, taking a deep breath. "I—I have to say something. Whatever happened between us, I want you to know that I didn't care about the cake or the gym either, or the fact that I bought a cheap dress off the rack and sewed on more lace and beads to make it look more expensive. All I wanted was a life with you. And...no matter what happened afterward, I just want you to know that."

"I do know," he said softly. He looked into her eyes, expecting to see sorrow and remorse, but they held only warmth and softness. Maybe she was remembering those long-ago sweet times when they'd loved each other so deeply. He certainly hoped so.

He cleared his throat and focused on the cupcakes. "Last one."

As she gave a little nod and closed her eyes for a last time, he placed a bite on her fork for her to taste.

And then her eyes flew open, just as he'd hoped.

"This is...cheesecake." And was that the tiniest moan of pleasure?

"With caramel-chocolate drizzle," he confirmed. Her favorite dessert. Well, when she used to eat dessert, that is.

"How did you..."

And that's when she started to cry.

Oh no. He'd meant to surprise her. To make her happy. Not this.

She was wiping her cheeks with the backs of her hands. "Dammit, Nick."

He looked down at her plate. "Does it taste bad?" He was pretty sure it was amazing, but he still wasn't sure why she was crying.

She smacked him in mock anger on the arm. "No, it's wonderful, and you know it."

"I thought you hated cake," he said with a big, self-satisfied smile.

"I especially don't hate *this cheesecake.*" She looked around.

"What are you looking for?"

"More."

"Here, take my half."

She did and finished it off in two bites. Then she wiped her mouth with a napkin. "Why did you do that?" She sounded happy and exasperated all at once.

He shrugged. "I wanted to remind you that cake is...fun." And maybe also that *they* were fun.

She took a napkin and dabbed at her eyes. "That's not fair." She punched him in the arm again.

A weird giddiness soared inside of him that she felt something for him that wasn't anger. And he hoped it wasn't just for the cake.

"I asked Mimi to sneak it in there." He hesitated before continuing. "If we got married now, I'd make sure you had ten layers of that for your wedding cake."

She shook her head. "I wouldn't—didn't—need ten layers of anything, don't you know that?"

Before she could cry again, he reached over and grasped her hand. She grasped it right back.

There she was, he thought as she looked at him tearfully. The Darla he knew. The one not afraid to feel things.

"I'm sorry," she whispered.

"For crying? Don't be," he said in a lighthearted tone. "Most women I know get emotional over cheesecake. Gets them every time."

She swiped at her cheeks. "You know I'm not crying over cheesecake."

Yeah, he knew. And he needed to stop joking. "Maybe we were too young and we messed things up, but I really loved you, Dar."

Nodding, she pressed her lips together, "I loved you too."

He gripped her hand now as if he was afraid to let it go. That if he did, she'd disappear forever.

In a way she was about to, wasn't she? California was across the country.

Mimi came in just then, causing them to break apart. "Any decisions?"

"Everything was amazing," Darla said, sliding her hand away. "We'll bring the box to the bride and groom."

Nick pointed to the cheesecake sample. "We'll take a bigger one of these to go if you've got one."

"I'll box it right up," Mimi gave a wide smile. "Cake tasting always leads to more business."

Darla gave him an astonished look. "A whole cheesecake?"

"Why not? We'll share it with everyone, if you want."

"You don't have to…"

"Darla," he interrupted, lowering his voice, "sometimes

people just want to do something nice for you. So let them, okay?"

She shook her head in disbelief. But she was also smiling.

He'd done a small thing that had pleased her. But he'd made a decision too, and it had nothing to do with cake.

He was going to use their time together to remind her of what they'd had. Of how it used to be between them.

And then he was going to try to win her back.

Because what Tony had said was right.

He had one more chance before she left for good.

Chapter 12

AT 10:00 A.M. the next day, Darla was waiting for her friends in Coffee by the Sea, drinking the largest cup she could buy, when her phone buzzed with a text.

Her heart dropped a little when she saw that it was Mackenzie's mom, saying that it was okay to come this afternoon to visit. She'd been nervous about it for the past few days, knowing that Mackenzie was in the middle of a cycle of treatment, an intense and scary time.

Darla had done her best over the years not to think of the ordeal she'd gone through—the long road her family and friends had walked along with her. She'd wanted to put the sickness and suffering, the worrying, the concern in her loved ones' eyes, behind her once and for all. She hoped she'd be strong enough to not let her own fears make her unable to help Mackenzie.

"Wow," Kit said as she slid into the booth across from Darla. "Why the gallon size?"

Darla smiled at her friend, who had on a nice blouse and pants, dressed for her work as a front desk receptionist at the county mental health center. "I need every drop. I've been up since 6:00 a.m."

Kit set down her phone and her own drink, a frozen chocolate chip cappuccino, her usual favorite. No judging, but it was almost as big as Darla's own drink. "Wait a minute," she said. "You who go to bed at two and get up at ten?"

"Yeah. Not anymore, thanks to a crazy plan Nick came up with to help me keep my productivity on target." She blew on her coffee, took a sip, and smiled. "He's a real tyrant."

Kit frowned and assessed her carefully. "Are you smiling at the coffee or at Nick?"

"Definitely the coffee," Darla said quickly. "And the fact that I actually got some words written today, even if I do feel like crawling into bed now." She'd started adding the mystery element into her story. She couldn't say she liked it all that much, but it was early yet. Not to mention the story still had no end. But she would come through and do this. She always did.

Darla tried not to think too hard about Nick's unfailing support. Or how her stomach had fluttered and pitched this morning when he'd walked in bright and early, tossing a smile her way and whistling as he went about his work. Or about how a simple bite of cheesecake had nearly crushed her.

There hadn't been any more kisses, yet she felt an unsettled feeling, like she was getting caught in the power of an incoming tide. Every interaction with Nick seemed to be pointing them in a direction she was powerless to stop.

Scary.

"How's your studying coming?" she asked Kit. Kit had gone back to school to finish her psychology degree and had recently been accepted into a graduate counseling program. How she studied and worked while being a great mom to Ollie, Darla could only guess.

"I'm one exam away from my degree, and that's what's keeping me going," Kit said. "I've been sneaking my studying in between answering the phone at work, at Ollie's T-ball practice, waiting in line at the grocery store..."

"Wait. You study in line at the grocery store?"

"Yep. Everywhere I can. Even in bed with Alex." She took a sip of her drink and then set it down, smiling. "Except that's usually not very productive."

Darla covered her ears. "Okay, you can stop right there. Sounds like you've got things in check."

"Not really, but somehow it all works out in the end. At least, that's what I keep telling myself. It also doesn't help that everything at Ollie's school is coming to a head— soccer, drama, clean-up-the-school-grounds day, and kindergarten graduation. Attending these end-of-the-year celebrations is a full-time job. And as far as the wedding goes, I've helped Hadley pick the flowers, and Alex has found a great band. You doing okay?"

Darla decided to keep the conversation light. "I just came from the library," she said. She was so glad she'd taken the time to stop by. "It turns out my ancestor Amelia got local teachers to offer math and reading classes to the women in her home and worked with a lot of the merchants in town to offer job training. Which is amazing, but I'm also trying to find more information about her personal life.

The librarian is going to search the digital archives, isn't that cool? All I had to do was ask."

"That's terrific," Kit said. "But I was wondering more along the lines of your deadline, the wedding, and selling your house. Not to mention Nick."

"I'm struggling a bit with my current book, but I always find my way out of a bind." Darla made sure to smile and present a confident front.

Kit reached a hand across the table. Her eyes were watery. So much for light conversation.

"I'm really sorry you have to work during the short time you're home," she said. "Plus deal with everything else going on."

Okay, maybe her front wasn't that confident. Or something else was amiss. "Kit, I'm fine. Why are you upset?"

"It's no secret we *all* think you work too hard," Kit said. "Not that we aren't extremely proud of your accomplishments, but you are literally always working."

"Honestly, I'm having fun too. Don't worry about me." Darla made sure to grin widely enough to hopefully dispel Kit's fears. She'd always confided in her friends, but they all had so much going on it didn't seem fair to worry them even more. "Thank you for caring," she said sincerely, squeezing Kit's hand back. "And I just want you to know, you're going to make a great therapist."

"Ha! Only if I pass my finals." She narrowed her gaze at Darla. "You're sure you're okay?"

She held up her hand. "I swear I'd tell you if I wasn't."

Just then, Hadley joined them, carrying a zippered dress bag and a chai tea latte. Her phone was buzzing with multiple texts as she sat down. "It's Wednesday, the wedding's a week and a half away, and things are looking good—Tony's restaurant is doing the food, so that will be perfect. Flowers are set, band is booked, bartender is hired, and we've ordered our rings. Oh, and I picked up my mom's and my gran's dresses." She finally took a breath. "But I've actually got another dress to try on."

"Wait a minute," Kit said. "You already have a dress. It's pretty."

"I know," Hadley said a little sheepishly. "It's a long story. But I'm really excited about it. And I need your opinions, okay?"

The bridesmaid dresses, which they also had from over a year ago, were a different story. The three of them almost never kept secrets from each other, but in this case, Kit and Darla had vowed never to tell Hadley their true feelings. The dresses were peach colored with wide skirts that flared out and were topped with tulle, which made them even more poofy. Hadley had agonized over keeping costs down and being practical, so Darla and Kit had pretended to like them. Darla, being petite, couldn't help feeling like a giant cream puff in hers.

It didn't really matter. Because it was fun to see Hadley so happy. And this time was all about Hadley and Tony. As it should be.

Maybe Hadley caught them looking at each other because she said, "I feel like this wedding has ballooned into something I didn't mean for it to become."

"What do you mean?" Kit asked. "It's going to be small, intimate, and elegant."

Hadley didn't look convinced. "Everyone's busy pitching in, and...well, it's a lot more work than I intended.

And I sprung this on you all suddenly. In the midst of all the other things you have going on."

"We would tell you if we couldn't handle it," Darla said. "And it seems like all the important stuff is done." She paused and changed the subject. "What do you think of doing a clambake at my place next week? Maybe the Thursday before the wedding? Nick said he would bring the seafood." There was nothing like the familiar tradition of a New England clambake and a fire on the beach—and the friends had had many of them over the years. She very badly wanted to do this one small thing for her friends. "It will be our last time to relax and hang out before the wedding."

"We want to take you out for a little bachelorette party too," Kit said, tearing up and swiping at her eyes. Which seemed a little over the top. "See if the weekend before the wedding works. Sorry, weddings always make me emotional."

"You do know that this is the second time you've cried since we sat down," Darla pointed out.

Kit shrugged. "I am really emotional lately." She smiled at Hadley. "Probably because it's not every day that one of your lifelong best friends gets married to the love of her life."

Darla nodded in agreement. "You and Tony have waited a long time for this, and it's going to be a really special day."

"All right, you two," Hadley said. "I'll accept what you're saying as the truth. And I want to make sure that you know that I am unbelievably blessed to have you as my best friends."

"We love you," Darla said simply.

"And we're glad to help," Kit said.

"Speaking of that," Hadley said, "how's your personal construction manager doing?"

Darla laughed. Her friends were a lot of things, but subtle wasn't one of them. "He's not my—"

"He sort of is," Kit interrupted, which wasn't like Kit at all. "He's fixed anything that's gone wrong with your house—and a lot of things that haven't."

"I can't help it if he keeps volunteering for projects," Darla said. But even she could hear how bad that sounded. "Okay, okay. I could have said no. Maybe I should have," she joked, but she didn't really believe it.

"Nick's probably right when he says he can do the work the best," Kit said. "After all, Alex told me that your bathroom tile shipped from Sardinia. Nick pulled a lot of strings to get it, and it still took months to come in."

"Wait...what?" Darla processed that information. "Nick brought over some tile catalogues, and I flipped through and fell in love with some tile. But I never asked him to order it. Or tear apart my bathroom, for that matter."

"Even Tony knew how much you hated that bathroom," Hadley said. "Nick wanted to surprise you."

Darla's head was spinning. He'd ordered the tile she loved from fricking *Italy*? And it got delayed—he hadn't just put the project off? "I—um—I would have just told him to forget it," she said weakly.

"But he didn't," Kit said. "He wanted you to have it."

Darla gulped, suddenly feeling close to tears herself. "He surprised me with cheesecake," she whispered, and then immediately wished she hadn't.

Her friends both leaned forward at full attention. Kit's

brows had shot up, and Hadley reached over to turn off her phone ringer.

"You're glowing." Hadley looked way too pleased with herself.

"I am not." But Darla could feel the flush of heat in her cheeks. "We were in Mimi's," she explained. "We tasted all the usual cake flavors, and then he had Mimi put a mini cheesecake into the box."

"Not your favorite one with caramel-chocolate drizzle?" Kit asked.

"Yes!"

"Then what happened?" Hadley asked.

"Of course, I was shocked," she confessed. "Then he said that if he had a do-over, he'd make our wedding cake ten layers of cheesecake because I love it so much."

"And what did you say?" Kit asked.

"I said I didn't need ten layers of cheesecake."

Hadley frowned. "That wasn't romantic."

"The conversation turned…emotional," Darla continued. "We talked about how desperate we were to just get married. Nothing else mattered but being together." As she spilled all to her friends, her voice cracked. *Yikes.*

"You *said* that to each other?" Hadley's eyes were wide and a little shocked.

Darla nodded, unable to stop talking-slash-confessing. "He took me to the Dancing Crab. I—I think being constantly confronted by all these memories—not to mention Nick himself—is making me even more confused. And Nick seems to be taking every opportunity to remind me of things. He's always been the sentimental one."

"Does he want to get back together?" Kit asked.

Darla shrugged. "He said he misses our friendship."

Hadley snorted. "Your *friendship*? Have you given thought to that?"

"Yes, and every time I do, I think about pulling out the divorce papers to remind myself how painful that was." Then she thought of yet another reason not to get involved with Nick. "And you know what my mom says."

Kit lifted a finger and shook it, a gesture Darla's mom used all the time. "'Never make the same mistake twice.'"

"Right. And...there's one more thing." Now that she was on a roll, she might as well tell them what was really bugging her.

"Oh my God," Hadley said. "You slept with him!"

"No. We had this...moment. We were in my bathroom talking about the remodel. And then the talk turned serious and he...leaned over and kissed me." Her friends' eyes grew wide. "Then you showed up, Hadley, and that was it," she said quickly. "It happened so fast I'm almost doubting it happened at all."

"You doubt that Nick kissed you?" Kit asked.

Darla felt almost like they were in high school again, gossiping about their prom dates. But it felt so good to get everything off her chest.

"No, I mean—yes, he kissed me. Like, he brushed it off by saying that he got a little emotional and that he just wants to be friends." Her friends seemed to be holding their breath, waiting for her to continue. "I'm just taking all of this for what it is—a few very intense weeks I'm just going to have to get through. Plus, Nick is kind of a flirt. I mean, look at all the women he's dated. So I can keep this attraction in perspective. And if anything comes from this, it's that we might actually become friends again. That's a good thing, you know? It would help to heal some of the hurt."

"I just have to say one thing," Kit said, clutching her stomach. "Ugh, remind me not to order a drink with a billion calories in it for breakfast. Anyway, my advice is never say *never*. Because I said *never* when I first met Alex, but love found me anyway."

"Same," Hadley said. "Also, just to let you know, we used to be angry at Nick, but that was a long time ago. He's a great guy. If you think something might be there, maybe you should let yourself—"

"Okay, you two," Darla interrupted. She usually appreciated that her friends weren't afraid to disagree with her point of view, but not now. "I'm headed back to California right after the wedding. I need to keep moving forward, okay? Nick will always be hot, but I have to remember the big picture."

"Aha!" Kit pointed a finger. "So you *are* tempted."

"Of course, I am," she admitted. "But it's just leftover chemistry."

"Maybe not, because you *are* wearing the ring." Kit reached over and tapped on it. "Magic happens, babe."

Darla shook her head and withdrew her hand from the table. "When I feel tempted, I just think that, if he really wanted me, he would have sought me out, right? Because I've been here all along. He's in-between girlfriends, so maybe he's lonely."

"He doesn't have many opportunities to be lonely, Darla," Hadley said. "Tony tells me that Lauren keeps trying everything she can to get back with him. And he has lots of women asking him out."

"He hasn't really dated anyone since last year," Kit said.

"You did leave to forget him," Hadley said. "And it doesn't seem like that exactly worked. So just think, if you and Nick start dating, maybe you'll stay." Then she noticed Darla staring at her. "Okay, sorry, I couldn't help it."

Kit suddenly stood up, her skin tone appearing slightly greenish. "Oh my gosh. Hey, I think I'm going to—" Slapping a hand over her mouth, she rushed toward the ladies' room.

"What was that?" Hadley asked.

Darla counted on her fingers. "Tears, throwing up...Whatever it is, it might just be adding up to a big pink plus sign."

Hadley grinned widely. "The unexpected really can happen," she said. "You just have to be open to the possibilities."

* * *

Early that afternoon, Nick was walking downtown when he spotted Darla on the opposite side of the street, window shopping her way along Artist's Row. She'd passed the gallery featuring sea-themed paintings, the art shop that featured colorful jellyfish made from recycled two-liter bottles, and now she was looking in the window of the handcrafted jewelry shop, very focused on something in the window, all of which seemed a little odd.

Because the Darla he knew hated shopping with a capital H.

Even odder was how she looked when she finally turned around.

She seemed to draw in a shaky breath. And he'd bet his shiny new silver Toyota Tacoma that she was trying not to cry.

He crossed the street and approached her. "Darla, are you okay?" She didn't answer, but bit down on her lip instead. On instinct, he reached out for her.

She really was pale this time, no joking. And felt cold, despite the eighty-degree day. She swallowed hard and said, "I'm fine, just window shopping." Even her voice was shaky.

Frowning, he looked her over from head to toe. Ill? Heatstroke? Something worse? "You don't look fine."

Before he knew it, he was leading her across the street to a little café, steering her under one of the bright yellow umbrellas. Miraculously, she let him. "Sit down for a minute," he said. A command like that would ordinarily have drawn a protest, but she did as he said, which worried him even more. He gestured to a college kid who was waiting tables and asked her to please bring some water.

"Nick, you're embarrassing me." Darla placed a hand on her sweaty forehead. "I'm fine." Her voice was dialed way down.

He placed two fingers on the pulse point at her wrist. She was clammy, but he felt a good pulse. Or at least he thought that was what he was feeling. What did he know about medicine? He was in home construction. "Are you sick? Let me take you home."

Was it something to do with her health—like the

cancer? Did she get bad news? He catalogued a list of things in his head, things he'd read about long-term complications of Hodgkin's. Heart problems, lung problems, secondary cancers caused by the radiation or chemo...

"Please don't worry," she said in a quiet voice. She grabbed his arm, forcing him to look at her. "I'm just a little nervous. That's all it is. Okay?" When he managed a nod she said, "I was on my way to visit Mackenzie Pearson and her mom called me, warning me that she's having a hard time physically and mentally. It just—it just took me back to my own experiences, and I—"

"You're visiting her to give her some hope and inspiration?"

She nodded. "As one cancer patient to another."

He saw what was going on here. "You don't have to go, you know. Everyone would understand." It was so like her to jump in and help.

She shook her head. "No, I—I want to go. I just need a minute. Sorry, you caught me at a bad time."

The waitress rushed to the table with water. "Thank you," he said. Handing Darla the glass, he asked, "How about a Diet?" He wasn't even sure she nodded before he was ordering one. And thanking the waitress for her concern. He'd tip her well for scaring her.

"You hungry?" he asked as an afterthought, trying to think of something else he could do. Darla shook her head. "Do you need to put your head between your knees? Do you feel faint?"

"Thank you, but I'm really okay. Like I said, a bad moment—"

"You scared me," he said, his own voice catching. He

reached over and squeezed her hand. "I haven't seen you so pale since—"

She frowned. "Since when?"

He felt himself crack a smile despite his worry. "Since that time we were in that hot tub on vacation in Key West and we drank too much tequila and—"

She sent him a death glare, which made him breathe a sigh of relief. Because if she could get irritated, she was okay.

"The tequila came up," she said, "and that did not end romantically."

He chuckled. "No. But the next day, after the hangovers went away, we made up for it."

She tried to smile at his shenanigans. Which made him understand that she must be really hurting.

"Oh, sweetheart," he said. Because that was what came out. It was one of the few times he'd failed to screen his language or his emotions in front of her.

He hadn't said it to make her feel even worse, but tears welled up in her eyes. "Hey, just my luck," he said. "I'm trying to make you feel better, not upset you more."

That earned him the slightest smile. "You're doing everything to make me feel better. I'm so embarrassed." She glanced across the street. "I think those ladies over there recognized me and were about to ask me to sign a book. I hope they're not taking any photos."

Sure enough, two older women were standing across the street staring and pointing. Nick signaled that Darla was okay, and they moved on. "I think they were worried." Darla gave everything to her job and to her fans. She could be a human being for once.

"I have fifteen minutes to figure out how to comfort and reassure this young girl in the fight of her life when I can't even keep it together myself." She swiped at her tears. "Got any magical words of advice? I'm—a little lacking in courage right now."

That made his heart swell. Because she was asking him. Turning to him. Trusting him with her pain.

A tear ran down her cheek. On impulse, he caught it with his thumb.

Her cheek was warm and soft, and his hand froze. *He* froze. All he could do was look at her helplessly when what he really wanted was to take her into his arms.

And then, all of a sudden... he did.

"It's okay, honey," he said as he gathered her up. Her slight frame was light and seemingly fragile, yet she was among the toughest people he knew. The scent of her shampoo wafted up to him, the soft silk of her hair brushing against his cheek. And she felt so good that he wanted to stay like that forever. Except that he wasn't supposed to be thinking of himself.

"You don't have to be so strong all the time," he said quietly, his voice cracking a little. "Don't you know that?"

She didn't answer. But she let him hold her.

Which was incredible. They sat like that a minute, together, and it seemed that the whole bustle of the street, the cars, the kids laughing, people calling out to their friends on this bright sunny day, all seemed to fade away until it was just the two of them. Just Darla and Nick.

The way it should be, a voice whispered inside of him.

She was already sitting back, smoothing down her sundress. "I'm okay." She sounded like her usual, efficient, down-to-business self. "I—I just got overwhelmed for a minute. Sorry you had to see that."

"See that you're human and vulnerable? Please don't apologize for that."

"Okay," she said, looking him in the eye. Reaching for the Cokes, she slid one over to him.

As they sat and drank, she said, "I'm not sure what to say to Mackenzie—how optimistic to be, how honest. And I'm afraid I'm not going to be able to control my reactions. Did you know that the smell of alcohol practically gives me a panic attack? Also she's nineteen, Nick. Her whole life is ahead of her. Imagine what that would be like, having to fight this fight..."

He took her hand. It was the only way he could convey that he was here for her and he wasn't ever going to leave, without scaring her to death by actually saying it.

"I can't imagine what you went through," he said. "If it's too soon for you to be trying to help other patients—"

"She's from here. One of us. I can show her that if I got through it, she can too."

Searching for a distraction, he nodded to a handled shopping bag on the floor that she'd been carrying on her shoulder. "What's in there?"

"Just some fun things to help keep her spirits up. Now the only things I need are the right words to give her some hope."

He tried not to look at her in a way that would give away his feelings, which were all over the place. He'd gone from fearing for her health to being amazed that she'd finally dropped her tough front. And she was still letting him hold her hand.

He tried to be the man she needed him to be. "You don't need words, Darla. You're living proof that she can make it through to the other side." He gave a little smile. "Except you have to stop the shaking. That's just plain scary."

Darla managed a chuckle before she grabbed a napkin and blew her nose loudly. "Maybe I better lay off the Diet, huh? I also just had coffee with Hadley and Kit." She held out her hand to see if it was steady.

"Someone definitely needs to cut you off from caffeine for the rest of the day."

"Thanks for the caffeine assessment," she said, standing up. "And for the drinks."

He laughed. "All I did was seriously frighten the waitstaff."

"You did a lot more than that." She met his gaze. "I'm still coming to terms with life after cancer. Everyone says I'm cured, and they dismiss it—I mean, I *want* everyone to dismiss it—but the reality is a lot more complicated than that."

"I read about medical follow-up in Hodgkin's survivors," he admitted.

She looked surprised. "You did?"

He gave a careful nod. "Enough to know that it's complicated. But all you have to do with Mackenzie is focus on today. And be the hope she needs to see."

She blew out a big breath. "I really like that. I feel a lot better now." She looked relieved and more relaxed. "I—I'd better get going. I'm getting better at just saying thank you. So"—she shot him a bright smile—"thank you."

"You're welcome." He checked his watch. "I have a lunch meeting. Right here, in fact. Talk later?"

As she left and he stayed to pay the bill, he thought that Darla—the emotional, vulnerable one—was more and more the Darla he once knew. The one not afraid to tell him whatever was on her mind. The one who smiled at him and trusted him with her feelings because he knew her better than anyone.

How did he get *that* Darla to stay?

Chapter 13

WALKING INTO CAT'S Meow Books, Darla was instantly comforted by the familiar smell of books, some old, some new, and all wonderful. The bright, colorful displays made her want to grab a couple and make herself at home like the black cat who was curled up on a purple velvet window seat, sleepily watching the noontime crowds pass by along the sunny sidewalk.

Her happiness at being surrounded by books almost made her forget her nerves about meeting Mackenzie.

On the way to the front desk, she practically ran into a display containing her last five thrillers. And there, standing nearby, were the same women who'd been watching her from across the street. She felt bad for them. All they probably wanted was to meet her and have her sign their books, not witness a panic attack in the street. She never exposed her emotions in public, let alone had readers witness them.

"You *are* Darla Manning, aren't you?" A woman with gray hair approached, Darla's latest book tucked under her arm.

Darla smiled, banishing her worries into the background. "Yep, that's me." She never really got used to the attention her fame brought. Especially since three-fourths of her life involved sitting alone staring out a window making stuff up.

The woman next to her, who had bright red hair, added, "If it's a bad time—"

"No, it's perfectly fine." She understood that people were excited to meet her, and she loved talking with them. And she appreciated that they bought her books. So she tamped down her discomfort with being gushed over and pulled out a pen from her purse.

"I'm a huge fan," the first woman said, handing over the book. "Please make it out to Rosemary."

"And I'm Louise. We're sorry if you're having a bad day."

Darla looked up. She was touched by their kind concern, but in a way, it made her feel even worse. After all, it was Mackenzie who was having the hard time, not her. "Oh. Thank you," she said as she reached out for a book.

Rosemary, watching her sign it, said, "We came all the way from Chicago, and this was our number one thing, to try and run into you."

Aw, geez. She smiled. "Well, I'm very touched."

"We're sorry if we're being pushy," Louise said. "We just love your books. You're very kind. And…we hope everything's okay."

"And that man you were with back there," Rosemary said, "he was a real hottie patottie."

Darla let out an uncensored laugh, her tension suddenly dissipating. "He *is* a hottie patottie," she agreed.

"That poor guy moved so fast, he was practically tripping over his feet trying to help you," Louise added.

Poor Nick. She must have given him a scare.

"Is he someone special?" Louise asked.

She laughed again. "Yes, he's very special," she said without thinking. A week ago, she probably would have added under her breath, *A special pain in the ass.* But now...well, Nick had gone out of his way to do a lot for her since she'd come back. And she wasn't talking about construction work.

Maybe Nick was right, that it was okay to let people see you as less than perfect. These ladies had made her feel better just by giving her a laugh. She only hoped that she could rally the strength Mackenzie needed when Darla felt that she was far from the right person to help her.

Darla chatted with the ladies for another minute, giving them a few restaurant and sightseeing tips, and they insisted on hugging her goodbye. A few other people in the store started to notice something going on and began whispering among themselves as Darla headed to the main desk.

Michelle Pearson spotted her and waved, walking around the counter and guiding her to the back of the store.

"I'm sorry you were accosted as soon as you walked in," she said. "We'll make sure you leave through the back."

"Oh, I don't mind," Darla said as Michelle led her through a storeroom stacked with boxes, out the door, and across a gravel drive to a cute redbrick house. Bright-colored zinnias filled pots on the steps leading up to the back porch.

Michelle halted her steps. "Before I forget, I heard you were looking for some information about Amelia Manning."

"Oh yes." That was unexpected. "I found some articles about her women's home in the library. But I was also interested in her personal life. I was going to try the historical society too."

"In a town as filled with history as ours, we all work together on fun things like this. I'm using my connections to find a source for you. I'll let you know if I can find anything."

"Oh, that's very kind." Darla was surprised and touched that Michelle would offer to help at such a difficult time. "Thank you."

"Well, I can't thank you enough for agreeing to see my daughter." Michelle halted in the middle of the driveway. "Normally, Mac would be beside herself to meet you, but she's really down right now." She sighed heavily. "I guess that's why I still wanted you to come, because we were hoping you could wave a magic wand and give her some positive energy. But maybe that was an unfair ask."

Darla's heart started to knock a little in her chest. She pressed against it, as if to tell it to calm down, and then offered up a prayer. *Please let me help.*

Nick had to be right about the power of being there for someone. Her friends had certainly been by her side through thick and thin. She didn't actually remember much that they'd said to bolster her resolve during that difficult time. But they'd been present. Unfailingly. *That* was what had mattered.

"The Mackenzie we dropped off at college last fall is not the same person you're going to meet today," Michelle said. "Our old Mac was lighthearted, excited, always laughing. Ever since she discovered a lump above her collarbone last Thanksgiving, we've all been on a roller coaster we never wanted to ride."

What to say? That everything was going to be okay? Darla couldn't know that. She struggled for something positive and uplifting, but words failed her.

"She adores your books," Michelle continued. "She looks up to you as an author and as a role model. The fact that you've been through this too means more than you can ever know."

She broke down in tears. Instinctively, Darla hugged her. "It's a funny thing about chemo," Darla said, focusing on saying what was in her heart. "You're so wrapped up in getting through this journey that it doesn't fully sink in that you're fighting for your life until it's all done, when you finally have the time and energy to think. I didn't process it until much later. So you all might be more overwhelmed at the moment than Mackenzie is."

How could she use her experience to show this young woman that she could beat this? That there was a whole wonderful life waiting for her on the other side?

Life *was* wonderful. Sometimes, among all her worries and problems, she almost forgot that.

Michelle took a deep breath. "Mac had to leave college during her first semester, just when she was starting to make friends. Her new friends have been wonderful, but she thinks that they feel sorry for her, and she worries about not fitting in when she goes back."

"How many more chemo cycles does she have to go?" Darla asked.

"Two more. She'll be back at school in the fall. But her hair's gone, and she's worried about how she's going to look. That seems to be her biggest worry." She gave an ironic smile. "While her dad and I are just praying that the treatment works."

Being in her early thirties when she was diagnosed, Darla hadn't had to deal with worries about friends and boys. Although losing her hair had been awful. And so had the feeling of having to depend on other people to do things for you. Darla gave Michelle a squeeze and summoned her cheeriest voice. "Well, I have a few things to cheer her up. And I know from my own mom telling me this, that seeing your child in pain is the worst, most helpless feeling. Now that we're on the other side of treatments, she uses that as collateral."

Michelle lifted a brow. "Collateral?"

"Yep. If we disagree about something, she reminds me of how much she worried about me. That usually makes me give in to whatever she wants."

That made Michelle laugh. She led Darla into a cheery family room, where a teenage girl with glasses lay on the couch. She wore a maroon crocheted hat with a yellow-and-purple flower on one side, and several multicolored afghans with bright squares were draped over her. A gray cat was curled up in an indentation of the blanket over her hip.

Darla smiled, but underneath she was struggling to

breathe evenly because the flashbacks were returning in full force. She remembered the sickening, gut-twisting nausea. The exhaustion. The pure, overwhelming anger. And mostly, the feeling that you were never going to be the same vibrant human being again.

Cancer had made Darla a warrior—but not by choice. It had made her different than her friends, no matter how kind and concerned they were. It had given her scars on her body and on her spirit—ones that she was still acutely aware of every single day. These were the things she had in common with the girl lying on the couch in front of her.

"Hi, Mackenzie." Darla gave a little wave from the doorway. "I'm Darla."

Mackenzie gave a weak smile that showed a dimple. "Thank you for coming to see me," she said politely.

Michelle asked her daughter if she needed anything. Then she brought them some iced tea. "I'll let you two chat," she said. "Darla, will you say goodbye before you go? I'll be back in the store."

"Of course. Thank you." And then it was just the two of them. That's when Darla realized she forgot her shopping bag at the restaurant. *Great. No icebreakers.*

As Mackenzie pushed herself part way up on her pillows, she grimaced, clearly from pain.

"There's no need to sit up," Darla said as she took a seat in a chair next to the couch.

Mackenzie sighed but sat up anyway.

Darla decided to start right in. "Well, we share a common bond. One we wish we didn't have to share." That was awkward. She winced inside, feeling like she was messing up already.

"You don't look like you've had cancer," Mac said, sitting back against a pillow shaped like a heart that said "Mac" in bright pink script in the middle. She assessed Darla with a steady gaze, her brown eyes sad and maybe frustrated too. "And your hair grew back."

Darla ran a hand through her unruly curls. "My hair wasn't this curly before. Isn't that funny? My mom said it's like it was when I was four. Weird, huh?"

"Yeah, weird," the teenager said in a deadpan voice.

"Three years ago, I was lying in bed trying not to throw up, just like you." Darla was nervous, rambling. Should she tell her about the forgotten gift?

It occurred to her that in Michelle's desperation, she may have sort of forced this visit on her daughter. Which might be the reason for the chilly reception.

"Yep," Mac said. Dead silence filled the air.

"Look," Darla said, "I know your mom called me. And it's really okay if you aren't up for visitors today." She closed her eyes, willing herself to remember being in the same position. "That was the hardest thing about cancer treatment for me. Losing control. People making decisions for you. Even if they love you and are trying to do the right thing." Darla stood up. "I brought you something, but I was so nervous about coming that I forgot it on a restaurant patio. So I'm going to go now, but I'd like to leave you my number and come back at a better time, if you'd like me to."

She reached past a bottle of Coke on the end table to grab a pad of pink sticky notes and a pen. As she scrawled her name and phone number, she heard a sniffle.

Mac had her eyes closed, and a tear was leaking out of one of them down her cheek. "I'm really sorry," she said.

Oh my heart, Darla thought. But she completely got what Mac was feeling because she'd been there. She smiled and handed Mac a tissue box. "No, honey, *I'm* sorry. It's okay if it's a bad day for visitors."

Darla stood to go but there was a knock on the door. "Hello," Mac's mom said, sticking her head into the room. "Look who else came to say hi, Mac."

The door opened wider to reveal Nick, of all people, standing there, her gift bag in one hand and a small brown paper shopping bag in the other.

She was relieved to see the bag. But Nick was coming in to say hi, like he knew Mac?

Nick gave Darla a nod, set the bags on the ground, and walked right over to Mackenzie, arms wide open. "Hey, ZZ, it's been a while. I brought you something." He kissed her on the top of her cap.

Mackenzie blushed and gave a little laugh. "No one calls me that dumb nickname anymore except for you."

Yep, he knew her, all right. Darla made sure her mouth didn't hit the floor.

"Well, I always will," Nick said. "I hate to interrupt the visit with your favorite author, but I think you better open *my* present first."

"What did you bring me, Nick?" Mackenzie perked up, sounding animated and telegraphing Nick an affectionate look.

Darla stared at him, but he was too busy charming Mackenzie. He waved the paper bag in front of Mac and dropped it on her lap. Still smiling, she reached in and pulled out a bright yellow Popsicle box.

She showcased a huge grin. "You remembered."

Nick looked pleased. "Well, I know you'll only eat the purple ones, but maybe you can share the rest."

"Thanks." She tilted the box toward him, asking without words for him to open it.

He took the box, pulled out a purple one, and handed it to her. Then he grabbed a red one for himself and offered Darla one from the box. Just going with it, she chose orange.

He pulled up a chair next to Mac. "How are you doing?"

"Pretty crappy, actually," she said between licks. "But this hits the spot."

Nick picked up the other bag and set it on the coffee table. "Darla's great at cheering people up."

Mac looked from Nick to Darla. "I told my mom no visitors today because I look disgusting. But she insisted because she's so worried about me." She rolled her eyes.

Nick grinned. "Sorry about that, pumpkin." Which got him a weak chuckle.

Darla couldn't stand it anymore. "How do you two know each other?"

Nick smiled. "I happened to be the best babysitter in all of Seashell Harbor, right, Mac?"

Ah, so they went way back. And also, Mac was worried about how she looked? Well, what teenager wasn't?

Darla grabbed her purse. "I brought you a few things you can take a look at when you feel like it. I'm going to take off and let you two catch up."

Nick bent toward Mackenzie and whispered something Darla didn't catch.

"Wait," Mackenzie said. "Don't go."

Darla must have looked uncertain because Mac said, "I really want you to stay." She paused. "I look gross."

"Yeah, you're a real train wreck," Nick said, tugging on her cap. Mac gave him the evil eye. Then she looked in the bag. "You brought me scarves."

"Mackenzie, you look beautiful just as you are. But I get what it's like to have the company of a stranger forced on you—"

"Darla's not a stranger," Nick said quickly. "We're best friends."

Darla lifted a brow.

Mac surveyed them both. "I thought you guys used to be married."

"Yes, we were," Darla said while Nick, unfazed, gestured for her to sit back down.

Darla did, not because of Nick but because Mac was drawing scarves out of the bag. Yellow ones, red ones, green and purple and pink. Darla's family and friends had decided wilder was better. "These are so bright." Mac actually sounded interested.

"My mother bought most of them for me," Darla explained. "She was so determined to cheer me up that she bought the loudest, brightest colors she could find." Darla pulled out an especially bright geometric one with neon pink, frog green, and bright purple. "The theory is that when you look in the mirror and see wild things, you might feel a little bit...wild too. I guess what I'm trying to say is that seeing yourself in one of these can remind you of that little rebellious part of you that won't give up. The fighting part of you." Darla tapped her chest. "That part is deep inside, although it might be very quiet now. Whatever it takes to nurture that and keep it alive, do it." She cracked a smile. "Except fight with your mom. I'm not talking that kind of re-bellious."

Mac's mouth quirked up in a smile. "I love my mom and dad a lot. But they're both hoverers. Like, big time."

How could they not be, given the circumstances?

Nick looked at his watch and stood up. "I've got to stop by a work site before my lunch meeting." He kissed Mac on the head again and squeezed her shoulder. "Great to see you, ZZ."

She gave him a hug and a genuine, if weak, smile. "Thanks for the Popsicles, Nick. That was sweet."

"That's because *you're* sweet." She groaned at that. "Next time, we'll do ice cream sandwiches, okay?"

"Okay," she said.

"Hang in there," he said. "We're all rooting for you." Darla didn't miss a crack in his voice.

When he left, Darla pulled out more scarves, telling little anecdotes about them. The cat even got up and lay in the middle of them, rolling on his back amid the rainbow of colors. "I can show you how I used to tie them if you want."

"Midnight approves," Mac said, scratching her cat on the head.

Mac pulled out the yellow heart sunglasses and yellow cap. "Why did you bring these?"

"That was a gift from my best friends, who told me they needed me to channel some sunshine. They were desperate to make me laugh. My advice is to take everyone's help. Don't push anyone away."

Like you did to Nick, a little voice in her head whispered.

Back then, Nick had seemed desperate to help. He'd

offered to drive her to chemo and bring over meals. She'd said no to nearly everything, but then he'd often drop off food anyway. She'd been terrified to have him see her vulnerable. Weak. Afraid.

Come to think of it, today was the first time in years he'd really seen her that way.

"I don't want my friends to see me like this," Mackenzie said, touching her head.

Darla nodded. After the divorce, she'd been so angry. Felt so misunderstood and hurt. Being helpless on top of everything else was just...too much.

Mac lowered her voice to a confessional tone. "Sometimes I say no because I feel like they're just coming because they have to."

"It's hard for people who aren't used to needing help to accept it." She looked her straight in the eyes. "I'm one of those people. It's funny, sometimes I said yes because I felt bad for people feeling bad for me. But when I did let them help, both of us felt better, if that makes any sense."

She shrugged as she played with one of the scarves. "My boyfriend dumped me."

"That toad," Darla said in a low voice. Which got her a faint giggle. "If anyone abandons you when you're down, you can do better."

Mac brightened up. "Yeah, right?" That was the most animated Darla had seen her. "I don't really blame him though. He went to college to have fun, not date someone who had to leave school and lose all her hair. It was just too much."

Nick hadn't run away. Darla had *pushed* him out of her life. Once, she'd even taken an Uber to the infusion center because everyone was busy and she couldn't bring herself to call him.

Ugh. She'd been so prideful and stubborn.

Darla held up her thumb and forefinger in an *L*-for-Loser sign.

Mac gave a weak chuckle. "I was making these great friends at school," she said as she scratched Midnight between the ears, "and they message me and text me but now...I don't know. It's like they're just feeling obligated."

"No, Mac." Darla leaned forward to emphasize her words. "People don't know what to do or say in a situation like this, and sometimes it's just...weird. But don't stop texting them. Even if it's to show them something cute Midnight does or anything silly. Stay in touch, because soon you *will* be back."

She shook her head, heaving a big sigh. "That's impossible to imagine."

Darla gave her a firm look. "You *will* get through this." If only she could give Mac some of her own will and determination to help her through until she was strong again.

Mac's eyes grew watery. "I'll never be who I was before. I'm not even sure if I'm going to have anything in common with my friends anymore."

"I'm not going to lie," Darla said firmly. "You will be different. But in some good ways, I think. You'll know how precious every drop of time is with everyone you love. You'll be more focused on your goals. More compassionate. And...none of that means much now. Right now, all you have to do is use all your energy in fighting this. And just let the people who love you...love you."

Yikes. Darla felt shaky. She felt completely unqualified to give advice to anyone, much less a young woman—just a kid, really—in the fight of her life.

Darla had known this was going to be difficult. But she'd had no idea it was going to rattle her to her core.

She dug once more into the bottom of the bag. And gave her best sinister smile. "Just to give you a little bit of terror and triumph over evil, here's my latest book. It comes out in two weeks."

The girl's eyes lit up for the first time since Nick left. "An early copy of *No Time to Die*? Oh my gosh, I can't believe it."

"I signed it to you," Darla said. "And the next time I come, we can discuss it, if you want."

Mackenzie hugged the book to her chest. "Thank you so much. This really means a lot."

Funny, but Darla was thinking the same thing about Mac being excited about something. "When you feel up to it, I can tell you insider things."

"Oh, a private book club! What kinds of things?"

Darla gave a little chuckle. "Well, like I always name my villains after my worst one-dates."

"No way."

Mac's lids were drooping, and it was time to go. Darla stood. "It was great to meet you, Mackenzie."

"Thank you," she said in a quiet voice, still clutching the book to her chest.

As Darla hugged Mac and let herself out, she wondered how it was that facing this visit that was so dreaded and feared could somehow make her feel a thousand times more humbled and grateful for being alive than when she'd walked in?

She'd come to help Mackenzie, but it was she who had been given the gift.

* * *

As Darla turned back onto Petunia Street, she turned the ring on her finger, watching it catch and spread the rays of the warm summer sun. And realized that she just did a small, brave thing—brave for her, anyway—that might have been Amelia worthy.

She'd told Mackenzie to accept help and to let the people who love her love her. But Darla herself had such difficulty allowing the people in her life to do anything for her. Especially Nick.

Yet he kept coming back. Helping her. Doing things for her. Supporting her.

From finding fancy tile halfway across the world like it was her heart's desire, to finding her a Diet Coke when she was distressed.

She'd misjudged him at every turn. And she didn't need the fancy tile. But she did need to understand what was going on between them. And tell him how much his support had meant.

She was going to see him tomorrow at the clambake, but suddenly she was bursting with the need to tell him how amazing Mackenzie was and how his advice of just being there for her had helped so much.

Before she could talk herself out of it, she passed the

restaurant with the yellow umbrellas, scanning the patio for Nick. Sure enough, she spotted the back of his head as he sat at a far-corner table, his arm casually draped on the metal rail surrounding the elevated deck. She didn't want to interrupt his lunch meeting, but surely he was almost done by now? So she ran up the set of stairs.

Darla spotted him immediately. She was struck by his easy, relaxed posture. His good looks, his wavy hair blowing in the light breeze, sunglasses on. The man could certainly turn heads.

Except her heart jumped into her throat as she viewed his lunch companion…a woman. Not Lauren. A very pretty woman that she'd never seen before, with long dark hair, wearing a red blouse and red lipstick that stood out from a distance.

Oh.

Nick threw his head back and laughed so hard he had to clutch his chest.

Darla halted, momentarily frozen by a deer-in-the-headlights feeling.

"Would you like a table, Miss?" a waiter asked.

"Oh, hi, sorry," she fumbled. "I—I was just looking for someone. But I see they're not here. Thank you."

She reversed her steps, unseen, and walked quickly back down the stairs.

It suddenly struck her that he meant what he'd said about being friends. Regardless of the vibes she was getting as they spent time together, Nick was not interested in her.

Relief should have washed over her. After all, he'd asked for friendship, not a relationship. And his flirty behavior toward her was…well, remnants of their other life.

The disappointment that slowly seeped through her felt like a slow, thick coating of sludge, weighing her down, freezing her in place. She realized that her disappointment was based on the hope that she and Nick weren't done.

But in order for her to move on and live her life, she had to be done with Nick Cammareri. For good.

Chapter 14

"SO DID YOU make your word count today?" Nick asked the next day as he and Darla headed across her deck to walk down to the beach to collect grapefruit-sized rocks to set up the firepit for the clambake.

"Yep, I sure did," Darla said. "Nearly 2,500 of them."

"Oh, that's great," he said. "Glad you got some good work accomplished."

She nodded but didn't say anything more. He took that to mean her book was progressing and hopefully she'd enjoy their last night on the beach before the wedding, which was a little over a week away.

And speaking of the wedding, the deck looked great, if he did say so himself, thanks to his work sanding and staining it. In one corner lay the beginnings of the wooden arbor he'd started building for the bride and groom to stand under on the beach.

A warm breeze drifted in from the sea, blowing wisps of

hair around Darla's face and making the pale blue, flowy sundress she was wearing swirl around her ankles. The more time Nick spent with her, the more he couldn't seem to stop the optimism that filled him about their relationship. An impulse nearly overtook him to playfully gather her up and swing her around like he used to the many times they'd walked together on this beach.

Darla tossed a rock into the pit Nick had dug just above the high-tide line. Boss, thinking it was a ball, nearly jumped into the pit after it. Nick stopped him with a "No, Boss," after which the dog slunk away from the edge and walked around to Darla's side.

She wasn't very talkative today. Which he didn't get, because yesterday had been such a great day.

Maybe she felt uncomfortable that he'd seen her in a vulnerable state. But it had felt so good to finally reach her. They'd talked and shared, and he'd left feeling like they'd had a breakthrough in their relationship.

"So. It's going okay?" he asked, hoping she would tell him more. He tossed in another rock, frustrated that he couldn't seem to reach her again.

"The deck looks really nice," she said. "I know it will help sell the place. Although it wasn't in terrible shape to begin with."

He tossed several more rocks into the pit that he'd stacked up along the side. "I know, but I wanted it to be really nice for the wedding."

She smiled at that.

"What?" he lifted a brow.

"Just that you have your own streak of relentless perfectionism. You just hide it better than I do."

He threw his hands up in the air. "Okay, I admit it. I do want everything to be perfect for Tony's wedding. He deserves the best."

"You're a good best man. And brother." He saw a flicker of something in her eyes. But it didn't last long.

As happened so many times, what passed between them was so much more than words. She didn't seem angry, just closed off, and he had no idea why.

They set off down the beach with a wagon to gather firewood, a familiar pre-clambake ritual they'd taken part in since they were kids. Boss was beside himself, romping along the wave line, running toward the waves and then suddenly tearing away when the water covered his paws. Nick had to admit, for a giant dog, he was a big coward.

"How'd it go with Mackenzie yesterday after I left?" he asked. "I texted you, but you never texted back."

"Sorry, I—got busy." She seemed very focused on finding sticks. "She relaxed more with me after you left. Thanks for helping to break the ice."

"Sure. No problem."

They collected driftwood in silence for a while.

Then the devil got in him. "Is something wrong?"

Darla bit her lip, never a good sign. That always meant that she was holding back.

"Just for once, I wish you wouldn't do that." He couldn't keep the frustration out of his voice.

"Do what?" she asked with surprise. "I haven't said anything."

"I wish you wouldn't only tell me *part* of the truth."

"I've never lied to you." Her voice was heated.

"I'm not talking about telling lies. I'm talking about not letting me know what you're really thinking."

That seemed to throw her. She paused, seeming to choose her words carefully. Screening what she would say. Just once he wished she would lash out at him, let her words rip and tear. Because then he would know that she really felt something. But she stayed as calm and impenetrable as ever.

Over a large bank of sand, a few cars pulled up to a nearby beach parking lot. His brother got out of one of the cars and waved.

"We divorced for good reasons," she finally said. Dry, sharp words that cut him in an entirely different way. "And those reasons make it so that we can't ever get things back to the way they used to be. We've both moved on."

Ouch. "So you're saying we can't even be friends?"

She crossed her arms. "We can't go back to the way things used to be, no."

He circled his index finger in front of her face, something that he knew irritated her. "You're doing that chin thing again."

"What chin thing?"

"That stubborn chin thing."

She took a step back. "Stop reading my body language."

"Honey, I'll never stop reading your body language." Okay, that wasn't appropriate, but he was angry.

She shook her head sadly. "You really can't imagine a world where everyone doesn't cave to your charm, can you?"

"What's that supposed to mean?" he asked as she started to walk away.

"Sometimes the hurt is too deep, Nick. And it's better to just let things lie."

He touched her arm, making her turn toward him, and searched her eyes. What was she thinking? If only he knew. "No. I don't believe it's ever best to just let things lie," he said firmly. Okay, this was getting intense. He was operating only on instinct, which could be all wrong. But he couldn't stop himself from trying to reach her. "If I've done something to hurt you, I deserve to know."

Darla glanced nervously up the beach, where Alex and Tony were gathering firewood. Hadley and Kit were starting to walk down the sandbank to the beach. "Lower your voice," she said. "They'll think we're fighting."

"We *are* fighting," he said, throwing up his hands. "Well, let's call it a disagreement."

She dropped her voice to a harsh whisper. "We both said we'd keep our personal stuff from interfering with Hadley and Tony's happiness."

He started to say something but stopped. "Okay," he finally said, feeling a muscle in his jaw twitch from the tension. "Fine. We won't discuss it anymore."

She frowned. "What exactly are we not discussing?"

"The fact that you're afraid to lower your guard with me."

She gave him a look. "I am not."

"You run away—mentally, anyway—whenever we touch on a topic you don't want to talk about."

She waved her arms. "Do you blame me for not wanting to rehash the things that made us divorce in the first place?"

Their friends were fast approaching, and the last thing

he wanted was a spectacle. "We'll agree to disagree, how's that? And just get through tonight."

"Okay," she whispered back. "We'll get through tonight."

He stubbornly said his piece. "The easy, fun way we talked the other day—I loved that. It was like we were open and honest with each other for the first time in so long. Now, it's like you've turned off a switch. I just want to know why." He raked his hands through his hair in frustration. "I just…miss you, Darla."

If he thought his words would have her breaking down and admitting that she missed him too, he was dead wrong.

"You don't get to say that, Nick." She stood directly in front of him, her tone fiery, every word stinging.

Okay, so maybe she *was* angry after all. At least she felt *something*.

She lowered her voice, but not her fire. "Maybe every single man and woman in the world is attracted to your magnetic personality, and maybe I am too. Except the difference is that I got burned."

Her words felt like a slap.

He felt stunned. "I—wait."

But she turned away and ran to greet their friends.

Leaving her words ringing in his ears. But not the words she'd stung him with—the ones she'd let slip out. *Maybe I am too.*

* * *

As soon as Darla caught up with her friends, Hadley pulled her a little over to the side. "Is everything okay?"

"Yeah," Kit said, looking concerned. "You seem upset. We saw a lot of arm waving, like things were getting emotional between you and Nick."

Even the dog seemed unsettled, sitting stone-still a few feet away, his ears lowered. "Come here," she called, not wanting him to be distressed. He bounded over, and she soothed him with lots of pets and silly words, but her heart wasn't really in it.

She was trying not to hyperventilate from frustration. She was trying to project calm. For her friends' sakes. This was exactly what she'd wanted to avoid at all costs. And she was a lousy actor, but she channeled everything she could into getting her emotions under control. "We were just messing around," she lied, her heart still hurting. "Nick's about to start the fire. And it couldn't be a more perfect evening for the clambake."

Darla did her best to pretend that Nick was not the most irritating man on the planet. The one who drew her in and made her believe things she had no business believing.

Ordinarily, she'd just tell her friends what was going on. But she couldn't ruin this special time. And the truth was, she already knew what she had to do. For her own sanity, she had to get herself as far away from Nick as possible.

Hadley shook her head. "Uh-uh," she said. "Stop right there."

Darla's heart sank. Hadley was about to call her out. "Just because I'm getting married soon doesn't mean I have to avoid reality," she said. "You're not going to, like, burst my wedding fairy tale or anything, so please stop trying to protect me. Besides," she said with a little smile, "if it makes you feel any better, Tony and I have been squabbling all week."

"Why is that?" Kit asked.

"Wedding stress." She shrugged her shoulders. "Even though this is the least stressful way we could think of to get married. There are still just so many decisions that have to be made."

Kit gave Hadley a sympathetic look. "Well, it's all going to be worth it because you two are going to have a wonderful wedding." Turning to Darla, she said, "Hadley's right. We can both see something's wrong. So just come out with it."

The guys were gathered around the pit, laughing and starting the fire, which would burn for several hours to get the rocks hot before they added a bed of wet seaweed to steam the seafood. Darla let herself confess a little of what was bothering her. "Nick keeps trying to be friends. But we can't ever go back to the way it was. We can't act as if the past ten years never happened."

"So you're angry because he wants to be friends?" Kit restated in true therapist fashion.

Darla sighed heavily. "Okay, not just friends. Or maybe just friends." She threw up her hands in pure frustration. "I really don't know."

"I'm so confused," Kit said. "Nick wants to be friends, and that's upsetting? Or does he want to be more than friends, and that's upsetting?"

The friends of her heart knew that something was wrong and were looking at her with their usual kindness and concern. And that broke her, making all of the emotional turmoil that had been bubbling at the surface for so long spill out. "I saw Nick eating lunch with this gorgeous woman yesterday. I just...every time I feel myself letting him in, something happens that makes me feel like I'm a fool." Her voice cracked, and she swallowed hard so that she didn't cry. Which was ridiculous but...yeah. She'd really said what she felt. But it didn't bring her any peace, that was for sure.

"Are you sure that he was on a date?" Hadley asked. "Because Tony says he doesn't have a girlfriend."

"No. I— Look, he's allowed to date, right?" Darla tried to sort through her confusion. "But sometimes—a lot of times—I feel this attraction between us. But he's just outgoing and sort of flirtatious anyway, and I—"

She was going to say, *I get my hopes up.*

Oh no, she definitely didn't want to say that out loud. Or think it.

But it was true. She was disappointed. Everything between them had led her to think that he might be interested. Even though nothing had happened but a peck on the lips in the hallway.

She'd tried to ignore her emotions. Push them aside. But she couldn't stop feeling them. How could she stop herself from wanting him? Nick would be the death of her. She rubbed her forehead in frustration.

She wanted her ex.

She slapped her forehead. But that didn't knock any sense into her.

"Nick is jokey and funny," Hadley said, "but he doesn't go out of his way to flirt with women."

"I have to agree with Hadley," Kit said. "Maybe he

really is flirting with you. In any case, you know what you have to do." She made a hand sign that either meant a duck quacking...or she was telling Darla it was time to talk to Nick.

Hadley nodded in agreement.

"I don't want to be foolish," Darla said. "I don't want to make the same big mistake twice."

"Ask yourself what will happen if you let this go," Kit said. "Maybe you'll regret it the rest of your life if you don't try again with him."

"Right," Hadley said. "No matter what the outcome, act so you won't have regrets."

Darla hugged her dear friends. "Thank you for listening," she said. "I'm sorry this had to happen tonight."

Just then, the dog, who was very wet, brought her flip-flops back...make that one. The ocean probably ate the other one. He wagged his tail and jumped up and down excitedly as if he'd done her a great service.

"Thanks, Boss," Darla said, rubbing his head. He looked so pleased with himself that she couldn't help a small chuckle. "You're lucky you're cute, you know that?"

Darla was caught between a rock and a hard place. Unable to forget Nick but afraid to make the worst mistake of her life—again.

Chapter 15

AS THE EVENING wore on, Nick took it upon himself to keep the fire going. They'd had dinner, played bocce ball and a paddleball game, and he and Darla had managed to be cordial. She'd even smiled at him a few times and laughed at his jokes, but only because their friends were around. Now it was the time of the evening he'd been dreading.

Sit-around-the-fire time. Or, as far as he was concerned, *awkward* time.

Tony and Hadley sat together on a blanket, Hadley leaning against his chest. Kit and Alex sat propped against a large rock, his arm around her shoulder.

And Boss, who had somehow ended up with a blanket of his own, was snoring, belly-up, enjoying the soft breeze and the warmth of the fire.

Darla, who sat next to Boss on a striped beach chair

with her toes in the sand, fiddled nervously with her phone.

Nick unfolded a chair and placed it far enough from Darla to not look like they were together. But then he second guessed himself, worrying that it was still too close. So he asked, "This okay?" to which she nodded and answered, "Sure," a little too brightly.

He glanced at his watch. 9:00 p.m. It was going to be a loooong couple of hours.

"No matter how many years I live here," Kit said, glancing around the familiar beach, "I can't get over how beautiful this place is."

The moon was almost full, slung low in the ever-darkening sky, casting a golden trail of magic on the water. Nick had seen that sight dozens of times, but its beauty never failed to hit him straight in the gut.

His heart was hurting, but it was also full of love for this beautiful place. And for his friends. It was his feelings for Darla that were a lot more complicated.

"We grew up on this beach," Tony said in a reminiscing tone. "We knew all the secret paths, the best views...and the best places not to get caught doing things we weren't supposed to be doing."

"We snuck cigarettes in the rock caves," Alex said.

"Well, good thing that habit didn't stick." Kit made a face, waving her hand in front of her nose.

Alex grinned. "I thought I'd say that rather than talk about the make-out places."

That earned him a friendly swat. "I never made out on the beach as a teenager," she said, "but since the beach is right in our backyard, I can safely say that the sand is soft, but if you don't bring a blanket, it gets everywhere."

Okay, TMI. "Hey, aren't there laws against that?" Nick joked.

"*Querida*, you're worth breaking the law for," Alex said with a giant smile.

Everyone groaned.

"I never made out on the beach when I was a teenager either," Darla said.

"Yes, you did," Nick said before he could censor himself.

Darla jerked up her head, clearly considering strangulation.

Boss, sensing the tension, suddenly walked between Nick and Darla and planted himself. Possibly waiting to pick sides.

"Um, excuse me," Darla said, not seeming to be aware of the sudden silence or the fact that everyone seemed to be holding their breath, "but you were the only boy I went out with in high school, and we didn't start dating until spring of senior year. I think that I would remember if I made out on the beach with you. You must be thinking of another girl." She waved her hand in a *whatever* gesture.

Okay, he was about to dig his grave. But so what? What did he have to lose? He was sick of tiptoeing with his emotions around her. "No," he said calmly, "I'm not thinking of anyone else. It was after prom."

"Oh, that's such a cliché!" She was using her bossy know-it-all tone, confident of her case. "Don't tell me, you're going to say that we came out to the beach after prom with blankets and…and did things…and then watched the sun rise."

The dog looked from Nick to Darla and whined. Darla reached out and petted him, whispering it was okay, which Nick thought was interesting. Even more interesting, Boss scooched closer to her side.

"It must not have been very memorable, bro," Tony said with a smirk, "if she can't even remember—"

Hadley elbowed him in the stomach.

Nick tossed his brother a dirty look.

The dog barked and snuggled up to Darla, leaning against her leg and extending his neck to be petted more, the traitor.

Nick softened his voice for the dog's sake. "No," he said with measured patience, "we were not a cliché. Because you had a curfew. And your mother threatened my balls if I didn't have you back by 2:00 a.m."

Her eyes grew wide as recognition dawned. "We went swimming," she said softly. "I forgot all about that. The water was freezing." The dog dropped to the sand, belly-up. Darla indulged him by rubbing it. Lucky dog.

Yeah, it had been freezing. But he'd kept her warm. And he could tell by her expression that she was remembering that. If his smile looked a little smug, he couldn't help it.

"Just swimming?" Alex chuckled. "Great postprom date."

Nick shrugged. He wasn't going to go any further because it was no one's business.

"It really was a great date," Darla said, seeming lost in the memory. "You taught me to swim."

"Nick taught you how to swim after the prom?" Hadley asked. "I thought you finally learned in college."

She'd been terrified of the water ever since her mother signed her up for swim lessons when she was six and an inexperienced teenage instructor demanded she get in the pool. After that she wouldn't even dip a toe in the ocean or a pool for years. "You taught me not to be afraid of the water."

"Yes, but you asked me to teach you," Nick said. "You were ready for it."

"Somehow your lessons worked," she said. "That was kind of miraculous."

"Yeah, well, that's what love does," he answered, a bitter edge in his voice.

"Wait a minute, what about the making out?" Hadley asked. Being a bride had somehow made her very pushy.

"A gentleman doesn't kiss and tell," he shot back.

His gaze snagged with Darla's. For a flash of a moment, it was just the two of them, lost in an old memory. One that involved him stripping down to his boxers and her to a silky camisole and panties, and after she'd finally gotten up the courage to hold her breath under water, rewarding him by wrapping herself around him and kissing him repeatedly. *That* was the making out part.

And it had been so worth it.

"I'd forgotten all about that," she said. "I owe you an apology."

"Nah," he said. "But I'm glad you didn't forget."

They were brought back to reality by Tony popping a bottle of champagne and Hadley passing around glasses.

Tony raised his glass. "I just want to say thank you all for being here for us, through thick and thin. And for making time in your busy lives to help us to have a fabulous wedding. I can't think of anything better than spending my life with Hadley...and having you all to share life with." He raised a glass. "So, to friends. For being here for each other. We love you."

"We love you," Hadley echoed.

Everyone drank. Alex stood to give another toast. "We wish you a home filled with love, laughter, lots of dogs and cats and...kids."

"Yes," Kit agreed. "May you not be exempted from any chaos that comes with all of that."

"Life is short," Darla said, raising her glass. "So may you never forget that each day is a precious opportunity to love each other."

"All the happiness, bro," Nick said. "May you two never take a good thing for granted."

Nick immediately felt like he'd given a terrible toast. He blamed it on all his upside-down emotions and Darla's presence throwing him completely.

Dreading the thought of more snuggle-by-the-fire time and in need of finishing what was between him and Darla, Nick did the only thing he could think of to get out of there. He turned to his dog. "Boss, do you have to pee?"

"Woof!" Boss said agreeably.

"Care to come with?" he asked Darla, trying to sound casual when he felt anything but.

She was already standing up and walking across the sand, looking like she couldn't wait to get out of there either.

At last.

He heaved a sigh, and not just for being grateful to leave.

Because, he realized, it was finally time to come clean.

* * *

Boss came bounding over to Darla, shockingly with her long-lost flip-flop, excited for a walk. Nick called him back with a whistle, but he stuck to Darla's side. Which made her oddly happy that the dog chose her.

Could dogs give moral support? They were attuned to emotions, right?

"Okay, Boss," she said under her breath as she bent over and gave him a kiss on the top of his head. "I have to confess that I'm a little nervous about this."

Boss bumped up against her leg. Either as a gesture of solidarity or because he was big and clumsy—she wasn't sure which.

"I think my dog likes you better than me," Nick said when she caught up to him.

"He has great taste," Darla said. "Don't you, Boss?"

"Woof!" said Boss. Which made her send Nick a smug look. No matter what happened here, at least Boss was on her side.

"Which way shall we walk?" Nick asked.

"You pick," she said.

Nick pointed right. Which was the less crowded part of the beach, farthest from town. The evening was warm, a light, salty breeze blowing off the sea. But Darla had the feeling their walk would be anything but breezy and light.

As soon as they were out of earshot of their friends, Darla summoned her courage and got right to the point. "Sometimes I think that you're flirting with me." Nick turned toward her and arched a brow as they walked along the edge of the surf.

"What I mean is, I *know* you are, but I'm wondering

if it's serious. The kind that means something more than joking." She took off her flip-flops and let her feet sink into the warm sand. Let the cool water rush over them, at once shocking and familiar.

Nick halted. Boss bolted down the beach, headed for the surf, which she wasn't sure was a good idea, but Nick didn't seem overly concerned, fixing his gaze on her.

"Is your dog okay out there?" she couldn't help but ask.

He glanced briefly at Boss, who followed the surf as it retreated and then ran away as it rolled toward him, getting very wet in the process. This appeared to be a game, as he did it over and over.

"Yes, to both questions."

Her pulse began to pound in her ears. "Yes to Boss is okay," she said carefully.

"And yes to flirting." He locked his gaze on hers, which caused her heart to knock against her chest. And crazy hope to bloom there.

But wait. "I know that to you the teasing is just…casual. Like, maybe we fall back into it because of our history, but it has to stop." She waved her hand in the air. "Because it's too…flirty." But the real reason was that it made her think he meant it.

A frown creased his brow. "Did I offend you with something I said?"

"No, but…" She sighed. "I thought you wanted to get our friendship back."

"I lied. I want more."

Her heart lodged in her throat and stopped it up so she couldn't form any more words.

He reached out and touched her cheek. The contact made

her breath catch. His eyes held tenderness, which threw her even more and made her blink back sudden tears.

She was getting to be like Kit, crying at the drop of a hat.

Nick didn't say anything else. But she needed to be honest. "I—I went to find you after my visit with Mackenzie yesterday," she said. "I was excited to tell you about it, so I walked onto the deck of the restaurant and you were—you were eating lunch with a beautiful—"

"Friend," he interjected.

"Friend?" she repeated. "I mean, you've dated a lot of women since we've been divorced—"

He leveled his gaze at her. "Are you faulting me for trying to move on with my life?"

"No, I—I just want to understand. Because I—"

"Because you what?"

"Because I've been here all along." There. She'd said what she'd been thinking for months. Make that years. That was probably not a good thing because she might as well have told him that she was jealous. But at least it was the truth.

"You made it clear you wanted nothing to do with me."

She steeled herself, flexing her hands into fists. This conversation was becoming intense. "Well, it was clear you weren't interested in me."

"Darla, *you* divorced *me*." He spoke with emotion, with passion, but he looked more hurt than angry. "You served me with the papers. And you've done a lot over the years to ensure that I stayed far away."

She pressed her lips together to keep from crying. "What did you expect me to do? We had big problems. Ones we couldn't solve. And you...you left. *That's* when I filed for divorce."

He paced back and forth in front of her, his footprints tracking in the wet sand. Meanwhile, Boss found something floating in the ocean—something that looked like a giant stick—and started tugging at it.

Nick stopped pacing and faced her. "If I told you how many times I replayed that night over and over in my head—how many times I told myself I should have stayed. And again, how I should've ripped up those divorce papers and gone after you and told you I loved you. That we were worth more than anger or pride.

"I was jealous of your determination to succeed. Your focus. And the fact that…that you had a choice of what you wanted to do, while I felt trapped. I admit, I gave you a hard time about working. I didn't understand."

She shook her head. "I used my writing as an excuse. The more you wanted to go out and have fun, the more you grew impatient about me working all the time, and the more I hid in my work. I…I was determined to succeed no matter what." Her voice cracked. "I chose success over my marriage. I had no balance. And I felt angry that you didn't support my dream."

Oh no. The tears were falling freely down her cheeks now. She didn't want to relive this. But she had to if they were ever going to leave it behind. "The night you left was the worst night of my life."

"I'm sorry for all the pain, Darla." The emotions on his face were raw, and she saw that he meant it. "I'm sorry for being so immature. I was angry with my brother for leaving. Angry that I felt that I had to be the one to stay and help my dad." Looking directly at her, he said, "Mostly, I'm just sorry for quitting you." He raked his hands through his hair. "It was the worst decision I ever made."

Darla wrapped her arms around herself to try and keep it together. "We both made bad decisions. I'm sorry for underestimating you. And for hiding in my work instead of dealing with our problems."

He shook his head—in disbelief or sadness, she wasn't sure. "The woman yesterday was Kerri Adkins. Her husband Brad is on our crew and left the table a few minutes before you came. They asked me to be the godfather of their new baby."

"Oh."

He looked out over the water. They were enveloped in darkness now, as if they were the only ones on the beach. "I'm only interested in one woman. The one I've been flirting with lately. She's got it all—she's beautiful and kind and she just...gets me. And I can't stay away from her. Although God knows I tried." He paused. "I'm proud of you, Darla. So proud of who you've become."

He wanted her. Warmth rushed over her as his words hit her full force. "I'm proud of you too. You've done amazing things with the company."

He shrugged. "I made peace with who I am."

"You're not who I thought you were," she said, shaking her head.

"Darla," he said gently, "I'm a nice guy." He dropped his voice. "I've grown up."

"You're pretty hard to resist."

He slid his hands down her arms and gripped her hands. "I can't forget you. I can't forget *us.*"

Darla closed her eyes. She felt like she was living something she'd conjured up as she created scenes for a book. Something she'd imagined that was far too good to take place in real life.

She looked down at their intertwined hands. The warmth of his clear blue gaze, the gentle stroke of his thumbs against the inside of her palms, she felt it all, for the first time in a decade. She was hot and cold, weak and strong, confused and completely lucid, all at once.

"You remember that swim lesson?" he asked out of the blue.

There he was, reminding her again. Of everything. Making it impossible for her to resist. And of course, there they were, right at the part of the beach where he'd taught her to swim so many years ago. "Of course, I do."

"We left our good clothes on the rocks, remember?" He nodded over to where giant boulders formed a break line along the beach. "You held my hands just like this and lowered your head in the water. You trusted me."

"Yes. I trusted you."

"I'll never forget you standing there in the moon-light. You looked beautiful then. But you're even more beautiful now."

She said the honest truth. "I wasn't afraid with you."

"I had your back." He smiled, his eyes soft with remembrance.

"I know you did." She remembered it all so vividly. "I dunked my head and floated and then you made me swim forward with my arms. And afterward, I was so amazed and grateful that somehow you'd helped me conquer my fear."

Nick gave a soft chuckle. "I remember thinking how lucky I was to have you trust me—to teach you how to swim." He paused. "And to touch you."

"We didn't have actual sex for a while after that."

He shook his head, smiling. "No, but by then we'd learned each other's bodies really well, didn't we?"

She smiled right back. "Getting back into those prom clothes was so hard when we were all wet, remember that? I always felt that my mom knew everything the minute I walked in with my hair wet."

He chuckled. "That was probably the day she started to dislike me."

Darla didn't say it out loud, but she thought he was probably right. "She's always been very protective of me."

"I feel that way too, even though I know you don't need anyone's protection." He reached up and tucked a stray strand of hair behind her ear. "You're still the most beautiful woman I've ever seen."

Startled, she flicked her gaze upward. When she looked into his eyes, she saw...Nick. The same Nick she'd fallen in love with years ago. The man who got her like no other. The one she'd once trusted with all her heart.

She leaned in, unable to stop herself. He closed the space between them, their lips meeting in a shock of yearning, desire, and heat. Nick didn't hesitate, wrapping his arms around her, and at last, she melted into him with a sigh.

Nick's lips were soft and warm and wonderful. He kissed her slowly at first, taking his time, as if he were reacquainting himself with every inch of her mouth. He tasted familiar in a way she couldn't describe in any other way but wonderful.

His hand came up to her jaw, caressing it softly, and then he curled his hand in the hair at her nape and pulled her in closer.

She let out a whimper, drowning in the simple pleasure

of his touch. He kissed her like no man had ever kissed her before. Pressing herself against his hard body, she wrapped her arms around his lean waist as their kisses grew deeper and more desperate.

He leaned her against the rocks, planting a trail of burning kisses down her neck, whispering how much he missed her, how wonderful she tasted, how beautiful she was. She arched her neck, wanting more kisses, more murmured words. More of him.

As he nuzzled her neck and dropped his mouth lower, he reached the sensitive skin of the small horizontal scar several inches under her right collarbone where her port used to be buried—the device that delivered her chemotherapy and through which her nurses and doctors drew her blood.

She instinctively jerked back, reaching up to touch the bumpy ridges of the scar. As if she could hide such a thing.

"My port scar," she said, feeling warmth rush into her cheeks. "I got it taken out around a year after the chemo."

And there it was. Reminding her of things she'd almost forgotten. Things she couldn't put into words.

Worries welled up, dissipating the magical, awestruck feelings that had filled her up. Cancer had changed her, outside and in. She couldn't pretend it hadn't. She was wary, on guard, bracing for a great anvil to come crashing down on her dreams at any moment, so she'd better not be too happy.

"I—I'm not the same." She drew back. "Not physically, not mentally." Cancer had strengthened her, but it had definitely left its battle wounds.

He tipped her chin up so she had to look at him. "Neither of us are. We're *better*," he said determinedly.

His words touched her deeply.

But it was so much more complicated than that. How could she explain to him all that she'd gone through? That she wasn't the same simple, carefree young girl he fell in love with? How could she say that she had to learn how to embrace living all over again and seemed to be failing miserably? That sometimes she felt more afraid than fearless? Still more frightened than grateful?

Baring her soul didn't come easily. Especially when she worked so hard on a daily basis to put up a tough front.

"Hey, you two." They turned to see Hadley running toward them carrying a handful of long sticks, a wet Boss running at her side.

"We're about to toast marshmallows." She took in Nick leaning his arm on the rock behind Darla's head. "Also, I found this guy wandering off down the beach."

"Woof!" Boss said from her side, now on a leash.

Oh no.

"I had to give him a marshmallow to get him out of the surf."

That made Nick stand straight up. "Sorry," he said. "Thanks for getting him."

"Yep. Worst dog owner ever," Hadley said. She turned and called back over her shoulder. "See you up there. After the marshmallows, we're going to bank the fire and call it a night."

"We'll be right up," Nick said. "Thanks for finding Boss."

Darla started to walk back. "Wait," he said, running until he was at her side. "You've gone quiet. Don't shut me out," he said. "Please."

That almost broke her. How could it be that he was the most open and honest person she knew while she was constantly trying to tamp down secrets? She wanted to run straight back into his arms. Tell him that he was the only one she wanted. The only one she would ever want. But fear had frozen her voice, her heart.

"I—um." She had to clear her throat because her voice was so ragged. "You know, right after the wedding, I've got to head straight back to California to find a place to live and prepare for my new job." She couldn't look at him. "I'm sorry, but—I don't think it's a good idea to start something now."

Nick's dark brows pulled down in a frustrated vee. He spoke slowly and calmly—too slowly and calmly. "The quality of yours that I find most difficult is that you think you can get through life not needing anybody."

"That's not true," she protested. "I have great friends. I have—"

"Hear me out, okay?" he said calmly. "Anytime something's wrong, you shut down. You push people away. You are so determined to go it alone. What if other people need *you*?"

Completely baffled, she shook her head. "What are you talking about?"

"The people who love you," he said, never losing eye contact. "What if, by shutting yourself away, you're depriving them of loving you? Losing all the good times. The special moments. The laughs."

She wanted to tell him she was afraid. That she didn't know how to live without a giant shadow hanging over her head. But that sounded so weak. And one thing Darla never showed was weakness. And all her words got stuck in her throat.

Nick tugged at Boss's leash. Boss bristled at his loss of freedom. Nick smiled, a little sadly, and kissed her on the cheek. "I'm going to pass on the marshmallows. See you later."

Chapter 16

AFTER EVERYONE LEFT, Darla found herself sitting alone in the dark on her aqua heaven blue couch telling herself that she'd done the right thing.

She ran her fingers lightly along the ridged scar on her chest. One she saw every single time she looked in the mirror. The appearance itself didn't upset her; rather, the scar was a reminder that she would never be done fighting.

Unable to sit, she paced the great, hollow room, her footsteps echoing on the shiny wooden floors. Echoing! In her own home. It was a lonely thought. She walked outside onto the deck where a million stars were shining overhead. She filled her lungs with the clean, salty air. Listened to the waves lapping to the shore, a sound that always gave her comfort.

But she found no peace. It could have been the blizzard of the century for all the fine summer night registered.

Her first apartment, in college, had overlooked a brick wall. She might as well be looking out at that stark, dark nonview for all she saw.

All she could think of was the long, cold, empty prospect of a lifetime without Nick, rattling around in a house the size of a hotel. Her mother had warned her not to make stupid mistakes twice. But what if Nick wasn't a mistake?

And what if she would regret not acting now for the rest of her life, just as she regretted so many things about her past?

She couldn't bear more regret. Especially when it had to do with him.

Now she had a chance to change the story. Her story.

The key word being *now*. What if she blocked out her worries about the future and just stayed in the present? She was wasting all her time thinking of what ifs.

What if she could go to Nick and just give him...today?

Let the people who love you love you, she'd told Mackenzie.

That's what she wanted to do. She'd *survived* the cancer, but she was going to start *living* her life right now.

* * *

Ten minutes later, Darla found herself knocking on the door of Nick's little bungalow. It was late, after ten, the lights in her sister's house next door darkened except for the flicker of a TV from an upstairs bedroom. Her pulse quickened as she spotted a light on in Nick's living room, and she rapped louder.

Maybe she wasn't too late.

Maybe he wasn't too angry.

Maybe she hadn't blown it for good.

The door opened, and Boss bolted out to say hi, jumping around excitedly as if to say, *What took you so long to find me?*

Darla looked up from petting her hairy friend to find Nick's dad standing in the doorway.

"Darla, sweetheart," Angelo said, wearing a look of concern very much like his son's. "He's not here."

"Angelo!" she exclaimed. "What are you doing here?"

"I came over to watch the game, but when I got here, Nicky said he needed to blow off some steam. So I'm sitting with the Boss for a little while."

"Oh." *Where would Nick go to blow off steam? To go use power tools at one of his construction sites? To talk with his brother? For a run? The first two sounded a lot safer than jogging in the dark.*

"Aaaand it's a two-run homer for the Mets!" the TV announcer shouted in the background amid cheering from the crowd.

Angelo ran back into the house and stood in front of a large TV. "Will you take a look at that?" he exclaimed, waving his hands, caught up in the action.

Darla walked in, Boss squeezing through the door at her side. "Angelo," she said, tapping his arm, "where'd he go?"

"Oh. Sorry." He pulled his gaze away from the television. "He's working on the house. Told me he'd be back around midnight. I just settled in to watch on his nice TV."

She looked around, confused. "*This* house?" After all, this was the house he'd been working on, preparing for sale.

He seemed to struggle not to glance back at the TV. "No, the other one."

"There's another one?" Her first thought was, *Nick had another big project that he hadn't even mentioned?* That made her feel...well, she didn't even process it because Angelo's expression crumpled. He raked his hand through his thick hair, a gesture a lot like his son's. "Oh boy. I've done it now. I thought he'd told you by now."

She pulled out her phone, thinking of the fastest solution. "I'll just text him."

"He forgot his phone." Angelo pointed to a phone sitting near a lamp. "That's how I knew he must be upset."

Darla didn't really have a clue what was going on here, but she felt an urgency to get to Nick right now. "Nick and I are...trying to work things out. And...I panicked a little and messed things up, and I need to go see him right now. Can you please tell me where this house is that he's working on?"

Angelo heaved a heavy sigh. Then he made the sign of the cross. Which didn't exactly calm her down. "I'm going to tell you because I love you. I just pray that my son talks to me again."

Darla put her hands over her heart. "Angelo! You're scaring me."

"Rose and Bay," Angelo said. "I begged him not to buy it because that house is a financial risk and a disaster, but he said he had to."

"Rose and..." One look at Angelo's suffering face and Darla realized what was going on. Nick had bought her great-great-grandmother's house.

Impossible. Incredible. Undeniable.

For her.

She collapsed into the nearest chair, which happened to be a recliner that rocked a little as her butt hit the seat, startling her further. She rubbed her forehead, trying to understand. Rotated her ring, trying to focus on something for clarity. "Nick bought my great-great-grandmother's house—to flip?"

"It's because he's flipped for you, sweetheart. He said it was your house. It belonged to you and that you should have it."

"He…" Why would he do such a thing?

She stood up. "I—I have to talk to him."

"Annnd…that's a monster home run," the TV announcer yelled. "He knocked that ball out of the park!"

To Angelo's credit, he didn't even throw a side-glance at the TV. "You okay to drive? Want me to drive you?"

Darla shook her head and managed to flash him a little smile. He'd always treated her the way she imagined a father would treat his daughter. Even now, after all that had happened, he always found a way to make her feel loved. "I'll be okay."

"All right then, be careful. Drive slow. And tell Nicky I'm taking Boss Man home with me for tonight. So there's no need to rush back."

She raised her brows in surprise. "You're an optimist."

He shook his head. "Not really. I'm just an older guy who sees two kids who fell in love a little too young. And they've grown up."

"So you don't think I'm foolish?"

"The only thing that's foolish is not being honest when you've made mistakes. You ask for forgiveness when you do. And then you start again. I'm no expert, but I like to think that's a nice way for it to work."

"Even ten years later?"

"Even a hundred years later."

She shook her head. "You make it sound so simple."

He shrugged. "What can I say? I believe in happy endings. By the way, tell my son I hope he forgives me."

"Thank you, Angelo," Darla whispered as she stepped forward and kissed him on the cheek. "Now I know where he gets that romantic streak from," she called as she ran out the door.

She ran the six blocks to downtown without stopping, but she slowed to a walk along the main drag. Being high season, tourists were still standing outside Scoops with their last cones of the night and leaving Cam's Place in a few small chatting groups of twos and threes. The other shops had closed long ago as people in search of more nightlife headed to the bars along the beach.

Finally, Darla turned onto Rose Court. On the corner of Rose and Bay, the old house loomed, its wraparound porch looking more foreboding than friendly in the darkness. And speaking of darkness, the house itself was pitch-black, not a light on inside or out. She halted in the front, short of breath and courage.

The idea of walking up to the door seemed as frightening as a scene in a horror flick.

Actually, she'd written a scene exactly like this once. The heroine, who had a terrifying fear of the dark, learned that her sister had been kidnapped and taken to a run-down mansion and had to conquer her fear in order to rescue her from a basement crawl space.

Why did she write books that were so terrifying?

Although right now, facing Nick felt even more so.

In the end, she walked up to the front porch, cupped her hands over her mouth, and called his name in a voice that sounded more like a harsh whisper. She was, after all, in a neighborhood full of people, some of whom were probably heading to bed. "Nick," she called, a little louder.

A porch light flicked on at the house next door, a stately brick Queen Anne with riots of flowers growing in giant pots near the front door.

Uh-oh. That forced her to move along. But the prospect of walking up those peeling old stairs onto that beat-up front porch and knocking on the door paralyzed her. Just as the front door of the house next door opened, she ran around the far side of the house to the back, where, sure enough, a bare-bulbed work light shone through the panels of a pretty bay window. She heaved a sigh of relief as she caught sight of Nick inside, earbuds in and a pencil behind his ear, looking over some papers scattered on a wooden sawhorse.

He was working on Amelia's house. He'd bought it, and he hadn't told her. Which was wonderful and maddening in the same breath.

How could she be honest and vulnerable when he was keeping secrets himself?

Despite all her turmoil, that hot-construction-worker vibe hit her hard, her breath hitching at his utter handsomeness. His arms were spread over the surface of the wood, supporting his broad shoulders as he bent over his work. His wavy hair was obliviously mussed, probably from his habit of raking his fingers through it as he solved a problem. He was in his element, lost in whatever he was doing.

He grabbed the pencil and seemed to sketch something with it, the taut muscles of his arm moving as he drew.

She'd given him up willingly a decade ago. But fate had brought them together for these few brief weeks. She had to be honest with him, or she would lose him forever.

That thought gave her courage. Because she knew deep down in her heart that she could not bear that.

Now or never.

"Nick," she rasped louder, hoping the next-door neighbors weren't about to call the police for a prowler in the bushes.

No response. Knowing Nick, he was probably listening to a favorite like Queen or Metallica on high volume.

Was there a door? It was impossible to tell, as most of the house was shrouded in shadow. She searched around for a rock that wouldn't break a window, but there wasn't one in sight. So she did what she had to do—she pulled off her flip-flop and tossed it at the window.

Nick lifted his head, looking surprised. Before he could turn back to his work, she threw the other one.

He frowned, stepped to the window, and threw open the sash.

"It's me. Darla." She barely recognized her own voice, which came out oddly squeaky.

His eyes grew wide as at last he saw her. "Darla." He said her name on an exhale.

"I came to talk," she said. Then she held her breath.

All she knew was that being here felt like life or death.

He tipped his head to the right, pulled out his earbuds, and gestured. "Meet me at the door."

She exhaled a giant breath. He was going to let her in. And she hoped that meant into his heart too.

Just as soon as she murdered him for buying Amelia's house.

* * *

Nick walked outside onto a crumbling brick patio with weeds growing through the cracks. It was a dewy summer night, smelling like a mix of green growing things, the salty air, and the humid heat from the ocean, where waves lapped to shore just beyond the backyard. A perfect night, really. Now that Darla was here.

If he could only make her understand that he wanted to be with her through everything—good and bad. That she could trust him with her heart and her worst fears. That he wasn't going anywhere.

"How did you know where I was?" He stood with his feet apart, arms crossed, knowing he was busted, and he had a feeling just who ratted him out. He wasn't even surprised. He steeled himself against Darla's reaction.

But the truth was, he could never really steel himself against Darla. All he wanted was for her to let him in. But she had to be the one to figure that out. So he tried to prepare himself for anything, including the possibility that she just couldn't trust him—or herself—enough to get there.

She handed him his phone. "Your dad told me."

Of course, he did. Because the guy was more romantic than Romeo. Plus, he loved Darla.

"I might have sounded desperate." She settled her gaze

on him. "I came here to do my best to be open and not keep secrets. So I hope you'll do the same and tell me what in the world you're doing in Amelia's house."

"I didn't mean for you to find out this way." Darla was facing him, fire in her eyes, her hands fisted. But also looking like she might cry, so he couldn't read her at all.

It was her turn to cross her arms. "Okay, then, when were you going to tell me—this?" She waved her arms in the air, encompassing the house behind him.

This was not the way he'd imagined her finding out. He'd imagined a scenario much more romantic, that was for sure. He gestured toward a stone bench. "Sit down with me for a minute?"

To her credit, she gave a quick nod and sat.

A bad thought occurred to him. Maybe she wouldn't forgive him for going ahead with this and keeping her in the dark. Maybe his good deed would be an epic failure. What if he lost her again due to the very thing he thought would help win her back?

He couldn't let that happen. "A few months ago, this place went up for auction," he said as he took a seat beside her. "I went and looked at it and saw that it was a train wreck. I thought about having Carol call you and let you know it was on the market so that you could bid on it if you wanted."

"She did tell me about it," Darla said. "I thought no one bought it at auction."

Nick nodded. "The night before the auction, I couldn't sleep. I kept debating about it, knowing that I had the skills to fix it up and make it beautiful again. The more I thought about it, the more I imagined what it would look like restored to its old glory. Something to make your ancestor proud." He gave her a little smile. "Something to make *you* proud. And so I concocted a grand scheme. A surprise. I could buy it and fix it up. But then I thought that was all ridiculous, and you'd never forgive me if I did that without telling you. So I told Carol to let you know, and I didn't go to the auction."

"Carol called me," Darla said, "but it was right when I got offered the permanent position at Stanford. And she told me it was a complete redo from the bottom up. It didn't seem right that I should take on something like that if I was never coming back here to live. But it sort of haunted me that I didn't act on it."

"When no one met the minimum bid, I walked through it again and made an offer." Truthfully, he blamed it on the fireplace. Those tiles. He knew that they were handmade, and he'd never seen anything like them. And in his gut, he'd sensed that there was a story there—part of Amelia's story. One he felt compelled to learn more about.

Darla was pressing her lips together, and he couldn't tell if she was still mad or emotional in a different way.

Nick felt like he was in deep water with no life preserver in sight. The time had come to play his trump card and take the consequences no matter what they were.

Next door, the neighbor's porch light flicked on and off three times. Darla looked over her shoulder and dropped her voice. "I think we're keeping people up."

He ignored the flickering light and took up Darla's hands, looking straight into her eyes. "Darla," he said quietly, "I bought the house because you should have it. It belongs to your ancestor—therefore, it belongs to you.

I'm not even sure I was fully aware at the time why I did what I did, but I am now. I wanted to do something wonderful for you that was so amazing and so unexpected and so…big…that you'd understand that I would do anything to get you back." He took up both her hands. "I love you." He shook his head. He might be a fool, but it was too late not to be foolish. "I never stopped. I want another chance."

Chapter 17

DARLA COULD NOT stop ugly crying. Mostly from relief that she hadn't managed to push Nick away— although, looking back, she'd given it her best shot. Three thousand miles worth of shots.

Nick was smiling, and she couldn't help but smile right back through her tears. Not because he'd somehow done this crazy thing, buying her ancestor's house for her— she hadn't really even processed that yet—but because of what he'd just said.

The first time he'd said I love you, she'd been eighteen. He'd sounded just as sure, just as confident. And it had been just as unexpected—they'd been at a carnival and she'd been eating cotton candy, pink fluff sticking all over her fingers.

She remembered the disbelief. The awe. The realization that those words were both what she'd longed to hear and also what she feared the most, all at once.

The same exhilarating mix of emotions as always churned inside her. But this time she wouldn't be impulsive. She wouldn't get carried away, whisked into a relationship before either of them was mature enough to handle it. This time, she had alarm bells chiming and brake lights flashing.

"Nick, I—" She was still crying. And sucking up her snot, not very cool. "Listen," she said. "I have to say something."

He looked like a person who'd just spilled his whole soul on the kitchen countertop and had to watch while someone sifted through the pieces.

She looked him straight in the eye. "Having cancer changed me. I was in survival mode for so long. I'm still trying to wrap my head around the fact that I made it through, that I can take a breath and look around and enjoy life. I still feel like I'm in combat mode sometimes."

He was still holding her hands. "I can help you with that."

His earnest look made her heart pound, her knees weaken, and her skin flush with heat. She wanted to shrug off all her worries and throw her arms around him. But he was everything she wasn't—vibrant, hopeful, fully alive. And she was...so afraid. To make a mistake. To trust herself to leap. She struggled to find words. "I'm trying to get beyond the fear. But I'd be lying if I said I was all there yet. And I *know* I'm not ready to take someone else along on this journey."

Through her tears she could see that he was emotional too. She could hear it in his voice and feel it in the firm, secure grip of his hands over hers.

"We never talked about what that was like," he said,

"watching you go through all that you went through from afar. Not knowing whether or not you'd make it through."

She put a finger on his lips. "Don't. I did make it. That awful time is past. It's made me tough, but sometimes I forget that I don't have to be tough all the time." She had to say something else too. "I suppose I've always used toughness to mask my fear."

He touched her cheek. "I can help you with that too. And I'll take whatever you can give me. One day at a time."

"I just want to be normal. But I'm still afraid."

"Afraid to let me in, after all that has happened to us?"

She shook her head. "Afraid that this is all too good to be true."

Nick's eyes grew tender. "You don't have to do this alone anymore. Let me kiss you and love you and show you how happy I am to be with you. And how good we are together." He punctuated that with a kiss on the lips. Quick and brief and familiar. But also, somehow, brand-new.

The back porch light next door flicked on and off multiple times, more aggressively. "Hey, take it inside you two, will you?" a voice said.

"Sorry," Nick called over his shoulder.

Suddenly Darla laughed. More like snorted.

Nick laughed too. "I feel like I'm on your front porch again, and your mom's trying to get me to go home."

"And I just realized that we're standing in my great-great-grandmother's backyard, and it's a mess but it's also really beautiful." She looked around for the first time, not only at the overgrown grass and the crumbling brick of the patio but also at the deep inky blackness of the water, and tiny lights blinking from across the bay, and started to cry all over again. But this time, she was smiling too.

A mess but also beautiful. Wasn't that just how life was?

As he led her into the house, she knew in her heart that nothing felt so right. She felt like she was completing a puzzle with the one last long-lost piece that you suddenly find after searching for years. And then...snap. Everything finally made sense. As her eyes grew accustomed to the darkness, she made out a big, empty room that smelled like paint and drywall, lit by a lone light bulb. It might have been a kitchen, but just then Nick leaned over to kiss her, and she forgot to care where they were. She tilted her head up and closed her eyes in anticipation. But no kiss.

She opened them to find him staring at her intently, his eyes warm and full of feeling. "Darla, I want to make love to you. With you. And I'm okay taking this one day at a time. But I'm not in this just for sex. I want to make sure you know that."

A laugh escaped her. "We've been through too much trouble together for this to be just about sex." She reached up and caressed his cheek. It was rough, a little bristly, and a whole lot sexy. She traced the curve of his jaw, the angle so strong, so familiar. Her hands were shaking as if she were touching him for the first time.

His full lips turned up into a smile. "I don't know. Maybe not. The way we were together...all that trouble might just be worth it." He took her hand, brought it to his mouth, and kissed it.

His touch set blood rushing to her head, making the room spin around her. Inside, all her emotions were spinning too.

As their lips met, an explosion of heat spread all through her, all at once. She kissed him tenderly, thoroughly, and with passion until she lost her breath and her balance.

"How...how do you do that?" she asked, drawing back a little.

"Do what?" He looked puzzled.

"Kiss me like no one else can."

"Well, I *am* a really good kisser," he said in true Nick fashion. "But the real reason is, I know you." He looked deeply into her eyes. "I know that sometimes you like soft, gentle kisses. I still remember just how you fit in my arms. I know that you really like it when I drop kisses on your neck. But most of all, I know you on the inside."

His words terrified her and made her feel things deep down to her soul. "I'm sorry I let you go," she said as she moved closer, wrapping her arms around his lean waist. Tears leaked onto his shirt. "I'm sorry we lost so much time."

He kissed her head and smoothed her hair back from her face. "Maybe it took that time to understand what we lost. And maybe now we can finally look forward, not back." Mischief twinkled in his eyes. "Do you trust me?"

"Yes?" she said.

"I wish that didn't have a question mark attached, but I'll take what I can get." He reached behind her to the wall and flipped a switch. The solitary light bulb darkened, making the room momentarily go pitch-black.

Then he flipped on his phone flashlight and handed it to her. Which was a little odd, but she went with it. As soon as she took it, he scooped her up and walked with her out of the kitchen.

"I take that back," she said. "I trust you as long as you don't trip."

"So little faith," he said. "Shine that straight ahead, sweetheart."

That melted her. "This is starting to feel like a scene from one of my books."

"A scary one?" he asked, chuckling. "Don't answer that. Honey, if I have my way, this scene will be unlike any you've ever written before."

Good thing he didn't see her roll her eyes as he led her from the kitchen and through a short hall, until she made out the rectangular shape of a large room with a giant fireplace. Large double-hung windows lined one side. And that was about all she could see in the dark. "How do I know you're not taking me somewhere scary?" she asked, thinking of her heroine stuck in the basement again. Not exactly a romantic image.

He stopped in front of a fireplace. "You really should try writing a romance. That might get you on the same page as me."

He had no idea how close that was to the truth. As he set her down, she made out a large rectangular object on the floor. She bent over and patted it. "An air mattress?"

He lifted it and moved it over a few feet, more in the center of the room. "Sometimes I work late at night and crash here. It's really pretty comfy."

"Looks good to me." She unbuttoned her shirt and quickly tossed it aside. "I just hope my ancestor's not watching. I haven't even seen her house and look what we're doing here."

He pulled his T-shirt off and stood in front of her.

"You're a lot older," she said, shaking her head. "Practically geriatric." Geez, his six-pack had a six-pack. And he was easily the most gorgeous man she'd ever seen. Her mouth had gone dry, blood was whooshing in her ears, and her entire body was trembling in anticipation. "You really should work out more."

"What?" He opened his arms. "I'm in the best shape of my life."

She let out a sound. It was sort of a chuckle.

Without warning, he scooped her up. "Can we please stop talking now?"

Even in the dark, she could make out the tenderness in his eyes. She saw past the jokes, past the efforts to make her feel at ease. She just saw...him, the Nick she fell in love with so long ago. The kind, gentle man who would do anything for her—including buy an old, run-down house that would need years of labor and effort to make it shine. And the man who wanted her now just as he'd wanted her all those years ago.

"Dar, I never stopped wanting you," he said before he kissed her.

"I want you too," she managed as their kisses quickly turned greedy, frantic, and frenzied. They somehow made it to the air mattress, where he kissed her neck and tugged her bra strap from her shoulder.

As his hand hovered over her chest, he searched her eyes. Asking permission.

She sucked in a breath and gave a slight nod. Her heartbeat raced, half from pleasure and half from fear of everything this moment represented. Not the cancer, but the intimacy of sharing her experience with him.

Nick gently traced the crooked line of the scar. She felt every touch of his fingertips as he gently traced along her collarbone.

Then he kissed it. Kissed her scar. Not once but again. And yet again. Softly, with reverence.

The port had been her lifeline. It had saved her by conveying the chemicals that had killed her cancer cells. He was telling her, without words, that the scar was important. That without it, she would not be here.

Tears rolled down her cheeks, and he kissed those too. Tipping her chin with his finger, he made her look at him. "You're so beautiful," he said in a low, sweet voice. "I love every part of you that fought to stay alive because it worked. You're here. And we get a second chance."

He sought her lips and kissed her tenderly. When she reached up to touch his face, she found that he was crying too. And that was the moment.

The moment Darla knew she'd love him forever, although she said no words and made no promises.

She could never love another like this, with all her heart and body and soul.

She kissed him desperately, clinging to every bit of happiness that came her way.

Placing a hand on each cheek, she felt Nick's stubble, prickly-soft beneath her fingers. "Now we start new."

"Now we start new," he agreed as he rolled her over and kissed her on the lips. And she felt his smile against her face.

* * *

Hours later, Nick cracked open one eye and was surprised to find he was lying on a very hard floor but didn't remember drinking the night before. It was morning, as evidenced by the sun shining in slanted beams across the scarred wooden boards, birdsong loud outside the tall paned windows.

As he came more fully awake, he chuckled as memories of last night flooded his mind, sweet and powerful. Yeah, much better than a night at the bars.

Yes, his back was a little sore, but the rest of him felt light, buoyant. Elated beyond belief. *Happy.*

Darla. *His.* All night. And hopefully…forever.

That's how he felt, even as he sensed—no, he *knew*—that she wasn't ready to hear that declaration.

He patted the space beside him then turned to find the mattress empty—of Darla and of most of its air, hence the fact that he'd been sleeping literally flat on the floor.

He hadn't remembered to set an alarm or charge his phone. But he did remember that he had a financial meeting with his dad at ten, and judging by the bright light, he'd guess that it was probably somewhere around eight.

He looked around to find Darla sitting against a nearby wall. She was dressed, her hair up in one of those complicated buns only women can magically create, holding her phone.

"Were you just staring at me?" he asked. His voice sounded like he'd been up all night.

Which was pretty close to true.

"Yes." Her full lips curved up in a smile.

He tried to run a hand through his hair, but it was obvious he had I-stayed-up-all-night-having-sex hair.

So did she, but on her it looked...gorgeous.

"Have you been watching me sleep?" he asked.

"Also a yes."

"And what did you learn?"

"That you're really hot." She smiled at her own joke. "Actually, I already knew that. What I learned is, you still do that thing where you lie on your stomach and tuck your arms under your pillow. Cute."

Nick patted the remains of the air mattress. "I'd invite you back into my bed, but it seems to have disappeared."

"That's so sexy." She gestured with her hand. "I bet you say that to all the girls."

He laughed out loud. "Come over to my house, and I'll make you breakfast."

"I'd love to, but I'm meeting the girls at eleven to work on Hadley's dress problems."

"That sounds like fun." His tone indicated a question because he knew Darla hated deliberating over fashion choices almost as much as she hated missing a deadline.

"Hadley takes years to make clothing choices, and so I'm a little scared." She chuckled. "What's on your agenda this morning?"

He scrubbed his face and kept the sheet on his privates, which happened to already be asking for round four. "I'm meeting my dad for a business meeting." Outside the windows, the leaves of a giant maple tree swayed in the breeze, sunlight filtering through its branches. Birds continued chirping out their love songs. Only in an old neighborhood. The best kind.

"How long have you been up?" he asked, looking around for his phone.

She crawled over and knelt next to him. "Long enough to notice you still have that little scar on your chin from when you were fifteen, when you were showing off in the pool and knocked it against the diving board."

He touched his chin and smiled. "When I grow a beard, no hair grows there. How many of my other flaws did you discover?"

"I already know all your other habits. Like, you still like to spoon in the middle of the night. *So* annoying," she said with a twinkle in her eye.

He gave her an *excuse-me* look. "Um, I believe that was *you* spooning *me*."

"Oh, I forgot. Also waking me out of a sound sleep to...do stuff again."

"That was you too. The third time, anyway."

Her smile was bright and in that moment, she looked so beautiful that his heart squeezed.

"So...where does that leave us now?" she asked.

He intertwined his fingers with hers. She looked happy and jokey, but underneath he could sense that she was a little unsettled.

Frankly, he was too. Because everything about last night had been even better than all the countless times he'd imagined their reunion. "Just answer one question," he said, stroking the inside of her palm. "How are you feeling right now?"

She sucked in a breath. Squeezed her eyes shut tight. "I-I'm afraid that if I say how I feel, it will all go away."

He let out a breath he didn't realize he was holding. Because she'd just unwittingly told him exactly what he needed to know. And he was going to make it his mission to keep her feeling that way. He opened his mouth to say he wasn't going anywhere ever again. "Darla, I want you to know that I—"

She shook her head and put a finger to his lips. "Hey, handsome. No declarations, remember? Or you'll scare me away."

"Okay, I won't say anything. For now. But only because it's what you need." He tapped his chest twice and then extended his hand toward her in that old familiar way.

He'd done it without thinking, without expecting much reaction. Her eyes suddenly misted up as she took his hand and placed it against her cheek.

"Hey," he said, tucking a strand of hair behind her ear, "that wasn't supposed to make you sad."

"I'm not sad. You just surprised me," she whispered, her voice catching a little. "I'm just remembering all the times you've done that."

He shrugged, wanting to make light of it for her sake. Call it habit, call it an expression of his feelings, but the gesture that just the two of them shared had been automatic. "I did it without thinking," he said truthfully.

Casting him a tender glance, she kissed him quickly on the lips before getting up and walking over to the fireplace, which he was glad he'd remembered to drape.

"Why is the fireplace covered?" she asked, stepping back to view the paneled wood, which reached up to the ceiling. She was changing the subject, taking some space. But that was okay.

"I'm regrouting it." That was true. Showing her the house for the first time hadn't gone the way he'd envisioned, so he at least wanted to reveal this one his own way.

"That's the original woodwork," he said, getting up, throwing his jeans on, and joining her. "The house has got a lot of features that even I'm impressed with. Some of them even survived a bad '70s kitchen remodel."

He walked her around, showing all the details he'd kept to himself all these months, including a little domed sunroom filled with windows, lots of quirky nooks and crannies, and a garden filled with dozens of old-fashioned orange lilies.

"I wish Amelia would've left behind notebooks or diaries," Darla said, absently touching her ring as they stood at a window and viewed the bay in the distance. "She was such a strong person. I wonder how she accomplished everything she did." She looked around the high-ceilinged room. "Even by today's standards, a single woman with nothing, doing all this—"

"Pretty incredible." He wrapped his arms around her from behind and nuzzled her neck. "It runs in the family."

"I can barely hold my life together sometimes," she protested, even as she arched her neck so he could reach it better. "But she reminds me to be braver. Because I've got to have at least some of that determination coursing through my own veins, right?"

He placed his hand on her arm, gently turning her toward him. "You are the bravest person I know." She immediately shook her head. "Not just because of surviving cancer or how you built your career—but how you just keep forging onward. Always looking to be better. You've been a great example to me."

She put up her hands in protest. "Nick, please, no compliments—"

She hated being praised, but he wanted her to know something. "Listen—I—I mean it. After we broke up, I was forced to think a lot about what I wanted in life. I started to become more goal directed. Like you."

"You didn't need me to be an example," she said in a firm tone.

It was time to tell her what she'd done for him. "Yeah, I think I did. You know how I felt about my job—stifled."

Searching his eyes, she said, "So how did you get over that feeling? Clearly, you did, because you're about to take over the company."

Someday, he hoped. "It involved getting some therapy. Figuring out how to play to my strengths. Truth is, I love to manage. And multitask. And I love to be in charge. And build things. So getting my MBA was a way to do things *my* way—differently from my dad. And more efficiently, because he's all about the craft. He hates the numbers part."

"He's proud of you." She sounded so sure.

He shrugged. "Maybe. I'm not sure he's ever going to trust me enough to retire."

Darla frowned. "Why do you assume that? Maybe he's not retiring for another reason."

"What would that be? He talks like he wants to, but he won't do anything about it." Because he didn't trust Nick. But Nick didn't say that.

"I don't know," Darla said, "every time I talk to him, he can't stop telling me what a great job you're doing." She assessed Nick carefully, like she was debating whether or not to say more. "Maybe you should have a chat with him."

"Maybe I will. But enough about me." He really didn't want to talk about himself. "I just want you to use some of that ancestral bravery to take a chance again. On me." He took her hand and looked in her eyes to let her know he was dead serious. "That's all I'm asking. A chance."

"Weeelll...hmm." She tapped her fingers against her lips. "I'm almost sure, but is there any way you might convince me?"

"I have a few ways," he said. He gestured to his deflated bed.

She guided him over to the flat mattress and sat down, patting the floor beside her. "I can probably make you forget all about this hard floor."

He threw his head back and laughed. In that moment, for the first time in a very long time, Nick was truly and genuinely happy.

After all, he was with the one person who could make him that way.

He didn't know what he'd ever done to deserve a new beginning, but he was going to make certain not to screw it up this time.

As Darla drew Nick down to the mattress with her, he had to admit that she made good on her word.

Chapter 18

LATER THAT MORNING, Darla sat in a lounge chair on her deck, stretching out her legs and tilting up her face to the sun as she waited for her friends.

She tried to process what had just happened between her and Nick. There wasn't a word she could match to the feeling. But the closest she could come was the way she felt on a Christmas morning long ago when she was eight.

Filled with sorrow after her dad left, she'd dreamed of flying free on a sparkly blue bike she'd seen in the hardware store window. It was the color of the twilight sky with shiny chrome handlebars, purple and pink streamers, and blinged out with a bell. She used to go out of her way after school each day to stare at it. It seemed that she turned every sad emotion, every feeling of being abandoned by their dad, into dreaming of that bike. As if getting it and flying away on it would take her to a better place.

Having outgrown the rusted-out starter bike that was a hand-me-down from Rachel, Hadley always kindly let her ride her pretty pink one. But one day, Darla confessed her heart's desire to her sister, who told her every night as she let her into her own bed to snuggle, to close her eyes and dream of riding it as she fell asleep. Rachel said that if she could imagine her dreams, they would come true.

Looking back, Darla knew her sister told her those things to get her to stop thinking about the divorce. So she would stop having nightmares, stop being frightened. But the funny thing was...it had worked.

Rachel had made that dream come true for her. Even to this day, Darla wasn't sure how Rachel convinced their shell-shocked mom, now single and raising two girls on a shoestring budget, to buy that bike. But on Christmas morning, there it was, under the tree.

That bike became her freedom, her escape. And Darla got right on it and rode until winter finally set in and made it impossible. She brought it into her bedroom for safekeeping and then took it out into the biting March winds as soon as the snow melted. When she hopped on that bike, she was unstoppable.

That was exactly how she felt now. Awake. Like her life had finally started again. Like she could finally leave the past far behind and ride the wind into the future.

She tried to tell herself that getting back together with Nick was a whim that would never last. That somehow, through all the wanting, the fantasy had taken on a life of its own, soon to be deflated by reality. She felt certain that her mom, who had predicted the disaster the first time around, would predict it yet again.

Yet Darla felt completely alive. She'd never felt such joy in the simple pleasure of feeling the sun's warmth on her face. Or watching families trudge through the sand with canvas bags stuffed with towels, umbrellas, and coolers for a glorious day on the beach. Or in the warm, sweet taste of the cappuccino she'd treated herself to on the way home from Nick's.

She must have drifted off because she was roused from sleep when someone tapped the bottom of her foot. "Hey, wake up." Kit stood there in her bathing suit, a towel tucked under her arm. "Famous authors who fall asleep with their mouths open get their photos taken. Oh. And posted on social media."

"I'm in my own backyard," she said, struggling to sit up. "Give me a break."

She heard a camera click. Kit stood there with a self-satisfied grin.

"Did you get the drool running down her mouth?" Hadley asked, looking over Kit's shoulder. She was shuffling a brown-handled paper bag in one hand and a zippered dress bag in the other.

"I was only asleep for a second," Darla said defensively. But she ran the back of her hand along her mouth to check for drool just the same.

"I'm just teasing about the drool," Hadley said. "But you *did* have the best smile on your face."

Kit slid down her sunglasses to examine Darla's face herself. "Wait a minute. You're *still* smiling." She took another photo.

"Please stop that," Darla held out her arm. "Maybe I'm just having a really good day."

"Maybe you just had a really good *night*," Kit said smugly.

Darla put on what she hoped was an innocent expression. "What makes you think that?"

"Because apparently Nick had the same starstruck look on his face at their work meeting this morning," Hadley said.

"And he kissed and told?" Darla asked, suddenly feeling horrified.

"No," Hadley said, "but Tony guessed what happened, and Nick didn't deny it. I mean, come on, we saw you both last night. The tension between you two was thicker than my gran's honey."

"Alex told me Nick couldn't stop smiling the whole meeting," Kit said, suddenly hugging her. "Oh, honey. We're so happy for you."

Darla stood up. She really couldn't stop smiling either. "He's really wonderful."

Hadley clutched her chest. "Oh, I knew you guys would work it out!"

"Well, we've started to. But I've told him I'm not ready for serious." She couldn't even dare to think about permanent. "Plus...I've still got a job in California."

"Nick was okay with that?" Hadley sounded a little surprised.

Darla thought about what to say. "I need to work through some things, and he's giving me space. I—I have a lot of mental baggage from the cancer."

"You deserve happiness," Hadley said. "You know that, right?"

"Yes, keep working on it." Kit gave a thumbs-up and grinned. "All doable."

Darla, still smiling, said, "He did something pretty amazing. He bought my great-great-grandmother's house."

"Full disclosure," Hadley said, raising her hands, "Tony's known about it for quite some time."

"Full disclosure," Kit said, "I heard about it from Alex. But Nick really hasn't told anyone else."

Darla glanced from one friend to the other. "You two knew all along?"

"Well, we knew after the fact," Hadley said. "Nick told Tony that he felt that the house was yours. You should be the one to decide how it's used from now on."

"We knew how badly Nick wanted to surprise you," Kit said.

Darla shook her head incredulously. "He was very low-key about it. He said the house would definitely sell, so I could take my time and think about what I'd want to do with it. Of course, I'm shocked."

"It was a sweet gesture," Kit said.

"My head is spinning." Darla's pulse was racing too, and she felt happier than she had in so long. "But with all good things."

"Speaking of good things," Kit said, approaching the table, "I'm starving. What's in that bag?"

Hadley set the bag down on the patio table. CAM'S PLACE was written in green script on the side. "I'm not sure. Tony handed it to me, gave me a kiss, and said, 'Enjoy. See you later.'"

Kit peeked into the bag. "Ooh, I see garlic bread." She lifted her head and sniffed. "And I smell something amazing, like cheese and pasta sauce." She dug into the bag, shooing Hadley away. "We'll set lunch out while you try on the dress."

"Where shall I change?" Hadley asked Darla.

"My bedroom," Darla said. "And guess what? The bathroom's all done. Go take a look."

"Be back in a sec." Hadley took the dress into the house.

Darla's phone went off with a text. It was Mackenzie. Hey, Darla, you know how you said we could talk about your book? Well, I sort of had an idea. How about a little book club? Just a few of my friends.

Mackenzie sounded good. Great, in fact. And she was talking about friends. So if she was up for it, Darla was too. That sounds like fun, she typed back. Just text me some dates.

Feeling relieved that Mackenzie seemed to be doing better, Darla peeked into the bag. "Maybe if we have the food ready to go when Hadley comes out, this won't take an hour."

Kit high-fived her. "Have you tried on your dress?"

"Once, a month ago. It fits." Darla searched her head to think of something else positive to say but came up short.

"But?"

"Well, it's orange and...frothy," she said. "I look like orange Jell-O mixed with whipped cream."

"I think the formal name for the color is apricot. And what exactly do you mean by frothy?"

"You know." She waved her arms in a way that resembled a hula dance. "All that swirly material over the skirt."

"My dress is a little tight in the waist," Kit said. "And it's too late to get it altered. I'm going to be sucking in the whole evening."

"You're the thinnest of all of us."

"I used to be," Kit said. "Age is catching up."

Darla frowned. She wanted to say *pregnancy* was catching up, but she was afraid to open that up for discussion right before lunch. "It'll be okay," Darla said. "Hadley really loved the dresses, and the price point was right so...Jell-O it is."

"All good," Kit agreed. "What's life if you don't get to wear at least one poofy bridesmaid dress to your best friend's wedding, right?"

Darla pulled a bottle of red wine out of the bag followed by warm breadsticks wrapped in foil. "Uh-oh," she said.

"What is it?" Kit looked over at her.

"I'm sensing that this is going to be a delicious, carb-packed experience that will require a long nap afterward." She peeked into a container. "Aha! Lasagna. I was right."

"I could use a nap," Kit said a little too eagerly. Then yawned to prove it.

Darla set down the food. "You do look a little tired."

Kit shrugged. "Like you, there's a lot going on right now."

Just then, Hadley walked out of the house wearing a white satin sheath dress. She'd piled all her hair on top of her head and marched out barefoot, holding up the skirt so it didn't drag on the deck.

Kit grabbed Darla's arm. Darla heard her suck in a breath.

"Oh, Hadley," Darla said, grabbing Kit's arm right back.

"Honey, you're stunning," Kit said.

"Absolutely beautiful," Darla agreed.

Hadley was beaming. "I really liked the other dress," she said. "But this one...this just fits..."

"Like a glove," Kit said.

"Perfectly," Darla agreed.

"It feels like me," Hadley agreed, twirling a little.

She looked so happy and content. "You look radiant." Darla just had to say that, even if it was cheesy.

Kit shrugged and said resolutely, "When you know, you know."

Was that really true, Darla wondered? "But what about the other dress?" Darla, always practical, had to ask.

"So that's the weird part of the story," Hadley explained. "Someone saw my dress hanging on the rack about to be pressed and offered full price for it. That's when Meg Halloran called me from the bridal shop. She said this one seemed to be a lot like how I'd first described the dress I wanted." She pointed to the trim on the bodice. "See the tiny little pearls? I can't explain it, but this is the one."

Darla felt tears pricking behind her lids. "I don't know why I'm so sentimental," she said as she wiped her eyes. Maybe it was that all her senses seemed to be magnified today. Everything seemed brighter, more emotional, more *everything.* "I'm so happy for you. But maybe I'm a little sad too because...well, it just feels like everything is changing. I mean, in a few days, you'll be married. And Kit, you and Alex will be headed to the altar next." She paused, worried that the food was getting cold but anxious to get something off her chest. "I've been thinking about this a lot lately," she said, "with regard to men. Do you think it's true? That you just...know."

"Yes," they both said at the same time.

"You're both hopeless romantics," Darla muttered.

"So are you," Kit said. "You just don't admit it easily."

"What I'm really worried about is, why haven't I been able to shake Nick out of my system? Is it real? How do I know?"

"Nothing in life is certain," Kit said. She was speaking about the death of her husband, of course. "My grandma says that the funny thing about life is that it requires you to make all kinds of important decisions based only on what you know at the time."

"For me it wasn't about knowing," Hadley put a hand over her chest. "It was about *feeling*. I knew I could trust Tony with my heart."

Darla knew she trusted Nick. But something else was worrying her. "My mom won't take this well. She's never been shy about letting both Nick and me know that she's never thought he was good enough for me. But I can handle my mom. I wondered...I wondered what you two think about this? Because your opinions really matter to me."

"We've always promised each other that if we think one of us is dating someone we dislike, we'd tell each other," Kit said.

"My gran always said that if your friends hate your boyfriend, you should dump him immediately," Hadley said.

"We love Nick," Kit said, and Hadley confirmed that with a nod.

"Your mom might take it better than you think," Hadley said. "Because you'll be staying. I mean, you *will* be staying, won't you?"

"I—I don't know," Darla said. With everything going on, it had been easy to avoid thinking about leaving. "Part of me thinks being with Nick is absolutely right and the other part thinks that this is all just a fantasy." She paused. "The opportunity in California is amazing, and I would never give it up for a guy, but honestly, it was appealing because it was a way to avoid my feelings about Nick. So right now, I guess you could say everything is in a jumble."

"You're afraid to trust your feelings, I get that," Hadley said. "He's a good guy, Darla. You just have to figure out if he's the *best* guy for you."

Darla didn't say this out loud, but, miraculously, for the first time since she'd gotten sick, she felt like a normal, regular woman who'd found a once-in-a-lifetime chance. Not Darla-the-cancer-survivor wondering if she was ever going to get the opportunity to have a normal life.

Kit smiled. "It's simple. You're going to just be with him and decide if you can't live without him. And if the answer is that you can't, you two are going to figure out a way to make it work." She rose suddenly. "I've got to pee so bad. Be back in a sec." Then she ran to the house.

Hadley exchanged glances with Darla, but it was Darla who called after Kit as she was bolting. "Are you pregnant?"

Kit stopped briefly with her hand on the door. "Oh. I— I really, really want to be."

"So are you?" Hadley pressed.

"Well, I missed a period and my boobs hurt and I can only eat bread and water without puking."

"I think that's a yes." Hadley's mouth turned up in a barely suppressed grin.

Darla lifted a brow. "And the reason you haven't taken a test is..."

"I took one two weeks ago," Kit said, doing a little I've-got-to-go-now dance, "and it was negative. And to be honest, between work, my finals, and the wedding, I've been too busy to pick up another one. And to be more honest, I suppose I'm a little terrified. Like, if I'm this busy, how am I going to handle taking care of another little person?"

Darla narrowed her gaze. "You're going to handle it like you handle everything else. And the wild mayhem will be...wonderful."

"It's so funny," Kit said. "Ollie keeps bugging us all the time for a sibling. It's like he senses something's going on too."

"But you've got to take the test!" Hadley added. "Especially before we go out this weekend for our little bachelorette party."

"Okay, fine. I just don't—I don't want to be disappointed again. My exam is tonight, and then I'll deal with it, I promise."

"Are you taking prenatal vitamins?" Darla called as Kit disappeared into the house.

"On it," came her voice from far away.

"Okay, good," Hadley said to Darla, hiding the wine under the table. "Well, one thing is for certain. Looks like there are big changes coming for all of us."

Chapter 19

AT 9:30 A.M., Nick entered the Cammareri business office near the heart of downtown with two coffees in hand. He found his dad in the back office, sitting behind a giant oak desk, looking at something on the computer.

If he wasn't mistaken, it was a boat.

As soon as his dad became aware of Nick's presence, he clicked out of the website, revealing an Excel spreadsheet.

"Hey, Dad," Nick said, setting a large coffee down on the desk and taking a seat in a nearby chair. "What's up?"

"Just going over some numbers." He took the lid off the coffee and blew on it. "Smells like heaven. Thanks." He looked up from the cup. "You angry with me?"

Nick frowned. "Angry about what?" After last night, angry was the last adjective in the world he'd use to describe himself.

His dad's forehead crinkled up in worry. "Ah, you know. I spilled the beans about that house."

"It worked out," Nick said, grinning. "Darla had to find out anyway."

"What did she think about it?" He waved a hand dismissively. "Ah, never mind. I can see it all on your face. You're lovestruck."

"I'm not lovestruck." He took a sip of coffee to hide his smile. "I'd say she was pretty shocked." And maybe upset, but lastly, happy. And unbeknownst to Darla, he had more surprises to come.

His dad shook his head. "That's quite a thing you did, buying that house for her."

Nick shrugged. He knew it had been crazy, but it was worth it. Getting serious, he said, "I really care about her." He let that settle. "What do you think about that?"

Nick knew what he was doing. He was asking for his father's blessing. He felt that his dad still regarded him as immature, and it mattered that his dad knew he wasn't. A lot.

"I was heartbroken when you two divorced," his dad said. "Even though I always thought you married too young. But both of you have figured out who you are separately, so I think it's terrific. I've always loved Darla."

Me too, he wanted to say out loud, but everything was too brand-new. He let out a breath. "Thanks. That means a lot." If only he had the courage to ask his dad to trust him enough to retire and go buy that boat he wanted so badly.

"You make good decisions without needing my approval," his dad eyed him carefully.

Nick felt a stomach flip of anxiety. Here was an opening to talk, something that Darla had encouraged him to do. *Now or never.*

"The company's thriving," Nick said. "We're having to say no to projects because our schedule is so full. And I'm interviewing for a new accountant to fill Betty's spot when she retires." Maybe if he catalogued his accomplishments, his dad would understand what he was trying to say.

"All good things, Nicky," his dad said. "But don't forget the human touch. Make sure that when people call about a project or a problem, they talk to a person, not a machine. I've spent my life in this town. I think I know every single family."

That was quite a legacy. "You've taught us about getting along with people. I won't forget it."

His dad smiled and looked a little far away, like he was remembering. "I've been working in this company since I was fourteen, when I went to work with my dad. I still believe treating people with respect and getting involved in the community are the best ways to keep a business open. People trust what the Cammareri name stands for."

Yes, he got it. He'd done everything in his power to keep their sterling reputation alive and well. If only his dad would see that.

Silence fell. "So are you thinking of buying a boat?" Nick asked.

"Just window shopping." His dad shut down that discussion pretty quickly.

"You know, Dad," he pushed, "it's okay to slow down a little. I've got things covered."

Okay, he said something, but he'd lost the courage to tell his dad he was sorry for those difficult years when he was so unhappy. When he felt stuck. When all his options seemed to constrict down to one thing: family obligation.

"You know we won the bid on that big hotel project," he continued. "That's going to keep us busy for most of next year. And we've got another bed-and-breakfast remodel for fall. Oh, and I got an A in my business strategy class." He was on top of everything. Could his dad hear the translation, the real meaning behind his words? *I'm competent. Trust me. I'm sorry.*

"That's terrific" was his dad's reply.

This conversation wasn't getting them anywhere, Nick thought with frustration. So he rallied all his courage. "Is it because you don't trust me?" he blurted.

His dad swiveled his chair around to Nick and leaned forward. "I've been working since I was fourteen. I don't know how to shut it off." His dad reached over and patted Nick on the cheek, a move that gutted him. "This isn't about you. You're a good boy. And you're doing a fine job. But I need to decide for myself the right time to go. Okay?"

Nick exhaled. *This isn't about you.* "You know, Pop, when I was younger—"

His dad pinned him with his bright blue gaze. "When you were younger, you had some things to sort out, as we all do. And let me tell you something, life isn't something that you figure out once and you're done. Like it or not, we have to keep on figuring things out."

"'Listen to what your heart tells you. It's hardly ever wrong.' Isn't that what you always used to tell us when we were kids?"

"Now I know I'm getting old if my kids are quoting me back to myself." He stood up and hugged Nick. Relief washed through him like a rushing river, stripping him of years of mental muck. "You're too hard on yourself, you know that? Good thing you're back with Darla. She can straighten that out for you."

* * *

"Thanks for helping me carry everything," Darla said to Nick that Saturday afternoon as she lifted out the first of a bunch of boxes from the bed of Nick's truck in the out-patient oncology center parking lot. It was a week before the big day, and it felt really good to take a break from writing and help out with wedding stuff.

Mac's idea for a book club with a "few" friends had ballooned into using the pavilion between the hospital and the cancer center for a group that now included some cancer patient friends, a few college friends, and some book-loving staff.

So if Darla had felt nervous about meeting with Mackenzie, the fact that there were other teens battling cancer multiplied the nerves times ten.

"Eh, piece of cake," Nick said, tossing her a confident grin that melted her clear through to her toes.

"You know what? Mac sounded so great on the phone and so excited about this that I'm just going to roll with it." She paused, her stomach pitching. "I think."

He held out his arms. "Why don't you get things started and let me carry these in?"

She'd brought some older books to give away, book-marks, and some gift cards she'd bought from local merchants to give out for fun. But her publisher had also sent brand-new copies of her latest book for everyone.

She smiled and handed over the box. "Okay, Mr. Muscle. Thank you."

He stood there for a minute, looking strangely surprised. She had to admit he looked pretty cute in his Mets T-shirt with his ball cap turned backward. She reached up on impulse and kissed him, but he was still looking a little dazed.

"What? What is it?" she asked.

He shook his head in disbelief. "You just said *thank you*."

"Yes...so?"

"Without adding *I can carry my own books*. Just *thank you*. I like it."

She sent him a saucy look. "Well, you make it easy for me to just say thank you. And you've been there for me in every single way. And...I like that too."

"Ditto."

"What have I done for you?" she couldn't help asking. "I mean, next to someone buying a house, I feel like I'm paling in comparison."

He smiled, which could have just been polite, but she noticed that it reached his eyes too. "First of all, you don't need to do anything special. Just wanting to be with me is enough."

She rolled her eyes, even though now he looked awfully serious. And her heart rate kicked up.

"You always inspire me, don't you know that? Look at what you're doing today. You're here to talk about books, but you're really doing so much more."

She started to protest, but he shook his head. "Because of you," Nick said, "I started to talk with my dad about handing over the company and about retiring. And you should know that he told me he was thrilled we were together. He said he loved you."

"I love him too," Darla said without hesitation. Then she smiled. There was more she might have said, but he seemed to understand that now wasn't the time.

"So get in there and have fun," he said as they approached the sliding double doors of the cancer center. "And show these patients they can get through this."

"I need to warn you," she said. "There are going to be young women here. You might be an object of interest."

He laughed out loud. "Hey, I'm just the book delivery guy."

Her pace slowed. And worries came to her.

Nick stopped walking. "You've done this a million times. What's wrong?"

He could still read her better than anyone. "It's not about the books. It's about me surviving and doing well, while some of these women are fighting for their lives."

He considered that. "I'd tell you to stop worrying, but I don't think that's going to happen. You don't have to do some big thing. You just have to talk about the scary people in your books and have fun. Okay?"

"Okay." She smiled. "I knew there was a reason I asked you to come."

Darla walked through the infusion center and out onto the tree-lined patio, which was set up with round tables covered with bright yellow cloths. The staff had set out fruit and cheese and cookies and iced tea. Her heart nearly stopped when she saw that it was literally filled with people.

And all of them were wearing bright yellow headscarves.

Some of the women were obviously chemo patients. But there were others too, some Mac's age, some infusion center nurses or inpatient staff, and they wore the scarves in all kinds of ways—as a headscarf, as a bandana, as a warrior headband. Suddenly Darla noticed that every single scarf had her latest book cover printed on it.

Oh wow. It seemed that every time she tried to do something helpful, she unexpectedly got back a thousand times more in return. Mac came running down the aisle—yes, running—waving one hand at her. She looked thin and a little pale but she was wearing a huge smile. And she was accompanied by a red-haired young woman around her age. "Hi," Mac said, tugging on her own scarf.

"Hi," Darla said, breaking into a smile herself.

"I hope you don't mind, I told everyone to wear them." She handed Darla one. The cover of *No Time to Die* unfurled in front of her eyes, with a concerned-looking heroine nervously glancing behind her shoulder in a dark alley.

"I love it." Darla hugged her and then wrapped one around her own head. Which would make her curly hair a disaster, but oh well. She wasn't going to miss this for the world.

"This is my roommate, Flora," Mac said.

Flora was chatty, and she and Mac seemed to share in the excitement, so it became really hard to stay nervous. Nick, who'd gone across the room to talk with Roberta León, the longtime head nurse for the oncology unit, looked up and winked. Darla found herself not only relaxing but really enjoying herself.

"I did what you said," Mac said privately. "I invited my

college friends, even though I was afraid they'd feel sorry for me. And my mom helped me order these, aren't they fun?" She touched her scarf. "When I told my friends from the infusion center, they wanted to come too."

"You're amazing," Darla said, giving Mac a hug.

Mac shrugged. "Well, lots of us love reading books. Plus, everyone can't wait to meet you."

Nick walked over with Roberta. "Hey," he said, giving Mac a quick side hug, then addressing Darla. "I'm going to go pick up the pizza, and then I'll bring in the rest of the books. Sound okay?" His eyes were drawn to Mac's bandana. "Cool. Got any extras?"

Mac handed him one. "Thanks." He immediately tied it like a sweatband around his head, à la hot runner style. Darla laughed at him, and in return, he kissed her.

Then Darla was mobbed by a bunch of young women who wanted to eat pizza and talk about books—two of her favorite things. She sat in a chair in the front of the crowd.

"So *No Time to Die* is about two sisters who have a very complicated relationship," she began.

"He's so hot," a young patient said as everyone watched Nick carry boxes. "He and his dad remodeled my cousin's kitchen last summer."

"Is that your boyfriend?" someone asked.

"Yes," Darla said honestly.

Someone raised her hand. Judging by her appearance, she seemed to be in the middle of undergoing chemo treatments. "I have a question," she said. "What was it like dating after chemo?"

Darla shot a glance over to Roberta, who smiled and

gave a slow nod. Like she was leaving how to handle it up to Darla.

Her mind whirled. She didn't want to sound like she had it all together. On the other hand, she wanted these young women to know there was life beyond this cancer center. Beyond the treatments and doctors' appointments. That was way more important than talking about her pathological fictitious sisters.

"I mean, didn't you ever wonder if you'd be normal again?" the young woman asked.

"I asked myself that question every day for a long time," Darla admitted. "And some days, I still do," she added more softly. She thought carefully about what she wanted to say. "But you know what? Once you stop the treatments and you start to get your energy back, you slowly start to reclaim your life. Except with a lot more gratitude for every single moment."

"How did you feel about—about your body?" someone asked.

Okay, maybe she should've stuck with the pathological sisters. Because this was getting a little intense. "You might feel like you and your body have been through a war. And you might feel that you aren't the same person and wonder if you're ever going to get yourself back. You have scars. Maybe you've lost your hair." She touched her chest near her clavicle. "Sometimes I look at my port scar, and it brings scary thoughts right back."

Behind her, Nick placed what was hopefully the final box of books on the floor.

"What's dating like after cancer?" someone asked.

Darla felt herself turn red. "Well, I—"

Suddenly everyone burst out in laughter. She spun around to find Nick behind her, grinning and making a two-thumbs-up sign. A smile crossed his face and humor lit his eyes as he looked at her and sent her a wink. Then he walked up to her and gave her a quick kiss. In front of everyone.

Everyone clapped. And there was a chorus of *Awwws*.

Darla recognized it for what it was. He was giving her an out. Lightening things up.

Darla turned to the room full of people. "I don't believe getting through this is about being strong. Mostly it is just hanging in there day by day, moment by moment."

A young woman with sleeve tattoos raised her hand. "I'm here because I love your books. But I actually do port-scar tattoos in my shop. I do flowers, inspirational sayings, whatever you might want. And I've got a grant to do them for cancer patients, so everyone should feel free to stop by."

This book discussion wasn't what Darla had expected in any way, but she hoped that anyone struggling would see that there was a good life on the other side. She was learning that herself.

"So, should we talk about the book?" Mac asked.

Oh, the book. The nasty sisters who disliked each other and had serious mental issues. That somehow seemed pretty anticlimactic. "Sure, but first..." She looked at Nick. "I think you might have to leave." He looked mock offended. "You're way too distracting."

Chapter 20

THE NEXT AFTERNOON, Darla was writing a love scene. It was tender and passionate and probably involved the best sex of her character's life. She found herself choking up and getting teary-eyed because the love scene had been a long time coming for the two star-crossed lovers in her story. The problem was that she couldn't bear to write the story according to plan, which would mean turning her hero into the villain of the story. Darla didn't want to spoil her couple's hard-earned happiness.

It wasn't lost on her that she was still clinging to her original idea of a heart-wrenching second-chance love story, writing the bits and pieces that could be included in either story. Also, she had to admit, the scene was eerily similar to something she'd just experienced with Nick—in tasteful, closed-door fashion, of course. But sooner or later she was going to have to buckle down and do the hard work of ripping the story apart.

She was struggling with what to do when Rachel's name suddenly popped up on her phone. When she answered, her sister said in a panic, "My supervisor just called. She's having trouble covering a shift and wondered if I could come in. It's Sunday, so it pays overtime, but Greg's stuck at work. Could you come over and babysit for a couple of hours? If you're too busy, I'll say no."

"I need a break. I'll be right over." Darla wasn't lying. She wanted to spend all the time she could with her nieces and nephew. Besides, she'd been at it all day, and her brain was fried.

Being with Nick had sharpened her sense of here and now, of not wanting to miss a single second of life.

She didn't even have to ring Rachel's doorbell before the door opened and she was greeted by three Disney princesses...and Wallis, who was wearing a string of Mardi Gras beads around his neck. Maisie was in a faux-satin-and-tulle blue skirt, Phoebe's was green with a mermaid tail, and Teddy was wearing a yellow one. And he was also carrying a lightsaber.

"Oh my goodness." She stooped to admire their costumes. "Look at you three!"

"We're playing princesses," Maisie announced.

"And Star Wars." Teddy added as they all dashed through the living room.

Rachel, in blue scrubs and practical clogs made for people who never sit down at work, as was often the case in the cardiac step-down unit, grabbed her backpack and headed for the door. "Thank you," she said, giving Darla's arm a squeeze on the way out. "There's a box of mac and cheese on the counter and some chicken nuggets in the freezer. Greg said he'd do his best to get home before nine."

"No rush. I'm looking forward to *Star Wars and the Princesses*," she called out as her sister ran to the car, tossing a quick wave behind her.

Darla called Hadley to ask if she and their friends could pick her up at Rachel's around nine for their little bachelorette party. Although with Kit feeling nauseous the way she was, Darla seriously wondered how that plan was going to end up. While she was on the phone, Maisie tapped her on the shoulder. "Teddy has to go potty, Aunt Darla. Phoebe and I will help."

"Okay, baby. Be right there." She turned back to her conversation as Maisie skipped away. Darla was confident that with all the potty practice, Teddy was in good hands—at least for another minute, anyway. "Rachel said Greg might even be home earlier. And yes, I bought a pregnancy test for Kit. Two, just in case. See you later."

Darla ended the call and tossed her phone on the couch before heading down the hall. Halfway there, she heard the alarming sounds of banging and screaming. Wallis was pacing before the closed bathroom door, whining nervously, no one else in sight. "Aunt Darla, Aunt Darla," came a panicked cry from one of the twins—Phoebe, she thought.

"I'm here," Darla said quickly and as cheerily as possible, even though her blood ran cold at the panic in Phoebe's voice.

"Open the door, Phoebe," Maisie said, her voice muffled from behind the door. Then, in a more panicked voice, she cried, *"Open the door!"*

What in the world… "Hey, everybody, I'm here," Darla said. "I'm coming right in!"

"Hurry," Maisie said in a high-pitched voice Darla had never heard before, "we can't get out!"

She heard sobs—from all three kids, no doubt. Forcing herself to stay calm, Darla tried the door. The doorknob was tight, un-jiggleable. She took a deep breath. "Okay, the door is locked. Just flip the little thingy underneath the knob."

Flip the thingy? How could she tell the kids what to do if she didn't even know the thingy's name? "The latch." Yes, the latch. The knob was smooth, patinaed brass, and besides what she'd just said, she had absolutely no clue how to troubleshoot this. Take off the door? Her mom had done that once when they were kids, but that was because angsty teenage Rachel had locked herself in her bedroom on purpose and refused to come out.

Don't panic, she told herself. The twins were definitely old enough to follow simple directions, weren't they?

"The doorknob broked," Phoebe said, sounding calmer than her sister. "Maisie broked it."

"I did not break it," Maisie cried. "I turned it, and it fell off."

Oh *no.*

"Okay, everyone," Darla said. "Stand away from the door."

The door was old and paneled and as solid as The Rock. Even though Darla got a running head start from across the hall and threw her entire body weight into the door, it didn't budge.

Rubbing her sore shoulder after that genius move, she

said, "Okay, I need all the princesses to act really, really royal. Do you all know what that means?"

"No, we're stuck!" cried Maisie. "We are stuck here with no food. Call the fire-people!"

Oh, the drama. "I can act royal," Teddy said confidently. "I have a lightsaber. I'm going to slice the door in half."

"Stop it, Teddy. You're stupid," Phoebe said. Then, presumably to her sister, she said, "Aunt Darla says we have to act like princesses. Princesses don't panic."

"Yes they do," Maisie said. "They yell for help, and the prince comes and gets them."

Wait—what on earth was her sister teaching these girls?

"Not anymore," Phoebe said. "We haveta save ourselfs."

"Listen," Darla said, more anxious that the kids were afraid than anything else, "I'm going to call for help, but I need us to sing a song so the help knows where to find us, okay? What song would you like to sing?"

Maisie started singing a refrain of "Let It Go" from *Frozen* while Darla sped back to the living room to grab her phone and punch in Nick's number. Poor Wallis, eager to be of service, charged right along with her. Nick picked up on the second ring. "Oh, thank God. I'm at Rachel's. The kids accidentally locked themselves in the bathroom, and I don't know how to get them out."

"What kind of lock is it?" he asked calmly.

"The old kind with the little flip thingy underneath the knob. I'm trying my best to keep them distracted, but they're upset."

"Keep them occupied for fifteen minutes." How could he sound so unfazed?

Darla stopped by her sister's desk in the kitchen and

grabbed a tablet of colored paper and a bunch of markers before running back down the hall.

The *Frozen* song had just ended. "I'm back," she said. "Uncle Nick's coming in just a few minutes. So until then we can make him a little card to thank him for getting us out." She rolled a blue marker under the door. "Who wants the blue one?"

"I want it!" Teddy yelled.

"Here come some more," she said, rolling a pink and a green marker under the door. Then she passed a few sheets of paper through.

"When's Uncle Nick coming?" Maisie demanded.

"It's okay, Maisie. It will be soon," Phoebe said in a comforting voice. "Here, you can have the pink one."

"Teddy doesn't have his pants on," Maisie announced.

"I don't need pants to draw," he said, stating the obvious. That made Darla smile a little.

"No, but you need pants because not having pants is gross," Maisie said.

"Hey, kids, Uncle Nick just texted me," Darla said. "He's on the way. You all better color fast."

What Nick had really texted was, Hang tight. Ten more minutes.

But it already felt like fifty. And she was running out of markers.

"Darla?" came a voice from the front hall, but it wasn't Nick's.

"Back hall, Mom," she called. "Guess who's here?" she said to the kids, using her isn't-that-incredible voice.

"Oh my goodness, is everybody all right?" her mother said in a panicked voice.

Darla put a finger to her mouth, whispering, "I'm trying to keep everyone calm. And yes, except Teddy won't put on his pants and Maisie especially is not handling this well."

"Hey, who wants to show Grammy their cards?" Darla asked through the door.

"Cards?" her mom exclaimed. "You have them making cards? Hey, kiddos," she called, "show them to me!"

Her mom knelt down to intercept a piece of paper colored with bright pink marker that suddenly flew beneath the door. She lifted it up. It read SEND HELP in six-year-old lettering.

"Which one of them did this?"

"That's got to be Maisie," Darla said quietly. "The fatalistic one."

"Oh dear," her mom said. "Maisie, honey, your penmanship has really improved. It's just beautiful. Write me another note."

"Grandma, we want *out*," Maisie said with an edge of desperation.

"Teddy just tooted, and it smells really bad," Phoebe said.

"I have to go poopy again," Teddy said, "but who will help me?"

"*I want out!*" Maisie yelled, punctuating her words by banging on the door. Darla and her mom looked at each other in horror.

"Sweetheart, please don't kick the door," her mom said patiently. "You could hurt your foot."

"Pee-*ew*," Phoebe said. "I'm going to use the bathroom spray. It's lilac."

"No, no, wait," Darla said, envisioning them spraying

each other in the eyes and choking on it in the enclosed space, for starters.

"Hold off on the spray, kids," her mom said in a commanding tone. "That can smell really strong without a window open."

"I'm out of entertainment options," Darla said to her mom. "What do we do next?"

"Do you want Aunt Darla to tell you a story?" her mom asked.

Oh no. "Mom, I don't know any kid stories," she said under her breath.

"You write stories for a living." Her eyes were lit up with humor, indicating that she was enjoying this a little too much. "Make one up."

"Okay, fine." Darla wracked her brain for an age-appropriate story but came up short. "How did you know to come?"

"Nick called me. He thought I could help keep everyone calm."

Nick had called her. To be with Darla. That was...nice. Knowing that calmed *her* down a little.

"Who wants to hear a story?" Darla asked.

"I'm busy," Teddy called.

"It's so stinky in here!" Maisie said.

"Okay, kittens," her mother said through the door, "we're going to have a contest. Who can meow the loudest?"

"I want a kitty!" Teddy said. "Meow!"

"Why?" Darla said. "They already have a pony."

"We don't have a pony," Phoebe said.

"You have Wallis," Darla said.

"Wahwis is *not* a pony," Teddy said.

"No, but he's as big as one," Darla loved up on Wallis, who looked ready to burst through the door to get to his kids.

First, they had a meowing contest and then a barking contest. Wallis kept pawing at the door. The girls got into a fight about whose picture was prettiest. And Teddy apparently pooped—and flushed—but lost interest in drawing completely, continuing to meow and bark and refuse to put on his pants.

Then Darla heard a distant thump, but it wasn't coming from the door. She and her mom exchanged glances.

"It's the window," her mom said.

Oh, thank goodness.

The kids suddenly began to scream and cheer. "Uncle Nick! Uncle Nick!" they yelled.

"Hey, you three," Nick suddenly said from inside the bathroom. Darla released a huge breath. "Ho ho ho, Merry Christmas!" he said in a deep Santa voice.

"You're not Saint Nick, you're *Uncle* Nick!" Phoebe said.

"I know, but I got into the house just like Santa," he said.

"Santa uses the chimney," Maisie pointed out.

"Okay," Nick said, "you want me to go back out and use the chimney instead?"

"No, no!" they all yelled. But not in a desperate way. Nick was joking, being funny, and putting everyone at ease, including Darla.

"I want to go down the ladder," Teddy said.

"Hey, hey, buddy, away from the window, now," Nick said. They heard the sound of a window closing and then clicking sounds as he fiddled with the lock.

"Can you get the door open?" Darla asked, leaning against it.

"Working on it," Nick said. "Whoa, hey, buddy, you are flashing the moon," he said, apparently to Teddy. "How about putting some pants on?"

Teddy laughed. "Okay," he said. "But will you wipe me?"

What a circus. Pounding noises ensued from behind the door. Suddenly, the click of the door unlatching was followed by the door creaking open. Darla practically fell into the doorway, and specifically into six feet two inches of muscled man. Nick caught her in his arms and smiled, while she wanted to cry with relief and only held off because of the kids. They poured out of the bathroom, hugging her legs, running to their grandma. Wallis, beside himself, started running circles around everyone.

Darla hugged and kissed each kid in turn and picked up Maisie, who was crying. "It's okay," she soothed. "Everything's all right. Don't be scared."

"I'm not scared," she said, burying her head on Darla's shoulder. Which was a little yucky because her nose was running from all the crying. "I broke the knob. It's my fault."

Nick hauled her into his arms. "Hey, Maisie, it's not your fault. In an old house, sometimes stuff breaks. Your dad and I are going to fix it and make sure that never happens again."

Teddy was doing a downward dog in the hall. "Wipe me, Uncle Nick!"

"Okay, little man. Let's get this business done." Nick handed Maisie back to Darla and ushered Teddy back into the bathroom, closing the door to take care of business.

And that's when Darla saw that her mom was staring at her in a peculiar way.

Like maybe she'd just been shocked by the sight of Nick

wiping a kid's butt. The easy way he handled everything and the obvious love he had for the kids was... well. It was making Darla's heart swell even more.

But she was worried about Maisie, who was still crying a little. Darla wiped her tears with her hands. "You were very brave. You know that, don't you?"

Her niece nodded slowly.

"Who made the help sign?" Nick asked, opening the door. Teddy squeezed out from around Nick before the door was even fully open.

"I did," Maisie said.

"Well, that's really something," Nick said. "You know what that means, don't you?"

She shook her head.

He gently tapped her head. "It means you were thinking. Solving the problem. Doing something to help." Everyone had gathered around. "All you kids did very well. So well, I have an idea."

"What's that?" Maisie asked.

Darla, ready to collapse from stress, couldn't wait for the idea herself.

"Why don't we go to Swenson's?" Mentioning the name of the popular beach burger place worked magic.

"Do we get a milkshake?" Maisie suddenly perked up.

"Of course, we do, Maisie." Phoebe patted her sister on the back. "Strawberry. Your favorite."

"I want fries," Teddy said, tugging on the leg of Nick's jeans.

"Okay, everybody," Darla said. "Get some shoes on."

"Thank you for calling me," her mom said to Nick as the kids scattered. "And for acting so quickly."

"I didn't have my ladder with me, or I would've been here sooner." He turned to Darla. "You okay?"

Darla nodded. But what she really wanted to do was to hug him. No, to crawl into his arms with relief and stay there for a long time. But her mother suddenly seemed very attuned to both of them, and she felt that she should have an opportunity to tell her what was going on with her and Nick rather than spring it on her.

She leaned in and gave Nick a kiss on the cheek anyway. "Thanks for the rescue." She purposely avoided her mom's reaction. Then she turned to the kids. "I'm starving. How about you all?"

"Do we have a vehicle with car seats?" Nick asked in a low voice.

"Rachel left me the van," Darla said. "We can all fit. Mom, you up for Swenson's?"

"You bet!" she said as she picked up one of Teddy's shoes from the middle of the hallway.

Just as they walked into the family room, the door opened, and Kit, Alex, Hadley, and Tony walked in. Ollie, Kit's adorable curly-headed six-year-old, flashed a big grin and ran straight over to his friends to join in the excitement.

Tony surveyed the room. "We came to help, but I see everyone's present and accounted for."

"Uncle Nick climbed into the bafroom like Santa," Teddy announced.

As the kids recounted the story, Darla took Kit aside. "That—um—thing you just might need to do before we go out tonight—it's on the counter near my purse. But if you use this bathroom, do *not* lock the door."

While everyone was chatting and helping the kids find their shoes, Darla pulled Nick a little ways down the nearby hall and wrapped her arms around him tightly. "Thank you," she whispered into his neck.

He slipped his arms around her. "Hello to you too," he whispered back. "But aren't you worried about your mom getting some ideas about us?"

"I'll talk with her. But I'm not going to hide, if that's what you mean." It was quiet and dim and private, the laughter of kids and the murmur of conversation from the family room softly muted in the distance. "What made you use the ladder instead of taking the door down?"

"Well, you know how old this house is. That door is so heavy it would require two people to get it off, and I figured the hinges would be pretty stiff."

"Thanks for the save."

He gave her a kiss and then quirked his mouth up in a smile. "I can say the same thing to you."

Her heart gave a little flutter, but she didn't want to misunderstand, so she said, "What do you mean?"

He shrugged. "Just that I'm really happy to have you in my life again."

Wow. Okay, so he really meant what she thought he meant. She beamed right back at him. "We've only been together one night."

She winced at her very bad effort to be light, to joke. He looked deadly serious. So much so that she felt a little panicky. "This isn't about sex," he said carefully and slowly. "It's about waiting, like, a hundred years for you."

A hundred years? She practically melted into a puddle right in the hallway. He was so sure, so confident. She yearned to strip herself of all her worries and free-fall right into all that confidence. But she was afraid to allow herself to hope for anything beyond the present. And she didn't even know how to begin to put that into words.

She pushed those thoughts away as she reached up and kissed him. Just a soft brush over his lips. But it wasn't enough. So she kissed him again, longer this time, their lips meeting and melding as he gathered her into his arms and pulled her deeper into his embrace. "You feel so damn good," he whispered against her ear, which sent a shiver all through her.

The sensible part of her knew that they should stop, that they were standing in the hall near a crowded room of people. She pushed weakly against him, trying to gather her wits, but all her senses were abuzz and her head was whirling.

And then someone gasped.

They broke apart to find her mother standing in the middle of the hallway staring at them. "Wait—oops—oh my goodness—you two are...together?"

Chapter 21

TRICIA STOOD IN front of them with her mouth open, and Darla had gone quiet.

Nick didn't want to speak for Darla, didn't want to put words into her mouth. Plus, they'd been together exactly one day. Although it had been quite a day (and night) so far, but still. That might be enough for him to say certain things, but he knew it might not be enough for Darla.

He wanted to support Darla in front of her mom, but he didn't want to anger Tricia.

Believe in me, he telegraphed to Darla, squeezing her hand. Believe in *us.*

"Darla," Tricia said, shock reverberating in her voice, "tell me that you two are not...dating."

She said *dating* like it was *cough syrup.* Or a raccoon in the garbage. Or a mouse you find in the cupboard as you're reaching for your box of cereal. Okay, this was going to be harder than he thought. Apparently, time didn't heal old wounds.

No, only talking could do that. He swore right then and there that he would show this woman that he was worthy of her daughter. Starting right now.

"Mom," Darla said, looking from her to Nick, "we...well. I—this is very new between us and we...we need time to figure some things out."

"I can't believe you two are actually going there again." Darla's mother crossed her arms and shook her head.

"Going where?" Maisie asked. "I want to go too!"

"Tricia, I think the world of Darla," Nick said. "And I hope—"

"Mom," Darla started again, "Nick and I—"

Just then the bathroom door opened, and Kit emerged, a determined look on her face. She walked up to them, huddled together in the middle of the hall, squeezing in between Darla and Nick and wrapping her arms around their shoulders. "I couldn't help overhearing, and I just want to say, that's so terrific, you two." She gave their shoulders a congratulatory shake. "Great news." She looked nervously at Darla's mom. "Tricia, isn't it incredible that they've found each other again? I think it's *amazing*."

She was flushed, breathless, and talking a mile a minute. And clearly trying to save the day.

Alex walked up and shook Nick's hand and slapped him on the back. "I can't think of better news." Then he said "Congrats, Darla," and hugged her too. Turning to Kit, he said, "Hey, I've been wondering what happened to you. I was afraid you got locked in there too."

Kit laughed nervously, just as Tony and Hadley joined

them. Tony put an arm around Darla's mom. "My brother is my best man, Mrs. M. And I trust him with my life."

"Me too," Hadley echoed.

These people were really pouring it on, rallying around them. As true friends do.

Darla's mom looked from Tony and Hadley to Alex and Kit and then to her daughter and Nick. Sighing deeply, she said, "Yes, but I just think—"

Kit interrupted, a strange move from her. "Hey, everybody, guess what." Her gaze darted around wildly. "I have some great news too." She turned to Alex, grasped his hands tightly, and smiled brightly. "I'm pregnant."

Whoa. The adults went silent as everyone stared at Kit. Nick could hear the sounds of kids laughing and chattering in the family room, oblivious to the new drama playing out in the hallway.

"You're...what did you say?" Alex wore a stunned expression. "I thought we were talking about Darla and..." His voice faded away.

"Thank God we aren't anymore," Hadley said poignantly.

"Yeah. It's true," Kit was smiling and tearing up at the same time. "I did the test twice."

"Oh, wow," Alex said. "That's what you were doing? Right now? Oh, wow." Then he took her into his arms.

Cheering and congratulations broke out. Even Tricia was laughing and happy crying along with everyone else. Nick hugged Alex and Kit, and then whispered a quick "Thank you" in her ear.

After a little while, Nick walked over to Darla's side. She cast him a wary glance, but he simply flashed a reassuring smile and turned to her mom. "I just want you to know I care a lot about your daughter. And I hope that you'll give me the benefit of the doubt." *Just this once.*

She drew a heavy sigh and gave Nick an I'm-warning-you kind of stare. "My grandchildren adore you. And so does my oldest daughter. And the girls." By "girls" she must have meant Hadley and Kit. "And there is one thing you did today that makes me think more highly of you."

"Getting that ladder was really nothing—"

"Oh, it wasn't that," she said, waving her hand dismissively. "You wiped Teddy's butt without blinking an eye. You took care of business with a smile on your face. That gives me hope that you've matured."

"So I'm on probation?" he asked hopefully. What was he going to have to do to win this woman over for good—climb Everest? Offer a free home remodel? Produce a grandchild? He was up for anything.

She pinned him with a stare. "I want the best for my daughter. The *very* best. Someone who loves her and treats her like the jewel that she is. Do that, and we'll talk again."

"Yes, ma'am." He wiped the sweat from his brow and went to join in the celebration.

* * *

"Kit, I'm so thrilled," Darla said, giving her a huge squeeze.

"…that you finally took the fricking test!" Hadley said, joining the hug. "But seriously, congratulations. It's wonderful news."

"Hope you don't mind that I'll be drinking drinks with

little umbrellas in them at our little bach party tonight,"
Kit said to Hadley.

"Hey, listen, it sort of fits into the theme of this
wedding where nothing is going exactly as planned."
Hadley grinned. "We'll make it work anyway. Also, I'm so
impressed by the timing of your announcement."

"You threw yourself on the pyre for me," Darla said,
sending Kit a grateful look. She had the best. Friends.
Ever.

"Oh, don't worry," Kit said, gleefully rubbing her hands
together. "I do consider this a big one in the bank of favors.
I'll be sure to remind you of it when I need one."

"I won't forget this." Darla's voice cracked.

"Geez, Darla, I was just kidding," Kit said. "Although it
really is time for your mom to let that one go."

"And take a look over there." Hadley pointed to where
Nick and Darla's mom were talking. "She actually just
cracked a smile." She turned to Darla. "Nick's won all of
us over. He'll win her over too."

"Fingers crossed," Darla said, then she got serious. "I
know this isn't the way you wanted to tell Alex."

Kit smiled. "Alex has been looking at me and shaking
his head for over a week now. So we pretty much knew.
And now we can tell Ollie." She added in a saucy tone,
"It *was* kind of clever to use a baby announcement as a
diversionary tactic, if I may say so myself."

Hadley turned to Darla. "I have a feeling we're never
going to hear the end of this."

"Well, I appreciate what both of you did," Darla said.
"Now my goal is to show my mom how happy I am, and
she's going to fall in love with Nick too."

Kit's eyes suddenly widened, her hand flying to her mouth.

"What is it?" Darla asked.

"Did it finally sink in that you're pregnant?" Hadley asked.

Kit shook her head. "It's not that. Darla, do you know what you've just done?"

"Decided I'll do anything including grovel to avoid a family feud?"

"No. You just admitted that you love Nick."

Darla felt her face heat up. "Well, I—I mean, you never really stop loving anyone…"

"I call baloney," Hadley said. Dropping her voice, she added, "And I'm only making that the G-rated version because there are children present."

"She's got a point," Kit said.

"Okay, fine." Darla smiled thoughtfully at her friends. "It's true."

She was in love with Nick. And maybe she'd never stopped being in love with him.

"Well, you need friends to push you sometimes," Kit said with a shrug.

"I love you both so much," Darla said. The three of them hugged each other tightly.

"Friends forever," Kit said, holding out her pinky.

"And ever," Hadley said, hooking hers.

"And ever," Darla added.

Nick approached them. "I hate to break this up, but the kids have been so good, and they want french fries, like, yesterday." He cracked a grin before hugging Kit again. "Congratulations. I'm really excited for you and Alex. And

Ollie." He hugged Hadley too. "And thanks for what you both did."

"Well, we like you," Hadley said.

Kit side-hugged him. "Yeah, we just can't help it."

"I can't help myself either," Darla said, smiling the widest she'd smiled in quite a while.

* * *

"What are you doing?" Nick asked the next night as he walked into Darla's bedroom holding two glasses of wine. They were about to go sit on the deck and relax, and he was going to show her the wedding bower, which was almost complete. It was the Monday before the wedding, and everything was perfectly on schedule, as planned. But Darla was kneeling in her closet, digging around for something, shoeboxes and shoes scattered all around.

He stifled a grin as the scattered evidence reminded him of a fact he'd forgotten...that she seemed to own almost as many shoes as she did books. "Just making a little surprise for Mackenzie for her chemo tomorrow." Her words came out muffled as she knelt in the back, bent low, giving him a fine view as she reached in the back for something. "Aha!" She popped her head out of the lineup of clothes. "Here it is."

What she held in her hands gave him a jolt. It was a box, square and about the size of a large shoebox, covered in green paper with a pretty gilded pattern.

Seeing it was a little jarring, because he remembered that box well. Years ago, a set of wrapping papers had caught his eye in a local antique shop where he'd been searching for fixtures for a renovation. Each paper had a different intricate pattern with bold colors and gilding. Maybe it was the fact that this particular one was covered with angels that had given him an idea.

Darla reached back in and pulled out a few more boxes, each with different, equally unique, coverings. There were six, each unique, one for each cycle of chemotherapy. She'd kept them all. That fact jolted him most of all.

"Every month," Darla explained as she examined the first box with a fond look, "one of these would show up at the infusion center right before my chemo. It got to be sort of a motivation thing. My nurse would hook me up to the IV and then give me the box. And I'd spend the next few hours rummaging through all the goodies inside.

"There was a little Connemara marble worry stone that I still keep in my desk to use when I'm stuck on an idea. Sometimes it would be Belgian chocolates or lotion. Oh, and a book. Every time, a different book to get lost in." She ran her hand along the lid. "And it wasn't just me who got goodies. There were often little surprises for everyone who came to the center that day—candles, fuzzy slippers, a simple craft, all kinds of creative things." She patted the box. "These little guys caused quite a sensation."

The boxes had been an act of desperation, something to distract her and surprise her and give her a break from thinking about the chemo. He'd done it at a time when things were rocky between them and she hadn't wanted to see him.

He remembered feeling helpless. Sending presents was fine, but it was a poor substitute for being part of her life back then.

"To this day, I don't know who sent them," she mused, "and everyone in the chemo center thought I had a secret admirer. The cards attached always said, *From your biggest fan.* But no one ever came forward, even when I thanked people on social media. The obvious sender was Julia, but she flat-out told me that it wasn't her. I always thought it was such a selfless act of kindness, doing something so thoughtful and never taking credit."

Nick wondered if he should say something, because he didn't want to lie, even by omission. They were building trust, and he didn't want to jeopardize that. But he was in awkward territory here.

It was me. I sent them. Because I never stopped loving you.

That seemed too intense a declaration for now. But he would tell her, someday. Yes, of course he would.

He took her into his arms. "That's how we feel about people we love. We'd do anything to take away their pain."

Darla nodded, her eyes filled with emotion. "She's so young, Nick."

He rubbed her arms. "She'll come through it stronger, and you'll help her."

She laid her cheek against his chest.

The gesture bowled him over. Little by little, Darla was letting her guard down. Yes, he'd always loved her. But he wanted her to be okay with that. And he was making it his mission to show her that it was okay to enjoy everything about life—and maybe realize that she loved him too.

He kissed the top of her head and hoped she'd feel it in the way he held her tightly to his heart.

"Dar, I feel...I feel like I did the first time we were

falling in love. Like it's just...right." He prayed that wasn't too much, but he just couldn't help saying it.

"I feel like that too." Her voice was low and hoarse, almost a whisper. "Like we've been given the gift of a second chance."

It did feel like a gift. Emotion swelled up inside of him. His heart thumped loudly in his chest, a sense of anticipation spreading like a warm buzz all through his body. "Take a chance on me," he whispered. "Just let it all go. Whatever the future brings, we can handle it together."

They stood together long enough for him to see the humor of having a serious discussion in a closet. Darla looked up and said, "My mom doesn't hate you, you know. She just doesn't trust men."

"Hey, I got a smile out of her. That's a reason to celebrate." He paused. "But I think she does still sort of hate me."

"She'll come around."

He smiled at her confidence. "I'm going to do everything I can to make that happen."

"I want you to know that I don't share her doubts." Darla held her breath.

Yes. "I don't either."

After a minute, he took a look around. "This is a huge closet. Kind of reminds me of that dorm room I had on the west side of campus."

"That was a utility closet with a bed," she said. "It had a breaker box in it, remember? It wasn't even supposed to be a dorm room."

"I kind of liked it. It was very...functional."

"Functional?"

"I was in charge of the electricity to the entire floor. And it was private." He raised a brow and shot her a pointed look.

"You're ridiculous." She laughed and shook her head. And then he took his time to remind her that closets were very multifunctional spaces.

As their lips joined and he gave in to the dizzying rush of warmth that never failed to overtake him when they were together, Nick recognized the magic between them for what it was. What he'd been looking for his entire life.

Chapter 22

DARLA AWAKENED SUDDENLY in the middle of the night. She was in her bed and, fortunately, not on the closet floor, she thought with a smile. She wasn't sure what exactly woke her because the room was silent except for the soft lapping of waves on the shore, a sound she loved and which often lulled her right to sleep. Even Boss, who was sprawled paws-up at the bottom of the bed, was breathing calmly. Her gaze alit on Nick, lying on his stomach, hair tussled, sleeping peacefully, and she was filled with an ache so intense it hurt.

She wanted to freeze this moment, this happiness, forever.

When she looked at him, she could see all the makings of a life teeming with family and friends and children. *A full life.*

The bedside clock read 4:00 a.m. Restless and now wide awake, Darla slid out of bed, walked over to the sliding door, and let herself out onto the deck, grabbing her phone off of the dresser and her robe on the way. Outside, she stood at the decfk railing, taking in the majestic view before her. The clouds were busy, rolling past the stars, a powerful and majestic sight. The calm sea was lit by a sliver of a moon that created a silver-spun trail on the water. *See that trail?* Her mom used to say. *That's how the angels lead people to heaven.*

Darla stretched out on a recliner, pulling her robe more tightly around her at the slight chill from the middle-of-the-night breeze.

Reading was always a good cure for insomnia. As she opened her phone to find her e-reader app, she noticed that she had messages. One was from Hadley, which said simply, Four more days! Followed by hand-clapping emojis. Another was from Mackenzie, telling her that she'd found a few more people interested in attending book club next time, and asking if that would be okay. She smiled at that one. And the third message…well, the third nearly stopped her heart.

It was from Dr. Ag. Hi Darla, the message read. Sorry I missed you. Please give me a call me when you get this. We need to discuss a test result.

Darla found a missed call. That and the message were both from early yesterday evening, an unusual time for the doctor to call. If Dr. Ag had a request, usually her nurse practitioner, Kim, was the one who called, and always during business hours.

That was the thing that got her the most. An after-hours call from Dr. Ag herself on a Monday. It practically screamed that something was wrong.

Good thing Darla was sitting down because all her forgotten fears roared back with a vengeance that made her dizzy.

She'd been so busy with Nick that she'd forgotten all about her phone for hours.

In fact, she'd been so busy with Nick she'd forgotten...all about the cancer. Forgotten that it would follow her everywhere, haunting her like a ghost. Robbing her of her happiness. Her worst nightmare.

Darla tried to read, which was always her balm when she was upset, but the words were little dancing blurs, and she was unable to pry her mind from focusing on the worst.

At 6:00 a.m., she crept into the bedroom to grab some clothes and took a long run on the beach, something that always helped organize her thoughts and help her make a plan of action.

But it was all she could do to hold on until seven, when she finally felt that it wouldn't be too early to call. She was about a quarter-mile from home when she stopped running, caught her breath, and punched in Dr. Ag's number.

Dr. Ag picked up immediately. "Hi, Darla," she said.

"I—I didn't see your message until the middle of the night. I have to say I'm unnerved." Darla held her breath, waiting for Dr. Ag to say something like, *Oh, it's no big deal. And can you sign a book for someone?* But she knew it wasn't going to be that simple.

"I was trying to spare you the worry by calling you directly," Dr. Ag said, "so I'm sorry for that. Would you be able to stop by the office this morning so that we can talk in person?"

"To be honest, Dr. Ag, I'm sort of freaking out." Darla paced the beach. Around her, a few early-morning joggers ran by with earbuds in. A group of seniors power walked by, laughing and chatting. "Please, could you just tell me right now?"

"Yes, of course. There's a little density on your mammogram. It's very small. But it's an area of concern."

An area of concern? "Like, a tumor?"

"It could be benign. Did you hear that, Darla? It could be nothing. I want to be certain you heard that. But it requires follow-up."

"Follow-up, like another mammogram? Or a CT or MRI?" She knew all the fancy tests. She'd been through them all before.

"Well," Dr. Ag began, which made Darla instantly realize that the answer wasn't simple. "I've already talked to one of our breast surgeons, and she recommends an ultrasound-guided biopsy. The breast radiologist can do it at one today at the hospital. Are you free?"

Today? *The Tuesday before the wedding?* There were so many last-minute things to help Hadley check on—flowers for the bower that Nick made, tables, dinnerware, chairs and a runner for the beach, all of which were going to be delivered to her house...not to mention her looming deadline. "I— um—well, yes, I can be." She had to be—if Dr. Ag thought the test was important, she would do it. Simple as that.

"Great. It's a very simple procedure done in the radiology suite with local anesthetic. The radiologist passes an ultrasound-guided needle right where the abnormality was on the mammogram. She'll take a small sample of tissue through the needle."

Needles and tissue samples were simple? "Will I find out the result right away?"

Dr. Ag continued in her calm, matter-of-fact tone, which was both reassuring and frightening at the same time. "The pathology takes a few days to come back."

A few days.

Darla's heart sank. She'd have to live with the uncertainty for that long and have to wait it out. She closed her eyes to get a grip. "Okay." Her throat had gone dry. She was shaking all over, and not from the light breeze off the water.

The waiting game. The bets on the odds. The breath holding. She was back to square one. Just when she'd finally managed to forget.

And maybe this was a selfish thought, but the timing was awful. Weddings were supposed to be joyous and fun-filled celebrations. How would she be able to celebrate with this hanging over her head?

"You—you're scheduling this today just to get it over with, right?" she asked. "I mean, I'm just—" Was this more urgent than Dr. Ag was letting on?

"If you want to wait until next week, that's perfectly fine. But I know how difficult it is to wait, and I thought I'd give you the chance to get it done quickly."

"Yes, of course. I—I want to get it over with." Yes, she wanted to get the pain of waiting finished as soon as possible, wedding or no wedding.

She blinked back tears. Nick. She needed Nick. She wanted to take shelter in his wide-open arms.

Slowly, she realized what she'd known all along. This was how her life was going to be, living from one scare to the next. And he would surely suffer with her.

"Darla," Dr. Ag said softly, "I want to tell you something, not as your doctor but as a friend."

"Yes, I'm listening," Darla said, trying to sound normal. But tears were rolling down her cheeks. Good thing it was still early and not many people were out on the beach.

"This happens routinely. Worst-case scenario, if it is something bad, chances are that it's going to be caught early. That's why we screen. And there's a good chance it's a benign growth, like an adenoma, which is very common in women your age. Okay?"

"Okay," Darla said, trying to sound upbeat but failing utterly.

"I'll be in the hospital this afternoon, and I'm planning to stop by. So I'll see you then."

"Okay. Thanks for calling, Dr. Ag."

"You're welcome. I have one more word of advice."

"Sure."

"Don't go this alone. Share the burden with someone. Okay?"

"Thank you," she said, "I appreciate it." And disconnected the call.

It took another fifteen minutes of hard running before she could muster the courage to go home. By then she hoped that she was so sweaty and flushed from exertion that Nick wouldn't notice she'd been crying.

"Hey," Nick said when she walked in and pulled off her shoes. She found him in the kitchen, dressed for work, measuring out Boss's food.

Boss bounded over to greet her. Which she took as a great compliment, choosing her over breakfast. She said good morning in as playful a tone as she could muster, which came out dull and monotoned compared to usual. It must have convinced Boss, though, because he gave her a butt wiggle and ran back to chow down his breakfast.

"Look at you, up early and all healthy," Nick said, pouring her coffee and setting it in front of her with a quick kiss. "What's your day like?" He was busy loading the dishwasher and didn't seem to study her face too carefully, thank goodness.

"I—want to write as much as I can before I bring Mackenzie that little gift. And I think I might pop over and make sure Hadley's not overwhelmed."

"Hey, you okay?" He looked at her with concern. "You seem a little edgy."

What kind of talent was that, knowing at a glance what she tried her best to hide? How did he know her so well from the inside out? Also, he'd just called her *healthy*. Oh, the irony!

"Yes, I'm fine." She smiled widely, even though her heart felt like it was being crushed under the weight of the news.

What if she could no longer have mornings like this, where he made the coffee, handed her a mug with a smile, and gave her looks full of loving concern? How would she ever give this up? Give him up?

She went to him as he sat on the counter stool and put her arms around his neck. He pulled her into his embrace, his powerful arms surrounding her. Nibbled her neck. Made her laugh. She stood there for a long time, inhaling his clean scent, taking in every single sensation of what it felt like to be held by him so she could memorize it forever.

"You sure you're good?" He assessed her intently. "Deadline going okay?"

"Yes, fine. Just a lot on my plate today." And then she gave him what she hoped was a reassuring smile.

She knew only one thing for certain. She wasn't about to drag him into this nightmare too.

* * *

Darla somehow held it together long enough to see Nick off to work. But as soon as he left, she collapsed onto a kitchen stool, her head buzzing.

It could be nothing. It could be *nothing.*

She tried to cling to that hope. Prayed for it to be true. Wished it to be. But that little lump in her neck so long ago had been small and persistent, and it hadn't been nothing.

Everything she'd been through to fight for her life hadn't been nothing either.

She drew a big gulp of air. What if she had to fight all over again? Did she even have the strength left?

Cold dread froze her veins. It had been wrong to think that she could find happiness as easily as other people. As her friends had.

Suddenly, the walls began to close in around her, and she began breathing too fast. She grabbed her phone and keys and found herself running out the front door and down her street. At first, she just…escaped. But then she realized that she had had a goal in mind without even knowing it. She skirted downtown by using the back roads until she arrived at her sister's back door.

"Rach. You home?" Darla managed as she knocked.

Her sister came to the door, holding Teddy in one hand and a paper napkin in the other. She wiped something chocolaty off his face.

"Aunt DarDar," Teddy said with a mischievous grin that showcased his adorable dimples, pointing at her with one finger touching the screen door.

"Hi, Sweetkins," she said, pretending to eat the finger, which made him laugh.

Rachel scrutinized her with eagle eyes. It hadn't really occurred to Darla that, on top of being sweaty and disheveled from her run, she might also look panicked and terrified. The look on Rachel's face signaled that to be true. Her sister, like Nick, always had a special way of sensing her moods that was rarely wrong.

"Go play cars," Rachel said as she set Teddy down, giving him a playful tap on the butt. Then she opened the screen door and her arms.

Darla ran right into them and let out a sob.

"Oh, honey," Rachel said, rubbing her back in a familiar, comforting way, "if Nick did something—"

"It's not Nick." Darla pounded on her chest, trying to clear her throat. "Can I please have some water?"

She sat down at the kitchen table. Teddy was in the sunroom, busy for the moment. Rachel, always the over-achiever, poured her a tall glass of lemonade full of ice.

"I ran all the way around the bay," Darla said as she gulped the drink, "and then I headed over here without thinking. Thanks."

Rachel grabbed a bakery box and a couple of plates and sat down. "Have a muffin and tell me what's going on."

God bless her sister. Calm, in charge, and supplying food. Just what she needed. "I have to have a breast biopsy," Darla said as she sat. "Today at one. They found a suspicious spot on my mammogram." She patted her left breast. "I can't even feel it."

Rachel frowned, her medical brain at work. "What kind of spot?"

"Dr. Ag said it could be something or it could be nothing. That's why they need to do the biopsy."

"That's fair," Rachel said in a calm, authoritative voice. "It's great that she got it scheduled so soon. You won't have to wait long to find out."

Darla tapped her fingers nervously on the table. "It's going to take a few days to get the results."

"I'm sorry." Rachel placed her hand over Darla's. "With everything you have going on right now, that's tough."

Darla shouldn't have met her sister's gaze because that started her crying again. "I'm being dramatic about this, right?" Darla swiped at the tears. "It's not like me to cry. It's just all the commotion around the wedding and—"

Rachel squeezed her hand. "Honey, it sucks no matter how you look at it."

Darla crumpled her napkin into a tight, tiny ball. "I just felt that things were going exactly right for me," she said. "I actually felt for the first time like who I was before the cancer. I mean, I'll never be that person again, but I felt light. Not weighed down. And like everything might work out for me."

Rachel gave her an earnest look. "It will work out. You can't allow yourself to go to the worst-case scenario. It could happen to anyone, right? And these screens are meant to pick up their share of benign things, right? It might just be—"

Someone was patting Darla's arm. Not Rachel. She looked down to see sweet little Teddy at her side. "Don't cry, Aunt Dar." He pushed the muffin box close. "Have one. It's happy."

She scooped up her nephew and kissed his head, inhaling his fruity toddler-shampoo smell. He parked a truck on the table, next to the muffin box.

"Thanks, Theodore," she said. "Muffins *are* happy."

"I have one too." He pointed to the one on Darla's plate.

"You already had one," his mother said. "How about a glass of milk before we head to Grandma's?" Rachel got up to pour her son a cup. "I have to go to work," she said to Darla. "Is Nick going with you?"

"No," Darla said quietly.

Her sister closed the fridge door and gave her a long, hard look. "You did tell him, right?"

Before Rachel could launch into what Darla called an "Is that wise?" speech, Darla said, "I need to see this through myself first."

Rachel rolled her eyes. "Why do you have to go through this yourself? How are you not going to tell him?"

Darla heaved a sigh. She couldn't tell him. She wouldn't. "I'm just...not."

Her sister put the milk down in front of Teddy and shook her head. "Nick loves you. He'll want to know. I can only see trouble ahead if you keep this from him."

Teddy was gulping the milk, making little sucking sounds against his red plastic cup as he drank it down. Darla put her elbow on the table and rubbed her forehead.

She couldn't put into words, even for her sister, what was hurting her heart. Which was a lot more than just telling Nick about the biopsy. It was about living with cancer every day. The rollercoaster of it. The not knowing. The waiting. The hoping and praying for more life, more time, more *everything*.

If she told him, the illusion of normal would be gone.

It would give way to another reality—that she'd always be the one who would need more from him than he would ever need from her.

Rachel had heard versions of this before, and she'd always brushed off Darla's fatalistic thinking. *You survived,* she'd say. *Make every single day count and stop worrying about the future.*

Darla didn't want to sound like she was pitying herself. So she took a deep breath and pulled herself together. "I'm fine. I just got…a little emotional. It's just the wedding and my deadline and…"

"Are Hadley and Kit going with you?" Rachel wasn't giving up on this.

Darla focused on Teddy's truck as he drove it across the table.

"You haven't told them either, have you? How about Mom?"

Finally, Darla said, "Hadley is busy with the wedding, and Kit's just gotten some of the happiest news of her life. And Mom will cry constantly until the result is back. I'm going to…I'm just going to go do this and not worry everybody. That's it."

"Darla, I'm always here for you." The sympathy in her sister's eyes made Darla want to break down all over again. "I only want to comfort you and make things better for you. But I have to say, this independence thing of yours is just...going too far. Give your friends—and Nick, for that matter—more credit. They love you and care about you."

"I know, Rach. I know." She forced patience into her voice. "I've got to handle this my way."

"I don't agree with 'your way.'" She made air quotes. "You're not an island. I don't know why you think it's so awful to let other people help."

"Rach. Please."

"Okay, okay." She reached over and hugged Darla, hooking a strand of stray hair behind Darla's ears, like she used to do when she was fixing her pigtails long ago. Then she refilled her lemonade. "I've got to get ready to go."

"Thank you for being here for me." Darla forced a smile. "And now I'm going to play with my nephew," she said, giving Teddy a squeeze.

"*I'm* your ne-pew." Teddy stuffed a bite of Darla's muffin in his mouth while his mother's back was turned.

Rachel saw Teddy chewing and shook her head at her son, who grinned and took another bite. "I'm going to see if I can get off and meet you at the hospital."

Darla couldn't help smiling at Teddy's antics. She cast a grateful glance at Rachel. "I appreciate it, but please don't. I'll be okay." She helped Teddy down and hugged her sister. "I don't know what I'd do without you."

She'd handle this, just like she handled everything else that came her way, but she could no longer pretend she was a normal woman leading a normal life. And that broke her heart almost more than worrying about her biopsy.

Chapter 23

"OKAY, ALL REGISTERED," the woman at the radiology suite check-in smiled as she handed Darla her insurance card and ID. As Darla slid the cards back into her wallet, she couldn't help thinking that at book club just a week before, she'd never have believed that she'd be on the patient end of things so soon. As she got up and turned back to the waiting room, she heard someone say, "You're cutting it a little close on time, don't you think?"

She looked up to see Kit shaking her head and tapping her wristwatch. Hadley was next to her, frowning and standing with her arms crossed.

Lots of feelings raced through her. At first, she was stunned, embarrassed, relieved…and ready to murder her sister.

But her second thought was, *I'm not alone.*

"What are you two doing here?" she managed through tears that seemed to come out of nowhere.

"No one should have to go through this by themselves," Kit said.

"My sister—" Darla began.

"...couldn't stand the thought of you going through this alone," Hadley said. "She even tried to call off work, but they needed her."

Rachel. Always with a big heart. And sometimes with a tad too big of a mouth. Darla couldn't decide whether she wanted to strangle her or offer to take her kids for a long weekend. Because now that her friends were here, everything felt a lot better.

"Why didn't you tell us?" Kit asked.

"It's not a big deal. It's not surgery or anything. I can even drive myself home afterward." Minimize, minimize, minimize. Darla just couldn't help herself.

"Um, yes, it *is* a big deal," Hadley said. "Because it's scary. Why would you want to go through something scary without us?"

"Well, you're getting married." Then she pointed to Kit. "And you're pregnant. And let's face it—" she threw her arms up in the air—"breast biopsies are a buzzkill."

"We are your friends through thick and thin," Kit said solemnly.

Hadley nodded. "Stop trying to protect us from things just because you don't want to cause us worry. You're more important than a wedding or a baby announcement or anything else going on."

Darla stabbed the air. "See? I didn't want to make a big deal about this. I just—I just want to get it done and over with."

Hadley hugged her then, and Kit did too. Which made Darla cry even harder. As she wiped her eyes, she said, "I don't even know why I'm crying. It's just a stupid little procedure." But she did know. She was crying for her newfound happiness. And praying that it wouldn't vanish into thin air.

"We love you," Kit whispered. "And we're sorry you have to go through this. But we're going to be right here."

"Every step of the way," Hadley added.

Darla swallowed back tears. "Thank you," she whispered. Now that they were here, it was as if all her emotions had let loose.

"There's just one thing," Hadley said. "Where's Nick?"

Darla tried not to wince.

Kit picked up on that immediately. "Darla, no! You didn't."

Hadley whistled. "I'm assuming not telling him was intentional?"

Darla pressed her lips together tightly.

Kit rummaged through her purse and pulled out her phone. "You can remedy that right now. Here."

Darla shook her head. "I—I'm not ready."

"He loves you," Kit said. "Anyone can see that."

"I don't want to go back to being 'Sick Darla,' if that makes any sense. I want to be 'Normal Darla,' without all these problems."

"Excuse me, Ms. Manning?" A friendly nurse in pink scrubs walked up to them. "I'm going to take you back and help you to get ready for your procedure."

"Okay, honey," Kit said, "good luck. We'll be right here when you're done."

"And we're driving you home," Hadley said. "Whether you can drive yourself or not."

"And if you're very good," Kit added, "we'll even stop at Scoops for a treat."

Darla had to chuckle. As much as she'd done her best to do this on her own, she had to admit she had the best friends—and sister—ever. And as for telling Nick...maybe she wouldn't have to, so she could make their wonderful, happy bubble last as long as possible.

* * *

Three nights later, at a little get-together on the evening before the wedding, Nick raised a glass of beer at the Sand Bar. It was just after dark, and he was sitting with his brother and Alex after all their other friends had gone. "I'd like to toast my brother. You're a great football player. And now you're the ultimate teammate by getting married. You're going to make a great husband and maybe, one day, a great dad."

"To a long marriage and a happy life," Alex said, lifting his glass.

"Thank you," Tony said. "Let's also toast to a healthy baby and mom." After that, Tony said, "We need to toast to you too, Nick. How are things going?"

Nick couldn't help the smile that crossed his face. "I'm going to tell Darla that I'm all-in. Like, committed. I feel in my heart that she is too." He wanted to make it official. He wanted to marry her.

"Wow, that's great," Alex said.

"Yeah, bro," Tony said. "Congratulations. Glad to hear it."

But he had something he wanted to ask his best

friends. "What do you guys think about me…us…doing it again?"

"Getting married again?" Tony clarified.

"I feel like that's where we're headed." He looked at his brother and his best friend. "I'm not seeking reassurance. Just…your blessing." It was important to him that they thought this was a good decision. That they were behind him. Although he was pretty sure they were.

"It seems clear that you two still love each other." Tony smiled. "But if you get married again, I'm afraid I'm going to have to ask for one thing."

Nick frowned. "What's that?"

"I get first dibs on best man."

Alex held up his hands. "I would never stand in the way of blood brothers. As for you and Darla, I think you two are very *simpáticos*."

"You mean like compatible?" Nick asked.

"More than that," Alex said. "Like, meant to be together. Bringing out the best in each other." He grinned. "I'm really happy for you."

They talked a little more. Had a couple of beers. Enjoyed a local band. When they headed back to Darla's to pick up the women, Nick was the first to walk up and onto the deck to find all three of them gathered together, excitedly discussing something. He couldn't help smiling, wondering what the cause was for the huddle. Even Boss, who he'd left with Darla, was sitting at Darla's side as if he were listening too. As Nick got closer, he saw that Darla was pouring over her phone.

"Is it from Dr. Ag?" Hadley asked. "Tell us already!"

"Great news," Darla said, holding up the phone. "My biopsy was negative."

"Amen!" Hadley said. "I'm pouring more wine."

"Wonderful news," Kit said. "But no fair about the wine!"

As the women hugged and cheered, Nick's head started to spin. The sound of his own blood rushed in his ears. Did he hear that right? Surely, he must've misunderstood. Momentarily stunned, he halted his steps, but he couldn't just stand there in the middle of the deck, so he cleared his throat to make his presence known.

Darla was the first to turn her head and spot him, blinking twice, as if she was caught by surprise. If it hadn't been so dark, he'd swear she was blushing. Which made him nervous.

"Hey," he said softly.

"Nick! Hi!" she said a little too excitedly.

Hadley and Kit fell silent, another bad sign.

He gestured behind him. "Hey, we just got back. Tony and Alex told me to let you two know they're waiting in the driveway."

Darla's friends shot her concerned glances, which she fended off with a smile.

"How was it?" Hadley asked Nick.

Nick managed to say something about having a fun night out. Then he and Darla walked the women through the house and said their goodbyes.

Darla closed the door and faced him. She was pressing her lips together. He waited for her to meet his gaze.

"What biopsy?" he asked.

* * *

Darla's stomach tumbled, a wave of nausea hitting her hard. She told herself she was okay. The scare had passed.

All was well. She could spare Nick the stress and make light of the whole situation.

But it wasn't well. *She* wasn't well. The scare had been upsetting and, well, scary.

And even if she'd squeaked past this one, there was sure to be another. And another. A lifetime of scares, the trade-off she must accept for being cancer free.

She opened her mouth to speak, but the sound that came out was tiny and hoarse. She suddenly needed water, so she walked into the kitchen and poured a glass. Boss followed her in and nudged her knee as he often did, knowing that the cabinet with his treats was nearby. She opened it and tossed him one, buying time to collect her thoughts. He dashed with his prize to his bed, where he happily crunched on it. She couldn't meet Nick's eyes, focusing instead on the backsplash, which was also a bad place to look, because he'd made it for her and it was beautiful. He'd done so much for her.

What could she possibly do for him?

Let him go, a voice in her head sounded insistently.

Which made her swallow back tears. Anything but that. It would break her.

Nick was still waiting patiently, but something in his eyes had dimmed. He looked on edge and wary.

She flicked her gaze to him from across the counter and plunged in. "I—I had a mammogram last week as part of the routine screening my oncologist does, and it showed an unusual density. So I got a needle biopsy a few days ago—but it turned out okay."

It sounded so awful, like telling him had been an afterthought. An oh-by-the-way comment dropped to a casual friend, someone not close enough or important enough to be entrusted with that information in real time.

He was the *most* important.

All she'd really wanted was for the wonderful bliss they'd been experiencing not to come to an end.

He stood there, so handsome in his worn gray T-shirt and jeans. And so angry. She could see it in the set of his jaw, which was clenched so tight it was practically vibrating. And in the way he stood so rigidly, as if shielding himself from a blow. And in the hurt in his eyes as he said, "So you had a suspicious finding, and you had to go and get a needle stuck in you, and you told your friends, who support and love you. But I had to find out by accident?"

She tried not to flinch. She deserved his anger.

Darla stood across from him and forced herself to look into his eyes. "Nick, please let me explain."

He tapped his fingers against his jeans. Harsh tapping, indicating beyond a doubt that he was furious. He moved his arm in a big swoop. "Please, be my guest. I'm listening."

Her mind was racing. She wanted to tell him how wonderful the past few weeks had been. So wonderful she'd forgotten all about being different and everything that came along with that.

She opened her mouth to speak, but just then, she saw an image in her head. Of her with the next biopsy. The next abnormal lab. Or, God forbid, the next lump—somewhere. In her thyroid, in her breast, somewhere else. The next cough. The next... whatever.

He'd never leave her. Out of honor. And compassion.

She would always be the weak one, the vulnerable one. The one always taking, not giving. How could she offer him a life like that?

"I—we just got back together, and I didn't want to trouble you with all the commotion before the wedding." She held her breath. Tears pricked at her lids. And her heart cracked in half as she forced the words out of her mouth. "Plus—we—we're just having fun, right?"

He jerked up his head.

Her heart stopped. Was she really going to do this?

It appeared that she was. Inside, the pain cut her in half, threatening to double her over.

Nick's color was high, and he looked stunned. "Having fun? Is that what you think we've been doing?"

She swallowed hard, willing herself not to choke up. "I mean, it's been great for these few weeks, and you'll always be special to me, but it's time to be practical. I mean, I'm leaving soon, and..." Unable to go on, she glanced away.

What was she doing, breaking up with him right before the wedding? Breaking up with him at all?

Better do it now, that inner voice said. He was already angry. Best to cut the ties quick.

"Leaving soon?" His brows shot up in surprise. He raked his hands through his hair and blew out a frustrated breath. "I mean, I guess I assumed you might be rethinking that. You've decided to go?" He scanned her face, searching for evidence of the lies she kept telling, but she steeled herself. Made herself a wall.

Darla was really good at that. That was her superpower.

"You're shutting me out," he said, calling her bluff.

She froze, forcing herself to stay calm. "No, I—I've just been thinking about us. We—we're complete opposites. I'm intense, you're laid-back. You're an early bird, I'm a night owl. I'm always working and—and that's not going to change. Julia called me today, and they want me to sign another contract, isn't that great?" She forced a lilt into her voice that she hoped mimicked excitement. "So between that and moving and teaching…I just don't think we could ever make it long-term."

Darla summoned every ounce of strength she had left to finish the job. She spoke slowly and carefully, delivering the death blow. "We'll always have this amazing chemistry but—but I just don't think the rest is going to work out. I'm sorry, Nick." She was blathering, talking too fast in a chipper voice while inside she was coming apart in a million pieces.

Devastated. She was completely devastated.

He kept examining her like she was under a magnifying glass, as if he could find the crack that would be able to prove that she was lying. But she didn't crack—on the outside, anyway. She held her head up and made her face expressionless, and after a long while, he gave a resigned sigh.

It worked. But she felt physically ill. Her head was buzzing, her stomach was churning, and she felt like she was about to throw up.

"Okay, Darla. Fine." Nick scanned her face, as if looking for something, anything, that would stop this avalanche from crashing down. "If that's the way you want it, that's the way it will be." He walked to the door, pausing with his hand on the knob.

Just make it ten more seconds, she told herself. She braced herself, vowing not to break down until he left.

But he dropped his hand from the knob and turned back to her. "No."

She looked at him in confusion. What was he doing? *She'd* broken up with *him.*

"I'm not going to accept this." He pierced her with his bright blue gaze. "The fact that you have to fight health battles isn't an excuse to not love someone—not to love *me.* You don't get to choose for me—to spare me from whatever you think I need spared from." He threw up his hands in frustration. "I already chose. I love you, Darla, and I want you forever. For a lifetime. So now *you* have to choose. But don't hide behind your cancer."

Good thing her vision was so blurred that she didn't even see him walk out the door. She only heard it close with a final, absolute click.

He'd called her bluff. He'd somehow known that this was about the cancer and then he'd acted just as she'd thought—he would never abandon her. But he had no idea what he was signing up for. It was better to spare him that and let him find a normal life.

Darla walked to the front door, listening to the finality of his footsteps as they clattered down the stairs. She leaned her back against the door and slid down until her butt was on the floor. Boss ran up and joined her, certain it was a fun game. "I'm so sorry, Nick," she whispered, choking on her tears.

Nick had been so distraught that he'd forgotten his dog. Boss, perhaps figuring out something was wrong, whimpered and put his head on her thigh. "You're a sweet boy," she said, doing her best to stop crying. "And I love you. But I just screwed that up pretty bad, didn't I?"

Just then her phone went off with a text. It was Mac's mom. Hi Darla, just wanted you to know Mackenzie's just been admitted with a fever. Will keep you posted. Appreciate prayers. xo

Darla lowered her head to her knees. A fever to a cancer patient—especially one whose immune system was weakened by chemotherapy—was terrifying.

Once, Darla had been in the hospital for a week for an infection that had entered her blood through her chemo port. And it had been scary.

She thought of beautiful, vibrant Mackenzie with her entire life ahead of her. Even as she prayed, she started to cry all over again.

This situation should have proved her logic. That life with or after cancer was a rollercoaster, and she was right to go this alone.

But as she buried her face in Boss's fur and cried, she only wanted one thing.

Nick.

Chapter 24

IT WAS ALMOST eleven at night when Nick knocked on Darla's mom's door. It was too late and showing up like this certainly wouldn't help to get him into her good graces, but he was beyond trying to do that. He needed her now for a different reason, for something only she could help him with. And he prayed that she wouldn't turn him away.

When Tricia answered, she was still wearing her nursing uniform. Immediately, she crossed her arms and narrowed her eyes.

"Hi, Tricia," he said as cordially as he could muster.

Her look was half concern and half surprise. He ran his fingers through his hair, which confirmed his suspicions—his hair was a wild mess like the rest of him.

"Hi, Nick," she said cautiously. "Is Darla all right?"

"She's fine."

She clutched her chest, relief evident. That drove home

that she loved her daughter. And also that Darla's health would be a concern for everyone who did.

Rubbing his neck, he thought it was time that they both made a step toward peace. "I came to talk, person-to-person. Do you have a few minutes?" He paused. Yep, surprise was definitely winning out over the initial shock of finding him at her front door. "It's important."

When she reached for the door, part of him expected her to close it. Instead, she held it open. "Come on in," she said, her expression wary.

Tricia used the remote to turn off her television, sat down on her yellow floral couch, and offered him a seat. He sat down on the edge of a chair, questioning his sanity, not to mention he was having flashbacks of being a teenager again, picking Darla up for a date.

Nick cast a nervous glance around. Paintings of flowers lined the walls. There was one of two little girls holding hands at the seashore, clearly a little Darla and a little Rachel. Tons of photographs of Darla, Rachel, Greg, and Tricia's grandkids lined the shelves and covered the top of an old piano against one wall. It appeared that was more like Darla than he realized. She surrounded herself with soft, emotional things that were in discord with her tough exterior. That meant she had to have a soft spot, didn't it?

He didn't know if he'd ever break through that tough outer shell, but he had to try. He had to understand what he was up against with Darla. Who better to ask about putting up walls than the person Darla probably learned that skill from?

"It's late," Tricia said, glancing at her watch, "and I have to be at work at six thirty in the morning, so whatever you came to say, you'd better say it fast."

Maybe Darla had pushed him away because she really didn't see a future with him. Maybe she'd meant every word. They *were* opposites. They both worked a lot. She *was* leaving.

The old Nick would have believed every word and backed down.

But the new Nick wasn't leaving this time until he had answers, whatever those answers might be.

Okay, *here goes.* All he had was sincerity, the wish to speak to Tricia directly from his heart. That gave him the courage to continue.

He took a big breath. "You were wrong about me, Tricia. For the most part." She started to protest, but he held up a hand. "Please, hear me out. When Darla and I were young, I was disgruntled with my lot in life. My future at the company was predetermined. I was jealous that she got to pursue her dream, and I didn't, and I took my unhappiness out on her. And when the divorce papers came, I was angry, and I let her go ahead with it. I didn't fight for her. I just signed them and said, *Fine, we're done.* But I should have fought."

Tricia's eyes widened, and he wasn't sure how to take that, but he went on. "Not fighting for her is the deepest regret of my life. Even after we were divorced, I kept finding ways to be near her, to do things for her—and I understand now it was because I never gave up wishing that we would connect again."

His feelings were the only thing that felt right, even when everything else was so wrong. Even though Darla herself told him that they were just for fun.

Something in Tricia's eyes softened the slightest bit. "Okay, Nick, I accept that you've matured. But why are you telling this to me and not my daughter?"

Nick hadn't expected this to be easy or for Tricia to cut him any slack. He just kept talking from his heart. "I found out about the biopsy, and I got upset. She said she didn't tell me because we were just keeping things light and that she'd be leaving soon anyway. But I don't believe her. That's why I came to see you."

She frowned, and her face went rigid. He knew he shouldn't have come. The romantic side of him was spinning unicorns and fairies instead of facing the cold, hard truth.

Tricia suddenly sat forward, her expression morphing into shock and worry. "What biopsy?"

Oh no. He had to admit that part of him felt relieved that she wasn't angry at him. "Darla didn't tell you?" She didn't even tell her *mom*?

"Nick, I—no." She ran a hand over her forehead. "She didn't say a thing."

"It was negative, and everything's okay." He hurriedly got that out of the way. "It was because of something on a mammogram. Apparently, she got it done a few days ago."

Tricia, who'd gone as pale as her white walls, clutched her chest. "Dear God."

He gave a wry smile. "Somehow, I don't feel quite as bad knowing she didn't tell you either."

Tricia rose from the couch and paced back and forth. She used her hands exactly like Darla did when she got excited. "She thinks she can carry all of this on her shoulders alone, and I don't know why. Actually, yes, in fact, I do." She flicked her gaze onto Nick, and he saw solidarity. Well, maybe a little, tiny bit of it. At least he hoped he did.

This is what he'd come for. To see if there was some way he could break through to Darla. To make her understand that nothing mattered to him except for being with her. "If you have a reason, I'd love to hear it."

This time, he wasn't giving up. He'd show Tricia, and more importantly, he'd show himself.

Tricia wrung her hands nervously. "When Rick and I divorced, he moved to Texas with his girlfriend. And he made lots of promises to the girls that he didn't keep. Oh, at first there were calls and presents, but after a bit, all that stopped. He even stopped picking up their calls, can you believe that?"

"Darla and I have a lot in common," Nick said. "We both have one very strong parent to make up for a very weak parent."

She sighed. "After Rick left, I tried not to show the girls how desperate I was—about money, about suddenly being left to manage everything on my own. I was overwhelmed. I didn't even have a job. I started out as a nursing assistant and worked my way through nursing school, did you know that?"

He shook his head. Tricia had worked in the ICU for as long as he remembered.

"I'm the queen of toughing it out. I didn't intend to pass the bad parts of that trait along, but Darla stopped trusting people early on. She learned very well how to face the world with a tough exterior no matter what was going on inside."

"I would never hurt her like that," Nick said. "These last few weeks have been—"

Tricia held up a hand. "Please let me finish. I think what happened back then made her resolve never to be dependent on anyone. To rely on herself."

Nick tented his fingers and tapped them together. "She's strong and independent." Those were the things that he loved about her.

"Yes, she is. But her cancer experience has sometimes made her dependent on other people out of necessity. I think she worries that she may have to face a health crisis again one day that might put her in the same situation."

He absorbed that for a moment. "If that's true, then she's shutting me out for my own good." Not because she didn't care. But, in her own way, because she cared too much. That was really messed up. But he got it. It was classic Darla. Giving, but never wanting to take. "In a weird way, it makes sense."

"You'll have to discuss it with her." Worry overtook Tricia's face. "You know, I stressed independence to my daughters. I never wanted them to get stuck in the same situation that I got stuck in. But maybe I went too far."

In that moment, Nick saw Tricia for who she was— a good mom, who'd done the best she could. Who maybe hadn't been perfect, but, unlike his own mother, had been there. "You've raised an amazing daughter," Nick said. "No matter what happens, I hope you and I can start again on a better foot."

Tricia swiped quickly at her eyes. "It's not good for Darla to think that she has to be alone. After all she's been through, she deserves the best." She spoke with passion, with love for her daughter, and of course, not without admonishment for him. "Someone who loves her and understands her. Who lets her be her best self, and who doesn't give her grief. Or give up on her."

Yikes. He was hoping he'd made some progress with her, but maybe not.

"I don't ever want Darla to face anything alone because I love her," he said. "I just need to get through to your stubborn daughter."

Tricia suddenly burst out with laughter. "She *is* stubborn, isn't she?"

She said it like she was proud. He almost said, *Like mother, like daughter,* but that would only buy him the doghouse. As he got up to leave, he realized that he hadn't gotten much reassurance, but at least he'd gotten some insight.

"Nick, I'm laughing because you finally told me you love her." She looked at him thoughtfully as she got up from the couch. "I believe you."

He looked her in the eye. "I'm not going to give up this time, Tricia."

"Wait," she said. "Please don't go yet." He must have looked confused or flat-out shocked at her invite. "Have a seat."

Stunned, he sat. She sat down next to him and placed her hand on his arm. "I have something to say that's been on my mind for a long time." Nick tried to prepare himself for anything. "I'm sorry I kept you away when Darla was going through chemo. I didn't want her to be upset, and she was so weak...but that was a decision I had no right to make. I was just so angry with you for putting her through all that heartache. And I felt like you'd tried to squelch her dreams." She fidgeted her fingers in her lap. "I suppose I felt that my ex did that to me, and I swore I'd never let it happen to my daughters."

"I couldn't be prouder of her accomplishments," he said firmly.

She heaved a shaky breath. "I know."

Inwardly, he released a breath too. Because she'd just apologized, and he knew that hadn't been easy. "I accept your apology." He paused. "So we're good?"

She nodded. She was crying.

That wouldn't do. He decided to try and lighten the mood. "I'm just not sure I can get used to calling you *Tricia*."

"Well," she said, "my full name is Patricia. That would be really formal, wouldn't it?"

He lifted a brow. "Maybe one day we'll work up to *Mom*."

She let out a hearty laugh. "You're all right, Nicholas," she said, wiping her tears. Then she gave him the first real hug he'd ever gotten from her.

* * *

The next morning, dawn light finally illuminated Darla's bedroom, giving her some relief that the horrible night was over with its attendant curses of tossing, turning, and not sleeping a wink. Telling herself breaking it off with Nick had been for the best wasn't working. She was still reeling from the hurt she'd caused him and the terrible things she'd said.

In addition to Darla's personal problems, Mackenzie's

condition was critical, and she had been admitted straight to the intensive care unit. Michelle had thanked Darla for her concern and asked for her prayers. She'd also asked her to please not come rushing to the hospital but to check in again in the morning. Darla vowed to text her as soon as it was a reasonable hour.

The big house was so quiet that she could hear the refrigerator humming, something she'd never noticed before.

Nick had come back for Boss, so as she got out of bed, no giant dog came bounding forward to offer her a giant dose of love to help her get through the day.

There was no Boss. And there was no Nick.

Darla forced down two cups of coffee, even though it tasted like sand. When she'd finally caffeinated herself into being awake, she grabbed her laptop and took it into her beautiful, untouched, un-lived-in office. And sat down for the first time at her shiny new desk.

Her too-clean desk, her un-tread-upon carpet, her plant shelves devoid of plants.

Signs of someone holding their breath. Make that someone *afraid* to breathe.

The first thing she did was open her laptop and dump an entire folder of papers over the wooden surface. She purposely mixed them up even more and sat back to examine the mini mess.

There. Now it looked like someone actually lived here. If only she could fix her life so easily.

Darla looked over her manuscript and let the hard truth wash over her. Today was deadline day, and she'd failed to fix it. She'd run out of time. And now that she was being honest, she wasn't going to, either. She understood now that a big part of her problem was that she hadn't wanted to change the story. She didn't want to turn it into a thriller. There was truth and heart in it as it was, but she hadn't delivered what she'd promised, what she was contracted to do.

But for the first time in her career, her looming deadline wasn't her most pressing problem. Nick was. She'd lied to the one man she cared the most about, the only man who would have her heart, who'd been nothing but good and kind and understanding.

And on top of all that, it was Hadley's wedding day. In a few hours, she was due to show up at Hadley's grandmother's house, where they were dressing and getting their hair and makeup done.

Hadley deserved to have the best day. The happiest day, with all of them fully celebrating with her. And not to have to worry about Darla's problems at all.

That made Darla hate what she'd done even more.

Amelia's ring, bulky as it was, knocked against her desk, reminding her of its heft. She took it off and stared at it. "You've been nothing but trouble since I put you on. My book is a train wreck and so is my life. You are no. Help. At. All." She tossed the ring onto her desk where it landed with a clatter among her scattered papers.

She walked over to the window and looked out at the ocean, always constant, always doing its job of bringing in those waves one at a time, 24-7.

She wanted a full life with a man who loved her with all his heart. But she wanted it as an equal partner. Not as someone who would always have to be looked after, watched over, taken care of, worried about.

Nick deserved better.

And she had no answers at all.

* * *

"Good morning," Darla said when she showed up in the ICU waiting room later that morning. She was terrified and hopeful, wanting to bring breakfast food, but what if no one wanted to eat? She finally decided to play it safe with coffee, showing up with a trayful of the good stuff from Coffee by the Sea.

Mackenzie's parents sat side by side on a couch, looking over an open newspaper that rested on a coffee table. It was a sweet scene, the two of them holding hands, Michelle looking over the left page and Jason the right.

It gave her heart a pang, seeing this couple who had weathered so much in a simple display of togetherness and love. Their quiet air of relaxed casualness also made hope stir in her chest.

"I brought coffee," she offered, holding up the carrier. The bulky shopping bag she was carrying knocked against her legs. They both looked up and smiled as she set the coffee down and leaned the bag against a nearby chair.

"Oh. Darla," Michelle said, rising to hug her. "Thank you."

"Real coffee sounds amazing," Jason said. "Not to criticize the trusty vending machine, but, you know..."

"Fresh-brewed coffee sounds like just what we need," Michelle agreed. "She's out of the unit, you know that, right?"

"Oh, hooray." Darla pressed her chest and exhaled a

sigh of relief. "Wonderful news." She gestured toward the bag. "I brought Mac a little something. For when she's up to it." She didn't want to be pushy. She just wanted Mac's family to know she was here.

"You might just have to deliver it yourself," Michelle said with a smile.

"Deliver it my—"

Jason nodded. "She woke up at 4:00 a.m. and asked her nurse for a Coke. We've been in there once already. But she's sleeping now."

Michelle nodded. "Weak and tired, but okay. The doctor said the antibiotics kicked in, and she's out of danger."

"Great news." Darla clasped her hands together. At least one thing was looking up.

An older nurse with dark hair pulled back in a bun appeared at the doorway. It was Roberta León from the infusion center, who was apparently covering a shift in the ICU. "Hello, Michelle and Jason. And hi, Darla. Mackenzie says she wants company and breakfast. And it had better be good company because we're going slow, bland, and mushy on the breakfast for now."

Michelle turned to Darla. "Why don't you go in? We're going to be here all day."

Roberta gave a nod. "Ten-minute visits for now."

Darla grabbed her shopping bag and followed Roberta to Mac's room in the step-down area. Monitors beeped and buzzed, and equipment on wheels rumbled down the shiny floors. When Darla entered Mac's room, she almost didn't see her among all the equipment and IV bags, which contained more LED lights than a Christmas tree. Mac lay half propped up on a pillow, fingers with glittery purple nail polish folded over the sheet. She looked pale and small with dark circles under her eyes, but she lit up when Darla walked in. "I'm so bored," she said. "They won't let me watch TV. Or feed me." She snuck a look at her nurse and then glanced back at Darla and grinned.

"TV after breakfast," Roberta said.

"You call green Jello-O breakfast?" Mac groused. "I hate green Jell-O. I like orange."

"Ha." Darla thought briefly of the whipped-cream-and-Jell-O dress she'd be wearing later today. But that brought other thoughts she forced herself to push away.

"I don't even remember coming into the unit," Mackenzie said.

Roberta did something to her IV tubing. "You slept all night." She sent Darla a wink. "It was so wonderful. A whole night without catching any of your sass."

"Well, guess what, Roberta. I'm ba-ack." Mac turned to Darla. "Like that guy in *The Boneyard* who sort of came back from the dead. He was super creepy." Mac looked at her nurse. "Do you read Darla's books? They're really scary. I love them!"

"I read romances," Roberta said. "I like the happy endings."

"I do too," Darla said a little too quickly.

Roberta looked up and frowned. "Then, girl, why do you write that scary stuff?"

Darla shrugged. "Writing about people getting justice against evil made me feel that I could conquer the bad guy." It suddenly occurred to her that maybe she didn't need to do that anymore. Maybe she didn't always need to be on the defensive, ready to fight the fight.

"I'm going to conquer the bad guy," Mac said. "You watch me." She smiled at Roberta. "Looks like I get to terrorize you another day."

"Lucky me," Roberta said with a smile.

Lucky all of us, Darla thought.

Darla lifted the shopping bag. "Do you feel strong enough to open your present now?"

Mac nodded enthusiastically, peeking in as soon as Darla set the bag on her lap. "What a pretty box."

Roberta stopped and looked as Darla lifted it out. The angels' wings and gowns were lined with sparkly gold that caught the light.

"Beautiful." She glanced up at Darla. "Is that vintage?"

"Yes," Darla said, "it's one of a kind, but the box is not the present. There's actually stuff inside."

"It's so pretty." Mac gestured for Darla to do the honors.

Darla pulled out fluffy white slippers with bunny ears that she put on Mac's feet. Mac immediately began wiggling her toes so the bunny noses twitched. Darla tilted the box so Mac could easily take out the lemon-scented soap and lotion. A journal. A couple of fun pens. A coloring book with inspirational sayings. And a book from another thriller writer Darla knew. And finally, a couple more random headscarves Darla had found in her closet.

"Thank you, Darla," Mac lifted her arms for a hug. "I love everything. But can I ask you something?"

"Sure," Darla said, hugging her back. "What is it?"

"My mom and dad look exhausted. Are they okay?"

Darla knew there was a reason that she loved this kid. "They're so happy you're okay. They're going to be fine."

"I decided to do what you said," Mac held the scarf to

her head like a warrior band. Roberta helped her tie it, draping the ends over her shoulder.

"Make yourself look scary?" Darla couldn't resist saying.

"I'm nurturing my inner rebel. And I'm taking everyone's help. And I'm going to get through this. Just like you did. I'm going to use all my strength to get well. Thanks for the fun stuff."

Mac was back. As sassy and determined as ever. Thank God.

Chapter 25

DARLA TOOK THE elevator down to the first floor of the hospital, to a peaceful atrium that she often used to visit during her stays here. This early on a Saturday morning, it was empty of people. She sat under the skylight, where the sun washed down on the vertical waterfall and surrounding tropical plants.

Mac was going to make it.

Relief felt like the water tumbling down the wall and splashing into the little pool.

Just let it go, she thought, wishing she could let her troubles tumble down and wash away too.

Darla let out a big breath. Despite all the sadness and confusion she was feeling, she felt so, so grateful.

She wanted everything for Mackenzie. She wanted her to go to college, make wonderful friends, change the world. Maybe even fall in love.

She truly believed that Mac would do all of those things.

She *knew* it.

When you loved someone, you wanted the best for them. You knew how much they had ahead of them to embrace. To not miss a single second of.

She'd gotten the gift of a second chance too, not just with the cancer but also with Nick.

But she was wasting so much time and energy worrying about battles she might or might not have to fight. She wasn't living in the here and now, but rather with fear hanging over her head, hovering like a giant anvil ready to drop. With a big, held breath, afraid to let it go. So when love came for her, no wonder she pushed it away.

She wouldn't want Mackenzie to be afraid to live her life. She wanted her to experience every single moment life had to offer.

Why would Darla wish anything different for herself?

She dropped her head into her hands as the logic of her own thinking hit her hard.

No one had their life wrapped up in a pretty bow and handed to them with promises that nothing bad was ever going to happen. The trick was to live despite knowing that nothing was ever going to be perfect.

"There you are," someone said. Darla looked up to see Roberta standing by the fountain, her arms crossed.

"Did I rile Mackenzie up too much?" Darla asked, thinking she might be a little irritated at her. "I'm sorry if I did."

"I love to see her riled up. But I'm a little concerned about you. Sitting here watching the waterfall when you could be out doing something a lot more fun."

"Just taking a moment."

"I recognized that box, you know. It's very unique."

"Those boxes helped me through my chemo," Darla said. "That's why I saved them all."

"Nick used to drop them off in my office days ahead of time," Roberta said. "He made me mark the date you were coming in for chemo on my calendar. And he'd call me afterward every single time to make sure you got it."

Darla sat up on the bench and blinked. "Wait—the boxes came from Nick?" From *Nick*?

"Oh my goodness, I'm sorry. He made me promise not to tell anyone."

Nick.

Of course, Nick.

"It's okay. At the time, we were barely speaking." The wounds from the divorce were still deep. But he'd found a way to love her even when she'd pushed him away. When she wouldn't allow him to express it.

She closed her eyes and swallowed hard as the truth finally sank in. So much of what he did for her was like that. From ordering tile that she loved to something simple like stocking her fridge when she first came home, to being there in every single way.

Until he'd finally had enough of her shutting him out.

Darla had told Mac that there was so much ahead of her to embrace. To not miss a single second of life. Yet she herself had wasted so much precious time. She'd closed herself off instead of opening her life to all the love and joy she could fill herself with.

She had to stop that.

She had to tell Nick how she felt. And tell him that one

day at a time wasn't enough. That if he'd have her, she was in it for forever.

* * *

Later that morning, Darla found herself once again at the door of her office, looking in. She took a breath and took a seat in the desk chair that was so brand-new it squeaked. For the conversation she was about to have, she was going to have to be an adult. In an adult space. One that she was going to stop being afraid of inhabiting.

She'd put her life on hold in so many ways. Maybe that was why she'd written such a strange book. Her soul just couldn't live on hold anymore.

Darla was about to push Julia's number on her phone when her doorbell rang. Her heart gave a jolt as she ran to open it, hoping beyond hope to see Nick, maybe just as distraught as she was.

She never expected to find Lauren, Nick's old girlfriend, standing there, looking uncomfortable. Her wild writers' imagination kicked into full gear, imagining Lauren telling her that Nick had left her, and that she and Nick were together again.

Before Darla's imagination really let loose, Lauren spoke. "I heard you stopped by the library," she said. "And, um—Michelle called me about a possible source. For stuff about your ancestor." She handed her a manila envelope. "We found it."

Darla was floored. Not so much because everyone had worked together to find information for her but because Lauren, of all people, had hand-delivered it. Lauren, who had barely spoken to her since she'd broken up with Nick. "Oh. You didn't have to come all the way over here. I could have—"

Lauren gave a little shrug. "I wanted to. Because it's exciting." She shifted her weight from foot to foot. "Your ancestor did a lot for our community." She cleared her throat. "For women too."

There was an awkward pause. "Would you like to come in?" Darla offered. "Have some coffee, maybe?"

Was she actually asking Nick's ex-girlfriend to come in for coffee?

Lauren shook her head, her pretty blond hair falling gracefully around her shoulders, perfectly in place. "Darla, I just wanted to say good luck with Nick. He's—um—a great guy. And—and I wish you all the best."

Whoa. That had been really brave. And nice. "Thank you," Darla said with sincerity. "Not just for the information. For coming over. It means a lot."

"Yeah, well, I gotta go." Lauren gave an awkward smile. "You're welcome." Then she headed quickly back down the stairs.

Darla closed the door. Her head still spinning, she tore open the envelope and pulled out a copied newspaper article. The title read "Old Kepler House Becomes Bloom House." *Bloom House?* It contained a photograph of women in early twentieth-century clothing sitting around a fireplace. The caption underneath read that they were knitting for charity, and it talked about many other community projects the women were involved in. Which proved what she already knew, that Amelia was incredible.

Next was a wedding photo. The woman had blond

curly hair much like hers, and it was piled up in a loose bun like the style of the time. She wore a long, lacy dress with a veil, and held a bouquet of roses. Next to her stood a dark-haired man with a mustache and a three-piece suit with a watch chain across his vest. Darla immediately noticed that she was wearing the ring. But on her right hand. On her left was a simple band. The caption read "Amelia Manning and Samuel T. Manning, married August 17, 1895."

The couple was very stark and serious, standing rigidly next to one another. If Darla was looking for reassurance that Amelia had a found a fairy-tale ending, this photo was not helping.

"Okay, Amelia," she said to the photo, "your hubby is cute, minus the giant mustache, but you don't have any magical answers for me, do you?" Not that seeing Amelia's happiness would guarantee Darla's, but for some reason she very badly wanted to believe that Amelia had had a great life.

Shaking off her thoughts, she sat down and focused on punching in Julia's number.

"What's wrong?" Julia said. "You never call. The last time, it was to tell me not to worry because you'd already plotted out the last two books in your contract and were turning them in earlier."

"This is a different kind of call." Darla gripped on to her phone for support. "I wanted you to know I've been dealing with some issues that are impacting my manuscript delivery."

"For *Stalker X*?" Julia asked, as if she hadn't heard right. "Are you okay?"

"I'm fine." Kudos to Julia, the best agent in the world, for caring about her first before the book. "But I—I'm not going to make the date."

"Oh." Dead silence filled the phone line.

Darla heard dismay and disappointment. Two things she'd always been determined to avoid. "I recently came back to my hometown to sell my house, but I ended up getting back together with my ex-husband."

"Oh." More ominous silence.

Darla barreled on. "One of my best friends suddenly decided to get married while I was home. And then I had a health scare. But then I got frightened and pushed my ex away, and I lost him. And…and I met a young cancer patient who loves my books, and she's amazing, but she ended up in the hospital and nearly died. But she's okay now, and she made me finally realize that I have to live my life differently." Darla took a deep breath. "And…there's one more thing."

"Darla, are you sure you're okay?" Julia blew out a *whew*. "Because that's *a lot.*"

"The final thing is that I didn't write the book I was supposed to write."

"Did you…did you write anything?" Julia asked.

"See, my ancestor had this ring, and I asked the ring to send me a book plot about a mysterious man. And sure enough, I came up with one. But he's not a killer or a stalker. He's…a romantic hero." She blew out a breath, grateful to finally have it out. "I wrote a book about two people who love each other but who screwed up."

"I'm not sure I'm following. You wrote a romance?"

"Yes. And then I realized that I've been terrified to let

myself be happy because I believed everything could be taken away in a heartbeat. And that's why I pushed Nick away. The only mystery is why I ever let him go in the first place."

Her voice cracked, and she started crying. "My best friend is getting married today and I…I have to tell you that if you want to see the book I wrote, I'll send it to you right now. But it's not anything like what the publisher wants. It's almost done, but it's missing an ending. I'm so sorry." She took a breath. "I also need you to know that I'm going to take six months off before I even think about signing another contract. And if I do, it's not going to be for a thriller. And…and that's about it."

"Wow," Julia said. "No more thrillers?"

"I want to explore…feelings. Emotions. Love. Because…because that's all that's important. And so is taking a little time off to enjoy life."

The line was silent for so long that Darla started to panic. "Are you still there?"

"Ha. Yes, I'm here. Frankly," Julia said, "I'm amazed it's taken you this long to need a break. Are you sure you're all right?"

"Yes. Physically, anyway. Except I may have lost the man I love for good. But I've come to realize that success is having people who love you. And who you love back. Because if you don't make time for that, you don't have anything."

"Darla," Julia said.

"I'm sorry about the book," Darla rushed to say. "I really tried to write the book they wanted. I just…couldn't. And I'm sorry I didn't tell you this a long time ago. I kept thinking that, with determination, I could dig myself out of the hole."

"Darla," Julia said again.

"Yes?"

"Please just send me the book you wrote," Julia said in a calm, professional tone. "I don't care if there's no ending."

"Okay."

"And take your time off. I'll tell Crime Scene. Okay?"

"Okay," Darla managed. Julia would look at the book. She was okay with Darla taking some time. The sky hadn't fallen when Darla asked for what she needed.

"I might be able to suggest a tenth-anniversary reissue of your first novel." Julia was already brainstorming, what she did best. "The one they're making into a movie. And you won't catch me saying this again because I've heard every excuse in the book from authors who are late with their books, but it's nice to know you're human."

Darla couldn't suppress a chuckle. Yes. Imperfectly, definitely human. With a life she'd finally chosen over her work.

* * *

Going to the hospital and calling Julia had put Darla way behind to join everyone at Hadley's grandmother's for lunch, hair, makeup, and mimosas. Yeah. She could definitely use one of those.

She hesitated in the driveway, trying to catch her breath and not look rushed, panicked, and stricken. Maybe she should call Nick? But how could she have such a serious discussion by phone? Would he even want to talk?

Should she text a, Could we talk later? in the middle of the wedding morning golf game the guys were playing? She honestly didn't know what to do.

But she did know that it was Hadley's wedding day, and Darla was going to make certain that the bride had no worries. She'd do her best to be fully present for her friend on this very important day.

On impulse, she decided to send the text. As she opened the back door of her car to grab her dress from the back seat, she dug in her purse for her phone to find it gone.

Ugh. She'd left it on her desk after her call to Julia.

"There you are." Kit motioned from the door. "Hurry up!"

As Darla rushed to join everyone, she had the feeling that once she walked through that door, happy wedding chaos was going to ensue, and she was determined to do her best to meet the challenge.

Sure enough, inside it *was* chaos, but not exactly happy. Hadley, who was normally cool as a cucumber, stood in the center of the tiny living room wearing her beautiful dress. Darla gasped, seeing her in the dress, making the reality of this day hit her full force. Hadley looked lovely. But she also looked rushed and panicked. She was surrounded by her grandmother, her mom, Kit, and Tony and Nick's sister Lucy, and they were all staring at her train with stricken faces. Darla set down her dress bag and her travel bag with her shoes and cosmetics. "What's wrong?"

She waved at Lucy, who'd just arrived from cooking school in upstate New York. Her dark hair was in a ponytail, and she was wearing a T-shirt that read CULINARY INSTITUTE OF AMERICA. Darla was struck by how much her big brown eyes were so much like Nick's. She greeted her with a quick hug as Hadley gathered up her dress and spread out the hem.

"Look what happened." She pointed to an approximately three-inch tear. "I tried the dress on one last time with another pair of shoes that I thought might be better, and I got my foot caught in the train."

Darla caught Hadley's distressed gaze. Poor Hadley.

"Gran, can you sew it?" Hadley asked.

Hadley's grandmother was sitting on the sofa and had already begun to assess the damage. "I just had my cataract done two weeks ago, and my vision is still a little shaky. How about you do it, Kit, and I'll coach you through it?" Kit was really good at any craft involving a needle, but her face had taken on that greenish tinge again.

"Do you need to sit down?" Darla asked.

Kit shook her head. "I'm fine," she said, a little shakily, but then she suddenly turned and headed to the bathroom.

"Oh my," Gran said. "This is so exciting! A wedding, a baby…Liz, how about you come and sew it?" she said to Hadley's mom.

Hadley's mom smiled and held up her hands. "Thanks, Mom, but you know that sewing needles and I don't get along."

Hadley's gran next fixed her gaze on Darla. "I think that Darla has the nerves of steel that we need right now."

Ha. That could not be further from the truth.

But as Darla said cheerily, "Okay, Mrs. Edwards, teach away!" and Hadley's gran ran to get her sewing kit, she hugged Hadley. "Don't worry," she said in the most reassuring voice she could muster, "We've got this."

Hadley burst into tears. "Thank you. Look, I can't wait

to get married. But there is just *so much going on right now.*" She dropped her voice to a whisper. "I feel that this whole wedding is cursed."

"No. You're not going there," Darla said firmly. "Once you see Nick—"

Oh no. Did she just say that? She rubbed her forehead and forced a chuckle. "I mean *Tony.*" But all she could really think of was Nick. "Once you see him," she hurried on to say, "all this other stuff will fade away. You work on being a beautiful bride, and let us take care of everything else, okay?"

Kit, who'd just returned from the bathroom, handed Hadley a mimosa. As Darla got to work threading a needle and listening to advice from Gran about how to make the stitches invisible, she forced herself to have a steady hand. She focused hard on each tiny stitch, praying that she had an opportunity to get to Nick. And that when she did, it wasn't too late.

* * *

"Are you sure you're more capable of tying this than I am?" Tony asked.

"Just hold still." It was later that afternoon, and Nick was alone with his brother in the same bedroom where he'd slept that first night at Darla's. Alex had gone to check on the setup outside.

As Nick struggled to tie his brother's bow tie, he found himself sweating. And shaking. And he felt like he was holding a greased pig for all he could make the loops of the bow tie actually . . . tie.

He had to stop and mop his forehead with a tissue. And he hadn't even put his jacket on yet.

"What's wrong with you?" Tony finally said in a tone that only a brother would use.

"Nothing's wrong." There was no point in getting into it today, even though Nick had never expected to feel so wrecked on such a happy day. "I just want this to look perfect."

Tony snorted. "What happened with Darla?"

"Nothing," he said flatly, finally making a bow. But it was lopsided, and he had to pull it out. Again.

His brother eyed him up close and personal as Nick went at it again. "Hadley told me about the biopsy."

Nick dropped his hands from the tie and stepped back. "Well, why didn't you tell me you knew about that?" he said in not the nicest way.

His brother pinned him with his gaze. "Because I like watching you suffer? No, I was just waiting for you to bring it up."

Nick glanced at his watch. "Well, you're getting married in half an hour. It's not a good time to discuss it."

Tony shrugged. Nick felt as though he was the one acting like a nervous groom, while his brother was as calm as the sea on a perfect summer day. "Sure it is."

"This day isn't about me." Nick knew that if he started to say what was wrong, he wouldn't be able to stop. And he wasn't about to ruin the amazing day his brother had waited so long to have.

Tony stepped back and placed his hands on Nick's shoulders, a move that gutted him. "Bro, I can't be happy unless you're happy, don't you know that by now? It's called family, right?"

"She broke up with me." Nick winced because he'd only managed to hold that in for two minutes. "I promise my feelings won't impact my job as your best man."

Tony rolled his eyes. Then he gently guided Nick to a couple of chairs and made him sit down. Even got him a bottle of water. "Darla broke up with you?"

"She said something about us being fine for a summer thing, but that we just wouldn't cut it long-term. And she's decided to go back to California."

Nick thought hard about the look on Darla's face as she said the words that devastated him. He'd tried to call her bluff because it seemed to be the pained look of a person who was hurting on the inside herself, but what if she'd been serious? "The thing is, I thought I knew how she feels. I saw it. I *felt* it." He started to drag his fingers through his hair but then remembered he shouldn't be doing that before the wedding. "I think she's lying."

Tony crossed his arms. "Why would Darla lie to you after all that you two have been through?"

"Because she's afraid of the future. Because she doesn't want to put me through all the things she's going to have to go through to monitor her health." It fit exactly with what Tricia had told him, and it fit with everything he knew about Darla—her stubbornness, her independence, and her selflessness.

He bent over, tapping his fingertips together. "I don't know. Maybe I'm just stunned. Maybe she means it, and I just can't wrap my head around it. She shut me out, and I don't know what to do."

"Did you tell her you love her?" his brother asked.

Nick raised a careful brow. "Not in a good way. In an I'm-leaving-out-the-door way."

"Look," Tony said gently, "I'm not sure how you convince her that none of that health stuff matters. It clearly matters to her, even if she does love you."

"I can't strong-arm her."

"No, you're right. You can't."

Tony gave a half smile. "But you can do what you do best. You're the romantic. Figure out a way to tell her so that she understands you have no choice but to love her for all eternity, so she might as well accept that and be happy."

It was Nick's turn to roll his eyes. "How on earth am I supposed to do that in the middle of your wedding?"

"What's going on in here?" a voice said from the door.

Their dad stood in the doorway. Maybe it was seeing him in a tux that made Nick view him for a flash not as his dad but as a handsome guy with his almost-white hair, tanned skin, and an athletic build. Alex was at his side, looking a little edgy. Gesturing outside, Alex said, "I'll go and make sure everyone's got a program…"

"No, you won't," Nick's dad said, wrapping an arm around his shoulder. "You're family too." He turned to his sons. "Don't you both look sharp?" He patted Tony on the cheek. "You don't look nervous at all."

Then he turned to Nick. "But you looked better that time you had the stomach flu." He shook his head. "I heard you two talking. Did you tell Darla that you love her?"

Why was everyone asking him that? "Not well enough."

"So do it better next time. Darla's a gem."

"Exactly," Tony said. "I told him he needs to tell her how he feels."

"That's always a good idea." His dad spotted Tony's untied tie and started to work on it. "By the way," he said over his shoulder, "I'm giving you my notice."

Did Nick hear that right? Of all times. "Dad, why are you bringing this up now?"

"Because I'm ready now to give retirement a chance. And you," he said to Tony as he tied his tie, "I'm proud of you too. Wait till you hear my speech. There won't be a dry eye in the house."

Nick caught Tony's anxious expression. Why should he get off scot-free? "You know, Dad, it's okay to make it short and simple. You don't have to strive for drama or anything."

His dad sounded resolved and confident. "Everyone likes a little bit of drama, don't you think?"

The retirement thing stunned Nick. But the fact that the wedding ceremony was fifteen minutes away gave him no time to think about it. Or to help out his brother, who was clearly worried his dad was going to turn his wedding ceremony into a dramatic reading.

Their dad turned to Alex. "And I'm proud of you too, Alexander. You're already a great father to Oliver. But now, you're going to expand your family." He handed something to Alex.

Alex glanced down. "You have business cards?"

His dad shrugged. "I'm offering my services as an officiant. Especially now that I have time to start a second career."

"It's his way of telling you to put a ring on it," Tony said, holding back a smile.

"I'm not judging what you young people do these days," his dad said, "but what are you waiting for?"

Alex laughed. "Mr. C, I've been asking Kit to marry me for a year now."

He shook his head with a *young-people-these-days* look. "I'm just so proud of all you boys."

"Love you, Pop," Tony said.

"Love you, Dad," Nick said.

Alex grinned. "Love you too, Dad."

His dad chuckled and clapped Alex on the back and then hugged each of them in turn. He saved Nick for last, tapping his cheek as he had his brother's. "I never doubted that you'd do a fine job taking over, Nicholas," he said. "But I have a piece of advice. Do you want to hear it?"

"Yeah, sure." Maybe? Not really?

"Do you remember what you told me when we talked about retirement? Now I can say it to you. Listen to what your heart is telling you. It's hardly ever wrong."

He looked into his dad's eyes. He saw someone who believed in him. Who always had. He was the only one holding himself back now. "Thanks, Dad."

He'd loved Darla forever. He'd made a promise to himself that he'd never give up on her again. And he certainly wasn't going to now.

Chapter 26

THE STRAINS OF a violin drifted up from the quartet on the beach, each pure, sweet note stabbing Darla's heart as she stood at her bedroom door. In front of her, the deck was adorned with beautiful bouquets and candles ready to be lit on tables for the reception. The stair railings were draped with thick boughs of fragrant white flowers leading the way to the beach, where a white runner was laid and two sections of chairs were now filled with family and friends. The blue sky was already showing off wisps of salmon and gold as it slowly turned to indigo on a picture-perfect summer evening.

All Darla had to do was walk onto her deck, down to the beach, and up the white runner between the groups of chairs until she took her place among the wedding party. And somehow not look at Nick in the process, or she'd surely burst into tears.

Hadley walked up next to her and peeked outside. She

was a vision in her perfectly form-fitting dress, and she was smiling a radiant smile.

"You look so beautiful," Darla said. "But more importantly, you look really happy." Her voice cracked a little before she could stop it, making Hadley scrutinize her for the first time that day.

"Everything okay?" she asked. "I mean, I know you're thrilled for me. And you're right, I am happy and totally ready to do this. You just seem a little off."

Darla forced the smile of a lifetime. "I just can't believe it." She gave a little shrug. "Look at us. All grown up."

Kit, who somehow looked beautiful even in the frothy peach dress, smiled softly. "All grown up," she agreed. "Remember how we used to play brides?"

"And hate boys?" Darla said. And that was the problem, Darla thought. Her life would be so much simpler now if she'd continued along those lines.

The music changed to a lyrical song with soaring notes, indicating that now was the time. Hadley's parents joined her, each taking an arm. "Let's go get you married," Darla said, squeezing Hadley's hand and giving a nod to Kit. Then she got into place, placing a photograph-worthy smile on her face. Just as she was about to walk across her deck and down the steps to the beach, Kit sucked in an audible breath. Darla turned in time to see her reach into her bouquet and eat something.

What the...

"It's a cracker." She shook her bouquet a little to reveal a little baggie tucked in along the stem of her bouquet. "Don't worry, I'll be fine."

All righty then.

With a shared look among the three of them that seemed to sum up the meaning of a lifetime of friendship, Darla led the procession.

She tried to remind herself that none of the guests would be focused on her. But it didn't help much. Because only one person mattered, and without having to look, she felt his steady gaze burning through her intensely enough to make the white roses and baby's breath in her bouquet shake.

She was going to lose it. She knew she was. The song was a classic, swelling piece about loving someone forever that stabbed her in the heart. As she rounded the turn at the back of the chairs and prepared to walk down the aisle, she couldn't help glancing up, and sure enough, there was Nick, staring at her with brows furrowed. She dropped her gaze, swallowed hard, and focused on not tripping down the aisle.

What a mess she'd made. She wasn't sure how she was going to make it through the next hour. And would Nick ever speak to her again?

She smiled even wider, bit down on the insides of her cheeks so she wouldn't cry, and focused on checking out the other guys. Tony looked calm and at ease. Alex winked at Kit, who was apparently still in the game. Nick looked so handsome in his black tux that her heart hurt. They soon all made it to the front, where Nick's dad stood tall and official, and lined up on either side of a podium.

Kit's adorable son, Oliver, held hands with Bernadette, Lucy's four-year-old daughter, and both hammed it up, smiling and tossing petals down the aisle.

The music suddenly changed to "Pachelbel's Canon."

Hadley swept elegantly down the aisle, happy and radiant and resplendent, just as she should be, and joined Tony in front of the podium. The wedding party turned from the audience to face Angelo. That put Darla right next to Hadley.

"Welcome, family and friends," Angelo began. "We're gathered here today to join Hadley and Tony in holy matrimony."

Darla was so focused on trying to breathe and not cry at the same time that she missed a lot of the poignant and sometimes funny anecdotes about Hadley and Tony that set everyone to laughing.

Good friends did readings. Angelo did more talking. But Darla only seemed to hear the soft squawking of seagulls calling to each other as they glided high above or the quiet rolling of the waves. But nothing could soothe her spirit.

What a fool she'd been to let the love of her life go. To push Nick away like he didn't matter. When he was *all* that mattered.

She wanted to live life with him, by his side. Every single day. She wanted to wring life dry until it ran out. No matter how short or long a time that might be.

She was jolted to attention by the uncomfortable feeling that someone was looking at her. Nick caught her eye and was giving a little nod toward his dad. It was enough to get her to suddenly pay attention to what Angelo was saying. "When you meet your person, that one person who gets you and that you can't live without, you'll do anything in the world to be with them. No matter what the struggles, no matter the past pain, *nothing* can keep you apart. This, my dear friends, is what love is. It's not a bargain to only take the good times. Or something you can opt out of if you think life is going to be too much trouble. Love simply is unavoidable."

Angelo stopped and stared at his son. Not Tony. Nick.

Darla blinked. This couldn't be, like, some kind of message—could it?

Nick shifted his weight, the color high in his cheeks.

Angelo cast a glance at her too before he continued reading. "Your partner's happiness is your happiness, and their sadness is yours as well. No one and nothing can separate you, because you already feel everything they are feeling."

Panicked, she looked at Nick, who gave his dad a little smile and then nodded. Then he pinned her with his gaze.

Darla swallowed a sob. Because she saw what was happening. Angelo was talking in generalities, but Nick was making sure she took it to heart. He was telling her that he loved her, and he would no matter what. That she couldn't keep them apart because he already felt everything she felt. They were in this together.

There was a problem with the sob swallowing. It wasn't silent. In fact, it came out like a giant choke and a sniffle at the same time that she was powerless to control.

Hadley grabbed her hand and squeezed tightly. The fact that Hadley understood and was supporting her in the middle of her own wedding was horrifying. "I'm so sorry," she whispered.

Hadley gave a little shrug and a smile, seeming to take it all in stride.

Angelo continued with the ceremony.

Darla looked over to find Nick surveying her intently. Everyone and everything around them suddenly seemed to vanish—the people in their summer festive best, the beach bathed in golden light, the spectacular sunset occurring as a backdrop to the beautiful scene. And Angelo and the wedding taking place right in front of them. She looked directly into his eyes. She didn't deserve his forgiveness. But she had to ask for it. "I'm sorry," she mouthed.

For a moment, she wasn't sure he understood. But then, in slow motion, he did something at once familiar and astonishing. He discreetly placed his hand across his heart, tapped it twice, and pointed his finger at her. It was subtle and quick, but enough that she knew exactly what he was doing.

His corny sign. Except now it wasn't corny. It was just right.

I love you, he mouthed back.

She let out another sob. But this time, she covered her mouth so she didn't interrupt the wedding.

Nick loved her—she knew that. Yet he'd somehow forgiven her, even when she tried to ruin everything. She hadn't lost him for being stupid.

Immense relief wracked her body.

"Anthony," Angelo said, "please take the ring you have selected for Hadley. As you place it on her finger, please repeat after me." Tony and Hadley exchanged rings, gazing into each other's eyes, their love for each other evident.

"I now pronounce you man and wife," Angelo said.

Hadley smiled from ear to ear as she gazed into Tony's eyes. "Finally!" she said, grabbing him by the lapels and pulling him in for a giant, enthusiastic kiss amid clapping and cheers and whistles.

As they headed down the aisle to more cheers, followed by Kit and Alex, Darla knew she wouldn't be following them. She ran straight over to Nick.

Clutching his arms, she said, "I'm so, so sorry. I promise I'll never keep anything from you again." She took a deep breath. "I need you, Nick. I love you. I always will."

"Forgiven," he said, wrapping his arms around her and holding on to her tight, "as long as you never shut me out of your life again."

Her tears were endless. She wiped her nose with the peach tulle overlay from her skirt. Still, she had to tell him one thing. "I just want to make sure you understand—"

"That you love me?"

"No, that the road ahead—"

"Is unknown," he said quietly, holding her arms. "For everyone, may I remind you. That's...life."

"Right." She swallowed hard. "So about that. I'm going to work really hard on being happy in the here and now."

The sound of his chuckle made relief flow through her, washing away all her distress. "Honey, I'm going to keep you too busy to worry about any other things besides me."

"I want to make you just as happy as you make me." He'd done everything for her. To make her happy.

"Finish your deadline because I have all kinds of plans to make with you."

She rested her hands on his chest. "I...I don't have a deadline anymore. I turned in the story I wrote. It's a love story, and chances are I'm going to lose my contract. And I'm saying no to California."

"Oh," he said. "How do you feel about all that?"

Darla threw up her hands. "Wonderful!"

"Well then, let's not waste another second." Nick tugged her to him. The warmth of his body and the feel of his arms wrapping around her made Darla feel a sense of pure, unleashed joy. He kissed her slow and long, taking his time. She got lost in his embrace and trembly in the knees as she held on to him tightly and the world faded around them. He threaded his fingers in her hair, and she reached up and held his hands and kissed him back as good as she got.

"Um, excuse me." Someone cleared their throat. It was Hadley. "You two have been kissing for a while, long enough for us to come up with an idea."

Nick broke away from her lips, and Darla slowly came to realize they were surrounded by a group of people. Their people—Hadley and Tony, Kit and Alex, Nick's dad, her mom and Rachel—everyone.

"The officiant wants to know if you two want to get married right now," Tony said, tilting his head toward their dad.

"We've created a monster," Nick whispered to his brother.

"Nice to see we have an officiant in the family," Alex said. "Katherine, want to make it legal too?"

"Aw, that's so sweet." Kit smiled as she snuck another cracker. "I really want to. But is it okay to wait until I know I can say 'I do' without throwing up?"

Alex put his arm around her. "I love you," he said.

"I don't have a ring," Nick said, patting his pockets, as if one would magically appear.

"Are you serious?" Darla said. "*Now?*"

"Why not?" Nick said.

Kit reached out her hand. "Will this do for now?" She was holding Amelia's ring. She turned to Darla. "I went in the house to use the bathroom and I saw it on your desk, and I just put it on. Maybe I had a feeling or something."

There was the ring, catching the last rays of light from the sunset.

"I'm sort of feeling like this is a setup," Darla said. "An officiant, a ring…"

Nick's dad chimed in. "Don't forget the heartfelt words the officiant chose to make you two realize you're right for each other."

"Doing everything we could to get you two together these past weeks was hard work," Hadley said, pretending to wipe sweat off her brow.

"Right," Tony chimed in. "Did you two really think we would argue about tasting cake?" He gave a little snort.

"I have another confession," Hadley said. "It's a big one."

"What is it?" Darla asked in a wary tone.

"We thought that having the wedding would sort of throw you two together and make you realize how perfect you are together."

"It was all worth it to get our two favorite people to realize they need each other," Kit said.

"And worth it to try to get you to stay," Hadley added. "And it's my wedding day, so you can't be angry at us, right?"

Darla looked at Nick. "How could I be angry when I rediscovered the love of my life?" At that moment, she felt only pure joy.

Nick looked at each of their friends. "You people are real pains, let me tell you. But I have to say thank you, from the bottom of my heart. You're the best friends anyone could have."

Darla looked at the ring and then looked at Nick.

Smiling in a way that somehow brought to mind that same one many years ago that day in the library, the smile that made her fall in love with him the first time, he took the ring from Hadley. Then he dropped a knee into the sand. "Darla, will you marry me?"

"Of course, I will," she said, her heart full. "But right now? Here?"

"Do it!" his brother called.

"We don't want to take away from your day," Nick said.

"It won't take away," Hadley said. "It will amplify our happiness to know you're happy too."

"I call co-maid of honor with Rachel," Kit said, raising her hand. "Since Hadley's a bride."

"That makes me the best man," Alex said. He nudged Kit with his elbow. "Want to hook up after the wedding?"

"What are you talking about?" Kit said with a tone of mock horror. "I can't even last ten minutes without barfing."

He shrugged. "The best man always hooks up with the maid of honor."

She laughed as Alex leaned over and kissed her on the cheek.

Nick took Darla's hand. "What do you say, sweetheart?"

"I'm just going to go with it." She smoothed down the peach dress. "I say yes." She turned to Nick's dad. "Marry us, Angelo," she said, grabbing Nick's hand.

"I forgot one thing," Nick said. "Hey, Tricia," he called. "Do I have your permission to marry your daughter?"

"Not yet," she said, walking up from the front row. "I need to borrow Darla for a minute." Tricia grabbed Darla's hand and took her aside.

"Mom, what are you doing?" Rachel said, a look of worry on her face.

Tricia dropped her voice. "No one should get married in a dress they don't love."

"That's really sweet," Darla said. "But I don't care about the dress. I just want to marry him. You love Nick, right?"

Tricia broke out in a grin. "Yes, my darling, I love him too. Especially since he got you to stay."

Suddenly, Darla was standing in front of Angelo, surrounded by her friends and family, with Nick firmly by her side, unable to control a giant grin. Everything she loved, everyone she loved, was here. Her sense of gratitude knew no bounds.

Angelo put on his glasses and read from his phone. "We rejoice with them in their delight of finding love with each other. Love bears and believes in all things. Love hopes in all things, endures all things. Love has no end." He looked up from his phone. "Do you promise to love and cherish each other forever—again?"

"I never stopped," Nick said with a huge grin. He turned to Darla. "Except this time, I'm never going to let you go."

"The answer is 'I do,'" his dad said.

Nick smiled, looking tenderly into her eyes. "I *definitely* do."

"I do too," Darla said. She squeezed Nick's hand tightly. "And I'm never going to let you go either."

Angelo smiled. "May you wake each and every morning and fall in love all over again. And now, I pronounce you man and wife."

"I love you," Nick whispered as he brought his lips to hers.

"I love you." Darla kissed the man she'd always loved in front of all the people she loved. Then, just as the sun was setting in a glorious array of color, they broke into a run down the aisle, because what was conventional about this wedding? Darla had the feeling that their life together wouldn't be either.

The candles were glowing, the sky was glowing, and Darla's heart was glowing as, Nick's hand in hers, they kept running down the beach, into the surf, and straight into their future.

Epilogue

AFTER DINNER AND dancing, Hadley and Tony ran through the sand, down a bright aisle of sparklers and cheers to a waiting limo that took them straight to the airport for their honeymoon in an undisclosed destination in Tuscany. Alex took Kit home to rest. And Nick took Darla straight to Amelia's house.

"I have a surprise for you," he said, guiding her carefully up the stairs with his hands over her eyes.

"Is it a present?" she asked in a worried tone. "I don't have a wedding present for you yet."

"It's just something I've been working on," he said. They got to the porch, but it was pitch-black. "Keep your eyes closed for another sec." He ran into the house and turned on his tripod work light to cast some light through the windows.

"Okay, you're good." Nick held his breath as Darla caught sight of the swing he'd drilled into the ceiling. One of those big, cushy ones that you could lie down on with your book and even take a nap on.

He watched as she surveyed the empty run-down porch and the lonely orange lily Lucy had potted on impulse to place near the swing.

"There's a lot more to do," he said hurriedly. Maybe what he'd done was ridiculous. But he had a point to make. One he had to make sure she got.

"The paint is peeling, there are water spots on the roof, the middle step is sinking, and—" she bent down to check the plant, "the flower needs water."

Okay, maybe this wasn't such a great idea after all.

She grabbed his arm and turned him around, wearing a huge smile. "I'm kidding. I *love* it." She jumped into his arms. "I've always wanted a swing like that, to sit with some tea and a book and watch life go by."

"That's exactly the point." He led her over and sat down, taking her hands. "I want us to take time to just sit every day. To have a glass of wine. To wave to the neighbors. To be grateful for what we have. To spend time just being together. This is a way for us to do that."

Darla smoothed the blue-and-white-striped cushions. "Let's make a promise to spend a few minutes just talking and being together every evening, no matter how busy we are."

He nuzzled her neck. "Sounds perfect. But maybe we need a hot tub or something, because sitting out here is going to get cold in the winter."

She smiled and arched her neck so he could kiss it more easily. "Nick, I've been thinking about this house, and I wondered what you thought of something."

He looked up. "Sure. What is it?"

"I wanted to do something to honor Amelia's memory. But it doesn't involve us living here."

"Oh." He sat back and scanned her face.

"Would you be disappointed if we didn't?"

He thought about that. "I guess I assumed you'd want to, but to be honest, I don't care where we live. Although my dad might not be thrilled if I move into your place. Unless I rename the company and start renovating more modern homes. Which might actually be fun, now that I'm thinking about it."

She took up his hands and looked into his eyes. "I had a dream that I turned this house into something kind of amazing again. Something to benefit the community, just like Amelia did."

"A writer's center? Something to benefit women?" She shook her head. "Then what?"

"A cancer wellness center. A place for support groups, counseling, fitness programs, family services—somewhere that would help not just people living through cancer but their families and significant others too."

It sounded exactly like Darla. And it sounded exactly right. "I can't think of a better way to honor Amelia." He gestured to the house. "Speaking of Amelia, there's something else I want to show you."

"Something else?"

He stood up, and, helping her up, gestured into the house. "Come on in."

Nick's heart began to beat hard in his chest. This was the secret he'd been holding for so long. He hoped that Darla would understand it for what it was—a message that he would be beside her no matter where life took them.

He walked her from the foyer into the big room with the fireplace, still draped with a sheet, the air mattress now propped up against a wall. He moved a folding chair to the middle of the room and motioned for her to sit.

"This is a big reveal?" She lifted a questioning brow.

"Just sit tight."

He walked over to the sheet and tugged it. It fell off the mantel into a cloud of dust on the floor, where Nick quickly whisked it aside. "Ta-da," he said, gesturing with his arm.

* * *

Darla stared at the fireplace. Well, more specifically, at the tile surround. Every single tile contained a beautiful, uniquely painted flower.

"You redid this." She looked from the tiles to Nick. "It's beautiful."

"All I did was regrout," he said with his usual humility. "I didn't touch the tiles. They're really unique, aren't they?"

Darla walked up and examined each one. A rose. An iris. A daffodil. A lily. And so many more.

He nodded. "I think that was Amelia's thing," he said. "She had everyone who stayed here make one before they left."

"Bloom House," Darla said as she traced the flower patterns with her finger. "That's what they called this place. Amelia helped people to bloom." She straightened up and looked at Nick. "That's what I want to do."

"Do it," he said. "Use this place however you want to continue her mission."

She was flooded with love for him. He got her—her connection to Amelia, her determination to do something good for others. "I will," she vowed. "I promise."

She went to hug him, but he walked her straight back to the fireplace. "There's more." Pointing to a tile with a blue-and-yellow iris on it, he said, "Tap on that."

She looked at him quizzically.

"Just play along, okay?"

She half smiled and half frowned, having no idea what he was up to. "Like this?" She tapped, and nothing happened.

"Come on, you can do better than that."

She tapped harder, and sure enough, the tile popped open, revealing a dark rectangular space behind it.

She tried to see in, but it was completely dark. "A secret compartment?"

"Stick your hand in there."

She immediately withdrew it to her side. "I'm afraid."

"Like, that something's going to grab your hand and not let go?" he asked, barely suppressing a laugh. "You've been reading too many of your own books."

"No. I'm afraid of what I'm going to find."

He gave her an irresistible grin. "Don't be afraid."

Summoning her courage, Darla reached in and pulled out a rolled piece of paper. It was yellowed and dry and had a distinct old-paper smell.

She shot Nick a questioning look, and he nodded for her to keep going.

Walking over to the floor lamp, she read:

In this place, people learned things that helped them to become independent, to work, to contribute, to make a good life for themselves and for their children.

I came here never dreaming that I would find a new beginning for myself. To whomever reads this—I hope this house helps you to find yours as well.

Love reigned here.

Amelia Manning, 1938

"1938?" Darla looked up at Nick.

"She died in 1940." Darla paused to do the math. "So she would've been around seventy-eight."

"Samuel died in 1938," Nick said. "He built the secret compartment. Pretty fine craftmanship too. Just like the rest of the house."

"You know about Samuel?" Darla frowned. She wasn't getting how it all fit together.

"Oh, I know about him," Nick said. "They were married for forty years."

"Wait a minute." She looked up from the paper, shocked. "She married her contractor?"

"Smart woman," he said, looking very pleased. "You Manning women have got great taste in men—what can I say?" He looked at her with mischief in his eyes. "I found a bunch more of these tiles. So if everyone who came through here made one, it's pretty clear those two helped a lot of people get on their feet."

Then Nick handed her an old photograph. "This was in the box with a note that said, 'My beloved Samuel, you built us a beautiful life.'"

"Oh my," Darla said. "That's so sad."

"No, it's not," Nick said, smiling. "They had a lot of happy years together. Look at it."

"This looks just like the one I have except"—she carried it to the light—"they're laughing." Baffled, she looked up at Nick. "They're *really* laughing. I've never seen an old photo like this."

"Smiling in photos wasn't really socially acceptable."

"But she didn't throw it away, did she? She hid it. I love it!" She looked at the couple. "They look so happy and in love. It seems like he's whispering something in her ear. I wonder what funny moment they just shared."

Nick reached into the space and pulled out yet another paper. "Be careful with this one—it's really old."

Darla held it carefully in her hands. "It's an obituary."

Nick nodded. "Read it."

"'Samuel Tobias Manning, age eighty, died yesterday of natural causes. Beloved husband of Amelia, he could often be found doing repairs at the women's home he built and they both managed for the past forty years." She stopped reading.

"I like Tobias for a boy's name," he said.

Darla nodded. "I kind of like Samuel too."

"And of course Amelia."

He walked her over to a window at the back of the house. "It's dark, but there's a house over there."

Darla squinted into the darkness. "I'll have to take your word for it."

"You can't see it very well through all the weeds. But it's on the bay."

"Close to Kit and Alex's?"

"Two doors down."

"What's it like?"

"Old. Lots of curves and crannies. Probably needs a lot of work. Maybe we'll go have a look. If you want to, that is."

"A modern house is nice," she said, "but there's something irresistible about one with a history..."

Just then her phone buzzed with a text. "Well, what do you know. My publisher wants my book. Except I need to write the ending."

"I can help you with that." He gave her a sweet smile and held her in his arms.

She looked into his eyes, which sparkled with mischief, and whispered, "I already know the ending."

He displayed a tiny frown. "What is it?"

It was so obvious. She gave him the widest grin. "...and they lived happily ever after, of course."

"Sounds like the perfect ending," he said. And then he kissed her.

Author's Note

Thank you for picking up Darla's story! I've enjoyed spending time with these three women and their amazing friendship. I'm sad to say goodbye, but such is a writer's life.

I wanted to thank my friends who have shared their experiences of surviving and living with cancer. Many thanks as well to my dear writing friends who are always there to prop me up and keep me going. Thanks to my agent, Jill Marsal, my amazing editor, Alex Logan, and the wonderful team at Forever. The biggest thanks is to my husband, Ed, who helps me to survive the roller-coaster ride of creating a book—and somehow still manages to make me laugh.

A special thanks to my oldest and dearest friend, who I met in the third grade. Debbie, I am blessed to have you in my life.

Dear Readers, I hope you've enjoyed reading about these friends and their journeys to becoming their best selves. Many thanks for reading my books. Please don't hesitate to drop me a line. I love hearing from you!

Miranda Liasson
December 2022

About the Author

Miranda Liasson is a bestselling author who writes about the important relationships in women's lives as well as the self-discovery and wisdom gained along the way. Her heartwarming and humorous romances have won numerous accolades and have been praised by *Entertainment Weekly* for the way she deals with "so much of what makes life hard…without ever losing the warmth and heart that characterize her writing." She believes that we can handle whatever life throws at us just a little bit better with a laugh.

A proud native of northeast Ohio, she and her husband live in a neighborhood of old homes that serves as inspiration for her books. She is very proud of her three young adult children. And though every day she thinks about getting a dog, she fears a writer's life may bore the poor animal to tears. When she's not writing or enjoying books herself, she can be found biking along the old Ohio and Erie Canal Towpath trails in the beautiful Ohio Metro Parks.

Miranda loves to hear from readers!
MirandaLiasson.com
Facebook.com/MirandaLiassonAuthor
@MirandaLiasson